Take My Love

BROOKE MONTGOMERY

willow branch mountain

suggested reading order

Take My Name (#1)

Take My Love (#2)

Take My Kiss (#3)

Take My Soul (#4)

Take My Hand (#5)

Each book can be read as a stand-alone and ends in a happily ever after. However, for the best reading experience, read in order.

When I'm in your arms, you're the only thing that matters
    It's you and I won't let this feeling fade
    Whenever we touch in that moment, all else shatters
    And I hope that you know
    You can take all my love
    My heart is just for you, you know it's true
    You can take all my love
    Baby, my soul yearns for you

take all my love
Reed Wonder, Aurora Olivas

playlist

Listen to the full *Take My Love* playlist on Spotify

Friends Don't | Alexander Stewart, Lauren Spencer Smith

Fix What You Didn't Break | Nate Smith

Take All My Love | Reed Wonder, Aurora Olivas

DAISIES | Justin Bieber

The Good Ones | Gabby Barrett

Castle | Haven Madison

The Fate of Ophelia | Taylor Swift

Restless Mind | Sam Barber, Avery Anna

What Could Go Right | Thomas Rhett

Caramel | Conan Gray

Opalite | Taylor Swift

Crazy Stupid Love | Blake Proehl

Ordinary | Alex Warren

Man I Need | Olivia Dean

author's note

Willow Branch Mountain is a fictional town set in northeastern Tennessee. The characters speak in a Southern dialect, which is reflected through their dialogue and inner thoughts. Outside of that, the narration is written in standard American English to ensure clarity and a smooth reading experience.

Welcome to Willow Branch Mountain Equine Ranch & Luxury Camping Resort

The town of Willow Branch Mountain, Tennessee is home to twenty-five hundred residents and is nestled in the Appalachian Mountains between Doe Mountain, Forge Mountain, and Iron Mountains—a landscape surrounded by peaks. Willow Branch Mountain is one of the highest valleys in the state. We're just a few miles from the Virginia and North Carolina state lines.

Enjoy a cozy couples getaway in the mountains with luxury cabins, domes, glamping tents, or leisure treehouses. Spend the day horseback riding, trail walking, cliff diving, biking, or ziplining and then enjoy a romantic dinner at the Summit Views Restaurant! We have massage therapists on-site, ready to turn your room into a sanctuary, and a hot tub for you to enjoy after. Relax and reunite with your partner during your stay!

Don't forget your welcome basket loaded with self-care essentials, including goat soap from our family-owned goat soap business—Langston Soapworks, a spa-inspired candle, snacks, and books. If you need anything while you're here, don't hesitate to reach out to The Branch Haven so someone in guest services can bring you whatever you need.

Meet the Langston family:

Grady & Lindsey Langston
the parents

Aunt Josephine "JoJo" Langston
paternal aunt

Warren Langston
the oldest child and son

Posey Langston
the oldest daughter

Colton "Colt" Langston
the middle child

Bodie and Bellamy Langston
twins, the youngest

Job positions:

Grady & Lindsey
Owners

Aunt JoJo
Restaurant manager at Summit Views

Warren
Ranch Operations Manager

Posey
Goat farm manager at Langston Soapworks

Colt
Resort Operations Manager

Bodie
Ranch hand

Bellamy
Resort Concierge

Find all of our current information at
willowbranchmountain.com

We hope you have the best time!
-The Langston Family

See map on the next page!

Willow Chalet
Zipl... Are...
Willow Peak Stables
The Branch Haven
Ranch
Resort
Wil...

Summit Views
Restaurant

Willow Falls River

lls Bridge

prologue

Silas

EIGHT YEARS AGO

"YOU NERVOUS?" I smack my childhood best friend's shoulder, staring at his reflection in the mirror.

He adjusts his tie after his mother commented it was crooked.

He's in a fancy-as-fuck all black tuxedo, moments away from walking down the aisle to his high school sweetheart.

"Nope. Been waitin' to marry Maze since I was fifteen." Warren grins like a lovesick fool as he folds his collar down. "And gettin' to spend the summer with her before she goes back to college is somethin' I'm not takin' for granted."

"So…lots of baby makin' practice." I smirk, squeezing his shoulder once before releasing him.

He probably won't come up for air until she leaves.

"Don't worry, we'll still hang out," he reassures me, but I'm not holding my breath.

We've been friends since elementary school. Most of my middle and high school summer memories revolve around him and Maisie. Riding on horses or four-wheelers through his family's ranch, swimming in the river, camping in the woods, throwing bonfire parties—we've been inseparable.

It was a shock to no one when they started dating at fifteen and later got engaged.

Unfortunately, that made me the designated third wheel. But I didn't mind, *usually.*

"It's fine. I'll just have to find someone else to take your place until I getcha back."

"The fuck you will."

I chuckle at his aggressive taunting voice because he knows he has nothing to worry about. I can keep myself busy with work for a few months while the newlyweds stay glued at the hip. It's not like I have anyone else to hang out with in the meantime besides my older sisters.

Making friends and dating never came easily to me, especially as a nerdy kid who didn't hit puberty until my senior year of high school. Even now at twenty-one, I've still never had anything serious.

Warren and Maisie set the standard, and I haven't wanted to settle for anything less.

Not to mention the one girl I have a crush on is strictly off-limits.

She's two years younger and Warren's little sister. *The biggest fucking cliché.*

Posey Langston is breathtaking, is always the life of the party, and has my same zero risk o'meter. Hell, she's more ballsy than anyone I've ever met. I'll try anything once, but she'll do it twice just to prove she can.

Being raised on her family's ranch and resort has made her fear nothing. From zip lining, to cliff diving, and standing upright while her horse runs forty miles an hour, she's always had an adventurous spirit.

Although she tagged along with us sometimes, I never saw her as anything more than Warren's sister. But last summer changed everything. She had a bonfire with some friends and they roped me into a game of Truth or Dare.

After a few drinks, someone dared her to kiss me. I figured she'd find a way to get out of it and say she thought of me as a brother, but then she straddled my lap and stuck her tongue down my throat.

I was in such shock, the only thing I could do is grip her hips and kiss her back.

We never talked about it, but ever since, she's been the star in all my private fantasies.

Something I've actively tried to get over, but so far, no such luck.

The secret glances and blush that spreads over her cheeks anytime I'm near tells me she's not over it either.

"Hey, I know you'll be busy with best man duties and flirtin' with all the single ladies, but if you can, keep an eye on Posey for me? Some guy she was datin' broke up with her a couple days ago and she's been pretty upset about it."

Fuck. I didn't even know she was dating anyone.

"What exactly do you want me to do?" I ask cautiously.

He doesn't know about my little obsession. Otherwise there's no way he'd ask me this. Warren's the oldest of five kids and very protective of his siblings. Posey can hold her own, but I'm not sure he'd approve of me dating her. It'd be a risk in the event we didn't work out and then he'd be stuck in the middle between wanting to kick my ass and protecting his sister.

"She's gonna sneak alcohol at some point—which is whatever—but could you make sure she doesn't overdo it? I don't want her to leave with some random dipshit or find a closet to cry in. This is, like, the third guy in the past six months so she's feelin' kinda low."

My jaw locks, keeping the words I want to say inside so I don't reveal my secret.

"Yeah, no problem. I'll make sure she gets to her room safely."

Everyone's staying at this fancy-ass hotel since Maisie's parents are rich snobs and wouldn't let them get married at the ranch. But all that matters is he gets to marry the love of his life, so Warren hasn't complained.

"Thanks, man. I appreciate it." He smacks my shoulder, the goofiest smile splitting his face. "Time to find my future wife."

The sickly in love couple are doing a first look before the ceremony, so it's a private moment between them and the photographer. I wait in the dressing room with Warren's brothers who are the other groomsmen. Since they're all younger than him, they look more bored than excited.

"Okay, it's time," the wedding planner announces, eagerly clapping.

Watching my best friend tear up at the love of his life walking down the aisle has me choking back my own emotions.

Their love is so rare and inspiring that it's hard not to be envious they found it so early in life. They have years of shared memories from their youth, and now they get to grow together into adulthood and make endless new ones.

They have that forever kind of love that nothing or no one can get in between.

"Picture time!" one of Maisie's bridesmaids calls out.

My gaze catches Posey's who, despite being upset about her breakup, has been smiling and looking bright-eyed all afternoon. Her blonde hair is pulled up, exposing the nape of her neck. A strand falls around her face and she delicately twists it with her finger to keep it curled.

She catches me looking at her and gives me a lingering look down my tuxedo before shifting toward Bellamy, the youngest Langston sibling. She's only thirteen, but Warren and Maisie wanted all their brothers and sisters in the wedding party.

"If Mrs. Callaway tells us to smile one more goddamn time, I'm gonna stick one of my four-inch heels through her eye..." Posey's low muttering next to me has me choking back a laugh.

It's been an hour and a half of moving to different spots and posing in various positions throughout the venue and in the courtyard while Maisie's mother continuously scolds us to straighten our spines and show more teeth.

Add in the June Southern heat, it's been a miserable time.

"No shit. My cheeks hurt," I say, rubbing my hand along my jaw and stretching it out. "I think she's the worst Momzilla I've ever seen."

"More like, of the century. I dunno how Maisie deals with her."

I shrug since I honestly don't know either. It's probably why she was so eager to move seven hundred miles away for college because her parents are overbearing and try to dictate every aspect of her life.

Before I can respond, we're being directed toward the reception ballroom. We're doing a grand entrance before the happy couple enters as husband and wife.

"Hey, in case I don't get to talk to you until later, save me a dance?" I say before being yanked to the end of the line beside the maid of honor.

Posey glances over her shoulder with a smirk, and I give her a wink of confirmation.

I tell myself I'm watching out for her the way Warren asked, but deep down, I want to recreate that kiss I haven't been able to get out of my head in the past twelve months.

POSEY

My alarm blaring somehow sounds in the distance and inside my head at the same time.

Which, I might add, is fucking pounding.

"Make it stop..." a deep rumble near me has my eyes sprinting open wide and confused.

Scanning the hotel room, I quickly realize it's not mine and locate my phone on the floor next to a pile of clothes.

Oh God. I'm naked.

And the guy next to me with only a thin sheet covering his bare ass is Silas Mathiesen.

My brother's best friend.

Someone I kissed a year ago on a dare that I'd wanted to kiss since I was twelve.

It's embarrassing how long I've had a crush on someone I know I can't have, which is why I keep putting myself out there to get over him but haven't had any luck.

Inching down the bed and falling off the mattress like a clumsy sniper, I crawl to the offending noise and quickly silence it.

I set my alarm before the ceremony so I gave myself enough time to shower and get ready for the farewell brunch. Mrs. Callaway made it clear to the wedding party we were to attend before the out of town guests leave and the newlyweds go on their honeymoon.

But with my current situation of being in my brother's best friend's hotel room, naked and hungover, I consider skipping it.

Unfortunately, it'll be suspicious if I don't show up, and I don't need my parents or siblings to come looking for me, so I suck it up.

Grabbing my dress and heels, I tiptoe to the bathroom. Memories flash of the seductive way he lowered my zipper and pressed his soft lips to the nape of my neck as it pooled to my feet. I was left in only my panties since the gown has a built-in bra.

He slowly licked his bottom lip while his gaze flooded with heat, lapping over my bare skin as if he couldn't wait to touch and taste every inch of me.

It was the first time being exposed to a man and not feeling insecure or self-conscious.

When I look in the mirror, my face is flushed and hair is matted from his fingers tangling through it all night. My chest rises and falls in quick breaths as I try to steady my racing thoughts of what we did.

My body's sore in a way I've never felt before. A delicious ache between my thighs that reminds me how big he felt and how deep he was inside me. He stretched me in a way I've never experienced but he went slow and gentle so it didn't hurt as much as I was expecting.

Once I could take all of him, he continued his tender movements and kissed me in between. Down my neck and between my shoulder, leaving a small purple bruise where he sucked a little too long.

His hands felt incredible on me too.

So big and firm, he palmed my ass to bring my hips closer to his, hitting that sweet spot deep inside. Then he palmed my breasts and played with the nipples before sucking them into his mouth.

Every touch and kiss set my body on fire.

We stumbled a bit at first, both tipsy from the open bar, but once we found our groove and pacing, it was the best and most surreal moment of my life.

One I'd like to repeat over and over, but until we can talk about what this means, I don't know if it meant as much to him as it did to me.

Silas is a good-looking guy, but he doesn't date much.

He was the nerdy kid in high school, but that's what I liked about him. Even when he teased me, I secretly liked the attention.

But then things changed when my boyfriend, Calvin, picked me up for prom and Silas punched him so hard, he broke my date's nose.

I spent my senior prom night at the ER with Calvin and then he never talked to me again after that.

Silas's explanation was that Calvin told the entire baseball team he was gonna pop my cherry in the bed of his truck that night and then add me to the team's sex ranking chart, which is as disgusting as it sounds. I don't know where Silas heard that from or who, but he picked the worst fucking time to do something about it.

Silas and I didn't talk again until last summer when my friends pressured him to join our bonfire and then dared me to kiss him. Feeling tipsy and bold, I straddled his lap and did what I'd wanted to do for years. But then we never talked about it and I assumed it meant nothing to him.

Which seems to be the story of my pathetic dating life.

I can't keep a guy interested in me longer than a few months before they give me the "it's not you, it's me" bullshit speech.

That's if I get one at all.

Between that and being ghosted, I'm starting to wonder if I should give up dating until I'm thirty.

But after the mind-blowing orgasm Silas gave me, I'm not sure I want to wait years to experience that again. This time, we're going to talk about it because I know last night meant something to him, too.

Once I've finger-combed my hair and wiped off the mascara smear under my eyes, I grab my shoes and walk out of the bathroom. Silas rolled onto his back, giving me a perfect view of his abs and the happy trail that leads below the sheet.

He has a half-sleeve of tattoos that I've admired since he got it done. He wants a full sleeve, so there's more ink he needs to get done, but it's attractive as hell as is.

Deciding to wake him up since I don't know if he set an alarm, I poke his shoulder and mutter his name.

"It's after ten. We gotta be downstairs in an hour," I remind him.

He releases something like a groan, and I take that as confirmation he heard me. I don't have time to babysit him, so he's going to have to get himself up.

"Don't be late or Momzilla will burst into flames…" I laugh but then immediately regret it.

All the shots we took last night have my head throbbing.

Crossing my fingers no one is in the hallway to see my walk of shame, I walk barefoot to my room five doors down. I strip and jump in the shower. But when the hot water hits my skin, I frown at washing his touch away, although I'm hopeful it'll happen again.

After I'm dressed and rush to finish getting ready, I make it downstairs with a few minutes to spare. I smile at Maisie, who's glowing—although I doubt she got any sleep—and give her a quick hug before heading to the bar for a mimosa.

If I have to be around people for the next hour, I need alcohol to numb this hangover.

There's a line for the brunch buffet, so I pull out my phone and look through the photos from last night while I wait for it to move. Half of them are dark and blurry, but I can't help grinning at the ones Silas and I took on the dance floor.

"Surprised you made it." Warren's taunting voice grabs my attention in front of me, but he's not talking to me.

"You and me both," Silas replies, rubbing his temple.

They're oblivious to my presence behind them.

"Last time I saw ya, Posey and you were line dancin' and

takin' shots. She looked like she was havin' a fun time, so I appreciate you keepin' an eye on her. Better than her being lonely and depressed."

Warren asked Silas to keep tabs on me?

Why the fuck did he do that?

And who said I was lonely and depressed...

"Hopefully, it wasn't too painful for ya since she most likely cock-blocked you," Warren continues. "How late did y'all stay up?"

Cock-blocked him? If he only knew...or rather, I hope he doesn't.

Before I can interrupt and demand answers about putting him on babysitting duty, Silas clears his throat with an amused chuckle. "Nah. I barely remember anythin' after y'all cut the cake, so I'm not sure. I woke up like a half an hour ago and it's all fuzzy."

What? That can't be true.

"Alcohol amnesia, huh?" Warren snickers.

"Pretty much."

My heart bottoms out in my stomach when the realization hits that Silas was only hanging with me in the first place because Warren asked him to watch me. I should've known something was up when Silas asked me to dance after witnessing him turn three other women down.

But that's not what has my chest squeezing with anger and tears welling in my eyes.

Silas has no memory of slamming me against the elevator wall and claiming my mouth. The kiss was clumsy and passionate, and we laughed at nearly stumbling to the ground when the elevator stopped at our floor.

He has no memory of sliding his hands underneath my dress and asking if he can touch me. Nearly *begging* to taste me.

He doesn't remember that we had sex last night.

Or worse.

That he took my virginity.

chapter one

Posey

I'VE NEVER SEEN my brother so miserable and depressed. And I hate that there's nothing I can say or do to lift his spirits.

"You're comin' to Bellamy and Bodie's birthday party tonight, right?" I ask when I find him at his desk. He's the stables manager of the horse ranch and where his office is located.

He's ignored our sibling group chat all week and hasn't confirmed if he'd be there or not. The twins are turning fifteen and since they're the youngest, everyone makes a big deal out of it. Mostly, Mom and Aunt JoJo take any excuse to cook and bake all day.

"Yeah, I'll be there," he grumbles, not looking away from his computer screen.

His hair's longer than usual, messy on the top and overgrown on the sides. He hasn't shaved in weeks, which isn't abnormal, but he hasn't kept up with trimming it. The bags under his eyes

15

represent how much he's not sleeping without his wife next to him.

I'm honestly surprised he's kept up with his job at this rate.

Not that Dad would fire him, but if it got bad enough, he'd definitely pull him aside and talk to him about it.

Our property is split into two businesses. One side for the horse ranch and the other for the luxury camping resort. We rent out cabins, leisure treehouses, domes, and glamping tents. It's primarily for couples looking to respark their love or want an anniversary getaway. Since we're nestled in the Appalachian Mountains, we offer guided horseback riding, trail walking, ziplining, biking, and cliff diving. We also have massage therapists on staff who come directly to their rooms to help couples relax. Most of the cabins also come with an outside hot tub.

Everyone in the family has a specific job on the ranch and resort. The three oldest siblings work full-time, but since the twins are still in high school, they work part-time on the weekends. Mom and Dad manage the finances, admin, marketing, and most of the employees.

I appreciate my job but working with your siblings means we're always in each other's business.

"You want me to come get you when it's time?" I ask cautiously.

He lives in the trailer behind our parents' house on the ranch side of our property, which is where he and Maisie were living so they had their own space and privacy. It's only a few minutes away, but I hate that he's there alone now.

"No, I don't need a babysitter. I said I'll be there, I'll be there."

Ironic he says that considering he thought I needed one at his wedding.

After he and Maisie got married, they spent all summer together before she went back to New York City for her final year of college. They did long-distance for another nine months, she visited a few times, then after graduation, she returned permanently.

He was so happy and excited to have his wife back instead of video chat dates and late night texts. I couldn't blame him though but knew they'd survive through it. Watching their relationship over the years is exactly the type I've always wanted too. Madly in love, can't get enough of each other, and stupidly obsessed with one another.

Who wouldn't want that?

But then she got offered an apprenticeship and had to move back to pursue her dream in publishing. She begged him to come with her, but he wouldn't leave the ranch.

I think he secretly hoped she'd realize she couldn't live without him or didn't like the job as much as she thought and would return. He visited her once but said it was like going to another country and not knowing the language.

Maisie visited over Christmas, but even I could feel the tension between them. I'd never seen Warren so damn broken when she finally told him that if he had no intention of moving there with her, they were over.

That was three months ago.

As far as I know, they haven't spoken since the day she left.

"Alright, see ya there."

I spend the next few hours helping Mom set up and decorate the house so the twins return from school with it all ready to go.

My other younger brother, Colton, works full-time on the resort side, so I'm the only one around to help. He only graduated high school last spring and has been training to become the operations manager. Since I work as a receptionist at the Branch Haven where guests check in and out, my job's more flexible for me to take off or find coverage.

Although I don't plan to work there forever. I'm trying to convince my dad to let me start a goat farm so we can produce goat milk and use them for brush control in some of the pastures. I've been researching and putting together a business plan so he'll take me seriously.

He hasn't said no to the idea, so that's promising.

I grew up with horses and love riding, but I don't want to work with them all day.

My dream would be to fix up one of the older barns to house the goats and then open an online goat soap business. Since we give each guest at the resort a welcome self-care basket, it'd be another item to include as well, which would also help promote it. We could sell wholesale stock to retailers and so much more. There are plenty of small businesses in town that'd love to sell it.

Mom's all for it and told me she'll approve it even if Dad doesn't. But I don't think that's going to be an issue. He wants to make sure this is something I truly want to do and not invest in something I'll get bored of in six months.

"Maybe your brothers can help with gettin' that old barn restored this summer," Mom suggests after asking if Dad has given me an answer. Although he hasn't, she's convinced he will.

"That'd be nice since I have no knowledge of that sorta thing," I respond.

"I can't wait to cuddle all the baby goats," Aunt JoJo gushes, and I laugh.

"Me too."

Aunt Josephine's the chef and manager at the Summit View Restaurant on the resort side. She lives in the garage that my dad and brothers turned into an apartment for her after my uncle died.

When it's apparent that Warren isn't coming, I offer to go look for him. Everyone's in the dining room, waiting to eat, and he's nowhere to be found.

I'm shocked when I find Silas's truck beside Warren's and contemplate knocking or not. Silas and I haven't talked much since the wedding weekend—mostly because I have nothing to say to him—but every time I see him, I'm reminded of our night together that he doesn't remember.

Before I approach, the trailer door swings open, and I'm greeted by a scowl.

"What're you doin' here?" Warren snaps, throwing an empty beer can toward the trash bin before placing a ballcap on his head.

"You're late," I tell him, folding my arms and returning his attitude.

"That's my fault," Silas says, coming up behind him. "I didn't realize the time."

When my gaze reaches his, I swallow hard at the sincere way he's looking at me.

But I ignore it.

"Go figure," I mutter. "Let's go."

They silently follow me to the house but when Silas walks past me to get to his chair, his arm brushes my shoulder and sends an unwanted shiver down my spine. Instead of reacting, I pretend he doesn't exist during dinner, even when I feel his heated gaze on me.

Although everyone's ignoring the elephant in the room, I notice how much Warren drinks during the party. By the time Mom brings out the cake and we sing to the twins, he's on his fifth beer. He had at least one beforehand, so he's probably had over half a dozen by now.

He's the only one of our siblings who's legally allowed to have alcohol but Dad usually has some stocked in the fridge.

By the time the twins have ripped open every gift and left to play their new video games, Warren is half-passed out on the couch. Silas gets him to his feet but then stumbles with Warren's dead weight.

"Here, let me help," I quickly offer, standing against Warren's other side and wrapping his arm around me so I can hold him up.

"I'm fine," Warren slurs, barely keeping his eyes open.

"We better leave before my parents see him like this," I tell Silas.

They're cleaning up in the kitchen, and I usually help, but I was too concerned about Warren to leave him out here.

"Where're we goin'?" Warren's head bobbles from side to side as we shuffle through the back door.

"To your house so you can sleep off the killer hangover you're gonna have in the mornin'," I tell him.

"I'm not hungover..." he argues.

"Not yet," I mumble, hanging onto him tighter.

Silas and I manage to open the trailer door and get him

inside without the three of us falling. Warren collapses on his bed with a grunt.

"I'll take off his boots," Silas tells me, kneeling between Warren's feet.

"Do you do this for him a lot?" I ask after watching him effortlessly remove Warren's jeans and T-shirt.

"Sometimes...he's not usually this out of it, though. Can you grab a blanket from the closet?" Silas points behind me.

He shoves a pillow under Warren's head, covers him up, puts a trash can next to the bed and then sets his alarm so he's not late for work.

"I'll call in the mornin' and check up on him," Silas says before flipping off the lightswitch.

"I didn't realize he was this bad." I frown, wondering if he'll ever get through this level of heartbreak.

Warren's never been the blackout drunk type, but his drinking escalated after Maisie announced she was moving back to New York. Then got worse when she left.

"I overheard him drunk callin' her last weekend. Left her a long voicemail and she never returned it," Silas tells me.

"Oh, shit. Do you think they're over for good?"

When we walk through the living room, there are empty beer cans and trash littered on the coffee table. Silas notices too, and together, we clean up.

"I dunno..." He shrugs. "Warren can't live without her, that much is obvious, but he might have to."

"Warren won't give up. No matter how long it takes, he'll fight for her."

"You're probably right," he agrees. "He doesn't know who he

is without her. Even if she doesn't come back, he'll never move on."

The thought makes me sad because as much as I want to find love and have a solid relationship, I don't want to be that level of dependent. Though I can't blame him since he's loved her for the past eight years, the aftermath of being without her is destroying him.

Once the living room's picked up, I move to the kitchen and load the dishwasher. Silas and I work in silence, but there's an underlying current streaming between us that I try to ignore.

"I heard you and Kayden broke up," Silas blurts. "You doin' okay?"

My heart pounds at the sound of my ex's name. Another guy who treated me so well in the beginning and then randomly hit me with the "I'm not looking for anything serious" conversation.

"Yeah, I'm fine." I avoid his gaze while lifting the trash bag and tying it up.

"He wasn't good enough for you anyway."

My eyes lift to his dark ones and my brows pinch. "You didn't know him."

His shoulder lifts lazily. "If he couldn't see what a catch you are, he's not good enough."

"That's rich comin' from you," I snap before I can stop myself.

"How so?" He straightens his spine, crossing his arms.

Is he being serious right now?

"Forget it."

I shake open a clean trash bag before putting it in the bin, then grab the full one. Opening the door, I walk to the outside bin and throw it inside.

"Posey!" Silas shouts, and the trailer door slams shut behind him.

It's nearly pitch black out, the only light coming from the moon reflecting off the mountains in the distance. But when Silas and I meet in the middle, every inch of his face is tense.

I cross my arms. "What now?"

"Explain what you meant."

"No." Taking a step back, I swallow hard and try to settle my racing heart. "It was nothin'."

"You wanna talk about it finally?" He mimics my stance, folding his arms across his broad chest.

My guard lowers slightly. "About what?"

"Us havin' sex."

My stomach bottoms out and the pot roast I had for dinner threatens to come back up.

He remembers?

"I-I thought you had no memory of our night together," I say, too timid for my liking, but I'm thrown by his words.

"No..." His brows furrow in confusion. "I thought you regretted it."

"Why'd you think that?"

"'Cause you wouldn't look at me, purposely avoided me, walked away anytime I was with Warren..." He rambles off. "I figured you were embarrassed and wanted to pretend it didn't happen, so I didn't say anythin'."

"No..." I shake my head. "I was behind y'all in line when you told Warren your memory was fuzzy after the cake. And that you were too drunk to remember most of the night. I was also enlightened to learn you only hung with me 'cause he asked you to *babysit* me..."

"You heard that?"

"Yes. Were you lyin'?"

"Jesus Christ, Posey." He runs a palm through his hair, pacing in front of me before stopping to face me. "Yes, he asked me earlier that day to keep an eye on you, but I wanted to be with you anyway. And of course, I lied! I wasn't about to tell your brother I slept with his sister, especially before talkin' to you about it. Figured if I acted like I couldn't remember most of the night, he'd stop askin' me questions. I hoped we'd talk after, but when you avoided me for weeks, I got the memo. Assumed you wanted to forget it happened."

"So wait..." I hold up my hand. "You remembered everythin'?"

"Yes. I still do."

"Wow..." I blink a few times, trying to steady my breathing. "You were quite convincin', I guess. We drank quite a bit, so I thought you were tellin' the truth."

"I wasn't...and perhaps I should've tried harder to get you to talk to me, but I thought maybe you were avoidin' me 'cause..." He looks away, licking his lips. "'Cause it was bad."

"You thought it was bad?" I panic, replaying those memories I've tried hard to suppress.

"No! I thought *you* thought I was bad and that's why you wanted to pretend it didn't happen."

"Why would you assume that?"

"'Cause it was my first time..."

My brows pinch in confusion. "First time what?"

His expression flattens. "I was a virgin, Posey. You were my first."

I balk, scoffing. "Now I know you're lyin'."

"I'm serious. We were drunk, and I stumbled a lot. I figured you wanted nothin' to do with me 'cause I was bad at sex or I left you unsatisfied."

He couldn't possibly think that after how vocal I was the entire time.

"Not that I had anythin' to compare it to, but it wasn't bad. I didn't wanna bring it up and you think—"

"Wait, whaddya mean nothin' to compare it to?"

I stare at him in disbelief because I assumed he knew. "It was my first time too."

His nostrils flare. "Oh fuck, Posey. Why didn't you tell me that beforehand? I would've waited until we were sober."

"Why didn't *you* tell me you were a virgin beforehand?" I throw back at him.

We stare at each other, breathing heavily, and at a stalemate for who or what's to blame for not talking about what happened almost two years ago. Clearly, our communication skills suck.

"I was embarrassed," he finally says. "And then even more embarrassed when I assumed the worst and thought it wasn't good for you."

Rocking on my feet, I lock my arms behind my back to stop myself from reaching out and touching him. "I had no complaints."

He arches a brow. "So if I had asked you, would you have said it meant somethin' to you?"

My heart races as I contemplate how to respond. "At the time, yes."

He steps closer, invading the space between us with his large build. "And now?"

I swallow down the lump in my throat, struggling to fully

comprehend what's happening. "It's hard to say after spendin' all this time being angry about it."

He tips my chin, forcing my gaze to meet his. "I remember every touch, every kiss and moan of yours, Posey. It haunted me in my dreams for weeks."

My breath hitches, gasping for air at the words I never expected to hear from him.

"I do too," I admit. "I already have bad luck with dating, so thinkin' you had no memory of our night added to my insecurities."

He rubs the pad of his thumb softly over my cheek and it sends a shiver down my spine. "I'm sorry you overheard me say that, but if I had known, I would've cleared it up immediately. Ever since your friend dared you to kiss me two years ago, it's all I thought about. I didn't know if the feelings were mutual, and you being my best friend's little sister, I was too chickenshit to ask. I didn't want Warren to find out and deck me for makin' a move on you."

"They were mutual," I tell him, sounding braver than I am. "I've had a crush on you since middle school, but I didn't know if you only kissed me 'cause you felt pressured or if you liked me too."

His gaze moves to my mouth, and I stare at his, wondering if I'll finally get to feel his on mine again.

When he leans in, I do too, but then he releases a deep, almost regretful, sigh and rests his forehead against mine. "After our night together, I thought we'd finally admit our feelings. But then we didn't and I had to eventually move on."

I step back, finding the remorse on his face. "Whaddya mean?"

"I'm datin' someone now. It's new, but I owe it to her and myself to see where it goes. I don't wanna be the guy who cheats. You deserve better than that. So does Gwen."

My blood boils with fury at the emotional whiplash. "Why did you bring it up then?"

"'Cause I wanted answers! Maybe that makes me a selfish asshole but there was no closure."

"*Closure*?" My voice raises with frustration.

"I never knew why you left that mornin' and acted like it never happened, so yeah…it was time we got it out."

"I tried wakin' you!" I push against his chest, annoyed with how close he is to me, but he doesn't flinch. "Told you we had an hour to get down to the brunch, then I left to shower and get ready."

"Okay, *that* part I don't remember…" He frowns. "But everythin' else I do."

"Maybe it's better this way. Warren needs us right now and being together would've made things awkward with Maisie leavin'." I shrug, stepping around him, but he grabs my arm to stop me.

"I'm sorry I hurt you, Posey. I wish I could go back and fix it."

And I wish he never told me.

I'd rather believe he had no memory of us than knowing he remembers everything because even now after admitting we had feelings for each other, I still get let down. If this ache in my chest is only a fraction of what Warren's been going through, then I don't want any part of it.

"Good luck with your new girlfriend." I pull my arm out of his grip and walk away.

chapter two

Silas

PRESENT DAY

Eight Years After The Wedding

"AUNDREA, PLEASE. DON'T DO THIS," I plead for the fifth time, feeling helpless and desperate as my fiancée packs her suitcase. She carefully removes a shirt from the hanger and folds it neatly before adding it to the others.

"It's not workin' out, Silas. It hasn't for a while and neither of us have wanted to admit it, but if you're honest with yourself, you'll see I'm right." She glances at me with pity in her brown eyes. "Better to realize it before the wedding than after."

The wedding that's scheduled to happen in two weeks.

I hear the words coming out of her mouth, but I can't comprehend how she can say them so cold and emotionless as if they aren't driving a dagger through my aching heart.

"You'll thank me once you realize how wrong we were for

each other. Once we spend some time apart, you'll realize movin' on was the right choice."

She says it like she already has.

"How can you say that?" The anger building in my chest threatens to spill out. "I've gone above and beyond to do everythin' to make you happy. Shit, I changed jobs to work with your dad since you said I didn't make enough money. I gave up my apartment to move into your fancy-ass house 'cause you said mine was too small. What more do you want?"

She zips up her Louis Vuitton bag before setting it on the floor with a thud. It's the first time she's using it since it was meant for our honeymoon. It took me six months to save up the money to buy it for our anniversary and now I'm wishing I hadn't.

No matter what I bought her, it was never enough or something her father couldn't buy her without having to max out a credit card. Though I tried to make her happy in other ways, I shouldn't be surprised at her expensive taste when we met on a sugar daddy dating app.

Warren dared me to sign up when we were drunk one night, and after I dared him to pierce his dick, I couldn't chicken out. But I never thought I'd match with someone and it'd turn into more.

She knew I wasn't *rich* before our relationship progressed and she reassured me it wasn't an issue. We fell in love and that's why I proposed. I wanted to spend forever together. But maybe that's why I was so blinded by how she treated me, always wanting more than I could give her and pushing me to be someone I'm not.

"I'm gonna stay at a hotel while you pack your things, but please be gone by Monday."

"That's it?" I throw up my arms still in disbelief. "You're throwin' away two years with no emotion?"

She wraps a dark strand of perfectly straight hair behind her ear and purses her red-stained lips. "We haven't been intimate in six weeks and the last time you tried to be spontaneous, you took me out into the woods to have sex in the back of your truck. We're not compatible."

"It's the busy season! Your dad has me workin' overtime," I explain, although she already knows since she's the receptionist at his home construction company. "And I made up for the woods incident, didn't I? Not much I can do when I don't get home until after eight and then gotta be back to work at six. Then you go out with your friends on the weekends, so..."

"I always invite you to come with me and you rarely do."

"That's 'cause none of your friends can hold their liquor and I always end up babysittin' 'em. Why the hell would I wanna do that every weekend? Especially since you ditch me most of the time and end up on the dance floor surrounded by other men."

"God forbid I wanna let loose and hang out with my friends," she says dramatically. "I'm not gonna apologize for havin' a social life."

"You know that's not what I'm sayin'." I fold my arms across my chest, staring down at the woman I asked to marry me only a year ago. Admittedly, things have shifted between us in the past few months, but I thought it was pre-wedding stress.

"It doesn't matter anyway." She shrugs mindlessly, lifting the suitcase handle and walking toward me. "I'm sorry for hurtin' you, I truly am. You're a great man, but not the right one for me and that's why I can't go through with it. I wish you the best."

She leans up in her four-inch heels and presses a soft kiss to my cheek. "Bye, Silas."

If she were truly apologetic, she wouldn't be giving me a two-day notice to move out. On top of that, I'm going to have to find a new job. There's no way I'm going to walk in each day and see her behind the reception desk, pretending we weren't supposed to build a life together.

After a couple days of packing boxes and feeling sorry for myself, I finally load up my truck and drive away from the place I've called home for almost two years.

I haven't had the energy to tell Warren or my family, but they'll find out soon enough. From either a "change of address" text or showing up and begging them to let me stay with them.

Before I chicken out, I drive to Warren and Maisie's house. I feel bad invading their Sunday together, but after what I dealt with when Maisie left, he owes me.

Thankfully, Warren put his energy into building his house and stopped drinking so much. He refused to date or move on from Maisie even after she sent him divorce papers several times.

She returned a few months ago, demanding he finally sign them so she could marry another man. He asked her to give him one week to prove they were still meant to be together and make her doubt getting divorced. I thought he was crazy for thinking she'd change her mind, but she did.

They're in a much better place than they were seven years ago. Although they're newly reunited after being estranged for so long, you couldn't tell they spent time apart. Still madly in love and obsessed with each other.

I knock twice on the door and am greeted by Warren's sleepy face.

"Silas?"

"Hey, sorry it's so early. Can I come in?"

His rooster crows in the distance. He has half a dozen chickens in the fenced-in area next to his cabin. I'd usually say hi to them, but I'm not feeling it today.

"Yeah, of course." He steps back so I can enter and then closes the door behind me. "Everythin' okay?"

It's been a couple weeks since we last saw each other but since my bachelor party is supposed to be next weekend, we've been making plans over text. Two weekends ago, Maisie threw him a surprise birthday party and he was suspicious when Aundrea didn't come with me. I didn't tell him we were going through a rough patch because I was hopeful it was only temporary.

"Not really," I admit, following him into the kitchen where I smell bacon and sausage. "This wasn't somethin' I wanted to tell you over the phone."

"Shit, that sounds serious." Warren crosses his arms and leans against the counter while I sit at the breakfast bar. "What happened?"

"Aundrea called off the weddin'."

Even saying the words aloud has my lungs burning and my chest aching. It still doesn't feel real.

"Shit, dude. Do you know why?"

"Things have been rocky for a while. She says we're not compatible and basically said it was better to end things before the weddin' than after. I have a feelin' she wanted a wealthier version of me and not the me who worked ten plus hours a day. I guess she had enough of me not being able to give her what she wanted—a sugar daddy."

Warren gives me a look that resembles the same look I used to give him: *pity*.

And I hate it.

"Yeah, so...now I'm out of a job and place to live."

He cracks a few eggs and starts scrambling them.

Before he can respond, Maisie enters with a wide grin. "Two hot men in my kitchen and the delicious smell of food? Have I died and woken up in a romance novel?"

I'd laugh if my heart wasn't shattered into a million pieces. She's a literary agent and loves reading, so I'm used to her talking about books.

"Mornin', baby." Warren gives her a quick kiss before sharing the devastating news. "Aundrea and Silas broke up."

She gasps, directing her gaze toward me. "Oh my gosh, I'm so sorry." She wraps her arms around my shoulders, and although I appreciate the sentiment, it makes me feel like an even bigger loser.

"He needs a place to crash for a bit," Warren tells her. "We could set up an air mattress in the library or living room until he finds his own place."

"I don't wanna be an inconvenience," I argue, especially

since I know they're fucking every single chance they have. They've been making up for lost time, which is why I haven't seen my best friend very much. "I can stay at a motel."

"Absolutely not." Warren shakes his head, handing Maisie and me a plate of food. He knows I can't afford it either, but I'd rather go into debt than hear them having sex every night. "We'll figure it out."

"What about Posey?" Maisie asks, and I quickly shake my head, but she ignores it. "She has a spare bedroom, and did I hear you need a job? She was just tellin' me she's still lookin' for extra help at the goat farm."

"Maze…that's not a good idea," Warren warns.

"Why not? It's perfect! He doesn't wanna sleep on an air mattress anyway."

Warren glances at me, and I sigh. "She'll never agree to it."

Maisie furrows her brows. "How come?"

"Posey's not his biggest fan," Warren tells her. "She crushed on him all through high school and teased her like a little sister. But when he never reciprocated those feelings, she refused to be 'round him."

That's not *exactly* the truth…but I don't correct him.

"That was years ago. Surely she's not still upset about it." Maisie glances between us.

"Trust me, she is," I say, stabbing a piece of my sausage. Posey and I rarely cross paths, but when we do, she avoids my gaze. "She hasn't talked to me in years."

"*Years?*" Maisie gasps. "That can't be right."

"It's true," Warren confirms, sitting next to her with his food. "Posey deemed him enemy number one. Anytime he's with me, she leaves or blatantly ignores him."

Maisie's quiet for a moment but has a look of determination on her face. "Hm…I'm gonna call her. Doesn't hurt to ask."

She pulls out her phone, and I already know it's not going to go well.

"Good mornin', my favorite sister-in-law," Posey singsongs, sounding happier than I've heard her in ages.

"Hello to *my* favorite sister-in-law." Maisie grins as if this greeting is the norm between them. "I have a big favor to ask."

"Okay, shoot."

My heart pounds, and my palms sweat with nerves. There's no way she's going to agree but a small part of me that hopes she does. Even if it'd be awkward, it'd be better than staying anywhere else.

The last thing I want to do is go to my parents with my tail between my legs and ask if their thirty-year-old son can move home.

It's bad enough I have to tell them the engagement is off. I'd like to have some dignity left.

My older siblings are married with small children, so it's not like they have room for me either.

"It'd mean a lot to both me and Warren, so please remember that," Maisie tells her, and I brace myself.

"You're pregnant? And you want me to be the godmother? I accept!"

Maisie snorts. "No, not quite. We have a friend who could use a place to stay while they look for an apartment, so would you mind a roommate?"

"Depends…" Posey's drawls. "Who is it?"

Maisie's gaze meets mine briefly before responding. "It's Silas."

"Are you fuckin' kidding me? Not happenin'. Please tell me you're jokin'."

I close my eyes at the anger in each syllable as her voice goes up an octave.

"Did your asshole husband ask you to fuck with me?"

"Posey, I'm being serious. Aundrea broke up with him and he has nowhere to go."

Ah yes, that doesn't make me sound desperate and pathetic.

"That's literally not my problem. He can sleep with the goats for all I care."

"Posey," Warren's deep voice bellows. "He can hear you."

"Motherfuckers! I hate y'all."

"It's fine," I blurt, not wanting them to fight on my behalf. "I'll figure somethin' else out."

"Time to get over your unrequited crush, Posey. You're the most forgivin' person I know. Why can't you let this go?" Warren asks.

The line goes silent, and I wouldn't be surprised if she hung up.

"Posey?" Maisie furrows her brows.

"It wasn't unrequited," she murmurs softly but loud enough for them to hear her.

Warren's eyes snap to mine as if demanding answers, but I chicken out and avert my gaze.

Fuck.

"What the fuck does that mean?" Warren barks. "Please tell me it doesn't mean what I think it means."

"It was a long time ago," Posey admits. "I have valid reasons for hatin' him, but if you wanna know why, ask him."

And then she hangs up.

Leaving me to deal with one red-faced Warren who's glaring at me.

Silence fills the air as I focus on the food in front of me, knowing he won't drop it, but wishing he would.

"Told ya she wouldn't agree to it," I mutter.

"You have a lot of explainin' to do."

I set my fork down and blow out a breath. "It's not what you're thinkin'."

Unless it's that I had a one-night stand with his sister, then it's exactly what he's thinking.

A memory that's haunted me for years, even worse when I found out she thought I'd forgotten about it and learned it was her first time.

Maisie scoots closer to me with a wicked grin. "Tell me everythin' and leave nothin' out."

Warren snorts and rolls his eyes. "But please limit any gross details…" He holds up his palm. "As her brother, I don't wanna know *everythin'*."

"Well, I do, so you can plug your ears," Maisie says eagerly. "Start at the beginnin'."

I tell them the truth—from the dare that led to our first kiss, to the night of our hookup, and then what happened almost two years after that. I admit I fucked up and should've communicated with her a lot sooner. And even when I thought I was doing the right thing by not making a move that night because I was dating someone else, I wish I hadn't told her I wanted to see how things worked out with Gwen.

We only last two months, but at that point, Posey wouldn't give me the time of day. She blocked my number and social media accounts. Then she started seeing some guy shortly after.

I ruined my chance and regretted it ever since.

"You need to apologize," Maisie tells me. "Make amends. Not 'cause you need a place to stay, but 'cause it's overdue and you owe her one. And you never know..." She smirks at Warren. "Sometimes apologies can lead to somethin' more."

Warren winks at her, and I gag at how sickly in love they are now, but I'm happy for them. They deserve it after what they went through and how long he waited for her.

"I don't think an apology is gonna fix how she felt when I rejected her," I admit. "Although I could blame Warren for most of my behavior."

"Me? How the fuck am I included in this?"

I chuckle. "You were a drunken mess. There was no way you'd be okay with me datin' your little sister. You'd either kick my ass and threaten to kill me if I hurt her or you wouldn't wanna see us together 'cause you were so miserable. You would've been in the middle and already weren't in a good place."

"Ooh, I vote for that. Put all the blame on Warren." Maisie giggles.

"Oh no..." He folds his arms. "If I'm being name-dropped, then so are you."

"I wasn't even here!" she argues.

"Exactly," Warren points out. "You broke my heart and it had a ripple effect. Now you deal with the consequences."

Maisie rolls her eyes. "My heart was broken too, but I didn't go and drink myself stupid."

This time, Warren rolls his eyes. "I eventually slowed down."

"Alright, lovebirds..." I hold up my hands so they stop

arguing on my behalf. "I'll apologize, but it probably won't do any good."

"Even so, at least then you can say you tried." Maisie grins. "And the offer for you to stay here is still on the table no matter what."

Her words cause me to glance down at the breakfast bar I'm currently eating at and wonder if they've done it here.

Knowing them, no surface in this house is safe, so I desperately need Posey to forgive me.

chapter three

Posey

"BATMAN, you little shit. Get over here." I chase behind the buck who somehow got loose and when I finally catch up to him, laughter echoes behind me.

My spine straightens when I recognize who it belongs to.

What the hell is he doing here?

You'd think after I basically word-vomitted my distaste for him on the phone yesterday, he would've gotten the hint.

Apparently not.

Maisie texted after I hung up to tell me Silas explained his side of the story but she wanted mine. I gave her the short version, which was similar enough to Silas's, so she knew he was telling the truth even if it made him look bad.

I might have overreacted a bit when she asked about him staying in my spare bedroom, but I was so taken off guard that my anger and frustration with him came out before I could stop myself.

"Posey."

The deep timbre of his voice saying my name sends a shiver through me, which I *hate*, but can't deny after all these years he still has an effect on me. Even if it's unwanted.

I've spent the past eight years trying to forget him. *And the details of our night together.*

"Whaddya want, Silas?" I ask harshly, opening the gate and directing the goat inside the fence. I need to get back to work, but I don't want him to follow me inside the barn.

"I was hopin' we could talk."

When I spin to face him, I regret it. His tight T-shirt shows off his muscular biceps, with one arm now full of tattoos, and the rest of him looking hot as usual.

But there's a pitiful sadness about him. His expression is full of remorse that I'd usually ignore.

I've purposely avoided having to see him because I knew my traitorous heart couldn't handle it. You'd think after all this time, I'd get over my attraction to him.

"So talk…" I demand.

"Could we go somewhere? Maybe for a drive or walk?" He shoves his hands in his pockets and sweat builds along his hairline.

He's nervous.

Good.

I place my hand on my hips. "I'm workin' right now."

My shirt's covered in coconut oil and my hair smells like lye and hay. The last thing I want is to be in close quarters with him while I reek of chemicals.

"Do you get a lunch break? I could come back."

"Not really." I shrug, losing my patience. "I'm shortstaffed."

"Are you hirin'? Could I apply?"

I bark out a laugh, crossing my arms. "You need a job too?"

"Unfortunately, yes."

Pinning him with my stare, I contemplate how to respond. "Do you have any experience?"

"I was a contractor for the past two years and built houses. Before that I worked in construction. I don't have goat-related experience, but I'm a hard worker who's used to being in the heat for long hours. I'm also a quick learner and will catch on to whatever you need me to do."

I consider his words for all of three seconds. "So you're a city boy thinkin' you can work a ranch job."

His forehead wrinkles in protest. "I wouldn't necessarily—"

"It wasn't a question."

His mouth snaps shut.

"Sorry, I need someone with animal experience, but thanks for stoppin' by!" I turn on my heel to walk away, grabbing an empty bucket on my way to the barn.

"Posey, wait. Please?"

The desperate plea in his voice has me stopping in my tracks.

"I'm sorry. I'm truly, so very sorry for how things happened between us. If you give me a chance, I'll prove it to you. And I know that my word might not be enough, but I'll do anythin' to make it up to you."

He thinks I'm still mad about what happened years ago. Although a part of me is upset that my first time having sex is tainted with the memory of thinking he didn't remember and then dangled the possibility of being together in front of me like a carrot before telling me he was dating someone else, it's not the only reason I've stayed away from him all these years.

"Anything?" I spin around, arching a brow.

"Yes. I'll do all the grunt work and more. Whatever you need."

That gives me an idea.

"Fine, I'll give you a week trial."

His eyes widen in excitement. "Seriously?"

"Don't be too happy yet. You'll be beggin' me for mercy by the time the week ends."

"It's a goat farm." He chuckles. "How hard can it be?"

Oh, Silas Mathiesen…you're about to eat your words.

"Do you have any idea what we do here? No, you don't, so let me fill you in…" I continue speaking before he can interrupt me. "I'll walk you through a typical day for my staff. Aside from the basics of feedin' and carin' for the goats, we milk 'em, then clean and maintain all the equipment. We monitor their health and wellbeing on top of maintainin' farm records for each goat. Then there's breedin' season."

"Breedin'?"

"Yes, when a mommy goat and daddy goat love each other, they make a baby goat. Well, technically, they're called kids. But anyway, keep up." I sigh, regretting my decision already. "There's filterin' and pasteurizin' the milk, which then gets distributed— some for goat milk we sell to local businesses and some we freeze for goat soap—which is another whole process from beginning to end. It's a lot of hands-on and teamwork. It's messy and dirty but—"

"I can handle it," he states confidently.

"Fine." I can't believe I'm about to say this. "Can you start now?"

He licks his lips, glancing down at his clothes. "Uh, sure."

"Great. Let's go."

He scrambles to follow me into the barn and before I can warn him to watch where he walks, he steps in goat shit.

"Don't wear your favorite boots to work next time," I demand. "You'll need waterproof rubber boots. Somethin' easy to rinse off and walk through mud."

"I didn't know you'd—"

I raise a brow that dares him to argue with me.

"Noted. I'll be more prepared tomorrow."

Looks like he's a fast learner, after all.

After introducing Silas to the staff, I give him a pitchfork and shovel, then put him on mucking duty.

"Hey Ian," I call him over from where he's watching Silas.

He's my right-hand man who's been with me since day one. When I got the approval from Dad to open a goat farm, I hired Ian to help me get things started. He supervises most of the staff while I run the goat soap business, Langston Soapworks.

"Yeah, boss?"

"Remember how Sheila broke your heart when she started sleepin' with your stepbrother?"

He deadpans. "Yeah?"

"And how you wanted revenge on 'em?"

He crosses his arms, studying me. "Where you goin' with this?"

"I want you to give Silas the revenge treatment. He should be cryin' and wantin' to quit by the end of the week, got it?"

A smirk forms across his tan face. "Do I get to know why I'm torturin' this poor man?"

"Let's just say, he deserves it." I pat him on the shoulder. "And you get to pretend he's Kyle. Or Sheila. Hell, both if you want."

Ian's stepbrother not only stole his fiancée from him but then knocked her up while they were still engaged. He's worked through it, mostly, but there's still some resentment left inside him and he's dying to take it out on someone.

His grin widens. "You're evil, Posey."

"Trust me, it'll be good for him." I wink, and he walks away shaking his head, but I know he's gonna enjoy it.

Silas thinks working on a goat farm is easy peasy and we're about to show him exactly what it takes.

I should take the highroad or at the very least be professional.

But if he wants to make it up to me, then he can start by getting dirty and sweaty.

Walking down to my office at the end of the barn, I grab a cold water bottle from the mini fridge and a work shirt from the cupboard. Even if he's here for a week, I don't need him passing out on my watch. Then I find some spare boots that may or may not fit him before finding Silas knee-deep in straw.

"Here," I say, grabbing his attention. "You'll wanna bring a tumbler or jug of water with you from now on. That way you can refill it throughout the day, but for now, I brought you this." I hand him the plastic bottle.

And that's as professional as he's getting from me.

"Thanks." He opens it and chugs half of it down.

"I guessed your sizes, so hopefully the shirt and boots fit. If not, well, too bad since it's all I had."

The corner of his mouth tilts up slightly. "I'll make it work, boss."

"Don't call me that," I snap.

"Oh, I thought I was supposed to." His gaze shifts to Ian, which means he overheard him calling me that.

"Ian's the farm supervisor, so you'll report to him. He's the only one who calls me that. He thinks it's funny." I shake my head. "Technically, my father is the boss since he pays the employees. I manage the goat soap business."

"Got it." Silas smirks, yanking off his T-shirt and giving me a full view of his chest.

His full tattoo sleeve of flowers and vines spread across his shoulder and down his pec, merging into a compass surrounded by roses and trees. It's breathtaking.

"When did you get that?" I blurt, unable to take my eyes off it.

His chest was bare the last time I saw him shirtless.

He follows my gaze, looking down. "About five or six years ago. After I finished my arm, I wanted somethin' larger on my chest."

"It's a compass."

My eyes snap to his. He knows I have a thing for compasses ever since my great-grandmother passed hers down to me when I was in high school. Her house was covered in compass-themed decor. Every time I see one, I think about her and how much of an impact she had on my childhood, which is why I got my own compass tattoo.

I was her first great-granddaughter, so she spent a lot of time spoiling me and teaching me random things about life. Her husband died before I was born, so I never met him, but she loved talking about him.

The night we hooked up, we talked a little about his tattoos, and I confessed I wanted one, but since then, he hadn't seen it.

"Do you like it?" he asks when I grow silent.

I hate it.

It's too similar to mine.

"What made you get that, Silas?"

He throws the work shirt over his head and adjusts it right above his buckle. It's a smidge short but it'll do for the few days he'll be here.

"I dunno...just liked the way it looked, I guess."

He's a bad liar.

I finally snap out of it and stop staring at him. "Okay, back to work. Ian will tell you what to do from here on out."

"Where're you goin'?" he asks before I can walk away.

"I work mostly in the back with Amaya makin' soap and doin' the marketin' for the business."

"Who's Amaya?"

"She works with me. I'm sure you'll see her 'round."

"Okay, cool."

I nod once before walking away but then Silas gently grabs my shoulder. "Posey."

"What?" I say harshly without realizing it.

Even though there's chaos surrounding us—people coming and going, goats bleating in the distance, and the noise of milk machines echoing from the other room—the moment my eyes lock with his, it stops. I don't know why he has this hold on me, but the silence is deafening when we're locked into each other.

"Thank you for givin' me a chance. I know we haven't talked in a long time, but I promise to work hard, stay out of your way, and do a good job. You'll hardly know I'm here."

Doubtful.

I swallow, licking my lips and lowering my gaze to break the spell. "Do you still need a place to stay?"

I hear the words come out of my mouth but I don't know why or how they do without my permission. Mentally slapping myself, I close my eyes before opening them and finding Silas staring at me.

"Yeah, I do but—"

"You can stay in my spare bedroom, *temporarily*, until you find your own place."

"Seriously?"

"You gotta follow my rules or I'll kick you out."

He grins. "Of course."

"We'll go over 'em later." I step past the wheelbarrow to walk back to my work area.

"See ya then, roomie!" he calls out, and my back stiffens.

"Most definitely, do not call me *that*," I shout over my shoulder and find him laughing.

Oh God. I regret this already.

"Who's the new hottie?" Amaya asks after watching Silas's poor attempt at running away from a few goats trying to eat his jeans. We took a quick break to eat before going back to pouring soap.

"Silas. But don't get any ideas. Work relationships are strictly prohibited," I tell her while recording a video of her wrapping soap bars for the social media page. The ones with music do the best, so I don't have to worry about talking or background noise.

Most of our sales come from online orders, but we do wholesale for a few shops in town so the local customers don't have to worry about shipping. The sample-sized soap goes into the resort self-care welcome basket, so those get separated.

She snorts. "Since when?"

"Since always. Especially when there's a power imbalance. It's unprofessional and could lead to termination."

"You're makin' that up."

"I am not!" I click off the camera and turn toward her. "It's in the employee handbook for the ranch and resort, which includes the goat farm."

"I don't recall signin' anythin', so I think he's free bait." She waggles her brows, and I snort at her implication.

"Well, you did, and he's not. Plus, he's on a week trial. You might never see him again after Friday."

I wouldn't be surprised if Silas was interested in her. Amaya's sweet and gorgeous, and knows how to have a good time. Although we didn't go to high school together, she's been a loyal friend and employee ever since we met a few years ago.

Her long brown hair is pulled up into twin space buns with a few loose curls in the front. It's adorable and cute, which is why I love making videos with her in them. They get the most views versus ones without her.

"In that case…" She seductively bites her lower lip. "He'll be eligible if you fire him."

"His engagement just ended. Maybe wait until he's not heartbroken anymore to hit on him."

"That's the best time! Get 'em when they're freshly wounded and lookin' for a rebound."

"Can we get back to work, please?" I ask pointedly. "We have five hundred orders to send out by Thursday and three new scents to make."

I set my camera aside so it doesn't get dirty. I do most of the editing at night after I eat dinner and then schedule my posts for the next day or two.

"I thought you were gonna hire more help for the summer season," she asks, grabbing more molds off the shelves.

Considering it's mid-August, the summer peak season is almost over.

"I wanted to but I haven't had time to go through job applications. Silas is only here 'cause he begged for a job, but I wasn't about to let him work directly with me, which is why he's now Ian's problem."

"Why? You two have history?"

I blow out a breath. "If I say yes, will you drop it for now?"

"Doubtful, but you can try." She smirks, pouring the liquid mixture into a mold before swirling it around with the other scent. Since it has to cure for four to six weeks, we're already working on fall-themed scents.

"Yes, okay? He's Warren's best friend. I've known him for years, but I've avoided him for several years now."

"That sounds juicy…" She cocks a brow. "Keep talkin'."

"Hard pass."

I put on my work goggles and gloves so I can add the lye to the frozen goat milk. It's one of the first steps we have to do before we melt the oils and mix them together. Since the soap has to stay in the mold for two to three days before cutting it, we're always making more batches to stay stocked.

By the time we finish at five, I'm ready to call it a day. Amaya and I worked nonstop to get things ready to package and ship out orders. Sometimes we stay a couple extra hours when we're behind, but I try not to make it a habit. Adding a third person would help speed up the process, but for now, we have things down to a science. We maneuver around each other and keep up without getting in each other's ways. Training someone new would take more time than we have right now.

"Posey?" Silas calls out.

"Back here."

"Oh damn, it reeks." He wrinkles his nose. "What is that?"

"A little bit of everything," Amaya responds. "Pumpkin pie spice, cinnamon apple cider, and lavender oatmeal."

Silas coughs, pulling his shirt up to cover his nostrils.

"Seriously?" I deadpan, staring at his muddy boots. "You smell like shit. Literally."

"Yeah, but I got used to that after a few hours. This is like being hit in the face with ten candles at once."

"That could be arranged."

Amaya snorts. "You get used to it."

He glances at me. "Doubtful."

"Suck it up 'cause I'm sure my house smells the same."

"Wait, he's goin' to your house?" Amaya asks, and I wince at the slip of my tongue.

"He's *temporarily* movin' into my spare room," I explain.

"Oh really?" If her grin were any wider, it'd stretch off her face. "You forgot to tell me that little interestin' tidbit when we were talkin' about him earlier."

And now I want to smack her.

"Y'all were talkin' about me, huh?" Silas smirks.

"Only about how annoyin' you are, so don't be flattered," I say before Amaya puts her foot in my mouth any deeper. "Are you ready to go?"

I already sanitized the work tables and washed up, so I grab my bag and walk toward him.

"Well since she's not gonna introduce us, I'm Amaya." She holds out her hand, and he happily accepts it. "Nice to meet you, Silas."

"The pleasure's all mine," he drawls.

I roll my eyes at the way his accent thickens.

"Great, now y'all know each other and we can leave." I push Silas into the hallway. "See ya tomorrow, Amaya!" I singsong, knowing she's going to have a million more questions for me.

"My suitcases are at Warren's, so can I meet you at your house? I should probably clean up first, too."

"Is that all you have with you?" I ask, walking through the barn and waving goodbye to everyone. There are a couple workers who start later in the day and stay through the evening so the day crew can leave before dinnertime. They also work the weekend shifts so the goats get milked on schedule.

"Yep. All the furniture was Aundrea's. She didn't like any of my stuff, so I put some of it in storage and got rid of the rest."

That's kinda sad considering he probably spent a lot of money and years buying his own things after moving out of his parents' house. And now he's starting over in a house that isn't even his.

"Okay, I'll leave the door open for you, so come over whenever you're ready. I'll get you a key, too."

"Sounds good, thank you."

"Mm-hmm." I avoid his gaze, uncomfortable at how heartfelt they look through me, then walk to my car.

I'm already dreading being alone with him—especially in my house—but I can't back out now. So I'll keep to myself and hope he finds his own place soon enough.

chapter four

Silas

YANKING OFF MY RUBBER BOOTS, I place them on the deck before walking through the door of Warren and Maisie's cabin. Then I unbutton my jeans and strip them off so I don't track dirt on the carpet. My shirt goes next since that's also covered in dust and straw. I hadn't expected Posey to agree to giving me a job, nevertheless, starting right away, so I was in my nice Wranglers and boots.

I texted Warren to give him the news and gave Maisie a heads up since she works from home. She's sitting behind her desk in the office when I find her.

"Hey!" Her eyes light up when she notices me in the doorway. "Why're you naked?"

"Excuse me?" Warren's voice echoes from her speakerphone.

"I'm not naked!" I quickly tell him before he rushes home and kicks my ass. He's normally home by now so I'm surprised he's not. "I didn't wanna track in dirt and goat shit."

Maisie beams. "How was your first day?"

"I'm certain Posey told that Ian guy to give me a hard time 'cause he didn't give me two seconds to breathe all day. Either he's a germaphobe who wants every speck of dirt cleaned up or Posey told him to purposely stay on my ass. On top of that, the goats kept chewin' on my clothes and chased me 'round the pasture until I tripped and fell."

Maisie chuckles, clearly enjoying my suffering.

"You'll get used to it," Warren says. "It takes a bit to get the hang of it, but I'm sure you will."

"Well, I'm certain she's hopin' I'll quit by the end of the week."

"I can't believe she agreed to let you move in too," Maisie says. "That must've been some apology you gave her."

"I did give her my best puppy dog eyes." I grin, but I'm just as surprised. "But if I suddenly go missin', don't be shocked if she puts a pillow over my head in my sleep and feeds me to the goats."

"Posey's very independent and headstrong. So, as long as you stay outta her way and don't suffocate her, she'll play nice," Warren explains.

I want to believe him, but there's a part of me that thinks she'll do whatever it takes to get back at me even if she acts like she's over it.

"I hope you're right. Well, I'm gonna shower, then grab my stuff and head over there."

"I should be home before you leave," Warren says. "Had to run to the grocery store to get steaks for dinner."

"Steaks? Well shit, now I wanna stay," I quip.

"Take your time, Silas. I'm sure Posey won't mind waitin' for you." Maisie winks.

Yeah, I'm sure she's eagerly awaiting my arrival.

I take a quick shower and change into clean clothes, then load up my bags. Warren's home by the time I'm ready to leave and I thank him again for letting me stay last night.

Even though the offer to crash there was made, I didn't want to invade their space. I'm lucky that Posey's letting me take her spare bedroom so it gives me more time to find an apartment in town. It'll be a bit of a drive to the ranch, but I'm used to commuting for work.

"See ya guys. Enjoy your dinner." I wave, opening my truck door.

"Hey, don't forget to see my dad and fill out paperwork so you get paid," Warren reminds me.

"Will do." Assuming Posey doesn't fire me in a few days.

"And if she ends up kickin' you out, you can always come back." Maisie smirks.

As I drive to Posey's cabin, it hits me how I've barely processed how much has changed in the past four days and in such a short matter of time. Aundrea was my longest relationship, and I thought we'd be together forever.

Now I'm pulling back the blinders and realizing I was more dedicated to our relationship than she could ever be.

I enter Posey's house, hauling in my suitcases, then set them by the door. Since I don't know her rules on shoes in the house, I take mine off and place them next to my bags.

"Posey?" I call out, walking through the living room.

The house is quiet and eerie with no lights on. Her car's parked in front, so she's here somewhere.

"Hello?" I say louder. "Posey?"

"Yeah?" She continues talking, but I can't make out the words.

I follow her voice to a door and open it so I can hear her.

Posey whips around, clutching a towel tight against her chest. "Ever heard of knockin'?"

"Shit, sorry." I smirk. "Though, nothin' I haven't seen before."

"Silas!" Her face goes red.

"You're all covered up. Except…" I arch my neck. "What's that?" I point toward the back of her thigh where a tattoo peeks out from underneath the fabric.

"None of your business." She attempts to hide it but I already saw the ink.

"C'mon, let me see. You saw mine."

She crosses her arms, tightening her hold. "All of yours?"

"No."

"Show me."

"Show me yours first."

Her lips twitch as if she wants to argue but then huffs and turns away. Looking over her shoulder, she carefully pulls up the towel. My eyes widen in shock at the compass design surrounded by flowers that starts on her left mid-thigh and continues up her ass cheek. I'm immediately jealous of the person who gave it to her.

"We have the same tattoo!" My jaw drops, amused. "It's gorgeous on you."

"No! You stole my idea!" She quickly spins back, hiding it from me. But I already engraved it to memory.

"I wasn't aware you were the only one allowed to get a compass tat."

She waves her finger, ignoring my comment. "Now show me your other one."

Lowering my sweatpants to my knees, I lift my boxer briefs and reveal the floral design on my right upper thigh. "It's nothin' special. I was bored."

"You really like flowers," she says, staring at it. "Didn't peg you as the slutty thigh tattoo kinda guy."

I pull my pants back up and straighten them over my waist. "Slutty thigh tattoo?"

She points toward it. "That's what that is."

"Is that what yours is too?" I quip.

"No, mine's on the back so it doesn't count."

I chuckle. "If you say so."

"I do. Now, can you leave so I can get dressed?"

"Sure thing, roomie." I shut the door behind me and hear her groan at me calling her that.

Grabbing my luggage, I bring them to my new room and set them on the bed. Sadness washes over me that my life is condensed in these two bags.

"Oh look, you found the right room." Posey leans against the doorway.

"I haven't been in here since it got remodeled." I helped Warren and his dad fix it up several years ago. It was a fun summer project. "Looks nice all decorated and furnished. I'm surprised they didn't end up usin' it as a guest cabin."

"They tried at first but once word got out that someone died in here, no one wanted to rent it out."

My hands freeze midair from pulling out my clothes. "What? Someone died in *here*?"

"Yeah, before the remodel," she explains. "But her spirit never left."

"Whaddya mean? Whose spirit?"

"The woman who died. Her name's Marjorie."

"You're fuckin' with me, aren't you?"

She's talking way too calmly about this.

"I'm being dead-ass serious. She likes movin' shit and openin' cabinet doors, so try not to freak out. I don't think she knows she's…" She lowers her voice. "*Dead.*"

I bark out a laugh, shaking my head. "Now I know you're messin' with me."

"Why would I lie about that?" she asks, defensively. "When no one wanted to stay here, I volunteered since I didn't wanna live at my parents' anymore. I needed more privacy."

"So this Marjorie…" I walk toward her, lowering my voice. "How do you know when she's *here*?"

"Things will go missin' or they'll be moved. Cabinet doors open after I've closed 'em. Sometimes things are left out that I already put away. She's usually harmless, but sometimes she lets me know she doesn't like somethin' or someone," she explains, walking through the hallway.

"*Someone?*" I follow her toward the kitchen.

"When I have friends or guys over. She'll flick the lights or slam a door to get my attention."

The silence lingers between us as I glance around the room for any weird movement. A cold shiver runs down my spine, sending goose bumps over my arms.

"Did you feel that?" I blurt.

"What?"

"Like a gush of air...cold air."

"No. But I wouldn't be surprised. She's not a fan of company." She shrugs, glancing over her shoulder.

"You couldn't have told me this little detail *before* tellin' me I could move in?"

"You didn't ask." She grabs a glass out of the cabinet, then opens the fridge.

"I didn't know that was somethin' to ask about!"

"Oh relax, you big baby." She pushes against my chest when I close the gap between us.

"You just told me this place is haunted and she doesn't like when you have people over. How should I act?"

"It's not *haunted*...it's spiritually-occupied."

I roll my eyes, moving out of her way when she nudges me back. "We need sage. And a priest."

She cackles. "For what?"

"To guide her into the light. Or wherever the afterlife is."

"Bellamy already tried that. We had a whole séance and even tried a Ouija board. Marjorie likes it here," she explains, pouring sweet tea into her cup. "And I like her too."

"Great, so I have to sleep in a house with two crazy women."

"Aren't you glad you asked to be roomies?" She brings the glass to her lips, smirking around it.

"Anythin' else I should know? You have a zombie livin' in the basement? A poltergeist in the attic? Perhaps a baby dragon in your bathroom?"

She licks her lips and my eyes track the movement. "No, but I have a pet rat named Teddy in my walk-in closet."

I squeeze the bridge of my nose. "Please be jokin'."

"Nope." She pats my chest before moving past me. "You're in the country now, city boy. Time to toughen up."

"Silas!" Posey's whispered voice above my head sends me into a panic, catching me off guard and thrashing against the mattress. My eyes struggle to find her in the dark.

"What the fuck?"

"Time to get up," she says, flicking on the lamp next to the bed.

"What time is it?"

"Six-thirty."

I groan, rolling away from her. "I thought we started at eight?"

"It's Tuesday, so we start at seven."

"Why?"

"Goat yoga at the Branch Haven every Tuesday and Thursday. We gotta load up the baby goats and bring 'em over, then back to the barn when it's over."

My eyes finally adjust to the lighting. I roll back over to find her in tight leggings and a pink sports tank. "*Goat yoga?*"

"Yes. And since you're the newbie, you get to be the demonstrator." She grins wickedly. "So wear pants you can stretch in."

"Wait, what?" I lift up on my elbows but she's halfway out the door.

"You heard me. Chop, chop!" She claps, walking down the hallway.

Groaning, I fall back on the mattress.

She's trying to kill me.

Once I'm out of bed, I change into sweats and a T-shirt, then find my running shoes. I have no idea what the hell goat yoga entails, but I have a feeling I'm going to regret finding out.

"Uh, Posey?" I glance around the kitchen, my mouth wide open in confusion.

"There's coffee in the pot. Help yourself," she calls from her room, then walks toward me. "And you should be grateful I'm sharin' my expensive beans with you."

"Is this supposed to be funny?"

"Whaddya mean?" She walks up to where I'm standing and finds what I'm staring at. "Oh."

Every cabinet door and drawer is wide open.

"Did you do this?" I ask, creeped out by the thought of the alternative.

"No, I swear. I haven't been in the kitchen. The coffeemaker's on a timer. I set it last night."

"You're tellin' me your ghost did this?"

"Marjorie," she confirms. "I told you she doesn't like guests."

I look down at her, scowling.

"Hey, you're the one who begged to live here." She holds up her hands.

"I didn't *beg*. Maisie asked on my behalf," I defend.

"Same thing. She'll get used to you...*eventually.*"

"That's reassurin'," I deadpan.

She clears her throat, bellowing out her words. "Miss

Marjorie, this is Silas. He's not here as a friend or boyfriend. It's temporary, so you don't gotta worry."

"Not even as a *friend*?" I smack my chest. "Ouch."

"Well, are we? Friends?" She moves into the kitchen, grabbing two tumblers before shutting the rest of the doors. "Workin' and livin' together doesn't automatically make us friends. We've barely had a conversation in six years."

"I thought we could be," I say somberly, grabbing the carafe. "Do you have creamer?"

"I have half-and-half." She opens the fridge and sets it on the counter. "And probably not."

"I guess that'll do." I pour some into my tumbler before tightening the lid. "And why not?"

"'Cause guys can never be friends with girls. They always sexualize 'em. And eventually when the fantasy ain't enough, they make a move and ruin the friendship."

"But we've already had sex. So it shouldn't be an issue to be friends, right?"

"I think being friends would complicate things."

"How so?" I challenge, leaning against the counter while she finishes making her coffee.

"We're gonna be late. Let's go." She walks off before I can stop her. "Do you wanna carpool?"

"Only if I can drive."

"Why?" She grabs her bag before opening the front door.

I follow her outside and wait while she locks up. "I've heard stories."

She rolls her eyes. "You're such a wimp."

"'Cause I don't wanna be a victim as you drive off a cliff?" I open the passenger side door and motion for her to jump in.

"That was one time and everyone was fine!"

Shaking my head, I close the door, then walk around to the other side.

"So what does goat yoga entail?" I ask, hitting the gas. "I don't gotta do any weird positions, do I?"

Her lips curve into a wicked grin. "I hope you're flexible."

chapter five

Posey

ONCE WE LOAD up the baby goats in the crates on the trailer, Silas drives us to the Branch Haven. The class is outside and has already started, so we back up to the gate of the fenced-in area and wait for the instructor to give us the go-ahead to take out the goats.

The first forty-five minutes are a structured class and then the remaining fifteen are when the goats roam free. The instructor usually demonstrates so they know how to pose to get the goats to jump on their backs.

Today, Silas gets to demonstrate.

"So what's the point of this?" Silas asks while we watch.

"Yoga improves flexibility and balance, it also helps reduce stress and anxiety. It's known to boost immunity along with strengthenin' your core and posture. Plus—"

"I meant the goat part, Posey. How do they help?"

"It's a form of animal therapy but it's mostly to add in a fun element, which reduces stress and leads to a relaxed and mindful experience. When a goat climbs your body, it helps increase balance and improve mood."

He snorts. "You read that off a pamphlet?"

"I helped with the marketin'," I admit. "And I'll have you know addin' goat yoga twice a week has increased membership by 150%. Anyone can sign up for it, not just the guests at the resort. So people from the surroundin' towns come each week."

"For fifteen minutes?"

I grin, shrugging. "People love baby goats."

When it's time, I open the fence and we usher them in.

Everyone sits in butterfly pose, smiling and laughing as the goats hop around.

Once the gate's closed, I bring Silas up to the front and roll out one of the extra mats.

"He's gonna demonstrate for you today," I tell Mila, smirking while I tie on my apron that's filled with treats.

"I'm what?" Silas whisper-hisses.

I nod toward the mat. "Downward dog."

"What is that?"

"Kneel on the mat with your palms flat and lift your knees up. Then straighten your legs and stretch back," I tell him in the easiest way he'll understand. "Although you can bend your knees a little if you need to."

His gaze pingpongs between Mila and me. "Why?"

"So I can have the goat climb on your back," I explain, then point at the mat. "Now do it."

Everyone's staring at us, so I give him an encouraging nod.

Reluctantly, he steps on the mat, gets to his knees, and looks at me. His stare is lethal, and I bite my lip to stop myself from laughing.

I motion for him to keep going and when he finally gets on all fours, Mila stands behind him and grabs his hips to align them.

"What the—"

"There, that's better." Mila pats his butt. "Now stretch back slightly and hold."

I walk around and find Silas glaring.

"Lookin' good, city boy."

Grabbing a handful of treats, I get one of the goats' attention and direct them to climb on top of Silas's back. His eyes widen at the added weight.

"Push on your tiptoes if you need to steady your balance," I tell him.

His posture isn't perfect but it's doing the trick. Mila instructs everyone to get into the same pose while I keep the goat in place with treats.

Once the goat jumps down, I give Silas's ass a little love tap. "You can rest now."

He collapses. "That wasn't any of the things your little marketin' bit said it'd do."

I scoff. "You didn't relax. You were too tense."

Walking through the class, I help with getting the goats to climb on their backs and bribe them with more treats. Mila directs the class into child's pose, lotus pose and then a plank— all ones that make it easy for the goats to climb them while they balance and stretch.

Giggles echo through the air as the goats hop from person to person, getting more treats and lots of pets.

Once the time is up, Silas helps me get them loaded back into the crates. Mila closes out the class and thanks them for coming.

"Well, that was…interestin'." Silas glances at me from the driver's side, taking us back to the barn.

"In a couple weeks, you'll easily hit that pose. Probably a few other ones too."

"Please tell me you're not gonna keep makin' me do that twice a week?"

"The women loved you! Pretty sure a few of 'em were throwin' heart-eyes your way. Now they're gonna expect you each time, so you gotta keep doin' it."

"I didn't agree to that…am I gettin' paid for this?"

"You're livin' in my house rent-free," I remind him.

He snorts. "Do *you* pay rent?"

"That's none of your business."

Dad wouldn't take my money even if I did offer to pay. He said he'll only take it when I buy land to build a house and since I'm nowhere near ready to do that, I'll take the free cabin.

"Fine," he agrees. "But then you're buyin' all the groceries. And I want *flavored* creamer. None of that half-and-half crap."

"What? No way. You probably eat twice as much as me." I scoff. "And what's wrong with half-and-half?"

"If I'm lettin' goats stand on my ass twice a week, that seems fair." He lifts a shoulder. "And it's borin'. I like a little caramel in my coffee. Or vanilla even. Pumpkin Spice when it's available this time of year."

I roll my eyes at his basic-ass tastes. "We'll go shoppin' tonight after work. But I'm only payin' for *one* creamer."

"Deal." He grins, backing up his truck in front of the fence. "Look at us compromisin' as roommates already."

"Mm-hmm," I mutter. "I wouldn't get used to it."

He winks before jumping out of the truck.

Following him, we get the baby goats back inside the fence, I put the crates away, and then he unhooks the trailer before climbing back into his truck.

"I gotta change and grab my boots," he tells me. "Can you let Ian know?"

"Yep." I wave him off, then go and find Amaya after telling Ian to give Silas a hard time for being tardy.

"Pumpkin Spice Latte or Pumpkin Pie Spice?" Silas holds up two creamer flavor options, glancing between both as if he's making the hardest decision of his life. "Which one?"

"They sound the exact same, so just pick one," I deadpan.

"No, the pictures on the labels are different. Look!"

He shoves them closer to my face, and I quickly grab one and throw it in the buggy. "There, let's go."

"Good choice." He smirks, while I move to the yogurt section.

"You like smoothies?" I ask, deciding if I should buy one or two containers.

"Yeah, sure. What kind are you gonna make me?"

I side-eye him. "Strawberry-banana with a pinch of rat poison."

"Oh, in that case, I'll pass."

Grabbing one of the tubs, I toss it in. "Anythin' else you need?"

"Beer?"

"Alcohol is on your tab, not mine." I walk toward the front of the store. "I'll meet you at the checkout."

"Hello, Miss Posey," Margarita greets while I load groceries on the belt. "How've ya been?"

"Good, and you? How's Millie?"

"Recoverin' well, though she hates wearin' the cone, it's stopped her from lickin' the wound."

I smile wide at that. "I'm so happy to hear that."

Margarita's pug got hit by a car last week and had to get emergency surgery. Her daughter set up a GoFundMe to help pay for it and it was funded in less than two hours by everyone in Willow Branch Mountain chipping in.

Mom and Aunt JoJo baked goodies, then Bellamy and I brought them over shortly after Millie came home.

"She enjoyed the treats your mama and aunt made her."

"Oh good! I'm sure they'd love any excuse to bake her some more."

"Mr. Mathiesen." Margarita's eyes widen as she glances between him and me. "You two shoppin' together?"

"No," I respond at the same time Silas answers, "Yep."

Margarita's knowing grin has me shaking my head.

"I'm lettin' him stay in my spare bedroom *temporarily*," I tell her.

"You keep sayin' it like that, I'm gonna start thinkin' you don't want me there," Silas quips, nudging me with his elbow.

Shooting him a glare, I walk away to bag our items.

Just because I'm taking the high road and letting him stay doesn't mean I want to be on friendly terms. Keeping him at a distance is what's going to help me get through this until he finds a place.

"Have you looked for any available apartments?" I ask him when he comes to help me.

"Between goat yoga and being haunted by your ghost, I haven't had time."

I snort. "You're so dramatic. If you want, I can help you look."

"You sound like you're tryin' to get rid of me only after two days…" He puts all the bags in the buggy, glancing at me over his shoulder with a shit-eating smirk. "But that can't be, right?"

"Perhaps I'm not being obvious enough," I mutter under my breath.

Margarita's smile stays planted in place when she tells me the total. I grab my wallet and scan my card, then take the receipt.

"Give Millie kisses for me," I tell her, then follow Silas with the buggy out of the store.

"I didn't want Margarita thinkin' we were together," I blurt, loading the bags in the back of Silas's truck.

"What?"

I swallow hard. "If I don't specify that you're livin' with me temporarily, she'll assume we're together. And if she thinks that, it'll get 'round town that we're datin'. Considerin' you were engaged four days ago, I don't wanna be known as the other woman. Or worse, the reason y'all broke up. So yes, I have to clarify or they'll call me a homewrecker."

"Okay, that's fair." He nods. "So you don't mind that I'm there?"

"Well…" I hand him the last bag. "Undecided. It's only been two days."

The corner of his lips tilts up. "I know you said being friends would complicate things, but if I promise to keep my hands to myself, we could be, right?"

It's not his hands I'm worried about.

It's my heart.

Closing the door, I inhale a deep breath. "If you don't make me wanna kill you in your sleep by the end of the week, then I'll think about it."

"Okay, deal."

Silas drives us downtown so he can get rubber boots in his size and some new jeans.

"Whaddya think of these?" He turns, lifts his shirt, and shows me his ass.

"Um…" I lick my lips at the tight globes in my direct view. "Why're you showin' me?"

He faces me, shrugging. "I dunno. Aundrea always wanted to see."

"They look fine to me. But you might want some looser ones since you're bendin' and movin' 'round a lot. Those look like one wrong move and they'll rip down the middle."

"Yeah, that would suck. Be right back."

He walks to the shelf at the back of the store, and I go back to doom scrolling on my phone. After a long day in the heat, I'm ready for a bath and pint of ice cream.

"Okay, I'm ready." He kicks my foot, grabbing my attention.

"Did you find everythin' you needed?"

He holds up the boots in one hand and three pairs of jeans in the other. "Yep. Found a few flannels too since Aundrea hated 'em and never let me wear 'em."

"Let you?" I arch a brow, eyeing them tossed over his shoulder.

"Well...she said I looked like a hillbilly lumberjack and wouldn't be caught dead with someone who wore one."

Karma needs to kick her where the sun don't shine.

Grabbing my bag, I follow him to the checkout. "Sounds like the woman's equivalent to changin' her hair color or cuttin' it after a break-up 'cause her man had a preference."

"I like my hair, so the flannels will have to do." He shrugs, setting his items on the counter. "Although..."

"No. Don't touch your hair. It's fine."

He slides a palm through it, shaking it out a bit. "You think so?"

I shoot him a glare at fishing for a compliment. "I just said it was fine."

"I love it!" the girl behind the register blurts. "It's a smidge long on the sides, but I could clean it up for you. I work at a hair salon on the weekends."

"Really? That'd be great since the one I used is my ex-fiancée's best friend and I'm pretty sure she'd shave it all off if I went to her."

She reaches over, threading her fingers through his strands. "Oh yeah, it'd be super easy. And your hair is so soft and shiny."

"That's called sweat," I say dryly, then nod toward the counter. "We have groceries in the truck if you wouldn't mind hurryin'?"

"Oh, for sure!" She reaches in her back pocket, then hands

Silas a business card. "Call or text to make an appointment. I'll *squeeze* you in any time you need me."

When she winks, I roll my eyes.

"Will do, thanks—"

"Michelle!" She grins wide. "Yours?"

"Silas. And this is my roommate, Posey."

"Oh, that's an adorable name," she gushes but it sounds like the way you'd tell a child their art project is a masterpiece when it's just smudges of different colored paint.

"I haven't seen you before. Did you move here recently?" I ask.

"About six months ago," she responds, folding his jeans and flannels into a large bag. "Everyone's been *so* nice here."

"I bet," I mutter, glancing down to her revealing lowcut top.

As a petite girl with B cups, I'd flaunt mine too if I had bigger ones like hers.

"Thank you, Michelle. I'll text you to make an appointment soon," Silas says, carrying the two bags of clothes while I reluctantly carry his boots.

"Sounds great! Have a great night."

"She seems nice," he says, loading his bags in the truck before taking the boots from my grip.

"Yeah, a real annoyin' ball of sunshine."

He snickers, opening my door, then closes it once I'm settled into the passenger seat.

"Am I okay to use the washer tonight or do you have plans to do laundry?" he asks when we're almost home.

"As long as I can use the dryer for fifteen minutes before bed, then go for it."

"Whaddya use the dryer for?"

"My comforter. I like it freshly warm."

"Every night?"

I snap my gaze to his judgy expression. "I get cold. Plus, it feels nice."

"Huh. I never thought to do that. Now I wanna try it."

"You're a brick wall of muscle. You probably radiate heat just fine."

"That's true." He nods, then glances my way.

"What?"

"Nothin'."

His sly smirk tells me otherwise.

I blow out an annoyed breath. "Just say it."

"You called me a brick wall of muscle. And you said my hair looked good."

"Oh my God…" My head falls back against the seat with a groan. "I said it was *fine*. And you know you're muscular. Did Aundrea never compliment you or somethin'?"

His eyes shift to the road. "Not really. She mostly pointed out what she didn't like about me and what I needed to change."

"You know that's not normal, right? Your partner should love you for you and not wanna change every little thing about you or only point out your flaws."

"I do know that but I wanted to make her happy."

"The right person will be happy with exactly who you are."

"I used to believe that. But I guess she warped my idea of what that means."

"Well, I'm sure Michelle would *love* to remind you," I drawl.

He chuckles. "Why do you say it like that?"

"'Cause she was flirtin' with you before knowin' if we were together or not."

"Did you want her to think we were together?"

"I didn't say that."

"Then what're you sayin'?"

"Can we just drop it, please? I'm starvin', exhausted, and I still have to edit a few videos tonight."

"Do you want me to cook you somethin'? I wouldn't mind."

I shift my gaze toward him. "Depends. What can you make?"

"I can make grilled cheese. Do you have soup?"

"I think so," I say. "But yeah, that sounds good."

"Perfect."

"Did you cook for Aundrea a lot?" I ask, grabbing our bags from the back once we're parked.

"No, she refused to eat my cookin'. She'd rather go out or order in and then expect me to pay."

"This is gonna sound rude but I gotta ask…" I walk into the house and he follows me to the kitchen. "Why'd ya stay with her so long? She sounds awful."

"I've been wonderin' the same thing, honestly. I think it boils down to likin' the idea of us together, settlin' down, and startin' a family. I ignored all her red flags 'cause I wanted someone to love, but I don't think she knew how to love me back."

That makes me want to hunt her down and find out what the hell is wrong with her.

We set the bags on the counter, looking at each other. "You deserve someone who will love you back. Even if it hurts right now, it'll get better."

"Thanks, and you do too."

"I'm not holdin' out hope since I can hardly find a guy to stay with me for more than a few months before they end it."

"I'm shocked they don't fall immediately in love with your bubbly personality," he quips.

Laughing, I playfully push against his chest. "I'm very nice, thank you."

"I've yet to witness it but if you say so."

I roll my eyes, putting items into the fridge. Then I roll them again when I grab Silas's bottle of creamer.

"If it helps any, I'm a pro at gettin' over a broken heart, so I can give you advice in that area," I say, shoving boxes of Mac 'n' Cheese into the cupboard.

"I'm all ears."

"The best way to get over someone is to date someone new."

He arches an unamused brow. "That's your *best* advice?"

"Okay yes, it's an obvious one, but I have more," I defend. "Get rid of all your photos together. Erase 'em from your phone and social media pages. Don't post anythin' wishy washy or depressive. Especially sad song lyrics. You want her to think you're doing better off without her and then you'll eventually believe you are. Buyin' new clothes was a good first step."

"Should I post a selfie in my new flannel?"

I bellow out a laugh. "Absolutely. She'll hate it."

"Okay, what else?" he asks as we continue bringing in more bags.

"If you haven't already, block her number. Don't give yourself the hope she'll reach out or the temptation to text her. Wallowin' is only acceptable the first forty-eight hours, after that, you only rot in bed as self-care."

"What's the difference?"

"You watch a funny show or movie, eat healthy food, and do a face mask. No cryin' allowed unless it's from laughter."

"And that works?"

"Foolproof." I grin, moving past him to stock the pantry. "And then you get up the next mornin' and the next day and the next…eventually, they're no longer the last person you think of when you fall asleep or the first person when you wake up. Your heart doesn't beat faster at the thought of 'em and you become indifferent when they do enter your mind. That's when you know you're over 'em and can move on for good."

He's in front of me when I close the door. I glance up and immediately regret it when I find his eyes glossed over and his expression too soft for my liking.

He knows I'm talking about him.

chapter six

Silas

IT'S TAKEN me six years to realize the gravity of how badly I hurt Posey when she realized I hadn't forgotten about our night together and then started dating someone else. Although it was miscommunication on both sides, I should've gotten over my fear of rejection and spoken to her about it sooner.

You don't talk about how to get over a heart break without experiencing it for yourself. So even if she gives me a hard time, teases me, and acts like she's over everything that happened between us, I'm going to find a way to make it up to her.

Better late than never.

"I wish I hadn't lied to Warren that day," I blurt when our eyes meet.

She looks up, her brows pinched in confusion. "What?"

"The day after his weddin'. The conversation you overheard. If I hadn't lied and said I'd forgotten most of the night, you never would've assumed I didn't remember. I should've made up somethin' else."

"It was a long time ago, Silas. No point in rehashin' the past." She moves to walk past me, but I grab her arm. Her gaze lowers to where my fingers wrap around her.

"But I did remember," I tell her, inching closer. "I just…want you to know that you'd be impossible to forget, Posey. Being the one to kiss and touch you, then later findin' out I'd been the only one to have you that way, I've kicked myself for fumblin' you ever since. And maybe that's why I've self-sabotaged and let someone like Aundrea treat me like shit."

She doesn't move, just stares and swallows hard, and I worry I've crossed the line. Posey stands behind a wall, using dry humor and sarcasm to protect herself, and it's starting to make sense why she pushes people away. Even if the guys are the ones to break up with her, it's because she's holding back to avoid getting hurt again.

From the way *I* hurt her.

"Posey?" I mutter softly when she doesn't say anything.

She finally blinks. "Well, it's a good thing we can be adults and move on from the past. Now you know you deserve better and won't continue the pattern."

This time when she moves to walk away, I let her.

Once I've picked up the kitchen and recycled our grocery bags, I pull out bread and cheese, then look for a can of tomato soup. I play music from my phone and get to work.

I sing along to my favorite song, and when I flip the first sandwich, the music stops, leaving me to belt the chorus on my own. When I tap my screen, it's paused. So I hit the button and bop my head when the music returns.

Thirty seconds later, it happens again.

"What the hell?"

This time when I press the play button, I watch as it pauses on me two seconds later.

Deciding the app must be glitching, I delete it and then redownload it.

While I wait for it to load, I prepare the next sandwich and lather butter on the bread. After it's on the pan with two slices of cheese, I check my phone and put my song back on.

Luckily, it plays normally and I continue singing.

Right when it's my moment to shine and hit the final high note, it shuts off again.

"Motherfucker," I grit between my teeth.

"She doesn't like that song." Posey's voice behind me causes me to jump.

"Huh? Who?"

"Marjorie. It's why she keeps turnin' it off."

With the spatula tight in my grip, I spin around and look for evidence of her. "She's in here right now?"

"Seems like it," she states without concern and opens the fridge. She pulls out the sweet tea and sets it on the counter. "She's in her eighties. She's not gonna like that hiphop pop stuff."

"You're fuckin' with me...it's a Wi-Fi issue, right? Right?"

She snickers, grabbing a glass. "Sure, the Wi-Fi."

I know she's lying, but I want to believe it.

"How's it goin' in here?" She peeks into the pan before I quickly flip it so it doesn't burn.

"Yours is in the microwave keepin' warm. Once I finished mine, I was gonna warm up the soup."

Inhaling deeply, I smell her shampoo and fruity bodywash, then realize her hair's wet.

"Did you shower?"

"Yeah, I took a quick one so you could get your clothes in the wash."

"Oh."

That's unusually nice of her.

"I'll probably head to bed at ten, so that should give you enough time to get your clothes out of the dryer before I need it."

And there it is.

"Sounds good. I'll do it as soon as I'm done eatin'."

Posey takes her sandwich and soup to the small table in the kitchen. I join her, but we're silent as we eat. As soon as she's done, I take her dishes and rinse them in the sink. While I load them in the dishwasher, she gets the coffeemaker ready and scheduled for tomorrow morning.

"Look at us actin' like an old married couple," I tease.

"Sounds 'bout right. No sex and sleepin' in separate beds."

I bark out a laugh. "Do you ever let your guard down, Posey? Or let yourself laugh and have fun?"

"Of course I do." She wipes down the counter where she spilled a little of the water. "Just not usually 'round men."

I'm sure that was meant to be an insult but it makes me chuckle anyway.

Posey disappears for the next few hours to edit her videos while I do my laundry and organize my closet to fit my new clothes. Since there's no TV in my bedroom, I sit in the living room and watch a rerun of an older show, hoping if Marjorie's really here, she'll approve and not mess with me.

At quarter to ten, Posey emerges with a white sheet mask on her face, her hair pulled back in some oversized headband, a pink plush robe that goes to her knees, and goat stuffies on her feet. She walks toward the laundry room with her massive comforter in her arms.

"What're those?" I pause the TV and grin when she walks through after putting her blanket in the dryer.

"Slippers. Christmas present from Bellamy. Aren't they cute?" She taps them together.

"Adorable. I wonder if they have my size so we could be roomie twins."

"Afraid they're sold out. They were a seasonal one-time sale," she states quickly without apology.

"Hmm." The corner of my lip tilts up at how bad of a liar she is. "Too bad."

"Yep. Thank you for dinner, by the way. I forgot to say that and didn't want you to think I was ungrateful. It was good."

"You're welcome, but I'd never think that about you."

"Okay..." She bites her lip. "Well, good night. As soon as the dryer's done, I'm gonna go to sleep."

"You look cute." I wave my finger around my face to indicate hers. "You have an extra?"

"You wanna wear a face mask?"

"Sure, if you don't mind sharin' one with me. The dirt and dust from the barn can't be good for my skin." I rub over my jawline dramatically so she'll take pity on me.

"Okay, hold on."

She leaves and returns a minute later with a small package.

"Lean your head back on the couch and close your eyes," she orders, and I happily oblige.

The cold wetness causes me to shiver as she smooths it across my forehead and cheeks. The pads of her fingers slide under my chin, rubbing the serum into my facial hair and down my neck.

Even if she's not meaning to, her soft touch drives me wild. It's taking everything in me to breathe normally.

"How long do I gotta keep this on?" I mumble, barely able to open my mouth.

"Fifteen to twenty minutes."

After she throws out the trash and washes her hands, I'm surprised when she sits on the couch next to me.

"Whatcha watchin'?"

I click play on the remote. "Golden Girls."

She looks at me and although I can't see underneath her mask, I can tell by the movement that she's smiling. "Marjorie loves this show. I'll come home to it playing when I never turned on the TV."

"That's what I was hopin'."

If I can't get Posey on my good side, the least I can do is get her house ghost on my side and to stop fucking with me.

When the dryer buzzes, she stays put to finish the episode. Then she returns without her mask and hands me a dry washcloth.

"Here, pat it dry," she orders after removing my mask for me.

I do as I'm told, then rub my fingers over my clean face. "My skin's never felt smoother."

"For ten dollars a mask, it better."

"For *one* mask?"

"Yep. But I buy 'em in bulk so it's a smidge cheaper."

"For that price, it better give me a shave job too."

She snorts. "Wait until you learn how much facials cost."

"Trust me, I know," I groan, thinking about the time I bought

Aundrea a gift certificate as part of her birthday gift and one session blew through half my budget.

As if she can read my mind, her expression shifts to one of pity.

"Well, thanks again. I'm gonna crash out too." I stand, and we go to our separate bedrooms, catching each other glancing over our shoulders before closing our doors.

"You ready to learn how to milk?" Ian asks a half an hour after I clocked in.

I smack my hands together to brush off the dust. "If you think I'm ready, sure."

Today's my fifth day working here and the last day of my week-long trial. Up until now, I've been on cleaning and feeding duties.

His grin turns wicked as he smacks me on the back. "Guess we'll find out."

This must be some kind of test to determine if I'll get to return on Monday. After yesterday morning's goat yoga, which I thought couldn't get any worse than what it was on Tuesday, Posey had me in a revolved triangle pose. On its own, it's already hard for a newbie, but add a goat standing on my back while I bend and twist my spine, my hips and thighs were screaming.

I sucked it up because I didn't want everyone to see me fail, especially since a few of them were recording me.

And of course, she teased me about being a city boy who needed to stretch more.

She's not wrong because I woke up stiff with a pinched sciatica and it still hurts.

As Ian leads the way to the milking area, Emily waits next to a stand with one of the goats tethered and a bucket of grain to keep it distracted.

"She's gonna teach ya how to do it," Ian says.

"Wait...I'm doing it by hand?"

I've seen them use a machine.

"Everyone has to learn how to hand milk before they use the portable machine. If there's an issue and they can't be used or we're down a machine, you gotta know how to do it on your own 'cause they're on a schedule since some only get milked once a day and the ones who are twice a day gotta be twelve hours apart."

He's explained some of the process to me where some goats will be in a dry period and some are still nursing their babies so they share the milk. But honestly, a lot of the production details go above my head.

"That gonna be a problem for ya, city boy?"

Posey's voice behind me has the hair on the back of my neck standing up.

I turn around to her smug face. "Of course not. I can handle it."

Amaya stands next to her, grinning wide.

"Good, 'cause it'll build a better connection between you and the goat and will make it easier when you switch to a machine."

"Makes sense," I agree. "But I didn't realize I'd have an audience."

"I couldn't miss your *first* time," Posey muses, crossing her arms and leaning against the wall.

"And I'm here for moral support," Amaya chimes in.

Those two are as transparent as glass.

"Go wash up." Emily nods toward the sink.

She's one of the workers and only a few years younger than Posey, but she's been more tolerable about me being new and learning about the job.

Once my hands are clean, I go over to where Emily sits on a stool next to the stand.

"Robin's a feisty one and is usually good during milkin', but you'll still wanna watch her legs in case she kicks."

"Kicks?"

"Yeah, especially if you're takin' a while. And you'll need to watch the bucket so she doesn't get her hoof in it and spill everythin'. You can use your forearm as a barrier if you need to."

"Got it."

"First thing you'll do is clean the udder and teats. This helps prevent contamination."

She takes a wipe and shows me what to do. "Don't be too gentle with the teats or it'll feel ticklish and then she'll most definitely kick you."

I wince. "Noted."

"You're gonna wanna get closer and watch my hands." She glances up at me, and I step toward her to get a better look.

"You wrap your thumb and fingers right above the teat to trap the milk and then squeeze. Don't pull down. You'll loosen your grip slightly to let the milk come down before squeezin' it again." She shows me, making it look effortless.

I notice the way her thumb doesn't move, only her fingers on the back. "The first few squirts you'll do in this small jar to make sure she doesn't have mastitis and look for blood in the milk," she explains, quickly examining it before putting the stainless steel bucket underneath the udder.

"In the event it does look weird, you'd empty her out and toss the milk. Then, let Ian know so he can examine her."

I nod.

"You can do both at the same time or rotate to give your hand a rest in between." She shows me both options. "Or if you prefer, you can do one hand at a time. Either way, it should only take three to five minutes per goat. You'll know she's done when there's only a few drops left and the teat will be soft and limp."

The worst combo.

As I continue watching her, more milk comes out. Her hands work so fast, I'm not sure how they don't get tired after continuous movement.

"Ready to try?"

"Um…" I glance over my shoulder at Posey. She gives me a little finger wave with a good-luck-asshole grin. Swallowing hard, I look at Emily. "Yep, I'm ready."

I've built houses, fixed plumbing in old-ass houses, torn out ancient flooring, and knocked down walls without breaking a sweat. I shouldn't be this nervous to milk a goat.

Emily stands, moving past me, and I sit on the stool.

"If that's uncomfortable, you can sit on the stand next to the goat. You have longer legs than me, so…" Her cheeks flush, and I notice how close hers are to my knee.

"I'll give this a try." I smile in return.

Once my hands are in position, I do as she said. I pinch the teat at the top and slowly squeeze. But nothing happens. I try again, making sure my grip is tighter before squeezing again.

"Try it faster." Emily leans in, wrapping her hand around one of mine and does the motion for me. She pulls our fingers up, then squeezes down. "It should be one fluid motion from top to bottom. Like this…"

She repeats it, but this time, I do it with my other hand too, finally getting the milk to come out.

"There ya go. Now try 'em at the same time."

She steps back slightly but close enough to brush my body with hers.

This time when I do it, milk squirts into the bucket. "How's this?"

"Good, now try doin' every other and see which one you like."

The rest in between is nice, but I think I prefer doing them at the same time.

"You're gettin' the hang of it," Emily praises, patting my shoulder. "In the event the teats point in different directions and the milk isn't gettin' into the bucket, you'll wanna make sure it's centered underneath and regrip a little so they shoot toward the middle. If that doesn't work, you'll have to do 'em one at a time and move 'round to the other side."

"Now do this twenty times in a row and you might be worth keepin'…" Posey taunts, coming behind me.

"It's the biceps," Emily hums, giving my upper arm a firm squeeze, and my spine straightens at the unexpected touch. "I bet these can do a lot more than milkin' goats."

"Do that again and you'll get written up for sexual

harassment." Posey's sharp tongue has my eyes bouncing between them, but I quickly avert them back to my hands.

"I touched his arm, so what?" Emily asks defensively.

"With words of sexual insinuation. Touchin' him without consent can make for an uncomfortable workplace for all employees."

"That's ridiculous. I was praisin' him for doing a good job, especially his first time."

"This isn't a kink club, you don't need to praise—"

"Maybe y'all should take this conversation into the office," Ian interferes, carefully wedging himself between Posey and Emily.

Considering I'm enjoying Posey getting riled up over me, I'd rather they stay and see what else she has to say.

"It's fine. I don't wanna file a report or cause any issues. I didn't take offense," I blurt, hoping to fizzle out the flame.

"See? He knew I wasn't being suggestive."

Well...

"My office, Emily."

Posey walks out, and Emily follows, sighing and rolling her eyes. I'm left with Amaya and Ian.

"Now what?" I ask once the milk starts dripping.

"Now you'll bring it over here to be filtered by one of the other employees and get the goat down. Bring her back to the pasture and grab the next one."

"Sounds good."

By the time I finish with the next goat, Emily returns with a faux remorse expression.

"Silas, I want to sincerely apologize for the sexual

implication of your large arms. I promise it'll never happen again and hope you can forgive me."

Her words come out genuine, but there's a glimmer in her eyes that tells me she knows what she's saying is absolute bullshit.

My gaze flicks to Posey standing ten feet behind her watching us with her jaw locked in place.

"I accept your apology, and of course, forgive you. No hard feelings."

"Great." She smiles wide, holding out her hand.

I look at Posey again, wondering if this is a test, and if I'm allowed to touch her.

Not wanting to leave Emily hanging, I shake it.

"Since that's over…" She steps closer, pulling her lower lip in between her teeth. "Maybe we could go out this weekend? As *friendly* employees?"

I don't have to look at Posey again to know she's shooting daggers at the back of Emily's head.

The third night at Posey's house, she finally listed off her house rules, which were mostly me doing all the chores and lawncare, but she never said anything about bringing home company. Plus, Emily's the only one who's been nice to me all week.

"Sure, I'd love that. But do you think until I get my first paycheck, you'd mind stayin' in and watchin' a movie? Then I promise we'll go out another weekend."

"I'm not payin' y'all to stand 'round and make weekend plans," Posey scolds.

"I'll give you my number later," Emily whispers before

walking past me and leaving me with a red-faced roommate who looks ready to kill me.

Or fire me.

Maybe both.

chapter seven

Posey

"SO…" Amaya prompts, nudging me when I don't react.

"What?" I ask, cutting through soap I removed from the molds earlier. Dealing with Emily slowed me down and now I'm trying to catch up.

"Don't act dumb with me, Posey. You totally jumped down Emily's throat for flirtin' with Silas."

"That's not true," I argue, slamming the cutter down harder than necessary. "She touched him inappropriately and made a suggestive comment. I would've called anyone out for that."

"Mm-hmm…" Her tone tells me she doesn't believe me but the policy is clear. I'm just following it. "Surprised you didn't fire her."

"I gave her two options. Get written up and apologize or get fired—same thing I would've done for anyone who crossed the line."

"I've touched way more than your arm and you never fired me."

Freezing mid-cut, I glare. "Maybe I should reconsider. You have smacked my ass before and that's definitely grounds for sexual harassment."

"Only 'cause you smacked mine first!"

I bark out a laugh. "Yes, but I did it after work hours. And we were drunk. See the difference?"

"Oh, so Emily can hit on him outside of work and you won't care?"

"Nope." I stack the slices of soap to one side before cutting some more.

"You're such a bad liar." She chuckles, but I ignore her.

Flirting is one thing, but once it turns into touching and suggestive comments, then it's a work violation.

After I've finished, I place all the bars on a curing rack and grab the next mold.

I wrap up for the day a little early since I don't want to start something new and not be able to finish it. I'm meeting my siblings at our parent's house for dinner, so I can't stay late.

With Silas and I carpooling to work, I can't leave until he's done. Ian's supposed to give me his final report on how Silas did this week, so I walk through the barn to find him.

But then I see Emily giving Silas her phone number and telling him to call her later.

"Silas."

His eyes meet mine behind Emily, but she quickly notices.

"Bye!" She walks away, leaving us alone.

"Are you done?" Silas asks, walking toward me. "I'm just finishin' up."

He's covered in dirt and straw dust, which is exactly why I make him strip down before walking into my house. The first time I suggested it, he had no hesitations. But then I regretted it. Now, I walk in before him and don't look back.

"Yes, but we need to speak in my office. Meet me there when you've clocked out."

I leave without another word and sit behind my desk.

"Hey, I'm done now." Silas comes in five minutes later, and I motion for him to sit. "Is this my week-trial review?"

The corner of his lip tilts up but there's uncertainty in his voice.

Standing, I grab the envelope with his check and hand it to him. "We didn't submit your information for direct deposit yet, so I wrote one out for you. I'm sorry it didn't work out."

"Thank—wait, what?"

"Today was your last day," I confirm, sitting back down.

"Why? I've done everythin' you and Ian have asked. I didn't fuck up anythin' and even hand-milked all mornin' yesterday and today. In fact, I took Ian's abuse all week, which I know you told him to fuck with me, but I never complained. And I let you put goats on my back while I was in positions I've never heard of before. What more do you need from me?"

Swallowing hard, I hate conflict but knew he wouldn't take the news lightly. "I assume my father went over the company handbook or told you to read it? 'Cause I have one with your signature right here..." I hand him the packet of pages.

"Yes, what about it?"

"Employee relations are prohibited. It creates an uncomfortable workplace and isn't tolerated. And since you're the one on probation, I gotta let you go."

"Who is it you think I'm havin' relations with?"

"Emily."

"I haven't touched her."

"Not yet, but you've made plans to see each other outside of work hours, which will then violate the policy."

"You don't hang out with any of your employees outside of work?"

I lick my bottom lip and his gaze lowers to my mouth. "Hangin' out ain't havin' relations with 'em. And unless you're sayin' Emily will keep her hands to herself while the two of you *hang out*, it's not the same thing. Especially if you had plans to bring her to my house. Employees datin' is a distraction and makes for an unbalanced team. It's why we don't allow it."

"Were you not the one who told me to get back out there so I could get over my ex? And now you're gonna fire me for doin' so?"

"It's not about that, Silas. Screw all the single women in Willow Branch Mountain for all I care. But not the ones who work here."

He arches a brow, leaning back in the chair. "Does that include you?"

I scoff. "You've just proven my point. Whaddya think happens when employees date and then break up? It brings tension and awkwardness into the workplace, so it's better to set the expectations upfront."

"Fine, so if I don't hang out with Emily, I can keep my job?"

I hesitate briefly. "Yes."

It's not that I want him to be without a job but seeing him every day is wearing me down when I've spent all these years trying to pretend he didn't exist. That made it easier to forget his rejection.

And the spiral of rejections I had after him.

He shakes his head. "She's the only person who was nice to me this week. It's not like I was plannin' to fuck her."

My spine straightens at his blunt words. "I was nice to you."

"No…you barely tolerated me. And you weren't exactly subtle about your dislike about me being in your house and workin' here. Ian didn't even say my name, just called me New Boy whenever he wanted to get my attention."

I hold back laughter because I didn't know Ian did that.

"I'll talk to him about that," I reassure him. "And tell him to ease up."

"So I can return on Monday?"

"Yes, as long as you don't violate the rules."

"Do I still gotta participate in being your goat yoga guinea pig?"

I smirk. "Surprisingly, the women like you. Class nearly doubled on Thursday than what it was on Tuesday."

"Fine." He sighs, dramatically rolling his eyes. "Wait, whaddya mean *surprisingly*?"

Chuckling, I shake my head. "A couple of 'em posted videos about you and it brought more attention to the class."

"So that makes me like…a pimp. A goat yoga pimp. I should definitely be gettin' paid." He crosses his arms.

Sighing, I lift my shoulders. "Fine. I'll add it to your next check. Happy now?"

"Are you gonna kick me out if I let Michelle cut my hair or we grab drinks after?"

"No." I furrow my brows in confusion, although I don't think he needs a haircut. "I don't care who you're romantically involved with as long as they don't work here."

"You don't?"

"As long as you don't bring 'em to my house," I quickly add. "Ever?"

"*Never*," I confirm, my skin boils hot at the thought of hearing him with another woman. I'd have to cut off my ears. "Either go to theirs or wait until you have your own place."

"Fine, I can respect that. It is your house."

"Exactly."

He squeezes the arm rests. "Anythin' else?"

"Yes, we're due for family supper in forty-five minutes so we need to clean up." I stand, grabbing my bag.

"I'm invited?" His face lights up.

"My mother told me to tell you, so yes. We're hostin' a weddin' for my cousin next month and it's all hands on deck to get it ready, so we're discussin' it tonight."

"Sweet, let's go."

As soon as we're home, I take a quick shower and dress in leggings and a tank top. We don't get together for dinners very often anymore since everyone's always busy with work or enjoying their downtime, so I'm looking forward to seeing them.

Even if Silas's there and they're going to bombard him with questions about working with me.

"You ready?" I ask, knocking on his door.

He opens it wearing only his boxer briefs.

"Why aren't you dressed?" I ask, looking up at the ceiling to avoid staring at his tattooed chest. "We gotta be there in five minutes."

"I couldn't figure out what to wear. Can you help me?"

"It's just supper."

"I know but—" There's insecurity in his voice, so I look at

where he's holding up two shirts. "It's still respectful to dress appropriately when invited as a guest. So which one?"

"Well, now you're gonna make me look underdressed."

I study both shirts, one a casual green button-up that goes nicely with his eyes and the other a black silk dress shirt that's far too fancy.

"The button-up will do," I tell him. "Wear it with dark washed jeans and your nicer boots."

"Great, thank you."

"Mm-hmm. I'll meet you in the truck."

I haven't driven my car all week, and I'm already getting too used to him driving me—which I shouldn't—but it's still nice.

We're the last ones to walk into my parents' house so everyone stares and claps, making a big dramatic deal about us being three minutes late.

"I can't believe you're still alive," Warren taunts, standing to greet Silas when we walk around the table. "I was about to go search for your dead body."

"What's that supposed to mean?" I ask offensively, taking a seat next to Bellamy.

"It means I know you." Warren raises his brow at me. "You don't play nice."

"Still breathin' but she did try to fire me earlier."

Dammit, I should've told him he couldn't bring that up.

"What?" Gasps echo throughout the room, and my eyes land on Maisie who's smirking wide because she knows more details than anyone else here.

Dad walks in and kisses me on top of the head. "Nice try, sweetheart. You can't fire him without reasonable cause."

"Which I had," I confirm. "Employee relations."

Everyone's gazes snap toward Silas who's sitting between Warren and Colton.

"I didn't do anythin'…" He holds up his hands in mock surrender. "A girl gave me her number and I said we could hang out."

"Ooo…" Everyone winces, shaking their heads.

"Yeah, yeah…I turned her down now."

"Weren't you just engaged last weekend?" Bodie asks.

"Posey's the one who told me to find a rebound." Silas points at me.

"Not from work!" I exclaim.

"You could always use a datin' app like Posey…" Bellamy blurts.

Everyone's gazes shift back to me, including Silas's who looks more conflicted than anything.

And now I'm going to kill her for bringing that up.

"I'm starvin', let's eat!" I reach for one of the dishes, but Aunt JoJo smacks my hand.

"We gotta say grace first," she reminds me.

Mom stands when the oven timer goes off.

"Any luck on the app since you scared away the last guy?" Colton quips.

He's two years younger so we often complain to each other about being in the dating trenches. His problem isn't finding girls who want him, it's finding one he actually likes. He claims even if he's attracted to them, he needs to have the gut *feeling* to pursue something more. Whereas my problem is men in general.

"If he didn't want an opinion on his…*manhood*…then he shouldn't have sent a photo of it askin' me to rate it from one to ten."

Maisie nearly chokes on her sweet tea the moment she takes a sip. "I'm scared to ask what you said."

"I'd rather you not say at all..." Dad pinches his brow, then steals one of the hot rolls from the pan Mom took out.

"I wanna know!" Aunt JoJo beams.

I shrug because it's not like they aren't used to hearing this by now. With three brothers, my parents have heard a lot worse.

"I told him it was hard to rate what I couldn't see and to send me another angle. He was too dumb to realize I was mockin' him, so he did. Then I told him that his dad should send me one instead so I know what it's supposed to look like."

Laughter echoes through the room.

"How'd he take that?" Maisie asks.

"He called me a sociopath, so I said, 'is that anyway to talk to your future stepmother?' Then he told me his father was dead and blocked me."

"Oh my..." Mom clutches her chest once she sets the basket of rolls down on the table and everyone cackles. "Maybe we should change the dinner conversation."

That's hardly the worst thing men have said to me on those apps. It's why I stopped trying because it was a waste of time. Even if things led to us meeting in person and dating for a bit, they always ended it once things turned sexual.

We finally bow our heads as Dad blesses the food. When I shift my gaze toward Silas, I find him already staring at me. I look away before it's awkward.

Once everyone has food on their plates, Mom talks about the wedding.

"Landen only gave us thirty days to plan this, so we need to stay organized. Everyone's gonna have a job, includin' you Silas." Mom winks at him.

"Yes, ma'am. Whatever you need."

I'd roll my eyes if he wasn't so damn polite.

"Why's the engagement so short? Is Ellie pregnant?" Bodie asks. "Is it a shotgun weddin'?"

Colton chuckles. "That's what we all said about Tripp."

That's Landen's younger brother who married Magnolia last year only four months after he proposed, but she just had a baby, so it was good she wasn't pregnant again so soon.

"No, she's not pregnant. She's trainin' for the National Finals Rodeo at the end of this year," Mom confirms. "But that's what you do when you're in love. You wanna get married as soon as possible."

Bellamy and I make gagging noises at the same time.

"I'm never gettin' married," Bellamy confirms.

She's been saying that for years.

"At this rate, I'll be fifty before I get married," I say, stabbing a piece of chicken with my fork and taking a bite.

"I still can't believe Ellie fell in love with him when she spent four years hatin' him," Colton adds. "That's gotta be some kinda superpower."

I snort. "No, just good ole amnesia."

"She lost her memory?" Silas asks. "How'd that happen?"

"Ellie fell off her horse while barrel racing. She hit her head just right and it knocked her out. When she woke up, they realized she'd lost part of her memory," I tell him.

"Not only did she forget she hated Landen, but him altogether," Bellamy adds. "He was a complete stranger to her."

"Except she had an instant crush on him as soon as she saw him," Warren says. "It was hilarious."

"Her memory eventually came back and she realized she had been wrong about him and they fell in love," I explain. "Or something like that. It's the strangest love story I've ever heard."

"Wow....that's wild. At least it wasn't the other way 'round where they were in love beforehand and she woke up forgettin' or hatin' him. That'd suck," Silas says.

"Knowin' Landen's persistence, he'd remind her why they were in love every day until she fell back in love with him." Warren chuckles. "I remember he'd call me so lovesick over wishin' she'd give him a chance."

I stare at my plate while I eat but I can feel Silas's heated gaze burning a hole through my head.

"And you were the same way over Maisie," Bellamy reminds him. "Admit it."

He shrugs. "Never denied it."

That's an understatement.

We continue eating while Mom and Dad go over everything that needs to get done in the next few weeks at the Willow Chalet. It's our large two-story cabin located on the resort side. It has a wraparound deck with ten bedrooms and fourteen bathrooms. Since we reserve it for large family gatherings or high-profile guests, it doesn't get used regularly. Landen and Ellie's families will stay there for the weekend, so the rooms need to be stocked and cleaned.

There's a big ballroom on the first floor, so it's the perfect spot for a wedding. They'll have the ceremony inside and when they're busy taking pictures outside, the staff will transform it for the reception. They usually help with the prep when we have events there, but with the short notice and cabins booked solid, they're already working overtime.

"Everyone needs to be in proper formal attire, so if you need new clothes, don't go shoppin' last minute," Mom warns. "I want the boys in suits and the girls in dresses."

Bodie groans. He hates wearing anything that isn't jeans and his dirty ball cap.

Bellamy doesn't look too thrilled about it either.

"And if you're bringin' a plus-one, you better let me know so we have enough chairs." Mom glances at Silas. "That goes for you too."

"Oh...I'm invited?" He bashfully points to himself.

"Of course! You're livin' here and you've been a part of the family for years anyway. If Posey ever lets you date without the threat of firin' ya, you should bring someone."

"Why am I the bad guy for enforcin' the policy that you two wrote?"

"I don't remember that part." Mom shrugs.

"It was added in after a couple broke up and it caused a massive fight amongst the other employees. They were all takin' sides and it was a whole mess," Dad explains. "Lost half the workers 'cause they refused to work with the one who supposedly cheated on the other."

"Okay, see?" I hold out my hand toward him. "Policy is there for a reason."

Maisie snickers. "Guess that means you and Silas can't date."

My eyes snap to hers and I glare at her in warning.

Shut up, for the love of God, shut it.

I never told Bellamy about Silas taking my virginity and don't need my parents finding out about it now either.

Aunt JoJo leans in closer and whispers, "Doesn't mean y'all couldn't sneak 'round."

"Oh my God." Shaking my head, I take a long, slow drink.

"After the wedding is over, we're gonna start on construction for the new childcare center," Dad announces. "So prepare for some louder than usual days while the land gets developed and while it gets built."

"You're buildin' that here?" Silas asks.

"Yep, so if you knock up a girl, you'll get free childcare workin' here."

Silas glances around as if he's waiting for the punchline.

"Mom requested the addition in hopes it'll force us to give her grandchildren," I explain.

"That's…only halfway true," Mom defends. "A lot of our employees have kids so it only makes sense to provide a place to bring 'em so they don't gotta worry about the added expense or not havin' a sitter. They'll be able to visit durin' their lunch breaks and not worry about a long commute pickin' 'em up after."

"I think it sounds like a fantastic idea." Silas beams.

"Thank you, honey."

What a kiss-ass.

I somehow manage to get through dinner and dessert without any of my secrets being revealed. Dad goes over specific tasks for each of us, including the day after for the farewell brunch and cleaning up.

"So…" Silas prompts once we're home. "Which datin' apps do you suggest I try?"

"You seriously wanna know?" I ask, shoving my comforter in the dryer.

"Yeah, I only have a few weeks to find a weddin' date and if Michelle doesn't work out, I'll need options."

"Um...I like Grindr. Lots of nice people on that one."

"Grindr? Okay, cool. I'll try it."

I close the door, then set the timer for fifteen minutes. "Good luck."

"Posey." He stares at me. "I'm not that dumb."

I burst out laughing. "Damn. Well...then don't ask dumb questions."

"Why was askin' you about datin' apps dumb?" he asks, following me out of the laundry room.

"'Cause I complained about how horrible my experiences have been and then you go ask me which ones you should try. Put two and two together, genius."

"Alright, fine. Then whaddya suggest?"

"You could go out to a bar?" I spin around quickly to tell him my next idea, but he's so damn close to me, we bump right into each other.

"Oh shit, sorry." He grabs my shoulders before I can fall on my ass.

"Distance, Silas. Six feet at all times." I push against his chest to move him back.

He laughs. "I didn't know you were suddenly gonna turn."

"I was about to tell you, we could both go out and help each other. Since I need a date for the wedddin' too, you be my wingman, and I'll be your wing woman."

Suspiciously, he raises his brows. "*You* wanna help *me*?"

"Why do you make it sound like I'm evil? You said you wanna be friends, right? And considerin' I didn't murder you this week, this is somethin' friends would do for each other."

He folds his arms, studying me. "And you're not gonna tell these girls that I have a limp dick, suck in the sack, or like to be pegged?"

I give him my best suggestive eyes. "*Do* you like to be pegged?"

"Hard pass...I'll go alone."

He walks away, but I quickly catch up to him.

"Oh, come on! This can be our first *roomie* night out." I use the same word he loves using but cringe a little when I do.

Not sure why I'm so hellbent on doing this with him, but maybe it'll make the awkwardness go away. I'll see him with other girls, he'll see me with other guys, and it'll be fine. We can be friends who live with each other and date other people.

Totally fine.

"Alright, but on one condition." He stands with his broad chest puffed out.

"You're givin' me the condition?" I mock. "What is it?"

"We arrive together and we leave together, which means you don't go home with anyone besides me."

"Uh..." My tongue pokes the inside of my cheek. "I thought the point was—"

"I don't wanna worry about you at some random guy's house neither of us knows. You'll be my responsibility if we're goin' together."

"I'm an adult, Silas. I can take care of myself."

"Even when you've been drinkin'?"

"I'm not a child. I've gone out before...several times, in fact."

"I don't doubt that, but I'd rather you be safe. Plus, you should make a guy take you out before goin' home with him."

"What if I bring him to my place?"

"If I can't bring people home, then neither can you. That rule should go both ways."

"But it's *my* house."

"And our rooms are close enough for me to hear you moan, and if I hear you scream out another dude's name, I'm kickin' the door down and beatin' his ass."

"That sounds melodramatic."

"Fair is fair, Posey. You either accept the terms or I'm findin' a date on my own *and* bringin' her here."

With a sigh, I give in to his stupid demands. "Fine, but you better not find me the nerdiest, dorkiest, lookin' dude in the bar."

"I thought you liked nerdy..." He waggles his brows.

And that's exactly why I don't anymore.

chapter eight

Silas

I HAVE no desire to find a date for the wedding, especially since I'm still processing my own getting canceled. If Mrs. Langston hadn't invited me herself, I wouldn't go. But if everyone else is bringing a date, then I guess I need one too.

In one week, I was supposed to stand at the altar and exchange vows with who I thought was the love of my life.

But now I realize it was a lie.

Aundrea's parents hired a wedding planner so there wasn't anything for me to do besides tell my family. After telling my parents and siblings the day after she left, they've given me space, but now they're on my ass for an update.

"Silas, darlin'!" Mom beams, giving me a hug. As soon as she pulls back, she smacks my cheek. "Why haven't you called?"

"Ma, was that necessary?" I rub my palm over where she hit.

"I've been worried about you." She walks to the stovetop and stirs the gravy. "Are you sleepin' okay? You look tired. Are you gettin' enough vitamins in your food? You look pale. How—"

"I'm fine, Ma. Got a new job and temporary place to live. Eatin' and sleepin' just fine."

Perhaps it should be telling that I'm not more sick over the breakup but mostly embarrassed that I didn't see it coming.

I glance around the kitchen that hasn't been remodeled since the nineties. Old wallpaper that's seen better days and a wood panel that goes midway down to the floor. Although it's outdated and no longer stylish, it makes me smile at the nostalgia from growing up here with my three older sisters. Our dad passed when I was thirteen from an aggressive form of lung cancer, so it's been the five of us ever since.

As the baby of the family and only boy, my mom's always been overprotective of me. My sisters too. Although I'm thirty, they treat me like I'm still a teenager.

"Where's the job and house?"

"I'm workin' at the goat farm on the Langston ranch. Warren's sister, Posey, runs it and she has a spare room, so I'm stayin' with her until I find my own place."

"Posey...which one's that? The blonde or brunette?"

I chuckle at why it matters. "Blonde."

"Oh, she's a cutie. Are you two..." She arches a suggestive brow.

"No, she barely tolerates me. We're just roommates."

"Well...doesn't mean that can't change."

"I wouldn't hold your breath. We're goin' out tonight to help each other find dates for her cousin's weddin' next month."

"A date? Shoulda told me. My nail lady has a daughter—"

"No blind dates." I quickly shake my head. She tortured me enough with that before I met Aundrea.

"You're not gettin' any younger. Your sisters were all married by twenty-five and had their first babies by twenty-seven."

I nod along because it's nothing I haven't heard before. They were thrilled when Aundrea and I got engaged and now they're going to try and set me up right away.

"Thirty ain't that old, Ma. Plenty of people in my generation are waitin' to get married until they're older."

"You wanna be fifty with a newborn? Trust me, you don't."

I snort, taking a drink of my pop that she handed me in between her ranting about my love life. *Or lack thereof.*

"Mama, leave him alone," my oldest sister, Celeste, walks in with my niece on her hip.

Mama puts her big spoon down, then quickly grabs Abbie from my sister's arms. "I'm just tellin' him he doesn't have much time to wait."

"Meanin' she thinks I'm gonna die sad and alone."

Celeste comes over to hug me and ruffles my hair. "You need a haircut."

"I'm gettin' one in an hour, actually."

My other two sisters, Sabrina and Corinne, come for lunch along with a few of their kids. Mom called for a family luncheon so we can discuss the tragedy that is my life.

"Have you talked to Aundrea since it happened?" Sabrina asks while we eat.

"She texted on Sunday before I left to leave her keys on the counter and that's it."

"Her family wrote a post on your engagement website that it was canceled due to a mutual split," Corinne says, curling her lip in annoyance. "Mutual, my ass."

"Corinne, language," Mama scolds, nodding her head toward the kids.

Corinne's only two years older than me, so we've always been closer, but she made it clear months ago she didn't like Aundrea.

"I think she had a side piece," Sabrina says. "It's already goin' 'round that she's datin' another guy."

"Who?" I ask.

"Some suit from Knoxville."

I scoff. "Probably an investor her dad knows. I wouldn't be shocked."

"An even better reason to move on," Mom exclaims.

"It's only been a week," Celeste reminds her. "Give him time."

"Thanks," I mouth to her when my mom continues talking about how I'm too good for a woman like Aundrea.

"He's livin' with Posey now."

"Warren's sister? She's adorable." Sabrina grins, reaching across the table to swipe a butter knife out of Henry's hand after he swung it around like a magic wand. "Is she single?"

"Uhh...yes, but—"

"You two would be cute together!" Corinne gushes, putting mashed potatoes on a fork to spoonfeed Nico who spits it right out.

Looking at my family, it's pure chaos, but I've never known anything else so it's almost comforting.

"We're just roommates," I repeat for the second time. "We agreed to keep things platonic."

"Why?" Celeste asks. "Do y'all have history or somethin'?"

When I stay quiet, my mom and sisters stop what they're doing and all stare at me.

"*What?* You never told me!" Corinne shouts, throwing a piece of broccoli my way. Daniella, my five-year-old niece, picks it up and throws it at her little brother.

"No throwin' food!" Sabrina catches it midair.

I'd laugh if everyone's attention wasn't on me again.

"It was a long time ago, okay? It was one time."

Their jaws drop and Mama's eyes brighten with ideas.

"But we're only friends now."

"Give it time…" Sabrina snickers. "I was *friends* with Reid once upon a time too."

"We're goin' to Honky's tonight to be each other's wingmen, so don't get your hopes up."

"Oh, can I come and help? Please?" Corinne smacks her palms together in a prayer gesture. "Oliver can watch the kids."

"Me too!" Sabrina smirks. "Celeste, you come too. We need a sister's night out."

"Oh God…" I groan, mentally slapping myself for telling them.

"I'm too old for that," she tells them. "Plus, I don't have a sitter."

Celeste's husband passed away a year after their youngest was born from a car accident and she's been doing it on her own ever since.

"I'll babysit," Mama offers. "The kids can sleep over. You deserve a night out."

"Really? You don't mind?" Celeste looks conflicted but she probably hasn't had a night out in years.

"Absolutely! You girls have fun. And watch your brother."

"Yes!" Corinne high-fives Sabrina. "The Mathiesens are hittin' the town!"

Just great.

I'm gonna need to give Posey a heads up or they'll be on her like cheese on pizza.

Once we finish eating and help Mom clean up, I say my goodbyes and tell my sisters I'll see them tonight.

Michelle's expecting me for my haircut in five minutes and there's no open parking available near the salon, so I have to jog half a mile to get there.

"Silas, you ready?" She greets me with a smile, and I follow her down a hallway to a private room.

"How're you doin'?" she asks, motioning for me to sit and then stands behind me.

"Good. You?" I ask into the reflection.

"Great but even better now that you're here." She threads her fingers through my hair.

Michelle plays with my hair and it puts me under a trance at how good it feels. Then she turns the chair and lowers my head into the sink to wash it.

By the time she finishes, I'm half asleep.

While she trims my hair, she talks the entire time, barely giving me time to respond before she says the next thing. She tells me all about why she moved here and that she's saving up money to go back to school to become a nurse.

Since I have plans with Posey tonight, and apparently my sisters, I suggest we meet for lunch tomorrow when she asks if I'm free tonight.

"Oh, I'd love to. There's this cute little cafe that has the best sandwiches."

"Willow's Corner Café?"

"Yes, that's the one!" She slides her fingers between my strands, checking the length.

"Sure, how's one?"

"I'll be there."

"Perfect." She softly brushes the hair off my neck once she's removed the cape. "And speakin' of apartments, there's a vacant one in my buildin' if you wanna use me as a reference."

Once we got talking, I told her a bit more about how I ended up living with Posey and that I'm hoping to find my own place.

"Where is it?"

"Just a few minutes away, which is nice since I can walk to both of my jobs. It's on Oak Street."

"Oh, those are nice ones. I'll check it out."

After I've paid, I head back to Posey's. We're not leaving until nine, so I've got the rest of the evening to do some laundry and cleaning.

"Wow, she didn't butcher it." Posey glances at my head, smirking around her spoon while she takes a bite of her food. "Looks good."

"Thanks." I scrub my palm through it and notice how much softer it is than usual. "We made a lunch date for tomorrow, so if I strike out tonight, all hope won't be lost."

"You're underestimatin' my skills as a wing woman."

"Not at all, but speakin' of that, I should warn you about somethin'."

She takes another bite before setting her spoon down. "What?"

"While I was havin' lunch with my mom and sisters, I told 'em about our plans tonight and now all my sisters are comin'."

"All of 'em?" She giggles. "You're in deep shit now."

Pulling out the chair across from her, I take a seat. "You're tellin' me. My mom says I better hurry up and find someone before I'm too old to raise a baby, which gave my sisters the green light to come help you find me a wife."

I leave out the part where they know we have history, but I didn't give specifics since they don't need to know.

"Wow...they sound more aggressive than my family." She stands, taking her dirty dishes to the sink. "Do you think they can help me find a husband?"

I bark out a laugh. "Don't give 'em the idea or they definitely will."

Although I hate the idea of Posey with another man, I know it's only fair to help her since she was so willing to help me.

"Are you sure there's nothin' goin' on between you two?" Corinne leans in with her drink straw between her lips.

We're standing at a bar table top while Posey dances with a couple guys my other two sisters picked out for her. She's in a tight black dress that makes it impossible to keep my eyes off her.

"Nope. She almost fired me yesterday and only gave me a chance in the first place 'cause I'm her brother's best friend. Before this past week, we hadn't talked in years."

"But if it were up to you..." She gives me a knowing look. "You'd hit that."

I nudge her, making her stumble and bump back into me. "Isn't that what you kids say?"

"You're not that much older than me."

"I know but I've been married since I was twenty-one. I haven't dated since I was eighteen. I'm outta the loop."

"You poor thing," I deadpan, chugging the rest of my beer.

"Hey, I've breastfed longer than some of your relationships."

"I didn't need that visual." I shake my head. "I'm gonna grab another beer."

As soon as I make my way to the bar, Posey catches up to me and grabs my arm. Her eyes are half-closed as she rocks back and forth between her feet.

"Hey! I found a girl for you. Her name's Gabby. Abby. Tammy? Somethin' like that. I'll introduce you when you come back to the table. Can you get us some drinks?"

Glancing above her head, I spot the woman at the table with my three sisters. *Fuck.*

"Sure, whaddya want?"

"I don't care. Somethin' fruity!"

"Okay, sure. You havin' fun out there?"

"Uh huh! The girl's really cool. Huge boobs. She started twerkin' and one of 'em nearly punched me in the eye."

I snort. "That sounds dangerous."

"I figured you liked big boobs. Or are you an ass man? Shit, I shoulda asked first." I've never seen Posey this bubbly before, so it's definitely the alcohol. "Either way, she has a nice ass too."

"I don't have a preference as long as we have chemistry."

"No doubt you two will." She pokes me in the chest. "Now hurry up before I steal her from ya."

She walks off, making my head spin.

I return to the table with their drinks and meet Sabrina's amused gaze. They pingpong between Posey and her new friend.

"Hi! I'm Jamie!" she shouts over the music and holds out her hand.

"Silas." I wrap my palm around hers. "Nice to meet you."

"You too."

"These are my sisters." I point to the three of them staring. Her shoulder-length black hair is halfway pulled up with long, dangly earrings that almost reach her collarbone.

Her tongue peeks out between her red-stained lips. "Hi, Silas's sisters."

"We're all here to find Silas a new girlfriend," Posey explains, speaking loudly over the music. "His fiancée just dumped him."

"Aww..." Jamie coos. "You poor thing."

"No, it's fine." I brush her off, slightly uncomfortable that Posey's telling her I need help in that department.

"We're also here to find Posey a date for a weddin' next month," I tell her, hopefully taking the heat off me.

"Really?" Jamie's eyes widen. "My brother's single! You two would totally hit it off!"

"Y'all could double date!" Celeste suggests, holding up her drink.

She's only on her second and she's already toast.

"Oh my God, yes!" Jamie screeches. "Did I tell you he's a fireman?"

Posey's jaw *literally* drops. "Um no...tell me more!"

As they gossip, I drink my beer and watch them. Posey's bright smile is hard to miss when she hasn't stopped laughing all night. It's a nice sound to hear.

Once they've finished their cocktails, they drag me and my sisters on the dance floor.

Jamie grabs my arms and positions herself in front of me, shaking her ass to the beat.

I lean into her ear. "How old are you?"

"Twenty-two. You?"

Fuck, she's young.

"Thirty." I turn her around so we're face-to-face, then draw her closer so we can hear each other. "Where do you work?"

"I'm a receptionist at my dad's law firm. I graduated college in May so I'm still job huntin' for the right position."

"That's cool. I just started workin' at Posey's goat farm."

"She told me! How're you likin' it so far?"

"Not bad. It gets hot and dirty, but I don't mind it."

"I'll have to come visit sometime." She trails her fingers up my chest. "You can show me 'round. I'd love to play with the goats!"

"Sure." I smile but it doesn't reach my eyes. "You'll have to give me your number."

"Gimme your phone!" She holds out her palm and I pull it out of my pocket.

As soon as she enters her contact info, she texts herself so she has mine.

"Hopefully we can plan somethin' soon." She hands it back. "I'm available most evenings after five and weekends."

"Sounds good, me too."

We continue dancing for several songs until I break away to get some water. Since I'm driving, I stopped drinking a while ago.

"My brother's comin' to pick me up soon. I'll introduce y'all."

"Tonight? I need to freshen up then." Posey takes her hand and drags her toward the bathroom.

"So this is fun…" Corinne drawls.

"Mm-hmm," I mutter.

"Jamie seems nice," Sabrina says. "Gorgeous too."

"Very," Celeste agrees. "Not a thought in her pretty little head though."

"You don't even know her," I argue. "She has a college degree and works at her dad's law firm."

"So? Sabrina has one too but still thought we had fifty-two states up until she was twenty-one." She chuckles, making the rest of us laugh too.

"Hey!" Sabrina pushes her shoulder slightly. "That's 'cause you lied and told me that so I'd fail my history test."

"Perks of being the oldest sister who already knew what was on the test." Celeste laughs.

"I say give her a chance…" Corinne says, nodding toward Jamie when she and Posey return. "And maybe a double date won't be so bad. If anythin', you'll get more experience."

"Yeah, you're right." I shrug, though I'm not looking for anything serious, it might help get myself back out there.

They announce last call and the girls flock to the bar for one last drink. I've lost count of how many Posey's had but there's no doubt she's going to feel it tomorrow.

Oliver arrives to pick up my sisters since they're all staying at Corinne's tonight. I help get them all in his truck as they stumble over themselves.

"Y'all have fun?" he asks.

"I think I'm gonna throw up," Celeste murmurs, her head bobbing from side to side.

"Why're you drivin' so fast?" Sabrina mutters, plastering her face against the window.

"I haven't even started the truck." Oliver shakes his head. "Y'all gonna be sick as shit in the mornin'."

I smack him on the shoulder. "Good luck with 'em. I gotta find Posey and Jamie."

"You brought two dates? Thatta boy." He smacks me back.

"Ha! Not exactly."

I tell my sisters goodbye and that I'll check in with them later.

Walking back toward the bar, I find the girls standing on the sidewalk and talking to some guy.

"Silas! Come meet my brother." Jamie waves me over.

When I get a better look at him, I notice his muscular frame and height are similar to mine, but I'd guess he's a few years older than me by the deep lines on his face.

"Hey, I'm Jackson." He nods when I stand between the girls.

"Silas, nice to meet you." I nod back. "So you're a fireman?"

"Yep, for twelve years now."

"You two have a big age gap?"

"Jackson's my stepbrother," Jamie confirms. "His dad married my mom when I was fifteen."

"Gotcha."

"Posey needs a weddin' date and I told her you'd love to go," Jamie tells Jackson.

"Yeah, that'd be cool. Text me the date so I can make sure I'm not on call that weekend."

I wait as Posey programs his number and she promises to text him tomorrow. Then I give Jamie an awkward hug goodbye.

"I'll text you tomorrow too," Posey promises to Jamie. "If I'm not pukin' my guts out."

"I'm sure you will be," I mutter, trying to pull her away so we can go.

People flood the sidewalks, walking to their vehicles, but I had to park down the street since the lot next to the bar was full.

"C'mon, Posey. Say good night."

"Night, I love you!" she calls out, walking backward.

"I love you too!" Jamie shouts before getting into her brother's truck.

Posey trips over her own shoe, but luckily I catch her before she can face-plant.

"Whoa, careful now." I wrap my arm around her waist, pulling her against me. "Can't have you showin' up to work on Monday with a black eye."

"No, I'm fine. T-totally fine," she stammers, barely able to keep her head up.

"I never realized how much fun you can be when you have alcohol in your system," I tease. "You're almost like a different person."

"That's not true! I'm always fun."

"Minus the stick up your ass."

"I do not have a stick up my ass!" She pokes me in the gut, hard, making me curl over. "You're the one who does."

I chuckle. "So whaddya think of this Jackson guy?"

"He's hot. Did you see his arms? His biceps are the size of my head."

"They're the same size as mine."

"No, his looked way bigger. Like save people from a burnin' house bigger."

"That doesn't even make sense."

"Don't be jealous."

"I'm not." I roll my eyes because I'm arguing with a drunken Posey who yesterday got pissed when Emily was admiring *my* biceps. "How old is he?"

"Thirty-five."

"That's a little old for ya, ain't it?"

"It's only seven years."

"Yeah, but it's interestin' that he's still single at his age. Unless he's been divorced."

"Okay, Mr. Nosy." She huffs. "He's been married before, yes. So at least I know he can commit. Unlike your ex…"

"Damn, low blow."

"I'm just sayin'! Don't knock him down until you actually get to know him better. Especially since I found you a banger of a date and I had to get my own with no help from you."

"I would've but you were glued to Jamie's hip."

It also wasn't easy with my sisters there, analyzing my every move.

"It doesn't matter anyway. Her brother seems cool enough for a weddin' date."

"Are you gonna see him before that since it's still weeks away?"

"Yeah, hopefully. Jamie says his work schedule can be hard to deal with since they'll work twenty-four-hour or forty-eight-hour shifts. I guess that's why his wife left. She hated it."

"And you don't think you'll have an issue with that?"

"No, I like my independence. And this way, we can get to know each other slowly. I'm in no rush."

When we arrived at the truck, I open the passenger side door and help her inside. She stumbles a bit, but finally manages to get her seat belt on.

"It was fun to hang with your sisters too," she says once I'm buckled in the driver's seat. "I can tell they really love you."

I smile, nodding. "Yeah, we're close and they've always been overly protective. They weren't a fan of Aundrea's though."

She giggles with a hiccup, leaning her body toward the window. "I knew I liked 'em."

Pulling onto the road, I drive us toward Posey's and soon the streetlights are behind us in the distance. By the time we arrive, she's passed out.

Instead of trying to wake her and make her walk, I carefully unbuckle and lift her in my arms. Unlocking the front door one handed is a feat but I manage it without dropping her.

She holds on tight around my shoulders, nuzzles her face against my neck, and sends a shiver down my spine. The Posey I know now—the sober version—would never willingly hang onto me like this, so I secretly enjoy it while I can.

"Silas?" she whispers when I pull back her covers and gently set her down.

"Yeah, it's me. You're okay. Just puttin' you into bed."

"Can you take my dress off first? It's itchy." Her eyes are half-closed as she slumps over.

"Uh...sure. Do you want me to get somethin' else for you to wear?"

"Just a T-shirt is fine. In my closet."

I find one with the ranch logo on it and bring it to her. "Can you lift your arms so I can pull off your dress?"

She manages to hold up her arms and I have to yank part of her dress out from underneath her ass before pulling it above her head. As soon as I have it off her, my eyes are drawn to her lacy bra and panties.

I shouldn't be looking.

Quickly, I grab the T-shirt and put it over her body, then tell her to push her arms through.

"Okay, lie down." I fluff her pillow before her head hits it. Then I yank up her sheets and comforter. "I'm gonna grab some water and a bucket in case you can't make it to the bathroom."

When I return, she's moved into a fetal position but she's shivering.

"Posey, you okay?"

"I'm freezin'."

"Do you have extra blankets?"

"In my closet."

I remove her comforter before adding one of the extras, then put hers in the dryer so it can heat up the way she likes.

While I wait for it, I find some pain meds that she'll probably need when she wakes up and a protein bar in case she gets hungry.

Bringing back her comforter, I place it on top and tuck her in the best I can.

"How's that?"

She moans quietly with a nod. "So much better."

I brush a few strands off her forehead, studying her gorgeous features.

"Your phone's on the nightstand, so you can text me if you need anythin', okay?"

"Mmkay. Thank you."

Her quiet words are barely above a whisper but I smile at hearing them.

Sleepy drunk Posey is sweet.

But I can't deny I like her snarky side too.

Leaning down, I kiss the top of her head. "Good night, Posey."

"Silas, wait..." she mutters before I can leave.

"Yeah?"

"What'd you think of Jackson?" she asks, her eyes barely open and her words slow and muffled.

"Uh...I don't really know anythin' about him." Besides his age and how much she likes his muscles. "Why?"

"He'll probably break up with me too."

I sit on the edge of the bed without touching her. "Why do you say that?"

"'Cause they all do." She rolls onto her side, inching closer. "They get sick of how long it takes me to finish."

My brows fly to my hairline and I blink. "Whaddya mean?"

"I can't come easily durin' sex. It takes me a long time to get there and after a while, they stop tryin' and finish without me. When I mention it, they tell me it's my fault. Although I can do it myself or with a toy."

I blink harder this time to make sure I'm not the drunk one hearing things. "Your exes didn't make you come, then blamed you?"

"Mm-hmm. So I suspect Jackson will do the same," she says in an adorable sleepy voice that almost sounds like she's given up hope. "I used to fake it but then realized if I never said anythin' they wouldn't know. Turns out they didn't care either way."

"Posey, that's..." I try to find the right words but I'm still in shock at how honest she's being. Sober Posey would never admit this to me. "Those aren't men you were datin'. They were boys who only cared about their own pleasure. It's better you didn't stay with 'em."

"You made me come durin' my first time," she confesses, and it sends a jolt of electricity down my spine and straight to my balls. "And I knew most women don't their first times so I wasn't expectin' to either but the way you talked me through it had me seein' stars and gasping for air. I guess that's partly why I hated you so much. You ruined all other men after you moved on without me."

I feel like a bigger bag of shit than I did before when she thought I'd forgotten about our night. Even worse when I started dating someone new and told her I needed to give that relationship a chance instead.

Though I don't know why she can't orgasm during sex with other men, a hint of pride puffs in my chest knowing I made her come for the first time and set the standard.

Now, I need to figure out how to help her fix it.

chapter nine

Posey

I HATE THROWING up with a passion. I've lost count how many times I've rushed to the bathroom to empty my stomach, but each time I do, Silas is there with water and a cold washcloth.

He tried holding my hair out of my face for me, but after the second time, I kicked him out of the bathroom. I'm mortified enough as it is, I don't need him to watch me at my worst.

"I brought you a few crackers and broth," Silas says, entering my room with a bowl in one hand and a small plate in the other.

"No way I can eat right now…" I groan, pulling the blankets up and covering my mouth.

"You need to get somethin' in your stomach to soak up all the acid." He sits on the bed next to me. "It'll help. Plus, you haven't thrown up in an hour. You might finally be done."

Reluctantly, I pull myself up and lean against the headboard. I can barely open my eyes all the way but take one of the crackers he holds up.

"You better never mention this to anyone, got it?" I take a bite, hating every second of chewing it. My head's been pounding all morning and the movement makes it throb harder.

He chuckles, holding up the bowl and spoon. "Open up."

I do as I'm told and swallow it down. "That's nasty."

"Says the person who threw up on herself..." He smirks, holding up another spoonful.

"I really hate you right now," I mutter, letting him feed me again but grunt at the awful dull flavor.

"Eat this." He gives me another cracker. "Then you can go back to sleep."

"I need a shower. That might make me feel better," I say, slowly chewing.

"Think you can stand that long? Maybe a bath would be better?"

"Fine." I don't bother arguing because he's probably right. "I've never been this sick from a night of drinkin' before."

"I'm startin' to wonder if you have the flu or some kind of stomach bug." He presses his palm to my forehead. "You're not feverish though."

"I hope not. I don't have time for that shit," I groan, rubbing my temples.

We have another busy week with getting orders sent out and more wholesale to deliver. Amaya can work on her own if she needs to, but it'll dramatically slow us down without both of us.

He sets the bowl on my nightstand. "I'll get the water ready, then come get ya."

"Silas, wait." He stands, then freezes and stares at me. "Thank you. I know I'm a big baby when I'm not feelin' well and not good at lettin' people help me. So, thanks for puttin' up with me and makin' sure I didn't choke on my own vomit."

The corner of his lips tilts up. "You're welcome. Plus, if I didn't, I fear Marjorie would fuck with me until I did." He winks before going to my bathroom.

Damn him for being so fucking sweet.

I drank way more than I normally do, but I was having so much fun with Jamie and talking to Silas's sisters. It'd been so long since I'd gone out, I didn't bother pacing myself and am now paying for it.

Jamie texted earlier but I haven't had the energy to respond besides a thumbs-up emoji confirming I was alive.

"Okay, I put every bath salt and soap I could find. Smells like Bath and Body Works threw up in there instead of you."

"Ha-ha, you're hilarious." I roll my eyes, swinging my legs off the bed, but then I get dizzy as soon as I try to stand.

"Whoa, hang on." Silas comes to my side and picks me up before I can stop him.

"I can walk!"

"Can you though? You couldn't even stand."

"But I stink." I grimace at the thought of how badly I must smell.

"Eh, it can't be worse than the goat farm."

"That doesn't make me feel better," I groan, and he chuckles.

He sets me on my feet in the bathroom and the cold flooring sends a shiver through me. I'm still only wearing a T-shirt, so my bare legs are covered in goose bumps.

"Do you want help with your shirt or gettin' in?"

"No, I'd like to keep some of my dignity."

He snorts. "I'll turn 'round so I'm still close in case you need help. Don't need you slippin' or drownin' on my watch. One ghost in this place is enough."

I sigh and wait until he's not looking before removing my shirt, bra, and underwear. The tub is overflowing with bubbles and looks like heaven. It's been a while since I've taken a bath.

As soon as I sink underneath the water and make sure the bubbles hide everything, I tell him he can turn around.

"Is it too hot?"

"No, it feels amazin'…" I lean my head back, moaning. "I'm gonna fall asleep in here."

"That's too risky but—" He moves throughout the room before holding up a face mask. "Figured you might wanna do one of these. Maybe it'll make you feel better. I can put it on for you."

I eye him cautiously at how thoughtful he's being. Considering I tried to fire him two days ago, he's acting like we've been besties for years.

"You're being awfully nice to me."

"Are we not friends? Or would you prefer I let you suffer alone?" He arches a brow, unfolding the mask.

"No, but I wanna make sure that we don't cross any boundaries. Especially if we're workin' together. We still have a code of ethics to follow."

"I have no plans of breakin' any of your rules. Plus, now we each have weddin' dates and can focus on gettin' to know 'em."

He places the mask over my face, softly and slowly adjusting it over my eyes and mouth. Once it's secure, he rubs over it to smooth out the bumps. His touch feels nice. A bit *too* nice.

"So you liked Jamie?" I ask once he's done and study him for the first time today now that my eyes are open all the way.

It doesn't look like he's shaved all week. The scruff on his jawline is longer than usual, but maybe it's one of his things he's doing because Aundrea preferred him clean-shaven.

"She's nice. We've been textin' a little today."

"Once I feel human again, I'll call her. She mentioned her brother in her last text, but I have no memory of meetin' him or what he looks like."

"Really?" He leans against the vanity, crossing his arms with an amused grin on his face.

His T-shirt stretches across his biceps and my gaze focuses on his tattoos. They remind me of the one on his chest that mirrors mine and it sends a weird sensation through me.

"Should I describe him for you?"

"Sure, maybe it'll spark my memory."

"He's about five-five to five-six. Stocky. Red hair. Long beard. Beer belly. Great smile."

I bark out a laugh because he's full of shit. "That's quite the image."

"Seems nice though, so I wouldn't write him off."

"C'mon, tell me for real."

"Fine," he drawls dramatically. "He's a fireman, so he's built as shit. Dark hair, trimmed, but no facial hair. An inch or two shorter than me."

"On a scale of one to ten…" I taunt, knowing he'll hate this. "What would you rate him?"

"Seriously?" He grunts, uncrossing his arms.

"Yes, help me. I can't bring an ugly date as a plus-one."

"If I *have* to rate him, then…a seven."

"Okay, I can work with that." I lean back further to keep the mask from sliding. "What would you rate Jamie?"

"Based on her looks alone, an eight. But her personality and our connection matter to me more, so until I get to know her on a deeper level, I can't determine our compatibility."

"From what I remember, she has a great personality. Very fun."

"Yeah, well…I need more than being fun. Anyone can be when they're tipsy."

He has a point.

"Are you gonna ask her out on a date before the weddin'?"

"She wants us to double date with you and Jackson first. I assume it's so she's not alone with someone she just met."

"That makes sense. Wait." *Speaking of date.* Something he told me yesterday hits me. "Didn't you have plans with Michelle today?"

"Yeah, but once I realized your condition, I told her we had to reschedule." He shrugs. "It's no big deal."

"Shit, I'm sorry. I should've said somethin' earlier. You could've gone."

"Nah, it's fine. I would've worried about you anyway, so I would've been lousy company. She mentioned her buildin' has an apartment for rent, so I'm gonna look into that and see if it's still available."

My heart drops a little because I'm getting used to him being here even if it's only been a week. It's nice not being alone all the time.

"You don't gotta worry about me, ya know? I can handle myself."

I don't want to be the reason he doesn't go out, especially knowing how his ex treated him. It's bad enough he's taking care of me like a sick child. When my younger siblings would get the flu, I always helped Mom and made sure they had everything they needed so she could still work and take care of everyone else. When I'd inevitably catch whatever they had, I toughed it out so no one worried about me.

"Yeah, so you've been sayin'…" he murmurs, shifting his gaze to the floor. "But I worry about my friends when they're sick, so it's best I stayed home."

I'm starting to understand why he and Warren have been best friends for so long. While Warren dealt with Maisie leaving, Silas was always there for him. Loyal to a fault and never gave up on him or made him feel bad for sulking. When Warren started building his A-frame cabin house for Maisie, Silas helped him during the evenings and weekends until it was done. Although he never knew if his wife would return, Warren didn't give up on making their dream house a reality.

"You're a good friend, Silas," I tell him. "But I'm still holdin' a grudge against you."

He throws his head back and laughs. The lights on my vanity shine behind him, making his smile glow brighter. "So you told me last night."

"Wait, huh? Whaddya mean?"

"You don't remember?"

I sit up, the bubbles sliding down my chest, his eyes following the movement. "What'd I say?"

"Oh no, if you don't remember, I'm not repeatin' it." He shakes his head. "I'm not fallin' for that trap."

"Just tell me what I said," I beg. "It can't be worse than me tellin' your sisters I haven't had sex in six months."

His eyes widen.

"Shit, you weren't at the table for that conversation." I close my eyes, inhaling through the little nose holes in the mask.

"I wasn't but that'd explain what you told me later."

"Silas!" I whine. "Just tell me or I'm gonna keep wonderin' and will bug you until you do."

"Alright...but you gotta promise not to get mad at me... *again*."

"Fine, I promise."

"Swear it."

Now I'm scared I told him something mortifying.

"I swear! Now spill."

His eyes lower to the floor while he licks his lips. He scrubs a hand over his jawline before meeting my gaze.

"You told me I ruined you for all other men 'cause they can't make you come during sex the way I did."

My heart pounds right out of my chest and the blood rushes in my ears as his words repeat in my head over and over. There's no freaking way I said that to him.

"Posey?"

"I'm gonna go drown myself now..." Closing my eyes and mouth, I sink down into the water until my head submerges. Maybe it'll erase all memory of the past twenty-four hours.

"Posey!" Silas yanks me up, the face mask sliding down until he removes it completely.

"Is there any chance you can pretend I never said that? Or I'll claim I was lyin'."

He sits on the edge of the tub, a brow pointed toward his hairline. "Were you?"

"Do we gotta discuss this? I was obviously out of my mind drunk."

"You said that's why guys keep breakin' up with you and said Jackson will too once he figures it out. Do you really think that's why?"

"I know it is. A few of 'em outright told me."

He grimaces. "You know it's not your fault, right? A lot of women have trouble orgasmin' during sex. Even when they try to do it themselves. The problem is—"

"Please don't psychoanalyze my vagina right now." I groan, lowering my body again and resisting the urge to stay under the water this time. Silas's way too happy knowing my secret.

"Then I'm gonna have to assume it's my super talented tongue and fingers…" He waggles his brows and waves his fingers. "Or that you only date losers."

Both. But I'm not admitting that to him or he'll never shut up about it.

"I didn't know what I was sayin', so you can't hold that against me. I was ten sheets to the wind."

He cackles. "The phrase is *three* sheets, but I guess ten sounds more accurate for you."

"And I'm back to hatin' you."

"Nice try, roomie. Admit it, you *like* me."

"I do *not*! You're a huge pain in my ass."

"That'd be a lot more convincin' if you didn't spend the last twenty minutes starin' at my arms and chest."

"Out!" I point toward the door.

Damn him for noticing.

He laughs harder now. "You don't want help gettin' out?"

"No, I'm hopin' I'll slip and fall to my death so I won't have to remember this conversation."

"And you called me the dramatic one?"

"Go!"

He pushes off the counter, laughing as he leaves and winks before shutting the door behind him.

I'm still mortified by the time I drain the tub and walk out in only a towel. Silas sits on my bed, scrolling on his phone.

"Would you rather I hadn't told you?" he asks.

"Yes. Ignorance is bliss and all that." I walk to my dresser and dig out some comfy clothes.

"But if I didn't tell you, I couldn't help you with your little... *problem.*"

I scowl over my shoulder, motioning for him to turn around so I can get dressed. "How exactly do you think you can *help* me?"

"Well...I managed to do it once."

"Yeah, about that..." I get my bra and panties on before sliding on a T-shirt. "How was it your virgin ass made me come my first time but no other guys seem to be able to?"

Or at least without a ton of effort and time.

"Uh...you don't wanna know the answer to that."

"Yes, I do. Tell me."

Once my pants are on, I sit on my bed and he stands in front of me.

"Posey, I'm certain you don't."

"Was it porn? 'Cause that wouldn't shock me. Most guys watch it."

"No. Although, I did read a few of my sisters' romance novels. Well, mostly the spicy parts."

I tilt my head down and remove the towel. Though I didn't wash my hair, I toss it up into a messy bun to brush through later.

"Okay, then what?"

He blows out a breath, crossing his arms and looking down at me. "You're not gonna get mad or threaten to fire me again?"

"That depends on what it is."

He sighs, relaxing his shoulders. "Your brother and Maisie were havin' sex years before I did and he gave me a lot of pointers."

Gagging, I nearly throw up again.

"I told ya you didn't wanna know…"

"Oh my God, this is worse than I could've imagined!" I fall back on the mattress, pulling a pillow on top of my face. "You've officially ruined sex for me. Now I will always think of how my brother taught you how to give me an orgasm."

"To be fair, he didn't know you'd be my first."

"Not helpin'!" My voice is muffled from the pillow but he chuckles anyway.

"Aren't you glad I gave you a good first experience versus a bad one?"

I throw the pillow toward him. "I wouldn't have known it was bad either way. At least not until I dated other guys."

"I'm not gonna apologize for knowin' what to do and makin' you come."

"Well, you should." I pout, leaning up on my elbows.

"Or you could just let me help you."

"You wanna be my sex coach, is that it?"

"I can talk you through how to tell your partners what you need in order to finish."

"That would be too awkward. I know how to do it myself. It takes a while, but I have more patience than the men I sleep with."

"I suspect they don't make you feel safe and secure or that you can trust 'em to get you there."

"Why do you assume that?"

"Do you tense up? Or feel in a rush to get there so they don't feel bad? Do they tell you how good you're doin' or praise y—"

"Stop," I blurt, needing his words erased from my brain immediately. "We're not doin' this."

"Friends help friends, don't they?"

"We've been friends for a week, so we can't go from not talkin' for years to sex tips."

"Why not?"

"'Cause it's weird! Amaya and I don't even talk about that stuff."

Bellamy and I do sometimes but she's only had a couple partners so we usually talk about how much we hate dating instead.

"That's a shame."

"I've come to terms with my pathetic sex life so it's fine."

He raises a brow, then licks his lips as he walks backward toward the door. "Alright, well...if you change your mind."

"I won't."

"Okay."

"My vibrator works just fine."

"I bet it does." His stupid smirk makes me want to throw something else at him. "But you might wanna keep it charged, then."

"Good night!"

He opens my bedroom door, smirking like he knows something he shouldn't. "Night. Sweet dreams, *roomie.*"

Groaning, I fall back on my bed and hope by morning it'll swallow me whole so I never have to face him again.

chapter ten

Silas

WATCHING Posey's face redden with embarrassment is my new favorite thing to witness.

She comes across so bold and fearless, it's nice to see her walls shatter a bit when she's vulnerable.

"Mornin'," I greet when she walks into the kitchen. "You look better."

"Well, I didn't spend the night throwin' up, so yeah, I'd hope so."

And snarky Posey is back.

She moves past me to make her coffee while I watch and hold back from commenting on our conversation yesterday. Although she kicked me out of her room while it was still a few hours before bedtime, I spent the rest of the evening finishing my laundry and watching TV. I heard her come out after I was in bed for the night, but I figured she wasn't up for company.

"I'll be ready to go in ten," she says, walking out without another glance.

It gives me enough time to make my lunch. There's a fridge in Posey's office so she keeps food stocked for when she's hungry.

The drive to the goat barn is silent besides the radio that's on low volume. Posey stares out the passenger window, ignoring me. I didn't realize she'd be so bothered by what I told her last night, but I'd rather discuss it and get it over with instead of worrying about it all day.

"Posey, wait," I blurt when she opens the door. "Can we talk quickly?"

"About what?"

"Well…how you can't even look at me for starters."

She finally shifts and meets my gaze. "I don't wanna talk about what happened or talked about this weekend, okay? I'd rather forget it."

"Why? Are you worried I'm gonna use it against you or somethin'?"

"I don't want you knowin' that personal stuff about me. After spendin' years tryin' to forget you, I can't let myself get too comfy with you in my life again. I appreciate what you did for me when I felt like shit but we should go back to the way things were before you moved in."

"You know that's not gonna be possible with me livin' there. Do you want me to leave?"

"No, but we can give each other space and make it work until you find a place."

I've looked online but everything so far is out of my budget or too big for one person. Even the apartment Michelle mentioned to me is more than I can afford.

"That might be a while," I admit.

She lifts a shoulder. "It's fine."

When she goes to leave again, I reach across the truck and grab her arm. "Wait. Please?"

She sighs. "I'm gonna be late."

"I apologize if I crossed a line and made you uncomfortable with the sex and orgasm talk. It won't happen again."

"Alright."

"Can we go back to being friends, please?"

She swallows, chewing on her bottom lip. "I'll try."

That's all I can ask for at this point.

"Okay, thanks."

I don't see Posey for most of the day, which isn't unusual since we're in two different areas of the barn, but I typically see her during lunch when she walks through.

Today they had me milking the goats with the machine, so it went faster. Afterward, we moved some of them to another pasture to clean out the brush. It's impressive how fast they work.

"I was talkin' to Jamie on my lunch break and she said Jackson's free on Saturday. She wants to know if we can double date and go to dinner," I tell Posey on the drive home. "Would you wanna go or would that be too weird?"

I tread lightly so I don't cross any boundaries or make things uncomfortable between us again.

"Sure, that'd be fine," she responds, and although she's not staring out the window this time, she's still avoiding my gaze. "As long as you remember neither of us can bring 'em home afterward."

"I wasn't plannin' to but I figured you'd wanna hang out with Jamie."

She shrugs. "Not if you two are datin'. I'd probably go to her place instead."

"Oh, right."

When we arrive at the house, I strip down to my boxer briefs as usual but this time she waits for me.

"Would you wanna go horseback ridin' with me?"

Her question takes me by surprise, but I'm delighted she asked. "Yeah, definitely. I'll get changed."

"Okay, I'll freshen up and be ready in a few."

I'm not sure what made her ask but hopefully it means this awkward tension between us will go away.

I haven't been on a horse in months, but growing up with Warren as my best friend means I know enough to get back on and be comfortable.

Once I've changed into jeans and one of my new flannels, I meet Posey in the living room. She's in jeans with a black cowboy hat on her head, looking cute as hell.

She hands me a bottled water. "Ready?"

"Should I wear one of those?" I point to her head.

She giggles, walking toward the front door. "You, in a cowboy hat?"

"Why're you laughin'?" I ask, offended.

"You're more of the baseball cap wearin' type, city boy."

I follow her outside. "Okay, what's it gonna take for you to stop callin' me that?"

Looking over her shoulder, she flashes a wicked smirk. "Grow up on a ranch or marry into one."

Catching up to her, I open the passenger side door and help her in. "Hmm..are you proposin'?"

She snorts. "You wish."

Grinning, I shut the door and walk around to my side.

"Thanks for invitin' me."

"Ridin' always helps me clear my head," she explains as I drive us to the stables. "And I thought you might enjoy it too with everythin' you're going through."

"I appreciate you lettin' me come." I grin, and she smiles in return.

When we walk inside the barn, we're greeted by Bodie who works at the stables with Warren.

"Hey, what're y'all doin'?"

"Gonna ride," Posey says. "Wanna join?"

"I've been on and off 'em all day, so no thanks."

Bodie takes guests trail riding in between taking care of the horses, mucking stalls, and training to become a farrier, so I don't blame him for not wanting to go.

Posey tells me which horse to take before grabbing her own. We cross-tie them in the aisle so we can groom them and put their tack on.

"Priest is a good horse. Warren rides him a lot," she explains, throwing her hair up and exposing her bare neck that I shouldn't be staring at for many reasons.

But I'll take it as a good sign that she didn't give me a bad one.

"Who do you have?"

"This is Blythe. She's a bit of a spitfire but she's a good girl, aren't ya?" She pats her back.

Once I have the saddle on, I ask Posey to double-check it for me since I haven't done this in a while. She yanks on one of the straps and tightens it a bit.

"You did good."

"Thanks," I say behind her. "I'm surprised I remembered after all this time."

"It's muscle memory. Once you learn it, it's hard to forget."

I smirk, thinking of something else that's forever engrained into memory. When she turns, we're only a few inches apart.

"What's funny?"

"Nothin'." I quickly wipe it off my face before she reads my mind.

She narrows her eyes, looking around us. No one else is here since the workers either left or are on the trails with guests.

"You can back up now."

"Oh right, sorry." I give her space to walk past me but notice the way her cheeks flushed at how close we were standing.

Once we're set, we untie the horses. I jump on Priest and she gets on Blythe.

"Ready?" she asks over her shoulder.

"Yep."

Or rather, I hope so.

Posey takes the lead out of the barn and toward the trails. Although it's later in the evening, the weather's beautiful. The sun's not high in the sky, but there's enough light to give us a few hours before we're in the dark.

"I wanna apologize for being short with you this mornin'," Posey says when our horses walk side by side. She doesn't look at me but there's sincerity in her voice. "I guess my mind and heart aren't on the same page when it comes to you. We went from not talkin' to suddenly being roommates and sharin' intimate personal details. It's a bit of a mindfuck, if I'm being honest, and gave me whiplash."

Her honesty takes me off guard, though I'm not surprised

she's struggling with our new arrangement. Posey likes to be in control, that much is obvious, and with me re-entering her life, she's having to come to terms with what happened between us.

"I appreciate your apology, but it's not necessary. I'm invadin' your home and personal spaces, it'd be a shock to anyone's system, especially someone as independent as you. I'll make sure to stick to PG conversations only."

"You don't gotta walk on eggshells for me. I agreed to being friends and to help you move on from your ex, so I should keep to my word without makin' it weird. We're roommates and employees, so it's inevitable our conversations are gonna get personal at times."

"You can always tell me when I cross the line. I won't be offended."

"I'm tryin' to get better at communication and not be so guarded. I guess it's a defense mechanism from years of feelin' inadequate in relationships." She finally glances at me, a soft smile on her glowing face. "But gettin' me drunk will always be a truth serum I'll regret the next day."

Bellowing out a laugh, I grin in return. "You never gotta be embarrassed with me 'cause I'll never use it against you or make you feel bad about it."

I suspect that's what her exes did when she explained her struggles or insecurities.

"That's why you're a good person, Silas. And why I get so frustrated thinkin' about how Aundrea treated you."

"Even though I'm a city boy?"

"Ha! Yep, even then." She gives Blythe a little kick and I do the same to Priest while we ride up one of the hillier trails, and thank God Priest knows what he's doing, because as he climbs up, I'm holding on for dear life.

"How ya doin'?" Posey asks a few minutes later once we're in a flatter area. "Ready to race back?"

"Wait, what? Noooo…" There's real panic in my voice because she has no fear factor and I have the luck of a squirrel crossing a highway. I'll fall off and break my neck.

"This is your time to prove you're a cowboy!" she calls out, standing up in the saddle stirrups and leaning forward. "Show me whatcha got!"

"No, I'm actually fine with—"

As soon as Blythe takes off, Priest mirrors her actions and bolts.

"Oh shit, no, no, no. Slow down." I pull back the reins, clinging tightly so I don't slide off, but that seems to be the wrong move because it only makes him go faster.

My ass bounces up and down the saddle, not looking anywhere near graceful as I catch up to Posey.

"He won't stop!" I shout, barely able to breathe in between trying to hang on and hold the reins, breezing past her and Blythe.

Posey flies up next to me and gets close enough to where she can grab the reins and pull back. "Whoa, Priest."

He finally slows down before my heart gives out, but I'm panting by the time he comes to a stop.

"You okay?" Posey asks.

I blink. "He tried to kill me."

She snorts. "No, you squeezed your calves after he saw Blythe runnin'. You told him to race."

"I most certainly did not!"

"Relax your body," she says softly, handing the reins over, although I'm reluctant to take them. "You're too tense."

"No shit. I almost died."

"Are you always this dramatic?" she teases, shifting Blythe over so there's space between us.

She adjusts the hat on her head, shaking out her long blonde hair that's lighter than it was years ago. Since her hair was in a braid all day and she took it out after work, the ends are wavy. I'm tempted to thread my fingers through it and feel the softness against my palm.

When she looks over, she catches me.

"Why're you starin' at me like that?" she asks cautiously.

"Lookin' at you calms my nervous system," I admit. "Sorry if that's weird."

"No, I don't mind." Her genuine smile sends warmth to my chest and my heart rate goes back to normal. "Not everyone gets used to the rush or likes it."

Posey guides us toward the barn, and I've never been more excited to kiss the ground.

"You okay to groom him? Otherwise, I can do it."

"No, I'm good now that the cloud of death ain't loomin' over me," I quip, knowing she'd laugh at my dramatics.

We work quietly, brushing our horses, and then I bring Priest back to his stall.

"No hard feelings, okay?" I give him a little pat, leaning against the gate once it's locked. "But I probably won't be back for a while."

"Meanwhile…" Posey's voice behind me makes me jump. "He's gonna tell his friends how much fun he had."

I bark out a laugh, following her to the tack room to put the grooming supplies away. "At least one of us didn't come back traumatized."

"Oh now you're milkin' it…" she taunts, setting everything inside while I wait.

I scoff once she closes the door behind her. "Says the person who couldn't even walk straight twenty-four hours ago."

She playfully pushes against my chest, but I don't budge. Instead, I grab her wrist and instinctively pull her into me. I expect her to step away or put space between us, but she stares up at me between her dark lashes.

"In case I didn't mention it, thanks for savin' my ass."

Her tongue peeks out between her pink lips before she nods. "Figured it was easier keepin' you alive than hirin' another new guy for the goat farm. Plus, a death on the ranch is never a good look."

"Oh, are those the only reasons?" I cross my arms, feigning offense.

She steps back, slowly walking toward the exit with a sly grin. "I guess you'll have to catch me if you wanna know!"

Posey takes off at a full sprint, holding onto her hat as she runs.

I can't help laughing.

That little shit.

By the time I get to my truck, I find her bouncing in the driver's seat.

"No, ma'am. Move over."

The last thing I need is her killing my transmission or damaging the clutch and having no money to fix it.

"I can't drive?" She sticks out her bottom lip. "We aren't that far from the house."

When I step onto the board, it brings us to eye-level. "Posey. Move over or I'll move you myself."

"Pretty macho for a guy who was weepin' for his life thirty minutes ago."

Weeping?

"You're gonna pay for that."

Wrapping one arm behind her and the other underneath her thighs, I haul her to my chest.

"No! I'm not movin'!" She tries fighting me, but I have an easy hundred pounds on her. "Let me go!"

Her squeals echo throughout the truck as she tries getting out of my hold. I dig my fingertips into her skin and tickle underneath her knees.

"Oh my God, stop that!" she yelps, unable to contain her laughter while I finally get a strong enough grip to bring her down with me.

She continues wiggling as I carry her in my arms, so I shift her body until I can haul her over my shoulder.

"Put me down, you caveman!"

"Nope, you didn't listen," I remind her, giving her ass a quick tap. "You asked for it."

"I'm so gonna get you back for this!" She smacks my back a few times before a throat clearing grabs our attention.

"Am I interruptin'?"

I was so lost in our stupid little game that I hadn't heard anyone approach. Quickly, I spin around to see whose voice it is.

And he doesn't look amused.

I set Posey on her feet and stand a few inches behind her. I'm like a deer in headlights, unable to move or speak, which makes me look suspicious as hell. Although we weren't doing anything inappropriate, I'm sure to him it didn't seem like harmless fun between roommates.

"Hi, Daddy."

chapter eleven

Posey

"WHAT'RE YOU KIDS DOIN'?" Dad asks, his gaze shifting from me hanging upside down to Silas's face.

He sets me on my feet, and I fix my shirt that rode up. "I took him ridin' and was tryin' to convince him to let me drive his truck back home."

"It's a manual," Silas explains. "And not in the best condition as it is, and since she wouldn't get out of the driver's seat, I had to carry her out."

"I can drive a manual!" I argue. "Even your crappy Toyota."

"Ouch." Silas smacks a palm to his chest. "Now you definitely aren't drivin' Brittany."

I roll my eyes. "Of course you named it."

Dad chuckles, shrugging. "Most guys do."

"You even gave it a basic bitch girl name to go with your pumpkin spice creamer." I shake my head. "And that's why you aren't a cowboy."

Silas yanks my hat off my head and places it on his. "I beg to differ. I rode your death horse and lived to tell the tale."

"Death horse?" Dad's eyes narrow. "Which one was that?"

"Priest. Nearly killed me when he wouldn't stop runnin'," Silas explains.

"He's being dramatic…" I jump up on my tiptoes to steal my hat back although he looked good in it. "There's not a scratch on ya, so quit being a baby."

Dad's gaze pingpongs between Silas and me.

"I rode up next to Priest and slowed him down before Silas could get thrown. He's fine," I reassure.

"Traumatized," Silas corrects, jumping into the driver's seat before I can again.

Dad snorts, then walks with me to the passenger side after Silas gets in the driver's seat.

"Y'all are gettin' along well, I see."

His questioning tone and raised brows are met with suspicion.

"We're just friends, Dad."

"Good, 'cause I'd hate to have to fire ya."

"*Me?* What about him?"

"You're supposed to know better being the boss's daughter. It'd create a power imbalance."

"You'd fire your own daughter?" I cross my arms, challenging him to say the words. Mom would never allow him to anyway.

"I'd fire anyone who violates the employee relations policy."

I can't tell if he's joking or not.

He opens the door for me and nods toward Silas. "Have a good night, kids."

"Night, Dad."

He winks before closing it.

"Everythin' okay?" Silas asks, one hand on the wheel while the other rests on the gear stick.

"Actually, no." I buckle myself in. "After I confirmed that nothing's goin' on between us, he said if there were, he'd fire me but not you."

He barks out a hearty laugh, shifting into first and driving onto the gravel road.

"I doubt it. You could sleep with all the employees at the farm and he wouldn't fire ya."

"Excuse me?" I smack his shoulder.

"Not sayin' you would."

"Well, if I'm gettin' fired, then so are you." I pout, folding my arms across my chest. "Otherwise it'd be sexist and I'd sue for wrongful termination."

"You know you're gettin' upset about a fake scenario where we're secretly sleepin' together, right? After we've already made it clear that's not happenin'?"

He chuckles again and I find it hard not to laugh with him.

"Okay, yes...but it's the principle of it. Say we were shackin' up. Why am I the only one who gets in trouble?"

"How 'bout this? I'll quit before anyone finds out. Then you get to keep your job and no one's in trouble."

"I know you're only tryin' to amuse me right now."

"Is it workin'?" He waggles his brows and flashes a wickedly handsome grin.

"No!" I can't help laughing because it absolutely is. "You need this job, though."

And I'm admittedly warming up to him to where I wouldn't want him to be unemployed because of me.

"I'm sure I could find a new one in this hypothetical situation."

"I'm sure Michelle could get you a job at that boots and flannel boutique," I deadpan.

"Is that snark I detect in your tone?" He pulls up to the house and parks.

"Nope. Total legit option." I grab the handle, but his next words stop me.

"Really? You want the person you're sleepin' with to work at a boutique with a bunch of hot women?"

"And now we're broken up." I jump out of the truck, slamming the door behind me.

Silas's laughter echoes through the air as he follows me up the staircase of the deck.

"Posey..." He stands directly behind me while I fight with the key to unlock the door.

His deep gravelly voice sends shivers down my spine but then he leans in and brushes his lips against my ear, sending my heart into overdrive. "C'mon, let's make up. We can't have our fictional relationship end. Marjorie won't like it."

It's impossible to stay pretend-mad when he's playing the role so perfectly.

"I dunno...perhaps you need a night on the couch," I taunt, walking through the doorway, but he grabs my arm and spins me around until my back plasters against the wood.

"Is that anyway to end our date?" he quips, tilting my chin to meet his humorous gaze.

I furrow my brows, lowering my eyes to his mouth when he licks his lower lip. "I never called this a date."

"Are we back to roommates now? Or—" He arches a brow, clearly unfazed by my antics.

"You think I'm insane, don't ya?"

He smirks, releasing his hold but stays close. "Nah, you're perfectly weird in your own way—a cowgirl who makes goat soap, has a house ghost, and hates flavored creamer."

"And makes up fake relationship scenarios 'cause I can't get a real date."

"You will, Posey." He steps back so I can shut the door. "We have that double date this weekend. Aren't you excited?"

Not really.

"Yeah, I guess." I set my hat down and go to the kitchen to make something to eat.

Once I have my sandwich and a yogurt parfait, I sit on the couch and go through my texts.

> JAMIE
>
> We have reservations at six for Mauricino's!
> I'm so excited!

> POSEY
>
> Sounds good! Can't wait :)

I wish I was as excited as she is, but it'll be nice to get out for the evening.

Jamie and I haven't texted a lot since I worked all day and then went horseback riding, so we're still getting to know each other. Jackson texted me once this morning but I never got the chance to respond.

JACKSON

Looking forward to seeing you on Saturday!
Hopefully, we can chat on the phone before
then. I'll be working for the next forty-eight
hours but we can text when we aren't out on a
call.

POSEY

Hey! Sorry for not replying sooner. I had a
busy day at work, but I'm home now. How's
work going?

JACKSON

No problem. It's been good. Went out on three
calls so far and now we're working on shit.

POSEY

I thought you only worked twenty-four hour
shifts?

JACKSON

I had to switch so I could get Saturday off, but
it's no big deal. I'll sleep Thursday and Friday
nights.

"Jamie told me this Italian restaurant is pretty fancy. Should I dress up?" Silas sits on the couch next to me with a plateful of pasta.

"Black slacks and a button-up will be fine," I tell him. "But I guess that means I gotta wear a dress."

"If I gotta dress up, then so do you." He smirks before shoving more food into his mouth.

I almost ask him if this is getting too weird that we're going on a double date with other people and both don't seem too excited about it. But I don't since he needs this. Aundrea really fucked up his head about with how she treated him and skewing his belief on what he deserves. So if I have to tag along for one awkward night, I'll do it.

"Crap, my phone just died in the middle of respondin' to her text." Silas tries to restart it. "It wasn't even on red."

"That's strange. I'll text her so she knows you aren't ignorin' her." I grab my phone but my screen goes black. "What the hell?"

"Yours died too?"

The TV changes shows without either of us touching the remote.

"Okay, what the fuck is goin' on?" Silas glances around, setting his plate on the coffee table. "This is a little too freaky for me."

"I'm not sure...Marjorie?"

"Oh please don't tell me your house ghost is doin' this?"

"She might be."

"There has to be another explanation." He stands, panicking while he grabs the remote and changes it back to the show I was watching.

"Maybe she's still not used to you being here."

"It's been a week. Why wouldn't she?"

"I dunno..." I shrug, continuing to eat my food. There's no anxiety streaming through me so I don't think she has bad intentions in whatever she's trying to tell us. "Maybe she didn't want us textin' 'em back for whatever reason."

"That—" He brushes a hand through his hair, looking flustered as he rubs over his jawline next. "That'd be ridiculous, Posey. Spirits don't have that kind of power to drain phone batteries and control TV remotes."

"How do you know? The sooner you accept she's real, the easier it'll be to understand why she does the things she does."

He pinches the bridge of his nose and sits. "I'm not sayin' it was her, but I'm not *not* sayin' it wasn't."

I chuckle, amused with how flustered he sounds. "You're gonna make her wanna prove herself even more now."

It's just after six in the morning when my phone vibrates with a call from Mila.

I usually keep my phone on silent, but she's on my list of people who can get through to me in case of an emergency. She sounds awful as she tells me she's come down with something and can't run the yoga class so she needs me to do it.

"Silas…" I poke his bicep, hoping not to startle him too badly. "Silas, wake up."

"Posey?"

"No, it's your house ghost, Marjorie. Get up before I slaughter you into a million tiny pieces and feed you to the goats."

His eyes pop open, and I grin at his adorable sleepy face.

"You're such a weirdo," he grumbles.

"Hey, you said you liked my weirdness."

"Don't recall that." He yanks the sheet up but I quickly pull it back, revealing his bare chest and boxer briefs.

"Don't make me bring Teddy in here to wake you."

"Your rat? Hell no."

"Then get up. Mila's out sick, so we gotta teach the yoga class today."

"Huh? *We?*"

He tries reaching for the lamp on his nightstand to turn it off, but I smack his hand away.

"My alarm hasn't gone off yet. Go away."

"We gotta get the goats on the trailer and out there by seven. It's too last minute to cancel. Plus, it's a packed class."

"What am I supposed to do?"

The corner of my lips tilts up. Most of the women are there to watch him, but he's too oblivious to notice or maybe he doesn't care.

"You get to help me do the poses and once the goats are released, I'll walk 'round with treats while you keep showin' 'em what to do."

"If I dunno how to do 'em, how am I gonna help?"

"It's a good thing I have cheat cards. So, c'mon, little Silas. Wakey wakey." I give his lower stomach a pat.

He quickly covers his morning wood but not before I see it.

I stare at his slutty thigh tattoo, wondering how badly it'd drive him crazy if I touched or licked it.

Oh God, who said that?

"I'm so gettin' you back for this," he mumbles, reaching for the blankets.

"Yeah, yeah. C'mon, I'll even make your coffee for ya."

"Okay, deal."

I smirk when he finally gets up.

After we hurry out of the house and load up the goats, we drive to the Branch Haven.

"Why're you so grumpy?" I ask, noticing the deep wrinkle lines on his forehead when he opens the gate for me.

"I didn't have time to stretch and everythin' already hurts." He moves his neck from side to side. "My thighs still hurt from ridin' yesterday."

"And this is why you didn't get to wear a cowboy hat," I quip. "You're too city boy."

"I still work blue collar, doesn't that count for anythin'?"

"You get brownie points for not being a total amateur. But let's see how you manage today."

I pat his chest before moving past him to set up our yoga mats. Since we don't need the goats right away, we keep them in the crates until it's time.

"Here." I hand him notecards of yoga poses. "Just follow me for the first part of class. Most of 'em will be distracted by the goats to pay attention to you anyway, so don't worry."

"I can't even pronounce half of these..." He flips through them. "And definitely cannot get my body to move like that."

I snort at how dramatic he sounds. "If you're vanilla, just say that."

He frowns. "I am not."

"Coulda fooled me," I quip, my cheeks heating at how intense he's staring at me.

He leans in closer, whispering hoarsely in my ear, "This might be inappropriate, so let's consider this as me providin' information to change your mind."

Swallowing hard, I lick my lips and don't move a muscle while he's mere centimeters away.

"I may not be a true cowboy who's worked countless hours under the sun, trained horses, or hand-milked goats for years, but I could effortlessly kneel between your thighs for hours without breakin' a sweat and still have enough stamina to make you finish five times before comin' up for air. I may not be good at plankin' or downward dog, or hell, even horseback ridin', but I'd fill you so goddamn deep, there ain't any amount of stretchin' that'd prepare you for the positions I'd put your body in. In fact, you'd be the one walkin' funny the next day."

My stomach twists at the way his voice deepens and wraps seductively around each word, making my heart rate kick up and my throat too dry to speak.

How the hell did he just whip those words out without a second thought?

"So you can continue callin' me a city boy by your standards, but you have firsthand proof I'm anythin' but vanilla."

When I finally get the courage to look at him, he winks. Before I can find my voice to reply, people arrive for class.

We greet them as they walk in and roll out their mats. I sit on mine, stretch out my legs, and reach my toes. Silas does the same, groaning as he struggles to lean all the way.

I keep a smile plastered on as I inch toward him so no one notices my sexual frustrations. "Just know I'm gonna pay you back for sayin' that to me right before havin' to do this."

"Why?" He waggles his brows. "Are your panties soaked?"

"Silas!" I hiss, nudging his arm.

He's far too amused.

"Just remember you started it."

"How so?"

"You called me vanilla. A man has every right to defend himself when being told they're borin' in bed."

"I never said that," I argue between gritted teeth.

"You did."

More people arrive and soon the class is full, so we'll have to finish this conversation later.

But he's about to be in tears after I put him through the intermediate positions.

Once I welcome everyone and explain that I'm taking over for Mila today, we start in Sukhasana pose to get everyone calm and relaxed. Then I lead them into mountain pose and walk them through breathing exercises.

"I'm sweatin' my ass off," Silas murmurs fifteen minutes later.

It's been comical watching him mirror everything I do, but at least he's trying.

"Can I take off my shirt?" he whispers.

"What? No."

"Why not? Y'all are in sports bras."

If he does, they're all going to be distracted and gawk at him.

"It's not the same thing."

"Well, too bad." He reaches behind his neck, and in one smooth motion, yanks his T-shirt off. As soon as his tattoos are revealed, numerous women's eyes widen in appreciation.

Silas uses his shirt to wipe his face and neck before glancing at me with a shit-eating smirk.

Shaking my head, I glare.

You just wait, city boy.

I direct the class into the camel pose, but this time, I stand so I can walk around and check everyone's posture.

"Keep your hips over your knees when you lean back," I tell Silas. "Touch your toes."

"I'm tryin'…" He grunts. "I'm not made to bend this way."

Standing in front of him, I smirk at him being on his knees.

"How's your stamina now, *cowboy*?"

"This proves nothin'."

"Keep your chest forward and move your hips out," I instruct.

"Yeah, that ain't happenin'."

"Just so you know..." I lower my voice and inch closer so only he can hear me. "You ain't hidin' *anythin'* in those sweats."

chapter twelve

Silas

SHE'S TRYING *to kill me.*

It's the only explanation for why she's walking around in goat-printed white booty shorts and a pink braless tank while cleaning at eleven o'clock on a Friday night.

It's taking every ounce of willpower not to stare and memorize every inch of her curves. She's always been gorgeous but living with her these past two weeks and getting to know her again has stirred up those feelings I tried so hard to bury after we stopped talking.

I should ignore them considering we're roommates and employee relations are prohibited, but it's impossible when she makes me feel alive again after the past two years of feeling like I wasn't enough. And if I'm reading her correctly, she's fighting them too.

Bickering and taunting each other has helped me deal with the break-up and not dwell on the initial shock and pain. I've gone through whole days without thinking about Aundrea.

That never would've happened if Posey wasn't distracting me with her house ghost and ridiculous yoga classes.

She's picking up the pieces without even realizing she's doing it. Instead of pitying me, she's reminding me I deserve better and helping me start over without shame.

I find her in the bathroom and shout over the music she's been blaring. "Posey, do you think we could turn that down a little?"

She's on her hands and knees, scrubbing the shower floor with a fierceness I haven't seen from her before. With an intense glare over her shoulder, I clamp my mouth closed.

Okay so…angry Posey likes to clean to loud rock music. *Noted.*

I walk away so my eyes don't linger on her ass and stay out of her way.

Once I'm in my room, I strip out of my clothes and get under the covers, trying to think of what she could be this upset about.

I'm not sure what happened while I was gone, but I'm afraid to ask at this point. She was fine before I left.

After work, I showered and drove into town to look at an apartment listing that Warren told me about since he knows the landlord. Then per my sisters' demands, I met up with them for dinner at the Willow Branch Grill. They're still worried about me since tomorrow's the day I was supposed to get married, but I'm honestly doing much better than I thought I'd be.

We ended up walking to one of the bars and having a few drinks, which is why I got home late. It was nice to chat and catch up without our mother interfering, but I'll see her in a few days.

When I got home, Posey was already in her aggressive

cleaning mode. I was tempted to ask if it was something I did or about what happened this past week but she didn't seem to be in the talking mood.

After making me suffer through two yoga classes this week, videos of me half-naked surfaced on social media with the background sounds of a cat purring and other trending music with sexual innuendos. She was less than amused when I showed her the comments of thirsty middle-aged women saying they wished they were a baby goat so they could climb me too.

Even though she purposely put me in hard positions, she blames me for removing my shirt when she told me not to, but I couldn't help it. The humidity and heat were excruciating—mix in the poses she was making me do, and I couldn't bear it any longer.

Even though Mila returned on Thursday to run the class, Posey volunteered me to keep demonstrating, and I once again removed my shirt when it got too hot—so honestly, she's the one to blame for making me participate.

It's not my fault someone recorded me without permission but she should be glad that it brought more attention to their goat yoga classes. The next several weeks are already booked out.

Warren's been giving me shit about it, as are my sisters, but now they're determined more than ever to find me a girlfriend.

Although I've been talking to Jamie and we're getting along fine, I feel nothing besides friendship toward her. She's beautiful and funny, and I'm sure she'd make a great partner—to someone else. I have a suspicion that kissing her would be like kissing my grandma.

Still, I'm going through with our double date for Posey's sake.

She won't go out with Jackson on her own, but hopefully they'll hit it off enough that they'll make a second date.

Even if the thought of them together makes me sick to my stomach, it'd be good for her to find someone who treats her right and makes her happy. The guys she's dated in the past have been residents of a flaming trash bin floating down a river.

When a loud commotion followed by a slew of curse words grabs my attention, I jump out of bed. The music's no longer damaging my ear drum but there's a mess of shattered glass on the kitchen floor.

"Shit, are you okay?" I kneel to where she's picking up the pieces. "Let me do this. I'll sweep it up."

She groans, clearly frustrated and annoyed with herself. "It's fine. I'll do it."

"I can help."

When our eyes meet, there's a fire behind hers, and I swallow hard at the way she's looking at me. But then hers lowers down my body, and I remember I'm only in my boxer briefs.

My gaze drops to her finger.

"Posey, you're bleedin'." I grab her wrist and hold up her hand before more blood drips on the floor.

"I'm fine," she insists. "The vase slipped and sliced me."

Not wanting to risk her stepping on the glass, I lift her up and set her down on the other side of the island.

"Silas!" she squeals.

"Where's your first aid kit?"

"Under the sink in my bathroom."

"Stay here," I order. "And keep your arm up."

She sighs. "You're overreactin'."

Ignoring her, I rush to grab it.

"It's really not that bad," she insists when I return.

"Better to clean it and make sure no glass got inside," I tell her. "Don't wanna risk it gettin' infected."

Grabbing one of the antiseptic wipes, I rub it over the open cut that's just below her knuckle before adding a little cream. Then I open a Band-Aid and wrap it around her finger. Once it's secure, I bring it to my mouth and kiss it.

"There, all better." I wink, then toss out the trash.

"Thanks, Dr. City Boy."

I snort, unable to stop my smile at her unamused tone even though her breathing picked up when I pressed my lips to her finger.

"Wanna tell me what made you so upset in the first place?" I stand against the counter across from her.

"No..." She lowers her gaze to her hands in her lap. "It's too embarrassin'."

"Well, now I definitely wanna know. Is it about those videos and comments?" They shouldn't bother her this much, but I can't figure out what else it'd be.

She folds her arms and the movement pushes her breasts up, tempting me to look, but I don't. "No, although now I gotta ban cell phones durin' class. It's gettin' outta hand."

"It was your idea to make me demonstrate."

"Not half naked!"

"You're basically half-naked there too."

She rolls her eyes because we've already had this argument. She'll say it's different because it's all women there and being the only guy meant I should've stayed clothed.

"If it's not that, then what is it? Maybe I can help."

She scratches behind her ear and fidgets with her earring. "I'm havin'…a woman issue."

"Like what? You have your period?"

"No." She blows out a breath. "While you were gone, I decided to participate in some *self-care* in the tub with one of my vibrators. And it wasn't workin'."

"The batteries died?"

"No!" Her cheeks flush while she looks everywhere except at me. "I've always been able to finish on my own. Either my fingers or a toy, even if it took a while, I could always get there. But tonight, I-I just couldn't and it pissed me off 'cause I feel more broken than usual. It's bad enough guys get mad about it, but how can I go on dates knowin' they're eventually gonna be disappointed?"

The stress lines between her eyes are evident and her nostrils flare as she speaks.

"It's completely normal to struggle when you're already tense. You gotta be in the right headspace, too. Don't be so hard on yourself."

I try to sound as sincere as possible because I appreciate how open and honest she is although she's embarrassed about it.

"It's hard not to when it's already somethin' I'm insecure about and now it's all I'm gonna think about the next time I'm with someone."

My jaw twitches at that thought, but I push it away.

"If it makes you feel any better, guys go through the same thing. We get insecure about performin'."

"But y'all always finish, don't ya?" She pins me with a knowing stare, daring me to argue.

"So…you rage clean to deal with your emotions?" I ask, genuinely wanting to know so I'm aware for next time.

She narrows her eyes.

"Not usually, but I'm sexually frustrated and it's your fault, so yes, I was tryin' to work through it by stayin' busy since I couldn't sleep."

"Wait, what?" I point to my chest. "My fault?"

"Yes." She crosses her legs, but I'm tempted to stand between them and demand answers.

"I don't see how that's possible." I've stayed within her friendship-only rules.

"My vibrator used to do the trick but ever since your little *I'm not vanilla* speech in my ear the other day, nothing is workin', and it's like being edged over and over with no finish line in sight."

I try not to laugh out of respect for her *problem* but I can't help it. She's seriously blaming me for this?

"It's not funny!" She jumps off the island, closes the gap between us, and pushes against my bare chest. "It's one thing when a guy can't make you finish, but it's torture when you can't do it yourself."

"And it's my fault 'cause of what I said?"

"Yes 'cause you said things that my vibrator can't replicate and my brain is no longer satisfied with a little buzz buzz action…now it needs words in my ear to get me there."

"That's 'cause you like being talked through it…and praised. I coulda told ya that." I smirk, leaning back with my arms and ankles crossed. "And I assume your exes didn't but now you've re-discovered that part of yourself."

"Well, it's stupid, and I hate you for remindin' me."

I can't believe we're in the middle of her kitchen having this conversation but I'm all for it if it'll help her.

"Posey…" I say cautiously, tilting up her chin and looking into her deep blue eyes. They're darker than usual since the only light in the room is above the sink.

"You like being told what to do durin' sex 'cause you're always in charge of every other aspect in your life. You're used to being in control to regulate stress and anxiety. But once you let go and relax, you thrive with the approval of satisfyin' your partner and doin' what you're told. This only works when you trust the other person and they make you feel safe enough to drop your guard. Otherwise, you stay tense and unable to give into what your body's cravin'."

"How can you possibly know that about me?" she asks as if she's offended I know her so well.

"You came undone in my arms the moment you trusted me to give you what you wanted. Every time I told you how amazin' you felt and that you were drivin' me crazy, you'd squeeze me harder. When I realized how much you liked it, I continued talkin' you through how good you were doin' and how badly I needed you to come. There was no hesitation when I flipped you in different positions 'cause you knew I'd take care of you. Being vocal is what you need to feel secure enough to let go. Otherwise, you can't turn off your brain to actually enjoy yourself."

"I can't believe you remember that from eight years ago." Her voice is softer than before.

"I never forgot, Posey. It's embedded into my brain like knowin' my birthdate without even havin' to think about it.

Maybe 'cause it was my first time, but I know it's 'cause it was with you. You set the standard for me."

She bites her bottom lip and my eyes follow the movement as her tongue peeks out and slides across it. "That's a lot to take in."

"Sorry if that's not what you wanted to hear, but I'll always be honest when you ask me somethin'."

"So..." She twists her lips a few times. "Does that mean you knew whisperin' in my ear durin' yoga would affect me and did it anyway?"

"Well..." I smile to myself that she's not denying I'm right about her. "I had to defend my honor after you insinuated I was vanilla and borin' in bed." My shoulders lift unapologetically. "I didn't realize it'd break your vagina."

Her eyes widen and she twists my nipple. "It's my clit, so I guess you don't know *everything*."

"Hey, that's attached." I cover my pecs to prevent her from doing it again. "And I know *exactly* where your clit is."

She groans but not before I catch her gaze staring at my groin. It's obvious talking about this has my body reacting to the memory of us together.

"Don't overthink what I'm about to offer..." I say cautiously, her eyes finding mine again. "But as I've said before, I can help you if you're up for it."

"How so?"

"If you need someone in your ear to talk you through it, then I can do that for you." Or as she called it before, her *sex coach*.

"That's against—"

I can tell she's about to argue by bringing up the employee relations policy.

"I'll keep my hands to myself," I quickly tell her, holding up my palms in a mock surrender. "You'll be the one touchin' yourself. I'll just be guidin' you until you get there."

"That might make things weird, don't ya think?"

I lift a shoulder, hoping she'll take me up on this. "It doesn't have to. We're adults and can separate business from pleasure, can't we? No touchin' or kissin'."

"I dunno…maybe."

Taking a step toward her, I bring my hand to her cheek and brush my thumb over her soft skin. "Do you trust me?"

She groans as if she hates to admit it. "Oddly, yes."

My heart pounds faster at her admission. "Okay, then turn 'round and put one hand on the counter."

It's going to take every ounce of willpower not to come in my shorts, but if it means making Posey feel better about herself, then I'll suffer through it.

"Slide your other hand into your panties and find your clit for me."

"Who said I'm wearin' any?"

I clear my throat to stop myself from moaning. "Posey."

"Fine, fine." She grins slyly over her shoulder before doing what I asked.

"Now tell me how it feels," I whisper desperately.

"So wet and needy. It's achin' for it," she replies.

Fuck.

I cage her in my arms, grabbing the edge of the countertop for support. My body molds around hers, making it easier for my lips to brush against her ear.

"Good…you're gonna explode all over your hand so I can steal a taste later, got it?"

She hums.

Since I can't touch or feel her, I'll talk her through imagining I am.

"Rub your clit, nice and steady, and imagine my mouth on you. Kissin' your thighs as I make my way between 'em and lick that slutty tattoo on your ass cheek."

"God, yes," she breathes out the words and sinks into me as the tension releases from her body.

"Then I'd fill your greedy pussy with my fingers while I teased your clit, flicking and sucking it until you couldn't take it anymore."

"Yes, *please*."

She continues touching herself, moaning while she pants through the euphoria.

"You're doin' so good, Posey. Stay focused for me."

"I am." Her back arches. "It's so good."

"Your body's so needy and responsive. And you're gonna give it what it wants, aren't you?"

"Mm-hmm." She nods eagerly.

"Perfect, now spread your legs…"

I move to give her room and she does immediately.

"Thatta girl. Slide your hand down and feel how wet you are." I lower my mouth slightly and press my lips to her neck, sucking lightly. "Is it ready for me?"

"Yes…God, yes."

"Now fuck that tight little pussy and tell me how good it is."

"It's so good…" she whimpers. "*Fuck*."

Her breathy moans are killing me, but I'm eating up every single one.

"How many fingers have you stuffed in that filthy cunt of yours?"

"Two."

"Can you add a third?"

"I'm not sure…"

"If you do, I'll give you a reward."

"What is it?"

No longer able to keep my hands off her, I fist the long strands of her hair and pull.

She whimpers at the sensation.

"And this." My other hand wraps around her throat, gently squeezing the sides. "But only if you say please."

"Yes, please…"

"Did you add a third?"

She nods.

"Tell me how it feels."

"So full."

"Such a good girl. Cover 'em in your juices so I can lick 'em off and see how sweet you taste."

"You want 'em now?"

"Yeah, bring 'em to me, but I want you to rub your clit with your other hand."

She obeys, switching them out.

"Keep rubbin' yourself…don't stop."

When she holds up her hand for me, I take it and groan at the familiar scent. My tongue reaches out and snags a taste before pulling her fingers between my lips.

Licking between them, I arch my hips.

"So fuckin' sweet." I suck on each one until it's clean. "Do you feel how hard you make me? That's all 'cause of you, Posey."

"I think I'm close…"

When she rests her palm on the counter for support, I tighten my grip on her throat.

"Don't hold back…the louder you are, the better and longer it'll last."

With my other hand in her hair, I pull her head back and expose more of her neck. Flattening my tongue, I lick the sweat up to her ear and suck on her skin.

"Oh fuck, I'm—"

"Let go, *baby*."

Her body shakes and stiffens as she rides through the waves of pleasure.

She cries out, moaning and panting as the orgasm takes over. Her eyes roll to the back of her head as she flails against me.

"Oh my God…" she whimpers once she catches her breath. Blinking, she glances at me. "That was intense."

Smiling proudly, I nod. "You did so good. Think you can give me another one?"

Her forehead wrinkles. "Yeah, right."

I laugh because her chest is still rising and falling dramatically.

"C'mon…it'll be good practice for you. Plus, it won't take you that long now. Your clit's gonna be super sensitive."

"Okay, I'll try."

My dick's so fucking hard, there's no way she can't feel the imprint digging into her back.

When she slides her other hand into her shorts, she doesn't wait for my orders.

"Shit, that's so raw." She licks her lips. "My hand's gonna cramp."

"Try flattenin' your fingers and rubbin' 'em back and forth… it won't put so much strain on 'em that way."

Her hips thrust into her palm and then she's rubbing her ass against my erection.

"Posey…" I warn, giving her hair a hard tug. "Unless you want my come all over your back, you gotta stop that."

"I'm so close but you need to take over before I lose my momentum," she pleads.

"You want me to touch you?" My breath hitches because I can't say no to her even if we agreed not to cross those lines.

"Yes…please? Just this once."

I want nothing more than to make her shatter to pieces and put her back together again.

"Okay, move your arm and spread your legs wider."

As soon as she does, my arm wraps around her waist and slides beneath her shorts.

No panties.

"Jesus Christ, you're gonna kill me."

Her swollen clit weeps the moment I touch it.

"Fuck, don't stop," she begs.

"I've barely started, Posey. You better hold on."

Although I wanna tease the fuck out of her clit, I bury my fingers in her pussy first. If this is the last chance I have to touch her this way, I'm taking full advantage.

She squeezes my fingers, and I groan. "Fuck, you're so tight…"

"That's so good, Silas…I'm—"

"Think you can come this way? Should I make you squirt all over me?"

"I don't think I ever have," she admits sheepishly.

"Good…another first I get to claim." I grin wickedly against her neck. "But this time, I wanna hear you scream my name."

I drive my fingers in and out of her cunt, thrusting deeper until her body seizes against me. My thumb reaches up to her clit, rubbing soothing circles while the other three digits bring her closer to the edge.

"Don't hold back, Posey. Ride my hand until you come all over it."

"I-I can't…it's so intense."

"Yes, you can…trust me. You're almost there."

She nods, squeezing her eyes and breathing through her nose.

"You're so perfect, baby. Being buried inside you feels like fuckin' bliss."

"Silas." Seconds later, her mouth pops open and she detonates. "Oh fuck…"

Her pussy tights and drowns my fingers at the same time, giving me exactly what I wanted. My spine tingles, unable to hold back my own release.

"That's my girl…holy shit." I continue sliding into her, but slow my pace as her body relaxes. "You drenched me."

I bring my fingers to her mouth. "Open up and suck. Taste how sweet you are when you let go."

Posey obliges, swiping her tongue between each one and groaning.

"My whole body feels numb…" she says, panting when I slide out of her. "Wait."

She spins to face me. "Do I get to help you out now?"

"What?"

Her gaze lowers to the waistband of my briefs but all I can focus on is how beautifully wrecked she looks.

"Oh, um…that's not necessary."

My heart's still racing at the reality of what just happened between us. I'm waiting for her inevitable freak-out when she comes to terms with it too.

"Why not? I let you touch me."

My tongue licks between my lips. "It's not that."

Her shoulders sag. "Then what?"

"I already…" I motion toward her. "When you…"

She peers up, brows raised. "Really?"

"You were rubbin' your ass all over me. It was impossible not to." I shrug. "I need a second shower now."

"Oh." Her face flushes and a hint of red warms her neck. "I should probably clean up too. And the kitchen floor! We never got to that."

"I already said I'd do it. So go ahead. Just be careful."

"Okay." She pushes off the counter, but it's her expression that causes me to reach out and stop her.

"Posey, wait."

Her gaze meets mine.

"Are we okay? I know things got more heated than they should've but I don't want you to think I took advantage when I promised I wouldn't touch you."

"No, I asked you to. It won't happen again, right? So we don't need to worry about it. But thank you…I appreciate the help. I'm less frustrated now." She releases a small laugh.

"Right, sure." I grin. "One friend helpin' out another friend."

"Mm-hmm. Except, you did call me baby."

I chuckle at her accusatory tone. "It slipped."

She arches a brow. "Twice?"

"I was in the moment, so sue me."

"Should I be askin' if you're okay?"

"I'm more than okay…" My voice involuntarily goes up an octave and I clear my throat to fix it. "Gonna sleep like a rock tonight."

She snorts. "Me too, I hope."

"Good night, Posey."

"Yeah, g'night."

Once she walks out of the kitchen, I grab the broom and dust pan, then clean up all the glass.

My heart rate doesn't slow down until long after my shower and I'm tucked into bed. Thoughts race through my head, keeping me from falling asleep, until a realization hits me.

I told her I'd always be honest when she asked me something.

However, that was a lie.

I'm not more than okay.

I'm devastated that I now have a second memory of her that'll continue to torture me for the rest of my life.

But I can't find it in my heart to regret it.

I can only hope she doesn't wake up and decide she does.

chapter thirteen

Posey

WHAT THE FUCK *was I thinking?*

I was drunk on lust and sexual frustration last night.

That's the only explanation for why I agreed to let Silas *talk me through it*. I shouldn't have asked him to touch me because now my brain and heart are more conflicted than before. But I can't seem to regret it either after he gave me one of the best orgasms of my life.

But Silas is off-limits.

I'm his boss's daughter. *His roommate.*

His best friend's sister.

It's against the rules and unless I want him to lose his job, we shouldn't be crossing the lines the way we did. Our double date is tonight so hopefully it'll be good for us to get back out there.

We can focus on other people who are interested in us instead of each other.

It'll be fun.

Now that I know what I need to finish during sex, I can tell my future partner and not be insecure about it.

Yeah, it'll be totally fine.

No reason things have to be awkward between us, especially since he's the one who offered to help me.

"Mornin'." Silas's hoarse voice makes me jump.

I didn't hear him enter the kitchen.

"Hey, hi. Mornin'." I swallow hard and it feels like razor blades cutting through my esophagus. I clear my throat and look at him, remembering the way his muscular body wrapped around me as his fingers slid into me.

Oh fuck.

No, no, no.

I need to snap out of it.

"How'd you sleep?" I ask.

"Great, never better."

"Yeah, me too."

His brows furrow as if he can tell I'm lying.

Although my body was more relaxed than ever, I only got three or four hours of sleep because my mind wouldn't stop racing. Or remembering how good it felt to finally be touched without anticipating disappointment. And dreaming about licking over his thigh tattoo.

"Coffee?" I ask to change the subject and get the dirty thoughts out of my head. "It's freshly brewed."

"Definitely." By his eager, desperate tone, he didn't sleep much either.

He moves to open the fridge at the same time I do so we bump into each other before either of us can open it.

"Shit, sorry," we say simultaneously.

"Go ahead," I tell him. "I was grabbin' your creamer anyway."

"Do you want your half-and-half?" He opens the door and holds it out for me.

"Thanks," I murmur, taking it from his grip.

The room grows silent and uncomfortable as we each make our coffees. My gaze slides over to where we were last night, on the other side of the island, where he made me come—*twice.*

He's fully dressed this time in sweats and a T-shirt but I've already memorized every bare inch of him. Well, besides what his briefs hid. I could've sworn I felt a piercing when his dick was digging into my back, but I was too embarrassed to ask at the time.

"Are you pierced?" I blurt.

Welp, no better time than the present, I guess.

Silas spits out the coffee he just sipped.

"Um..." He blinks hard. "Yeah."

"Hmm...I thought I felt somethin' but wasn't sure."

His tongue pushes against his cheek as he rubs along his scruffy jawline. "I actually have two."

"Interestin'..." My whole body sweats at the thought of what they must feel like.

Did someone turn on the heat?

"What kind?"

"A Prince Albert and Frenum. I've thought about addin' more to make a Jacob's Ladder but you gotta withhold from sex for at least two months, and since I was in a relationship, it didn't seem feasible." He shrugs. "But...I guess I could now."

My throat goes dry, and I bring the coffee mug to my lips with the image of his pierced dick in my mind.

"What made you get it in the first place?"

"Not sure you're gonna want that story." He grins, licking his lips.

"Why not?"

"It involves your brother."

"Oh for the love of God," I groan, rolling my eyes. "You two are insufferable."

"We were drunk…and I dared him."

"Of course you did." Chuckling, I shake my head.

"A few years after we did it is when I got the second one. He only got one but it might technically be two by the way—"

"Stop." I hold up my hand. "Do not tell me what he got, I'm beggin' you."

He chuckles and it feels nice to be laughing with him again.

"I've wondered if gettin' my clit pierced would help me…ya know, with my issue, but the long healin' time scared me. I also worried it'd get infected and make it worse."

His gaze lowers down my body before it snaps back to mine as if he hadn't realized he was gawking.

"The Prince Albert is known to enhance pleasure for both partners but a clit piercin' helps with personal stimulation, includin' those who have difficulty reachin' climax, so it's reasonable to think it'd make it feel better for ya."

"Now who sounds like they're readin' from a pamphlet."

His lips tilt up. "I did a lot of research before my second one."

"I wonder how that works when both partners are pierced. I'd be scared they'd catch on to each other."

"Not likely," he states as if he knows for certain. "Aundrea was pierced too."

And now I want to bleach my brain with that knowledge.

Maybe I'll get my nipples pierced instead. Although that sounds more painful.

"Good to know." I swallow down the rest of my coffee before setting the mug in the sink. "I'm gonna get ready for the day. Jamie and I are meetin' up to get mani/pedi's for our dates and then I'm hopin' to find a new dress for tonight. But I'll be back in time for us to drive to the restaurant together."

We haven't discussed plans for after dinner, and I haven't wanted to bring it up, but since we agreed to arrive together and leave together last weekend at the bar, I'm hoping that means they won't ask us to do anything after. Jackson and I haven't talked a lot this week. Either I was working or he was sleeping when he wasn't on shift.

"Sounds good. Hope y'all have fun." He leans against the counter with his arms folded over his chest with the mug in one hand and his legs crossed at the ankles. Silas looking at home and being comfortable is more attractive than I'd like to admit.

Although I wasn't thrilled about him moving in, I like him being here. He's fun to hang out with—even as friends—he cleans up after himself, helps with chores without me having to ask, and cooks. When we went grocery shopping a few nights ago, he picked out steaks and made them that night. They were the best I've ever had.

He mocked me for not knowing how to turn on the grill, and I teased him for overcooking the veggies, but we had a good time together. I contributed by making the side salads.

"Oh my God, hi!" Jamie engulfs me in a hug after running full force into me. "I can't believe it's finally the day!"

"Me too!" I squeeze her back, but I'm not half as enthusiastic as she is about this.

It's awkward now after what Silas and I did last night, but it's not like I can tell her. It was only a one-time thing anyway. There's no reason to get hung up on it when it won't happen again.

We walk side by side into the salon and get situated into the pedi chairs. It's been a long time since I've had one, so I'm glad she recommended it. We talk the entire time, and I'm grateful she's so easy to chat with because it soothes my nerves about the four of us going to dinner.

"Tell me some juicy things about Silas."

"Sure, whaddya wanna know?"

She spent the past twenty minutes telling me all about her brother and what a great guy he is. Just from the brief communication we've had, I don't doubt it.

"Anythin' and everythin'. Did you know his ex?"

"I only met her once but from what Silas has told me, she wasn't very nice to him and made him feel like he wasn't good enough."

"Wow, really? That's sad."

"Actually…their weddin' was set to happen today." I mentally smack myself because I forgot until right now and never asked how he was doing with it before I left.

"Well, hopefully he'll have a much better night out with us than he would've on his weddin' night." She giggles. "I'm so grateful Jackson and his ex didn't have kids so he wasn't stuck with her forever."

"How long were they married?"

"Four years but together for six."

"Has he dated since it ended?"

"A little but not much. He uses his job as an excuse to stay busy and avoid gettin' his heart broken again."

"Oh..." I frown at how relatable that is.

"Yeah, but don't worry! He's excited for tonight."

"That's good."

"How long was Silas with his ex?"

"Two years."

"The longest I've been with someone was eight months but it's not 'cause I haven't tried. The men 'round here aren't very marriage material. I'm lucky if they contribute to a conversation and ask questions versus me doin' all the talkin'."

I snort in agreement. "Tell me about it."

"Do you think it's too soon for him to date?" she asks once we move to get our nails done.

"No," I reply honestly. "I think once he realized how awful she'd been to him and deserved better, he knew it was time to move on. He only brought a few suitcases and his truck 'cause he got rid of everythin' else but he seems to be doin' okay. At least from what I can see."

"It's never too late to start fresh, so it's nice he has you to help give him that."

I glance away so she doesn't see my face heat.

Once our nails are done, we walk to one of the nicer boutiques in town and try on dresses.

"You look so hot in that! Definitely that one!" Jamie's jaw drops when I twirl in a black backless mini dress. My tattoo peeks out just enough so you can tell it's there. It has a high neckline that wraps around my neck and exposes my arms and shoulders.

"You don't think it's too much skin for the place we're goin'?"

I ask, glancing over my shoulder to look in the mirror. There's two thin straps that lead up to the neckline to hold it up but otherwise my back is fully exposed.

"No…it's perfect. You look amazin'."

"Okay, I'll get it."

Butterflies swarm my stomach at the thought of Silas seeing me in this. Even though he's seen me in less and has touched every inch of my naked body before, this dress is seductive and flirty.

I mentally slap myself when I realize I should be more concerned about Jackson's reaction.

Jamie tries on a few dresses and is gorgeous in all of them. Her dark hair looks best with the red dress, so she picks that one. It has a plunging neckline that shows off her chest without revealing too much. Silas will love it.

Once I find new shoes to go with the dress, we check out and hug goodbye. We have a few hours before our reservation, so I have enough time for an everything shower and to get ready without rushing.

When I arrive home, Silas's truck isn't in the driveway so I don't go looking for him. I didn't ask what his plans were for the day, so he could be anywhere.

"Posey?" Knocking on my bedroom door grabs my attention, and I turn down my music to make sure I heard correctly.

"Come in."

I'm on the edge of the bed, getting my shoes on when he walks in.

"I'm almost ready," I tell him, trying to buckle in the straps. "Okay. Done."

As soon as I look up, my mouth falls open.

Silas's wearing all black in a button-up with the sleeves rolled up, exposing his tattoos, with black slacks and dress shoes. There's a silver watch on his wrist that I haven't seen before but it looks sharp with his outfit.

All that's missing is a black cowboy hat.

"Wow." My eyes widen while I openly check him out. "You clean up nice, city boy."

Standing, I scrub my hands down my dress, smoothing the fabric beneath my fingers. With my heels, I'm almost as tall as he is and get an even better view of him. His hair is nicely done and his jawline is freshly trimmed.

"Thank you, but holy shit...that dress." His eyes slowly rake down my body.

As I spin to show him the back, his eyes widen in admiration.

"Fuck, Posey. You cannot wear that in public."

"That hot, huh? Maybe my failure datin' streak will finally come to an end." A girl can hope, but I'm not holding my breath.

His Adam's apple bobs when he swallows hard. "I dunno how any guy could resist you in that."

"Good to know." I chuckle, my cheeks and neck heating at his compliments. "We should go so we aren't late."

Grabbing my clutch, I follow him out to the truck where he opens my door and helps me in. Then he goes to his side and buckles in.

After ten minutes of driving, the silence is killing me.

"So what'd you do today?"

"Went to Warren and Maisie's for a bit. She was stuffin' the Save the Dates for your cousin's weddin' and he's buildin' the floral arch for the ceremony, so I helped him with that."

"Oh, that reminds me I have to get labels made and printed for the goat soap favors. Then we'll put 'em in cute boxes and bags."

"I can help with that if you need since it's all hands on deck. I don't mind."

"I'll probably wait until next weekend since we won't have time durin' the week, so I'll let ya know. Thanks."

"No problem."

We listen to music the rest of the way, but as soon as he parks, nervous flutters hit me.

"You okay?" he asks when he opens my door and I don't immediately jump out.

"Yeah, I just realized I'm gonna have to talk to someone who knows nothin' about me and go through the whole talkin' stage again."

He laughs when I pout.

"One look at you in that dress and he won't be able to talk 'cause his jaw will be on the floor."

"Silas!" Now I'm the one whose jaw is on the floor. "You can't talk like that."

"Why not?" He holds out his hand for me to take so I can jump down. "Just bein' honest."

"'Cause we're supposed to be friends."

He stands in front of me after locking his truck. "Friends can't compliment each other?"

"Sure they can, but not like *that*." I grip my clutch, trying to get my heart rate to go back to normal. "We agreed what happened last night was a one-time thing, so to avoid any further confusion between us, we should keep things strictly platonic."

The words confidently come out of my mouth but my brain disagrees.

"All I said was that his jaw would be on the floor 'cause of how beautiful you look." He steps closer and my eyes track the movement of his tongue peeking out between his lips. "And I meant it 'cause even if you're gorgeous every day, you're breathtakin' in this dress." His raspy voice makes me squeeze my thighs, but then he grabs a strand of loose hair and wraps it behind my ear, sending me into cardiac arrest. "He'd be crazy not to agree."

My eyes stay glued to his as my heart beats out of my chest.

Swallowing hard, I straighten my spine and put space between us. If I don't walk away now, I might do something I'll regret.

"We should go in and meet 'em so they aren't left waitin'."

He nods and follows me into the restaurant. Jamie's face lights up the moment she finds me and wraps me in a hug.

"You look stunnin'," I tell her.

Her hair's pulled halfway up with beachy waves down her back.

"Me? You're a fuckin' fox." She makes a purring sound, and I blush.

Jackson pulls me in next and kisses my cheek. "It's so good to see you again. That's a beautiful dress on you."

"Thank you." I smile wide at his tan cowboy hat. "Is that a Resistol?"

He swipes his fingers along the rim and tips it. "Yes, ma'am."

"I love it."

Jamie's laughter grabs my attention, and when I see her and

Silas chatting, jealousy I have no right to feel hits me in the gut like a punch I didn't see coming.

Jackson rests his palm on my lower back and leans into my ear. "I'll let 'em know we're here."

I force my gaze back to his and nod.

The dim lighting and candles flickering on the tables set a romantic vibe meant for lovers on an intimate date. A host in a white dress shirt and black slacks lead us to the back where it's quieter.

Jackson pulls out the chair for me, then sits to my right with Jamie across from me and Silas next to her.

"Your server will be with you shortly," he says after repeating the specials.

"Would you like somethin' to drink?" Jackson asks, handing me the alcohol menu.

"I'll take an amaretto sour," Jamie answers before I can.

"That sounds good. I'll do that too."

Silas's forehead wrinkles because we didn't discuss drinking tonight. He's probably thinking about last weekend when I went overboard and felt sick for two days afterward.

"I'm just havin' the one," I tell him.

"Me too," Jamie says. "Took me days to recover last time."

I laugh, relieved we're on the same page.

The conversation between the four of us flows smoothly while we eat. Jamie's easy to talk to and is good at asking questions and prompting Jackson to do the same. He asks about my goat soap business and my family. I ask about his fire station and the types of calls they get.

Silas's his normal upbeat energy and Jamie eats it up while

they talk about her working with her dad and how his first couple weeks working at the goat farm has been.

Although Jackson's been nothing short of a gentleman and is quite charming, there's nothing more than platonic feelings between us. And if I'm reading his body language correctly, he's in agreement.

"I'm dyin' to try their chocolate mousse cake. Do you wanna share a piece?" Jamie asks Silas.

"Sure, that sounds good."

They've been leaning into each other all evening and laughing. I'm relieved they're getting along and seem to be enjoying each other's company. They both deserve it.

"I think I'm gonna try the cheesecake," Jackson says, giving me the dessert menu. "Do you want anythin'?"

I was going to say no but I don't want to be the only one not eating. "I'll do the tiramisu. That's my—"

"Your favorite." Silas grins.

"Wait, how'd you know that?"

His expression changes as if he just now realized he said those words aloud. Clearing his throat, he pats his mouth with the cloth napkin. "You mentioned it once a long time ago."

The only time he would've been around when it was mentioned would've been in high school when Mom and Aunt JoJo were helping me make cookies and brownies for a club bake sale. We were talking about our favorite desserts and I'd mentioned mine.

He was always at the house with Warren, so it's possible he overheard.

But what a weird thing to remember after all these years.

"I've never tried it," Jamie says, playing with the straw in her empty drink glass. "I'll have to steal a bite."

"Me neither," Jackson adds.

"Y'all been missin' out. It's a rich treat with espresso-soaked ladyfingers and cocoa powder."

"Must be why you hate flavored creamer," Silas teases. "You prefer the bitter flavor."

"I never said I *hated* it. But if I'm gonna drink coffee, I want it to taste like coffee, not a pumpkin pie or latte."

"Oh, I love pumpkin spice!" Jamie exclaims.

Silas smirks. "Right? It's the best."

"No, I'm with Posey. Black coffee with a splash of milk is all you need."

I hold up my hand. "See? He gets it."

"Well, that's 'cause he's old," Jamie quips, and I almost forgot how much younger she is than us.

We all share when our plates arrive, which is fun and a great ending to our date. But I can't wait to get home and out of this dress. Although it's very flattering, I'd rather be in pj's and underneath my warm comforter. Teddy likes it too when I let him snuggle with me.

And that might be exactly why I'm single.

Choosing my pet rat's company over a man's.

When the check arrives, Jackson grabs it and pulls out his wallet. Silas offers to pay half but Jackson waves him off and says it's his treat.

"I'll get the next one," Silas offers.

Next one? Don't think so.

Once the server returns with Jackson's card, we head out.

Just as I'm thanking Jackson for dinner and nice conversation, Jamie interrupts us.

"It's still early. We should watch a movie!"

Silas walks next to me as we hit the parking lot and freezes at her words.

"Tonight?" I ask.

"Yeah! Maybe at your house?"

I swallow hard, trying to come up with an excuse as to why that's a bad idea.

"I'm game," Jackson adds. "I'm off tomorrow."

I don't mind hanging out with Jamie but it'll be awkward if she's all over Silas, making Jackson and me third wheels. Maybe I'll drag him into the kitchen to bake something so they can be alone.

"Sure, let's go," I say, walking toward Silas's truck.

"I'll follow you," Jackson tells him.

"Posey, wait!" Jamie catches up to me. "I'll go with Silas so you can drive with Jackson." She winks as if she's doing me a favor.

Before I can protest, she jumps into his passenger seat.

"Guess I'm ridin' with you," I tell Jackson with a weak smile.

Silas's gaze finds mine and he tilts his head as if to ask how I feel about this.

I give him a subtle nod to go ahead without me, then follow Jackson to his truck.

No reason it has to be awkward...*none at all.*

chapter fourteen

Silas

FUCK, *this is awkward.*

My arm's wrapped around the back of the couch with Jamie glued to my side while we watch *Cruel Intentions*. I haven't seen it in years but it's her favorite movie, so she insisted.

But now that I'm remembering the premise, it's a bit uncomfortable considering it's about stepsiblings and she went on a double date with her stepbrother.

I don't think Posey noticed the suspicious way Jackson kept looking at Jamie, but I did. Every time she'd lean into me, his jaw would tighten and his eyes would narrow in on her, but then he'd play it off by looking at Posey and smiling.

Perhaps I'm reading things wrong but there's definitely something weird going on between them that we're not privy to.

Jackson's on the other end while Posey sits in the chair next to him. When she excuses herself, she taps on Jackson's leg to follow her. I can't watch where they go without stretching my neck and being obvious.

"Oh my God, I love this part." Jamie snuggles in closer and places her hand on my thigh, squeezing it.

I should tell her this isn't working for me and I'm not interested in the way she seems to be, but I've never been good at dating.

Exhibit A: Telling Posey we couldn't be together because I was seeing someone else even though she's who I wanted in the first place, then letting her walk away.

Exhibit B: Not realizing how awful my fiancée treated me and allowing her to continue belittling me for two years.

"Do you have any popcorn?" Jamie asks halfway through the movie. "I could totally go for some."

My stomach has been in knots since Posey and Jackson left, so if I eat anything right now, I'll get sick. But at least this'll give me an excuse to get up.

"I'll go look."

Laughter echoes from the kitchen. They're standing around the island with items scattered everywhere. It's hard not to think about what happened between us last night when my gaze shifts to the exact spot she was standing.

"What're y'all doin'?" I ask.

"Bakin' muffins!" Posey grins, adding some crumble on top of them. "We wanted to give you and Jamie some alone time."

"Oh…" My heart races at how I'm going to get myself out of this. "Do we have popcorn? Jamie was askin'."

"In the pantry." She points behind Jackson.

"She loves salt and extra melted butter on top," he says once I put a bag into the microwave.

Posey hands me a large bowl and puts a spoonful of butter in a bowl.

"Who're you makin' these for?" I ask over her shoulder, inhaling the floral scent of her shampoo.

"I was gonna send a few home with Jackson and Jamie, then save the rest for us. Assumin' you like blueberry muffins."

"Are you kiddin'?" I smile genuinely for the first time since dinner. "That's my favorite."

Once the popcorn is finished with the extras, I bring it back into the living room and finish watching the movie with Jamie. She doesn't try anything beyond touching my leg but I do need to let her know I'm not interested in a second date.

"Wow...these smell amazin'!" Jamie exclaims when she sees the muffins.

I set the empty popcorn bowl in the sink and keep my distance from her, but subtly watch Jackson every time she moves closer to me. Perhaps he's an overprotective brother type but it's bordering possessive rather than protective.

"I saved some for y'all to take home. Warm 'em up when you're ready to eat and they'll melt in your mouth," Posey says, handing her a Ziploc bag.

"Thank you! Can't wait to try 'em." Jamie puts them in her purse that could double as a weapon with how big and heavy it looks.

Posey cleans up the kitchen while we chat and I quickly pitch in and load the dishwasher.

"Tonight was fun! Hopefully, we can do it again. Maybe go to the movies."

"Definitely!" Posey says.

"I'll actually be movin' soon, so I won't be able to for a while, but don't wait on me. I gotta go furniture shoppin' and get everythin' for my kitchen and bathrooms."

Posey stops what she's doing and glances at me. "You found a place?"

I swallow down the lump in my throat. "Yeah, the one I looked at yesterday. They emailed me a bit ago to tell me it was mine if I wanted it. It'll be available in a few weeks."

Warren knows the landlord and gave me a good reference. It's a smidge above my budget but I can make it work, especially if I find a different job that pays better. Not that I don't like working at the goat farm, but the wages aren't enough to be sustainable on my own. But finding a job around here is even harder than finding a nice apartment, so it'll probably take a while before I find something.

"That's so excitin'!" Jamie beams. "We'll have to throw you a house warmin' party. I could help you shop too if you want. I'm pretty good at house design."

"She is," Jackson agrees. "Should see what she did to my new place. Looks like a HomeGoods warehouse."

"You're such a liar!" Jamie flicks some of the crumble at him. "It's cute and cozy."

"Just what every single man wants," he deadpans.

I snort. "Thanks for the offer, but I think I'll be okay. I can't buy everythin' at once, so I'm gonna get the essentials first and go from there."

Posey avoids eye contact with me while the rest of us talk. If I didn't know any better, she's not happy about me leaving, which is confusing since she kept saying I was here temporarily.

Once we're done, Jackson asks Posey to walk with him to his truck, leaving me and Jamie inside the house.

"Thanks for tonight." Jamie slides on her shoes, adding a few inches to her height. "I had fun."

"Good, I'm glad." Nervously, I stuff my hands in my pockets and rock back on my feet.

"Would you wanna go on a second date before the weddin'? Maybe just the two of us?"

I swallow hard.

It's now or never.

"I wanna be honest and not lead you on…" I breathe out. "But I don't think goin' together is a good idea. You're gorgeous and fun, but I feel nothin' besides friendship."

"Oh." She sucks in her lower lip. "That's disappointin' but I appreciate you being honest with me."

"I'm sorry."

"No, don't be. I'd rather you tell me now than months from now. Plus, it'll save Jackson from wantin' to kick your ass." She giggles. "He gets overbearin' sometimes 'bout the guys I date."

That's one way to put it.

"I've noticed."

"Yeah…" She winces, waving it off. "But he'll be fine."

I open the door and walk her down the patio steps, then wait for Posey to return. Once she does, I follow her back into the house and lock the door.

"Did you want a muffin before I put 'em away?"

"No, I'm good. Still full from dinner." And the popcorn I stuffed into my mouth as an excuse to keep my hands busy.

"Okay, then I'm gonna get ready for bed."

"Posey, wait."

When she turns toward me, I freeze up.

"What?"

"Um…did you have fun tonight? You and Jackson seemed to be gettin' along well."

"Yeah, it was nice to get outta the house and have a nice dinner. Hope you didn't mind we left you two. Jackson and I couldn't talk without disruptin' y'all so that's why I suggested we go into the kitchen and bake somethin'."

"Oh, right. Makes sense."

"Did you have a good time?"

I scratch over my temple. "Yeah, it was fine."

She nods before walking away. I go through the house and turn off the lights and TV before going to my room. Moments later, Posey pads down the hallway, most likely putting her comforter in the dryer.

Although I'm not super tired, I get myself ready for bed, then get under the covers. Since I need a new bed, dresser, couch, and a bunch of other things, I start a list in my phone and look up ideas.

At some point I fall asleep and wake up when a banging noise echoes from somewhere in the house. When I check the time, I see it's after two in the morning. Posey should be long asleep by now.

Deciding to check it out, I walk out of my room and find every light on.

"What the hell?" I murmur, going into the living room to find the TV on. Although the volume's muted, the screen's flickering between channels, but the remote isn't where I put it.

Another bang comes from the kitchen and it's the last thing I expect when I get there.

Every cabinet and drawer is open, silverware scattered on the floor, and the flour bag Posey left out is tipped over on the counter.

"The fuck?" A wave of cold air makes me shiver.

I go to Posey's room and knock quietly before entering. As expected, she's passed out.

After turning the lamp on, I lean above her.

"Posey," I whisper, shaking her shoulder as gently as possible.

She doesn't move, so I repeat her name louder and shake harder.

Her eyes pop open and before I can apologize for waking her, she throws a right hook in the face.

"Shit!" Holding my nose, I stumble back and fall on my ass.

"Silas?"

I respond with a groan.

"Oh my God, whaddya doin'?" She kneels next to me, squinting.

"You punched me!"

"I was asleep and you scared me!" Leaning over my body, she peels my hand away. "You're bleedin'."

"No kiddin'…" I try to sit up.

"Hold on." She rushes to her bathroom and returns with a wet washcloth.

"I'm so sorry. I'm used to livin' alone and hearin' someone in the middle of the night made me go into fight or flight mode."

Keeping it on my nose, I stare at her and can't even be mad. "I'm glad you know how to take care of yourself, but goddamn, that took me off guard."

She chuckles. "Better be glad I didn't reach for my bat."

I'd laugh if it wouldn't hurt.

"What were you doin' anyway?"

Oh right.

"I heard noises and well…come and see." Standing, I lead her out and show her the living room and kitchen.

"You didn't do this?" she asks.

"Of course not. I was sleepin'."

"Shit." She glances around, worry etched in her features as she takes it in. "It's Marjorie."

"Posey, come on…" My shoulders sag. "It looks like someone broke in."

"No, she's done this before."

"You're serious?"

Did it get colder in here?

I'm still in only my boxers but there's definitely a chill in the air.

"Yeah, after I brought a date here. We were…hookin' up on the couch and I woke up the next mornin' to the same thing. I should've taken it as a warnin' sign 'cause he ended up being a complete fuckin' douche."

"Are you sayin' she's mad we had Jackson and Jamie here?"

She licks her lips, adjusting her top that rose up. "I think so. I knew she didn't like company but Jackson and I didn't even touch, so—"

"You didn't?"

"No…" She furrows her brows. "I explained how I didn't see anythin' romantic happenin' between us and he agreed. So to burn time, we baked muffins and he talked about his ex. I wasn't sure how things were goin' with you and Jamie, so I wanted to give y'all privacy."

"Oh…" I scrub my palm through my hair although it's already a mess.

"Did you and Jamie—"

"No, I told her the same thing before walkin' her out."

"Really? I thought y'all hit it off."

"As friends but nothin' more."

She spins before I can see her facial reaction.

"Hm...I dunno why she's so mad then." She starts closing the cabinets and drawers while I add pressure to my nose. It's sore as fuck, but I don't think it's broken.

This is going to sound dumb but I say it anyway. "Maybe she doesn't like the idea of us datin' other people."

"It's possible...especially after last night."

"Wait, you think she saw us?"

She shrugs. "Who knows? Marjorie will be quiet for weeks at a time and then will randomly let me know she's here."

This is getting too creepy.

"I'm startin' to think it's time to burn this place down."

"What? No!" She playfully pushes my shoulder before remembering I'm already injured. "Shit, sorry. How is it?"

I pull the washcloth back to show her. "Hurts like a son of a bitch, but I'll live."

"I'll get you an ice pack so it doesn't swell."

She digs into the freezer and hands one to me, but then her face scrunches.

"The thermostat...it's freezin' in here. She lowered it again."

Oh good, it's not just me.

"Oh shit—"

Without another word, she walks away and I'm too curious not to follow.

"Oh my God!" she screams when she goes into her walk-in closet. "Teddy!"

"What is it?" I go inside and see his empty cage.

"The cage's open and he's missin'!"

"*What?*" I scan the floor, moving my feet around to make sure he doesn't run over them.

"She's done this before and I didn't find him for three days." She opens each dresser drawer calling his name.

"Please be fuckin' with me…" I jump on top of her mattress, scanning the room.

"Stop being a baby and help me look for him." She moves throughout the room, looking underneath everything.

My eyes widen, stepping off the bed. "Where was he last time?"

"He showed up randomly when I was in bed. Most likely he's hidin' somewhere but he could get stuck in somethin' or get loose outside, so we need to find him."

"Are you sure that's not the better scenario for him?"

This time when she punches my arm, she doesn't apologize.

"I was kiddin', goddamn." I rub over my shoulder. "I'm already hurtin' here."

"We're gonna have to sleep together."

My brow etches at the whiplash. "Excuse me?"

"Sleep in the same bed," she clarifies. "To show Marjorie we aren't datin' other people. She's upset that we hooked up last night and then were with other people tonight."

"Posey, you can't possibly believe that. She's a *ghost*…"

And even that's questionable.

"You have a better explanation?" she snaps, marching out of her room and calling Teddy's name.

I wish I did.

"Okay, so you think snugglin' is gonna make her think we're

together?" I ask, following her through the house as she looks in and around everything.

"Of course you're a snuggler," she groans. "But it's worth a try. Maybe she'll bring him back or point me to him."

Once she's looked over every inch of the house, she throws up her arms. "I give up."

Stepping closer, I bring a hand to her face and lift her chin. "We'll find him. For now, we should get some sleep."

"Okay...how's your nose?"

"Stopped bleedin'." I shrug. "Hurts still, but I'll take some pain reliever."

"I am really sorry for punchin' you."

I give her a little squeeze. "I know."

I put the ice pack away and she adjusts the temp so we don't freeze to death. When we make it back to her room, she opens the covers and slides in.

"You're sure about this?" I double-check before flicking off the lights.

"Not like we haven't shared a bed before."

"Damn, don't sound so eager," I quip.

"Sorry, I'm exhausted and worried about Teddy."

I climb in next to her. "I understand. We'll find him, don't worry."

Her cold feet weave between my legs as she inches closer.

"What're you doin'?"

"I didn't warm up my comforter and now I'm freezin'."

"Oh, by all means, use me as a furnace." I laugh, though I'm not much warmer.

Deciding to say fuck it, I pull her into my body so she can drape her arms and legs over me.

"Better?" I ask when she nuzzles her face in my chest.

"Much, thanks." I hear the grin in her voice and can't help smiling too.

"Who knew you were such a cuddler?" I taunt when she sinks into me deeper.

"Shut up."

My chest vibrates with laughter.

Maybe I'm a fan of Marjorie, after all.

chapter fifteen

Posey

SILAS'S ARMS held and kept me warm all night. I haven't slept this peaceful in months.

And by the steel rod poking me in the back, it's now morning, but I have no desire to leave my bed.

A loud throat clearing grabs my attention and my eyes pop open.

In my attempt to move, I elbow him in the clavicle.

"Fuck," he chokes out, rolling over.

"Shit, sorry."

Wiping my eyes, I sit up and find Bellamy in my doorway, arms crossed, and brow arched.

"Mornin', sluts."

"This…isn't what it looks like."

"It looks like you beat the shit outta him." Bellamy walks in. "His whole face is bruised."

Glancing over, I find she's right. There's a purple bruise around his nose.

"That was an accident," I explain.

"Jesus, Posey." She shakes her head. "Y'all must be havin' some rough sex."

"She punched me in the face," Silas explains, throwing his legs off the side.

"Careful, you're half naked," Bellamy cheekily warns. "And you aren't hidin' *anythin'*."

My cheeks heat at exactly *what* she can see.

Silas quickly covers himself and sighs. "Christ, y'all are the same. I'm going back to my bed."

Bellamy laughs as he walks past her, messy bedhead and all, and stares at his ass while he leaves.

"Okay, perv. Stop starin'," I scold.

"His tats are hot." She waggles her brows, sitting on the edge of the bed. "So y'all hookin' up now or what?"

"No." I don't bother elaborating.

She scoffs, grabbing the pillow Silas slept on and throws it at me. "Bullshit."

"It's a long story, so don't ask."

"Oh, please. You're not gettin' away with that. Get dressed. We're late for brunch."

I mentally slap myself. I forgot about that.

One Sunday a month we meet up with Mom and Aunt JoJo for brunch at the Summit View.

"How much time do I have?"

"Ten minutes before they come and get you themselves."

Shit.

"And you're gonna tell me the truth."

Groaning, I rush to the bathroom to get ready. It's gonna take twice as many mimosas to get through this day.

As promised, Bellamy doesn't let up as she drives us to the restaurant. I give her the quickest brief from meeting Jamie and Jackson last weekend to Friday night and last night's activities. When I mention Marjorie, she laughs.

"You know y'all broke the employee relations policy," she quips.

"I'm aware," I deadpan when she parks. "So zip your mouth. He needs this job until he finds a new one."

"And when he does, will you finally admit you have feelings for him?"

"It's not that simple."

She's gonna flip when I eventually tell her we took each other's virginities.

She snorts. "You two are absolutely lyin' to yourselves."

I don't respond as we walk inside and find Mom and Aunt JoJo.

"Girls! Finally. Thought you weren't comin'." Mom stands, giving us each a hug.

"Sorry, I forgot to set my alarm."

"No worries, honey. Go get some food. We have drinks on the way."

When Bellamy turned twenty-one this past year, she was so excited to finally drink with us.

We head up to the buffet line and stack our plates.

"Hey," Bodie walks over with an extra chair and sits.

"Hi, sweetie," Mom greets with a smile.

"Whaddya doin' here?" Bellamy asks.

Although they're twins, they still bicker like regular brothers and sisters, but probably even more since they were forced to be glued at the hip growing up.

"What? I like mimosas and brunch," he replies, offended.

"You're invited anytime." Aunt JoJo pats his shoulder. "Go get some food."

Once he returns and we have our drinks, they get on the topic of Silas and his viral videos, and every time I try to change the subject, one of them brings it up again.

"I signed up this week just to watch him myself." Aunt JoJo smirks. "Think he's into cougars?"

"Oh my God," I groan, stabbing a sausage link. "Not you too?"

"I am!" Bodie smirks. "They're hot and always freaks in the sheets."

Mom's eyes widen in horror.

I snort. "Is this your way of tellin' us you're bringin' an old lady to the weddin' as your plus one?"

He frowns, messing with his already disheveled hair. "I wish…"

"I'll be your date." Aunt JoJo winks.

"Just what every bachelor wants to be known for…datin' his aunt."

Laughter echoes around us as we continue chatting, eating, and drinking. It's exactly what I needed after this past week, but I still feel guilty with Teddy missing.

"Before I take you home, can we have a serious talk?" Bellamy asks when we walk to her SUV.

"I knew this was comin'…" I murmur, hopping into the passenger's side. "Fine."

"You two like each other…and don't ya dare deny it," she says pointedly, pulling out of the parking lot.

"We have history from years ago. There's always been some

lingerin' feelings even though I tried to push 'em away, but with him in my house and at the farm, it's hard to ignore 'em."

"So, don't. Dad will get over the no employee relations policy if you're upfront and honest about it."

"It's not just that..." I fidget with my fingers, contemplating how much I want to share. "I'm afraid if I let him back in, I'll get hurt again. And after repeated datin' failures, I wouldn't be able to go through another heartbreak from him unscathed."

"You won't know until you try, and who knows, y'all older and wiser now, so it might be different this time. Do you think he feels the same?"

I lift a shoulder. "I think so, but he just got out of a long-term relationship with a woman who treated him like shit. I don't wanna be his rebound or be with me out of convenience 'cause we live together."

"That's your insecurity talkin', Posey."

"Okay, Miss Know-It-All," I tease, finally looking at her and she's grinning like she knows she's right. "Didn't realize you had so much datin' experience to share."

"Just 'cause I don't want the husband, babies, and white picket fence doesn't mean I can't offer my advice on relationships. You want those things but you'll never get 'em if you hold back at the fear of gettin' hurt."

I sigh because I can't even argue with her logic.

"You might change your mind, ya know?" I say when she gets to my house.

"About what?"

"Gettin' married, babies, white fence...you're still young."

She shrugs. "Maybe. But for now, I'm thrivin' in my single girl era."

I snort, then lean in for a hug. "Thanks for the ride. Love you."

"You're welcome, and love you too."

Before shutting the door behind me, she adds, "And I now require updates on you and your secret roommate boy toy."

"Oh my God..." I groan. "You did not just call him that."

"I've seen the goat yoga videos of him without his shirt..." She waggles her brows and licks her lips. "I just know he's hung like a horse. Better jump on that before someone else does."

"Bye!" I slam the door, shaking my head now that she's put that image in there.

The house is quiet when I walk in, which is good because I need time to think and process what's happened this past weekend. A bubble bath with my vibrator sounds like the perfect way to clear my mind.

Once my sexual frustration is taken care of, I'll be able to focus without thinking about his pierced cock.

Except when I lie in the tub, close my eyes, and turn on the high speed, it's all I can imagine.

Music echoes through the bathroom to stifle my moans but the closer I get, the more frustrated I become.

I get *right there* and then lose the sensation. Over and over again, I'm so close, one foot off the edge and about to fall, but then it vanishes into thin air.

"Goddammit," I groan, setting the toy to the side and falling back against the tub.

"Need some help?"

"Oh my God!" I almost jump out of my skin. "Don't ya ever knock?"

I pant and hold my chest at how badly he scared me. For a big guy, he walks around like a stealthy mouse.

"I did...and when you didn't respond, I got worried you were hurt or somethin' since I didn't hear the shower runnin'."

Okay, that's fair.

"I'm fine."

"Sounded like you were gettin' frustrated in here." He tips his head toward the vibrator. Leaning back against the counter, he crosses his arms and ankles, looking smug because he knows exactly why.

"Nope, just dandy in here."

"So you keep sayin'..." His tongue slides across his lower lip, and I can't help following the movement. "But maybe I can offer a suggestion if you're open to tryin' something new."

Even though my heart stopped racing from the jumpscare he gave me, now it's racing for entirely different reasons.

"Okay, I'll bite. What is it?"

"Mutual masturbation," he supplies simply. "Watchin' someone else get off can usually help your own pleasure."

"You want us to try that 'cause you think it'll help me?"

"Yep."

Hm...then I'll get to see his piercings.

After looking up the names of his, my search history now looks a lot different, but I'm still intrigued. So I might as well play along.

"You'll watch me and then I'll watch you?"

"No, we do it at the same time. We watch each other and could even race to see who finishes first."

"Well...I'll lose at that."

"Not necessarily..." He pushes off the counter, stalking

toward me. "Watchin' me will help you finish and watchin' you finish will *definitely* help me."

"Okay…" I can't believe I'm agreeing to this. "Since I'm naked, you should be too."

An amused grin covers his face. "Alright."

The moment he strips off his clothes, my fingers itch to slide between my thighs.

Speaking of thighs…

Good God, his tattoo.

I want to lick it.

"Ready?"

My gaze shifts up to see he's already hard.

I'm already salivating, but then he goes and wraps his large palm around it. I shouldn't be so mesmerized by the view, but I'm one thousand percent locked in.

"Are you gonna use your toy or your fingers?"

Blinking, I finally look at his face. "My fingers."

"Good…rub your clit while you watch me."

Gliding my hand down and spreading my legs, I do just that.

Silas strokes himself in a steady, firm pace and plays with his piercing at the tip.

Holy fuck, I want to stick out my tongue and pull him into my mouth.

"Focus on your clit, Posey. So wet and needy, aren't you?"

My throat's too dry to speak, so I nod. I can't pull my eyes away from how erotic he looks, pumping and twisting over his shaft. His veins are ready to burst.

"Now slide two fingers inside your cunt while you use the heel of your hand to rub against you. Tell me how good it feels."

His deep raspy voice is enough to have me purring like a cat in heat. "I-It's so full."

"Can you go deeper?"

"I'm tryin'…" I reposition myself and hook one of my legs up on the tub to give myself more room. "Oh fuck."

Silas walks over and watches the movement underneath the water. "Good girl, keep goin'…"

The build up resurfaces in my gut and tingles invade my stomach as a rush of pleasure flows down my spine.

So close…so, so close.

"Almost…" I murmur between catching my breath.

Silas reaches out and grabs my chin before sticking his thumb between my lips, forcing my gaze to his. I wrap my mouth around him and suck on it.

"Eyes on me. Don't stop…fuck that tight little pussy and tell me how good it feels."

I stare into his heated brown eyes and whimper.

Whimper. Like the actual noise slips out of me, but I don't feel an ounce of embarrassment about it.

"Such a beautiful sight, love. You're makin' me so hard and desperate to come for you."

And that does it.

I implode from the inside out, shattering every barrier that previously held me hostage, and scream through the intense orgasm that sends me floating to the ceiling.

"Holy shit, Silas…" His name slips from my lips as my eyes roll back from the relief I finally feel.

"Fuck, that was hot," he drawls in a deep raspy voice that could send a second strike of pleasure through me. "I'm almost there."

I rise to my knees, watching his hand stroke faster and can't help thinking how his piercings would feel so damn good inside me.

"Come on me," I blurt, the words barely out of my mouth before he throws his head back and tightens his grip. When his thighs shake, he groans out his release and spills it across my chest.

Watching his undoing is the hottest thing I've ever witnessed.

"Look at you," he murmurs in admiration.

Glancing down, I can't help smiling with pride at the mess he made.

"Sexiest pearl necklace I've ever seen." He winks before wrapping his hand across my throat, coating himself in his pleasure, then sliding two fingers between my lips. "Suck 'em clean, baby."

There he goes with that word again.

The post orgasm-induced coma has me obeying without objection.

"Can't lie, seein' you this way and at my mercy is makin' me hard all over again."

Licking my lips, the high from a moment ago simmers down and my heart catches up with my head. This was a bad idea. Now I'm more confused than before.

So much for coming in here to work through my thoughts.

"Don't get used to it," I deadpan.

"You can't always be in control, Posey. That's the whole point. Lettin' go is what gets you outta your head so you can enjoy yourself."

He grabs two hand towels and gives one to me.

"Feel better now?" He smirks, putting his sweats on.

"Actually, yes. Though, I'm still sad about Teddy," I admit.

"I'm sure Marjorie will guide him back to you soon. Maybe *this* will do the trick." He smirks proudly.

"So you finally believe me about her?"

"Well..." The corner of his lips pinch before he grabs his shirt. "Kinda hard not to unless you've been trollin' me this whole time."

I laugh. "Definitely not."

"Well, I'll let you finish your bath."

I nod, the awkward tension crawling back between us, making me want to stay in this tub for the rest of the afternoon.

chapter sixteen

Silas

"SO I HAVE A THEORY…" I hand Posey her half-and-half and once she pours some into her coffee, she gives it back, then I put it back in the fridge.

Although it's early, I've come to appreciate our little morning routine of getting ready for work, making coffee, and carpooling together.

"About what?" she asks while I grab my creamer and add a good amount to mine.

She sounds half asleep although she said she slept great last night.

After I left the bathroom and she finished her bath, we spent the night on the couch, watching TV, and chatting in between shows. It was nice. *Normal.* A few sneaky glances but nothing physical. Not like two roommates who helped each other orgasm.

I'm still riding the high from watching her unravel. Every

whimper, moan, and the way she came with my name on her lips has been on repeat in my head.

It haunted me in my dreams, and I woke up hard as fuck but didn't have time to do anything about it.

I'd be lying if I said I didn't want to experience it again. *And again and again.*

But I don't know where she stands on what's going on between us. If she still thinks I'm just *helping* her with her issue or if we're treading the line of forbidden territory so neither of us lose our jobs. Either she's really good at disguising her feelings or she has the self-control of a four-star general.

"Jackson and Jamie," I respond, quickly adjusting myself before she notices the tent in my jeans.

Tightening the lid of her cup, she furrows her brows. "What about 'em?"

"Well…" I tilt my head. "Ever watch stepsiblin' porn?"

"Oh my God…" She rolls her eyes, groaning. "It's too early for this."

"I'm serious! He's into her. Like in a not-so-brotherly way."

"Ew…but he's so much older than her." She wipes the counter before flicking off the lights.

"So? Some people are into that. Don't ya have a cousin who married her ex's dad who's twice her age?"

I'm pretty sure they had a baby last year.

"Yes, but Jackson and Jamie are basically family even if they didn't grow up together," she argues as I follow her out into the living room. "Wouldn't that be weird for their parents?"

"Probably, but as a guy, I could tell. He has feelings for her. Like beyond *sibling* love."

"No way." She shakes her head, grabbing her bag before opening the door.

"And I think she knows it too…" I continue as we walk out to my truck. "Why do you think she wanted to watch *that* movie?"

She bursts out laughing when I open the passenger door for her. "That's why you think they're doin' it?"

"No…" I say, rushing to the driver's seat. "But I think she knows his dirty little secret and she was tauntin' him with it. I also think it's why she agreed to go to the weddin' with me and suggested he go with you. See if he'd get jealous or not."

"Like a cat and mouse game?" She buckles in, then sips her coffee.

"Bingo!" I snap my fingers, shifting into gear. "Hundred bucks they're hookin' up or will be within the next few months."

She snorts, shrugging. "Alright, bet."

"Speakin' of the weddin'…" I drive us toward the goat barn with the sunrise peeking over the mountains. "After tellin' Jamie I wasn't takin' her, I'm not lookin' for another plus-one, so you don't gotta worry about tryin' to find anyone for me."

When I glance at her, she's staring out the window.

"Posey?"

She clears her throat. "Yeah, sorry. Um…I'm not either after cancelin' with Jackson. Not super interested in findin' a date with less than two weeks to the event. I don't think my younger siblings are bringin' anyone either, so we won't be the only ones ridin' solo."

"Does that mean you'll save a dance for me?" I say lightly, hoping she'll at least humor me. It's hard to get a read on her sometimes, so I have to prod a bit to find out.

Even if we're not supposed to date, there's no rule that says we can't dance if we keep it PG.

"Sure, they'll probably play somethin' that you can white boy dance to."

"Whoa, now. What's wrong with my dancin'? I thought my two-step was good."

She bursts out laughing and even when it's at my expense, it's my favorite sound in the whole world.

"I saw you at Warren and Maisie's weddin'…you looked like a snake was crawlin' up your leg or a bee was in your hair."

"Wow…" I teasingly drawl. "I must not have been that bad considerin' you ended up in my bed that night."

Her lips pinch in a firm line. "I was influenced by overly-priced champagne and tequila shots."

"So you're sayin' all I need is to get you drunk on expensive liquor and you'll dance with me?"

"Are you talkin' horizontally or vertically?" she says at the exact moment I take a sip of my coffee and choke on it.

"Jesus." I wipe my mouth. "Damn near took me out with that one."

When we arrive, I round the front of the truck and meet her on the other side before we walk in together.

"Have fun with your soaps," I call out like I do most days.

"Don't fall in goat shit, city boy," she taunts, walking toward her office. "But you still didn't answer me!"

"Guess you'll have to wait for the weddin' to find out!" I call over my shoulder and wink before going in the opposite direction.

After a long and hot day working and getting kicked in the shin, you'd think I'd fall asleep until my alarm goes off, but I toss and turn until nearly midnight.

When a loud bang jolts me awake not even thirty minutes later, I'm disoriented and confused if I actually heard something or dreamed it.

But then it happens again.

It doesn't sound like cabinet doors or drawers slamming closed or anything that Marjorie has done, so I grab the closest thing I can find that could cosplay as a weapon and tiptoe into the hallway.

The colored path of my lightsaber guides me through the house since it's pitch black—Marjorie usually turns on the lights when she wants us to know she's upset, so it's definitely not her.

When I hear it again coming from the laundry room, I quietly sneak in, then whip it around at whoever's in there.

"What the hell?"

"Posey?" I straighten my spine, recognizing her silhouette with the dim lighting behind her.

"Uh, yeah. I live here, remember?"

"It's almost one in the mornin'. I thought someone broke in. What're you doin'?"

She eyes the object in my hand. "And you were gonna what? Zap 'em into outer space?"

"For your information, it cuts and melts through things, so I could've easily killed an intruder with it." I wave it in the air to show her exactly what I could do with it.

"Right, clearly," she mocks, standing against the dryer with her arms crossed and a not-so-faint smile on her face. "You're such a nerd."

"Says the girl in goat stuffies…" I point the lightsaber at her feet.

"They're practical! They keep my feet warm."

"So is this…it guided me straight to you." I smirk before turning it off and setting it on the washer. "What're you doin' in here anyway?"

"I couldn't sleep so I came to warm up my blanket once more."

"And *I'm* the nerd?" I taunt, secretly admiring her cute pink pj's. Another shorts and tank set. Her hair's down and messy from her pillow, looking adorably disheveled.

"Wantin' a warm bed doesn't make me nerdy. You, on the other hand…" She lowers her gaze to my crotch. "Nice shorts."

Glancing down, I realize I'm in my Darth Vader printed boxers.

"They were a present," I defend.

She doesn't need to know that they were a gag gift from Sabrina last Christmas.

"Of course." She snorts. "Doesn't really help your case though."

"Fine…I'll take 'em off if they bother you so much." I shrug, waiting to see if she calls my bluff. But when she stands ten toes down, I follow through and lower them to my ankles, before kicking them off. "Better?"

She swallows hard, licking her lips and staring at my dick like she wants to eat it.

When I wrap a hand around my hard shaft and give it a few strokes, her breath hitches.

"Are you done pretendin' you don't want me as much as I want you?"

It's a risky question, but I'm done acting like we both don't want this.

When she doesn't respond, I back her up against the dryer and cage her in with my arms. Her lips part with a shallow inhale as if she won't allow herself to give in.

"Tell me what you want," I demand. "Use your words."

"We can't…" she murmurs, arching her hips into my erection.

"You'd be more convincin' if you weren't salivatin' for my cock." I tip her chin, forcing her gaze to mine. "Look at you droolin' for it."

"So? That doesn't mean we should break the rules."

"Who's gonna know, sweetheart?" I pluck her bottom lip out from between her teeth with my thumb. "I can keep a secret. At least until I find another job."

"I don't wanna lie to my family. They'll figure it out anyway. Bellamy already has."

I figured she did after catching us in her bed yesterday. Hopefully she can keep her mouth shut.

"So if that wasn't a barrier, you'd stop fightin' this?"

"I dunno…what is *this*? Beyond helpin' me with my *issue*, I mean."

"That's what I'd like to explore, Posey." I bury my face in her neck, sucking her skin and licking up to her ear. "I can't stop thinkin' about you. Obsessin' over you. Cravin' every inch of you. I know you feel the same. I can see it in your pretty eyes every time you look at me."

The sexiest whimper releases from her throat.

"Fuck, I wanna kiss you so badly…you have no idea how much I ache to taste your lips. But I won't cross that line until you beg me for it."

"*Beg* you?"

"That's right, *mama*."

She gasps, and I take that as a sign to keep going.

Sliding my hand around her neck, I suck harder on her clavicle. "Kissin' is intimate to me…it's more than a hook-up or situationship. So until you decide what you want us to be, my mouth stays below your neck."

"That's cruel," she hisses, pushing her body harder against me.

She's vibrating for a release.

"Let me taste you, then," she says, breathing harder between each word.

"You wanna suck me?" My cock twitches at the idea.

"Yes." She nods feverishly. "And lick your tattoo."

I blow out a laugh at her blunt honesty. "On your knees, love."

Spinning us, I lean against the dryer and spread my legs. She stares up at me—blue heated eyes between long dark lashes—and it takes all the willpower I can muster not to explode right now.

"Fuck, you're breathtakin'…" I grab a fistful of her hair. "Start slow."

She grabs my shaft, and my spine immediately tingles at that one soft touch.

Before swallowing me down, her tongue flattens on my thigh and licks over the floral tattoo.

I groan loudly at how erotic she makes it looks.

Posey on her knees for me. Kissing my ink, inching closer to where I need her.

Fuck, she's going to be the death of me.

"Be careful with the piercings," I remind her when she shifts her attention.

Posey's on me before I even finish my sentence. Her tongue slides up to the frenum barbell before swallowing the tip between her lips and teasing the Prince Albert ring.

When I tighten my hold on her, I tilt her head back and expand her throat. "Eyes on me. I wanna watch you devour my cock."

If this is the only time this happens, I want to etch it into my memory for the rest of my life.

She complies beautifully, teasing and tasting every inch while she gags and saliva drips down her chin.

"Jesus Christ, Posey. You're doin' so well…" I rub the pad of my thumb along her jawline. "Don't stop. Open wider and take all of me."

This time when I hold the back of her head, I thrust deeper, climbing closer to the edge and nearly tipping over when she chokes.

Pulling back, I give her time to catch her breath. "You okay?"

She nods enthusiastically, wrapping her lips over me again and keeping those hungry eyes locked on mine.

"Love the way you gag on my cock."

Her desperate whines as I feed her more and more of my length have the back of my thighs shaking.

"Touch yourself, pretty girl. Rub that needy clit."

Spreading her legs, she slides a hand beneath her shorts and moans around my dick when she finds that perfect little button. The sensation sends me into overdrive.

"Get your pussy wet and ready for me," I demand hoarsely. "I plan to taste you after this."

With a groan, she bobs up and down, finger-fucking herself, and soon, it's too much. Pulling back, I use my other hand to jerk myself until my balls tighten, and I release all over her chest.

"So gorgeous covered in my cum, aren't you?" I smirk, swipe my thumb through the mess, then push it between her lips. "Can't let this go to waste, can we?"

She eagerly licks it clean, those longing doe eyes never leaving mine.

Before releasing her, I coat more on my fingers until they're covered.

"Open up."

Instead of feeding them to her, I suck them into my mouth and taste myself. Then I lean down and spit it back into hers.

"Swallow," I demand.

She obeys, watching my every movement.

"How's that pussy? Is it ready for me?"

She nods.

"Good girl. Let's go." I pull her up, then take her hand and lead her toward the shower.

She's already a beautiful mess, but I plan to have my face covered in her cum next.

"In here?" she asks.

"Mm-hmm. Don't worry, I won't let you slip."

She strips off her clothing and joins me under the hot stream.

"Against the wall," I instruct, then kneel in front of her. "Hold onto me."

Lifting her leg, I prop it on my shoulder. Her hand flies to my head, directing where she wants me.

It only takes one lick to get addicted.

Breaching her pussy, I don't waste any time. I shove my nose into her skin, inhale her scent and commit it to memory before sucking her clit.

Reaching up, I cup her breast and play with her nipple until it pebbles. Gasps and moans release from her throat the longer I play with her pussy.

Pulling back briefly, I insert a finger and slowly tease her before curling it inside.

"Mm, yes…" She tightens her fist in my hair and her shallow breathing echoes through the air.

Heart pounding, I bring my mouth to the inside of her thigh, biting and kissing before adding a second digit and thrusting deeper.

"Oh my God, Silas…" Her hips push against me, seeking more. "Don't stop."

"Can you take another?" I ask, and she nods before I add a third one inside her. "So fuckin' tight, baby. Ride my hand while I taste you."

She rocks against me, groaning through waves of pleasure until her body shakes.

"Holy fuck…" she cries out, her voice laced in ecstasy, making my dick hard again. "I'm so close."

I peek up as she comes undone. Her head falls back, screaming through her orgasm as it coats my fingers and tongue.

She's the sweetest habit I've ever tasted, and I'm already greedy for another hit.

Once her breathing settles, I put her leg down so she can steady herself.

"Turn 'round, love. Hands on the wall."

Her chest rises and falls as she narrows her eyes in question.

"I'm not done with you," I tell her simply.

She listens without argument. Once her feet are planted securely, I grab her thighs and spread her cheeks.

"This goddamn tattoo, Posey," I growl out the words. "I swear to God."

I can hardly contain myself as I kiss and lick over the compass and floral ink that starts from the middle of her leg and rises up to her ass. It's the hottest fucking thing I've ever seen. Knowing it matches mine fuels me with a possessiveness I've never felt before.

Carefully, I inch back and pull her hips with me. "Bend at the waist so I can see you."

She arches her back, giving me the most delicious view.

"Fuck, mama. Look at you."

My hand cracks down on her right cheek, giving it a nice red glow.

She gasps. "Silas…"

Her little weeping noises are my new favorite.

"Are you okay if I touch you here?" I ask, sliding my finger between her cheeks and down to her tight hole.

"Yes, but no one ever has, so be gentle."

"Another first I get to have? Fuck, you spoil me."

At this point, I'm wondering if her exes knew how to touch her at all.

Better for me, though.

The water stifles her laughter, but I feel it in the way her body vibrates. My cock's begging for relief, but I don't give in. Not yet.

Slowly, I probe my thumb and kiss the delicate skin there. It doesn't take long for her to relax and give me full access to spread her wider with my tongue and taste her forbidden cherry.

Uncontrollable desire takes over, making me unhinged with need. Licking up and down her ass crack, claiming every inch of her, I can't stop touching her.

"Fuckin' hell. This is mine now, baby. Got it?"

She groans in approval.

Moving lower, I glide down to her pussy and steal another taste.

"Silas, oh my God…I think I'm gonna come again."

"Wait," I demand.

Getting to my feet, I wrap a hand around her throat, squeezing lightly until she tilts her head back against my chest.

Dipping my mouth to her ear, I whisper, "Cum on my fingers so I can fall asleep with the scent of your pussy on 'em."

With her palms flat on the wall and her back arched, I sink two digits into her cunt and curl them until I find her sweet spot. When I latch onto her neck, I suck hard and mark her so she can't deny who made her shatter so beautifully.

"So wet for me, mama," I drawl when she becomes breathless. "You ready to come?"

"Yes...God, yes."

"Say the magic word..."

Her gaze flicks to mine, fighting the urge to argue.

"C'mon, say it." I smirk, edging her closer as my hand thrusts faster. "Gimme what I want and I'll give you anythin' you ask."

Her eyes soften, desperate. "*Please*, Silas. I wanna come so badly."

I press my lips to her temple. "Since you begged so sweetly..."

If my fingers weren't filling her so full and my hand wasn't holding her in place, she'd probably kick me in the junk for taunting her. But since she can't, I'm taking advantage.

"Rub your clit for me," I demand. "I'm gonna add a third finger."

She whimpers with the double sensation and my cock digs into her back harder, not able to hold back much longer.

"Let go, Posey. I've got ya."

I feel it the moment her body gives in—her pulse kicks up and she releases the sweetest throaty moan.

"Holy shit." She collapses against me.

Grabbing her hips, I shift her body so we're face-to-face. As I push the wet strands behind her ears, my heart bursts at seeing how relaxed and sated she is.

"You okay?"

She nods, half out of it. "My legs are jelly."

Grinning, I turn off the water that's no longer hot.

"Wait." She licks her lips, then glances down at my erection. "I wanna get you off first."

"I'm fine and you're exhausted."

"But—"

I tip her chin. "Next time, okay?"

Because there *will* be a next time.

Grabbing a towel, I take my time drying off every inch before wrapping it around her, then grab one for myself.

Staring at her mouth, I contemplate breaking my own rule and kissing her.

"We should go to bed. It's late and we gotta get up early for yoga," she says, breaking the spell.

"Right." I swallow. "I'll grab your blanket for you."

I have to grab my shorts anyway.

She walks to her room, and by the time I meet her there, she's under the sheets.

"Ready?" I smirk, and she nods, then fan her comforter across her bed.

Once she's situated and tucked in, I dip down and press my lips to her forehead.

"G'night, Posey."

Licking her lips, her throat bobs. "Night, Silas."

I'm on the biggest high of my life when I crawl into bed, but it's quickly followed by dread.

I'd rather hold her all night instead of sleep alone but she'd never allow it since she's so hell-bent on not breaking the employee policy.

Starting tomorrow, I'm looking for a new job.

chapter seventeen

Posey

THE MOMENT SILAS kissed my forehead and flicked off the light, I passed out. But my alarm went off far too soon and now I'm dragging ass, but it was worth it.

It's going to be a double coffee kind of day, especially having to go to yoga first before an already hectic day. Amaya and I have to deliver orders to the local stores in town to stock them up with the fall scents. Tomorrow's the first of September and sales are nearly double than last month.

"I hope you made extra." Silas's sleepy voice behind me makes me smile, but I swallow and hide it.

"Workin' on it," I tell him, keeping my back to him.

After everything we did, I shouldn't be this embarrassed to face him, but I'm not usually a hook-up type. And when it has happened in the past, they'd leave right away.

Silas softly brushes the hair off my neck, his fingers skating across my throat, and burning my skin with his touch.

"Mm…" he groans, inching closer before pressing his lips below my ear.

It only lasts half a second before he pulls away, but my heart beats wildly at the subtle graze.

"I like seein' my marks on you."

"What?" My eyes pop open, quickly covering the spot with my palm and spinning around. "You gave me a hickey?"

He beams proudly. "Two of 'em from the looks of it. Although I'd have to examine your ass to see if there's more."

"Silas!" I push against his chest to look in the mirror. "I gotta go into town today!"

His chuckle echoes behind me.

When I go into the bathroom and look in the mirror, I gasp at the deep purple bruises his wandering mouth left behind.

"Oh my God…"

"Wear a turtleneck," he muses, leaning against the doorframe.

"In this heat, are you crazy?" I blow out a frustrated breath.

He shrugs. "Concealer?"

"That'll only make it look more obvious that I'm hidin' something." I scrub at my skin as if that'll erase it. "Ugh, what were you thinkin'?"

"You really wanna know?" His wicked grins assures me I don't.

"I'm gonna have to wear it down now and that's gonna suck in this weather."

"I like your hair down, so it's a win-win."

"Silas, I'm serious. This ain't good. I'm supposed to deliver soaps to retailers today. This is all your fault!"

"It's a hickey, not a bomb. Relax. No one's gonna say anythin'."

I roll my eyes. "You're so delusional."

When I go to walk past him, he grabs my arm and pulls me to stand in front of him. "So much attitude for someone who came twice last night."

My spine straightens, reliving the memories of how good it felt to finally get some relief that wasn't from my own hand.

But that doesn't mean he has to rub it in my face and be cocky about it.

"It might be cool for guys to have hickeys but the moment a woman has one, we're seen as promiscuous and not taken seriously. It's not a good look for someone who's supposed to be a professional."

"Alright, I'm sorry. Next time, I'll keep my mouth below your neck."

"There can't be a next time," I tell him although my head's screaming at me. *Liar!*

Instead of arguing with me like I expect, Silas crosses his arms and an amused smile spreads across his face.

"You'd be a lot more convincin' if you weren't squeezin' your thighs together like you're replayin' last night in your head."

God, I hate when he reads me so well.

I start to argue but something catches my attention out of the corner of my eye.

"Teddy!" I squeal, pushing Silas out of my way so I can quickly pick him up before he runs off again.

"Um...an excuse me would've worked just fine," Silas mumbles behind me. "And oh yay, the rat's back."

I pick up Teddy and nuzzle him with my face. "Where did you go? Are you okay?"

"He looks fine to me," Silas says.

Petting him, I feel his little ribs. "Aww...he's skin and bones. Look!"

I shove Teddy into Silas's chest, but he quickly holds up his hands and stumbles backward.

"Nooo...I'm good."

I scowl at him acting like a wimp.

"It's okay, Teddy. Mama'll take care of you." As I walk toward my room, memories of Silas calling me *mama* flood my mind.

No guy's ever said that to me before, and I had no idea it'd make me absolutely feral in the moment. Silas didn't hold back and worked my body better than anyone I've been with before.

And worse, he knows it too.

I never considered I had any preferences in the bedroom besides the desire to actually finish, but he's proved there's a whole other side to me I hadn't realized until now.

We have insane chemistry, and I fully trust him to make me feel good, but I'm still not a hundred percent convinced he won't break my heart a second time.

Once I get Teddy back in his cage and refill his food and water, I go to the kitchen to drink my coffee.

"All good now?"

"Yep, safe and secure. Even put a couple books on top of his cage so he doesn't get out again."

Silas stifles a laugh. "Marjorie opens cabinet doors and powers off phones. I hardly think that'll deter her from gettin' him out again if she wanted."

I blow out a frustrated breath because he's right. "Whaddya suggest then?"

"Get a snake and let Teddy be his snack."

"Silas!" I smack his arm, and he cackles trying to get away. "Gonna feed you to a snake instead."

"But then who'd be 'round to give you hickeys?" He waggles his brows, clearly proud of his comeback.

"I'm sure Jackson wouldn't mind givin' me a hand."

He snorts. "He's too busy jerkin' off to his sister."

I roll my eyes because I still don't believe it, but I certainly didn't need that image in my head.

"Let's go, we're gonna be late." I grab my bag and we walk out to the truck.

Except before he gets in, he pulls out a cowboy hat from the back and places it on his head.

"What's that?" I hate that he looks so hot wearing it. "Since when do you wear Stetson hats?"

"Since my fan club recommended I wear one to yoga." He smirks, buckling in.

"Your *fan club*?"

"The women in the comments of my videos. They suggested I wear one. Gotta give 'em what they want, Posey!"

"You're actually insufferable."

"This whole thing was your idea, remember? I'm just doin' my part to keep the classes filled."

"Oh, you're so full of shit. You love the attention."

With one hand on the wheel and the other on the shifter, he tilts his head toward me with a toothy grin. "Yeah, but the only attention I want is yours."

After an hour of Silas giving a show to the class and all the women hooting and hollering at him, I'm back in the barn with Amaya and packing up orders for delivery. It's not that I'm jealous they thirst after him, but he's turned my calm and relaxing yoga class into a Magic Mike cowboy-themed event.

No doubt there's already videos of him from this morning surfacing online of him in gray sweats and a cowboy hat.

I was damn near ready to kick him out.

"So...you ready to admit your feelings about Silas yet?"

"Huh?" I look at Amaya who's driving us into town.

"You've been starin' out that window for fifteen minutes and ignorin' me except when I said his name." She gives me a pointed look. "I've seen the videos. He's very social and charmin'."

"He's a nerdy extrovert," I correct.

"Have y'all kissed yet?"

"Technically, no."

"So that mark on your neck is..."

Dammit, I knew someone would end up seeing it.

I quickly cover it with my hair. "He sucked on my neck, but that doesn't mean anythin'."

She grins, glancing between me and the road, but the look on her face implies she knows I'm lying through my teeth. "And? C'mon, I won't tell."

"And…a few other things, okay? But he won't kiss me unless I tell him what I want. He doesn't do flings or whatever."

"That's a good thing, Posey."

"Did you forget about the employee rules? We can't date."

"So fire him, problem solved."

"He needs this job. And we live together until he moves into his own place. It'd be like skippin' the whole talkin' phase and jumpin' right into serious relationship territory. Then what happens when somethin' inevitably goes wrong? It's a disaster waitin' to happen."

"Why're you anticipatin' the worst? And y'all already have history, so of course it'll be different. There's no awkward phase when you've known him for years. I'd take that over datin' strangers any day. It's brutal out there."

"'Cause I don't wanna be a rebound and get hurt again. It's bad enough it happened the first time. A second time would send me over the edge," I admit remorsefully.

"You need to stop makin' assumptions and talk to him. Although I dunno him very well, I see the way he looks at you every time he swings by during his lunch just to say hi or when he asks if you're ready to go. He doesn't give off the vibes that he'd be playin' you either."

"No, he's not like that," I agree.

"So, I'm right." She smirks. "Why not just keep things on the down low and see how it goes? If it turns serious, tell your dad or make sure Silas has another job lined up before you do."

"I'm not sure how to deal with these feelings," I confess. "It's a huge risk, especially since he's Warren's best friend. He'd be put in the middle if things went south between us."

I'm already in deep, so might as well tell her everything.

"It's different with Silas compared to any other guy I've been with and that scares me. I completely fold when he touches me. Like…he'll tell me how good I'm doin' or how badly he wants me, and I just melt. He talks me through it so I actually finish and it's the hottest experience I've ever had."

"He found your praise kink," she teases, sticking out her tongue. "Don't be embarrassed. I have one too."

"You do?"

"Oh honey…where do I begin?" She giggles. "I also have a degradation kink. Be mean to me and I'll squirt all over you."

My cheeks heat as I laugh. "Oh my God. How am I supposed to look at you now and not think about that?"

"Maybe you should get some handcuffs or nylon rope so he can tie you up." She waggles her brows. "Oh wait…I bet I can guess another kink of yours."

"How? I'm just figurin' out my own as it is."

"You ever hear of a breedin' kink?"

"Yes."

"I bet Silas would love the idea of fillin' you with his seed and knockin' you up."

"Jesus, Amaya."

Why does the thought of him doing that make me blush?

"See, I knew it!" She points at my red face. "Tell him you want him to cum inside you and have his baby. He'll go *feral*."

"We're not even havin' sex!" I admit.

"But damn near close to it, right?" She shrugs. "Stop worryin' about the what-ifs and the rules for once in your life, Posey. You're a young, hot, successful woman. Have some fun!"

Amaya's words echo in my mind the rest of the afternoon. I

can hardly concentrate on anything else, and when we return from town, I can't even look at Silas when he waves to me.

Thanks to her, my brain is now trying to process what it is I want versus what I'll allow myself to have.

"Hey, Posey. Can we talk?" Ian knocks on the doorframe, grabbing my attention.

"Sure, I'll meet you in my office in a minute."

I remove my gloves and wash my hands before walking out. He's in one of the chairs and hangs up his phone as soon as I walk in.

"Delia's sick and the vet can't get here until tomorrow mornin'."

"What's wrong with her?"

I have a soft spot for Delia. She's a sweetheart and one I rescued from the side of the road five years ago. Some asshole didn't need her for milking anymore and dumped her.

"She's not eatin', but she's bloated and constipated. I tried gettin' her to drink and she wasn't interested. I put her in the sick pen for now so the others didn't bother her."

"Sounds like gastro issues." I try not to panic but goats can decline fast. "Let's try givin' her some hay and see if she'll eat that. And add some electrolytes to her water."

"Will do, boss."

"I'll stay with her until the vet comes, so you can go home."

"All night? Are you sure?"

It'll give me some much needed space to clear my head and this way she won't be alone.

"Yep, positive."

Once he leaves, I find Silas.

"Ready to go?"

"Go ahead without me. I'm gonna stay with Delia."

"Yeah, I heard she wasn't doin' well. Anythin' I can do?"

I still can't look him in the eyes, but now it's worse with Amaya's words lingering in my brain.

"Uh, no. I'll be fine. Not the first time I've pulled an all-nighter." I shrug.

"Okay..." he says hesitantly. "Do you need me to bring you anythin'?"

"Nope, I'm good. Thanks."

Before I can walk past him, he grabs my arm and pulls me into his chest. He brushes his mouth against my ear, and I feel his erratic heartbeat. "I'll be lonely without you, so text if you need me."

Swallowing down my emotions, the only thing I can do is nod.

chapter eighteen

Silas

THE HOUSE IS TOO quiet without Posey and I hate it.

Granted I didn't see her much today, but she'd been distant when we did see each other.

She's fighting her feelings, and I can respect her needing space to figure them out, but if I've learned anything from the last time, I need to be brutally honest about what I want.

But I'm afraid I'll lose her again.

And I can't let that happen.

Posey might not be ready to admit what she wants, but I am.

I spend hours applying to jobs and text a few friends for references. I'm experienced in construction, developing properties, project management, and building houses. There's no reason I shouldn't be able to find something within my area of expertise.

Eating alone after getting used to being with Posey in the evenings kinda sucks. She'd eat whatever I made, even when she made fun of me for screwing it up, and then we'd watch TV together. Sometimes, she'd read and I'd pull her feet into my lap so I could rub them.

Feeling restless and unable to sleep, I go into her room and grab her comforter and goat stuffies. I put the blanket in the dryer longer than usual so it stays hot and make a pot of coffee. If she's staying up all night, then I am too.

When I get to the barn, it's nearly pitch black inside, the only light coming from the back where Ian put Delia. I find Posey on the ground next to her, cuddled underneath a thin blanket, and passed out.

Instead of waking her, I fan out her comforter and climb in next to her.

She barely moves until I pull her body into mine.

"Silas?" she asks in the most adorable sleepy voice.

"Yeah, it's me. Go back to sleep, baby." I softly brush my finger down her cheek, admiring how gorgeous she looks without even trying. Her blonde locks are tied back with some loose strands around her face, and I slowly tuck them behind her ear so I can stare at her.

"I should check on Delia."

"She's sleepin' too. I can see her breathin' from here."

Posey's shoulders relax, and she wraps an arm over my waist. "If she wakes up, let me know."

"I will."

As she clings to me, I soak in the moment of getting to hold her this way. Nothing sexual, just soft touches over her arm as she buries her face in my chest. Her cute little snores are the perfect background noise to help me fall asleep too, even though I'm scared I'll wake up and this'll all be a dream.

My eyes pop open sometime later, and I hear Delia struggling to breathe. She's on her side but looks as if she can't get herself up.

"Posey," I whisper, lightly shaking her arm. "You gotta check on Delia."

She blinks a few times before realizing where she is. Abruptly, she sits up, then gets to her feet and walks over to the goat.

"She looked like she strugglin'," I explain.

Posey feels Delia's chest and stomach. "I think it's bloat. I'm gonna try somethin'…" She gets Delia upright. "I'm gonna get some bakin' soda and water. Can you massage her stomach for a couple minutes? It'll help with the gas."

I scramble to my feet. "Sure, yeah."

After Posey walks out, I lean over Delia and rub her belly. She makes a noise and looks like she wants to bite me.

"Hey, I'm just doin' what I was told."

Posey returns with a bowl, drenching syringe, and some gloves.

"What's that for?"

"Bakin' soda and water can help neutralize stomach acid, so I'm gonna try and squirt it down her throat."

"Do you want me to hold her?"

"Yeah, keep massagin' her stomach. She won't run off on me."

Posey's gentle with Delia while she administers the solution, and within ten minutes, she seems better.

"It's not a long-term solution, but hopefully enough until the vet checks her out."

Once Delia's asleep, I get back under the comforter and wait for Posey.

"Thanks for comin' and bringin' me my blanket," she says when I open it up for her to climb under. But this time she sits between my legs and lies against my chest. I'm propped up on a barrel of hay so we can both lean back comfortably.

"You're welcome." I cover us up. "I brought your stuffies too just in case you wanted 'em."

She chuckles, snuggling deeper into me. "Very sweet of you."

"I'm a very sweet guy."

"Mm-hmm," she muses. "Amaya and I talked about some interestin' things today."

"Yeah? You wanna share with the class or—"

"She thinks I need to get over my insecurity about relationships and the fear of you hurtin' me again so we can have a real shot at makin' this work. Then she said I have a praise kink…and possibly a breedin' kink."

My cock twitches.

"I felt that," she says, laughing and elbowing my stomach.

"I think Amaya just became my new favorite person," I quip. "So about these kinks…"

She shrugs. "Might be worth explorin'."

This time when she inches closer, I bury my nose in her hair and inhale. "I think I could accommodate that."

But I'm still not kissing her until she admits her feelings—even if it is giving me the worst case of blue balls.

"Uh, Posey? The vet's here."

My eyes slowly open until I realize where I am and see Ian in the doorway. His furrowed brow and narrowed eyes are aimed at Posey in my arms.

"Baby, wake up," I whisper in her ear so he doesn't overhear.

She startles awake. "Is she alive?"

Glancing over at Delia, I nod. "Her eyes are open."

"Oh, thank God." She whips off the blanket and gets to her feet.

I quickly follow so I'm not in the vet's way.

"Dr. Warner, thank you so much for comin'," she greets when he steps into the stall.

Posey quickly fixes her hair and clothes, looking adorably cute for sleeping in a barn all night.

Leaving them to it, I walk to the bathroom and relieve myself. I've had to go for hours and her pressing on my bladder didn't help, but I wasn't about to risk waking her.

Employees start arriving for their shift, giving me weird looks at me wearing my sweats and a T-shirt, I'm sure, but I don't bother explaining myself.

I need to shower and change, but I need to let Ian know first.

"Yeah, take your time," he says, but it's the suspicious look he gives me that has me concerned. If he tells her dad before I get the chance to find a different job or tell him ourselves, he'll fire me on the spot.

"Thanks, and we were only sleepin' just so you're aware. I brought her a thicker blanket and we fell asleep."

"Right."

"I'm serious. We kept an eye on Delia all night."

"So the hickeys on her neck weren't from you?"

Crossing my arms, I flex my biceps more than usual and stare him down. "Not sure that's an appropriate thing to ask about your boss's daughter."

"I hope I don't gotta remind you of the employee relations policy?"

"Nope, I'm well aware."

He purses his lips. "Good. Be back in twenty for your shift."

I resist the urge to knock him out and walk back to where Posey is in the stall.

"I gotta clean up and change, did you wanna ride with me to do the same?"

"We're gonna be a bit, so I'll have Amaya drive me home when I'm done."

"Sounds good." I wink before heading out to my truck.

Pulling out my phone, I realize it's almost dead since I didn't charge it all night, but it's the text from an unknown number that grabs my attention.

UNKNOWN

Hey, I've been seeing tons of your videos
online doing goat yoga and just wanted to say
I miss you. Hope you're doing well.

SILAS

Who is this?

UNKNOWN

Aundrea.

How? I blocked her number.

SILAS

Whose phone are you using?

AUNDREA

When my texts wouldn't go through, I
borrowed a friend's.

SILAS

I blocked you for a reason.

AUNDREA

I understand, but please just wait. I really think
we should talk.

SILAS

There's nothing to talk about. You said
everything you needed to say when you broke
off our engagement and gave me two days to
move out. And I had to get a new job.

AUNDREA

I know, and I'm so sorry for that. Truly. I'd like
to apologize in person.

SILAS

That's not gonna happen.

AUNDREA

I still love you, babe. Please. Give me a
second chance.

After hardly getting any quality sleep last night and working
all day today, I'm beat. Posey can barely stay awake while we eat
dinner. But the good news is Delia's doing much better after Dr.
Warner gave her some meds and helped with her bloating.

"This is so good, but I can't keep my eyes open." She leans back against the couch with the fork still in her hand.

"You're pathetic," I say with a laugh. "Let me help you."

I stab a piece of chicken with rice, then hold it up to her mouth. "Open."

Keeping her eyes closed, she obeys.

"Now chew."

"I can't believe I'm lettin' you feed me like a child."

"You like it," I tease.

"I'm too exhausted to even argue with you."

"Damn, you are tired then."

She lets me feed her a few more times before calling it quits.

"Will you lie on the couch with me for a bit?"

Her question takes me off guard, but I'm quick to respond. "Sure, which way?"

"On your back so I can snuggle into your side."

"Oh I see now..." I grin, getting into position. "You just wanna use me as a human body pillow."

A slow smile appears on her sleepy face. "Now you're gettin' it."

Opening my arm, she topples on top of me before wedging between me and the couch. Then she wraps her arm over my waist and bends her knee over my leg.

"Is this okay?" Her muffled words against my chest sends warmth through my body.

I tighten my grip, keeping her as close as possible. "You're perfect."

chapter nineteen

Posey

I CAN'T REMEMBER the last time I slept this hard and so good, but I wake up refreshed and energized for the day. When I peel my eyes open, I realize I'm in Silas's room.

In his bed.

Lifting up on my elbows, I glance around and try to remember how I got here. Then I peek under the covers to make sure I'm not naked.

It'd be a shame to forget having sex with Silas but luckily I'm fully dressed.

"Mornin', sunshine." He walks in shirtless, his sweats lying haphazardly down his waist. "Coffee's brewin' and breakfast is ready."

My gaze follows the path of his happy trail down to the noticeable chub between his legs.

"Um…" Trying to find my words, I'm distracted by how hot he looks. Freshly out of the shower and testing my limits. "How'd I end up here?"

"I carried you."

"But why am I not in my own bed?" I sit up, checking the time on the clock. We have to leave in thirty minutes to get the goats for another day of yoga.

"I tried but you clung to me like a baby monkey. I couldn't let you go even if I wanted to." He shrugs, digging through his dresser. "So I put you in my bed with me. Didn't realize what a cuddler you'd be."

There's humor in his tone, but I worry he wasn't comfortable.

"Oh...sorry if I hogged it all night. Not used to sharin'."

"Wasn't a problem. I loved it." He smirks at me over his shoulder before putting on his shirt.

I throw the covers off and stand, then stretch. "I'm gonna get ready."

"Okay, meet ya in the kitchen when you're done."

When I look in the mirror, I can't help but laugh at how wild my hair is.

Once I've brushed my teeth, put my hair up, and washed my face, I get on leggings and a sports bra. But then I decide if Silas can tease the shit out of me at yoga, then perhaps I'll do the same to him.

Grabbing a pair of spandex shorts, I slide them on instead. Although I don't have a whole lot going on back there, it'll be enough to drive him wild. Especially since my tattoo peeks out underneath.

As soon as I prance into the kitchen, I catch his gaze on my legs. They follow me while I make a plate of scrambled eggs and grab my tumbler of coffee.

"This looks delicious. Thank you." I take a sip, smiling over the rim that he made it just the way I like it.

"You're welcome." He tips his head to my legs. "What're you wearin'?"

"Shorts."

"You've not worn those to yoga before." His eyes lower to my ink.

"Well…if you can go shirtless and wear a cowboy hat for your *many* fans to record you, then I think me in shorts is the least of our problems."

He stalks over until he's in front of me, steals the tumbler out of my hand, and puts it on the counter before caging me in his arms.

"Is that jealousy I hear?" He dips his head close to mine. "You want a private show?"

I lick my lips before capturing the bottom one with my teeth. "Why would I be jealous?"

He buries his face in my neck, sending a shiver down my spine, and then another when he kisses below my ear.

"If you admit you're feelin' what I'm feelin', especially when I touch you, then I just might continue touchin' you. But the longer you deny it, the more I'll keep my hands and tongue to myself…" He sucks on the same spot where it's already bruised and digs his fingers into my hips.

"Silas…" His name comes out a whimper as my hands wrap around his biceps to hold myself up. "What about your job? It'll look bad if I break the rules after I've scolded others for it."

"Fuck the rules, Posey," he says harshly, tipping my chin so our gazes meet. "No one has to know while we figure this out privately together."

I'm pretty certain Ian already does, but I'll make sure he doesn't say anything to my dad.

"I've put in a dozen applications, so take that concern out of the equation. Jobs are replaceable." He inches closer, my eyes zeroing in on his lips. "You're not."

I hate the idea of him not working at the goat farm or doing goat yoga with me, but if it's between that or getting to be together risk-free, I'd take the former.

Swallowing down my fear, I nod. "Okay."

His brows raise. "Okay, what?"

"We'll keep it a secret until we're ready or you find a new job."

He rests his forehead against mine and sighs in relief. "Now tell me what else I wanna hear."

Feeling too vulnerable, I playfully pat his chest so he'll back up and give me room to leave. "We're gonna be late, cowboy."

"Not so fast, mama…" He effortlessly lifts me on the counter and stands between my legs. My heart rate kicks up when he dips his head, cups my cheek, and softly brushes his lips against mine.

It's over far too fast, and I whine when he pulls back.

"Silas…" My breathing picks up when his length presses into my thigh. "Kiss me, *please*."

A smile splits his face, reaching his brown eyes before he inches closer. "You beg for me so nicely, pretty girl. Just like I knew you would."

"Stop being smug."

He continues holding my face and stares at me like he's seeing into my soul. "Tell me you're mine, and I'll give you anythin' you want."

Even though I'm terrified as hell to give my heart away to

him again, Bellamy and Amaya's words of encouragement echo in my head. I'd rather be scared than regretful.

My tongue pokes the inside of my cheek before I finally get the courage. "I'm yo—"

He doesn't even let me finish before crashing his mouth down on mine.

Pumpkin Spice flavored creamer mixed with coffee invades my senses as his tongue massages with mine. Our bodies press together like a puzzle piece, wrapping my legs around his waist and pulling him closer.

He licks and sucks, inhaling every moan of mine, and leaving me breathless. Firm palms grip my ass and push me against his erection.

"Fuck, Posey. I'm gonna be hard all fuckin' day now."

Sloppy, eager kisses slide down my jawline and neck, stopping beneath my ear before he finds my lips again.

I groan at how good it feels to have his mouth and hands all over me like he can't get enough.

"Silas, we're really gonna be late now…"

"I know, baby. But I can't stop kissin' you."

I've waited eight years for this.

Lowering my hand between our bodies, I rub against his cock, wishing we could skip class today.

"Oh c'mon." He weeps, pushing his hips into me. "You're evil."

"Payback's a bitch," I taunt. "Now you'll have to keep your shirt on durin' class unless you want the outline of your dick all over the internet."

"I only did that for you, love. I like havin' your attention, remember?" He smirks shamelessly.

"You're such a shameless flirt." I shake my head. "Every woman wants your attention."

He presses a quick kiss to my lips. "But yours is the only one I want."

By some miracle, we get the goats to class on time and Silas gets his fifteen minutes of fame where he stretches and shows off his tats and muscles. But this time, it's not jealousy I feel.

It's admiration and pride.

They can stare at him all they want, but I'm the one he goes home with every day. While they watch him, he's looking at me.

And just to make class extra fun, I taunted him as much as I could by putting my ass in direct view of his face while a goat jumped on his back during downward dog. And anytime we were close enough, I stole soft touches against his neck and arms.

"You're gonna pay for that little tease…" he murmurs behind me before opening the passenger side door.

"Not sure what you mean," I say innocently, hopping into my seat.

"I'm sure you don't." He winks before closing it.

After dropping off the goats and trailer, he drives us back to the house to change. Amaya and Ian expect us to be late on yoga mornings, so they don't wait for us.

As soon as we walk into the house, I kick off my sneakers and go to change.

"Oh no, you don't…" Silas grabs my hand and pulls me to the couch on top of him until I'm straddling his lap.

"What're you doin'?" I squeal, holding onto his shoulders for support.

"We're gonna finish what you started." He lifts his hips and grabs onto mine. "Rock against me, mama."

"Right now?"

"Mm-hmm. Dry humpin' is another orgasm idea I was gonna tell you about, but now I don't have to pretend I'm just helpin' out a *friend*."

I laugh at how dramatic he sounds. "But I'm all sweaty."

"Don't care, love. In fact, I'm quite turned on by it as you can tell."

He pushes up into me again, and I hiss between my teeth at how good it feels against my pussy.

"Oh God…"

"Use me to get yourself off, baby."

I rock against him, the pressure sitting perfectly against my clit. He captures my mouth and slides his tongue between my lips, tasting and sucking, adding to the intense waves of pleasure.

"Fuck, you're so beautiful when you don't hold back." He kisses down my neck. "Take whatever you need from me."

"Touch me," I beg. "Take off my bra."

He pulls my arms up and slides it off before tossing it to the side. As soon as my breasts are exposed, he cups one and teases the peak.

"Yes…" I nod, leaning back. "More."

Dipping lower, he kisses down my chest until he sucks a nipple between his lips and drags his teeth over it.

I claw his arms and moan in between catching my breath. Silas kisses and sucks, cups my ass to ride him harder, and touches every inch he can get his hands on.

"I'm so close," I warn when the build-up intensifies.

"That's right, baby...don't stop."

It doesn't take much longer before I take off like a jet, flying through the clouds, and riding high. The pleasure shoots down my spine and doesn't stop until it reaches my toes.

"Oh fuck..." Silas fists my hair as he buries himself in my neck and shakes underneath me. He pulls me in for a deep, heated kiss and breathes out my name like a prayer. "Posey."

We're both panting and leaning on each other, neither of us moving.

"That was so hot," I murmur. "Literally. I'm sweatin'."

He chuckles against my neck. "Agreed. I need a shower."

"Me too."

But when I move to stand, he pulls me back into him.

"Just wanna make sure one thing's clear, love." He grips my chin, locking our eyes together. "You're mine and I'm yours, and I'm not lettin' you go this time. Got it?"

"You're really sure about this?" My insecurities flood back in. Even though I'm a risk-taker by nature, giving someone my heart isn't always a risk I can afford. "You were engaged three weeks ago. How do I know you won't change your mind?"

He shifts to one side, pulling out his phone from his pocket.

"Aundrea texted me yesterday from her friend's phone. Her last message to me was *I still love you, babe. Please. Give me a second chance.*"

Anger flows through my veins at the audacity she has to even reach out to him.

"Do you wanna hear how I responded?" He arches a smug brow.

"Shoulda blocked her again."

"Don't worry, I did." He winks. "After I sent her one final text that said, *You did me a favor by opening my eyes to who you truly were and what I deserved. Someone who doesn't try to change everything about me, appreciates the little things I do for her, and isn't afraid to be herself. And because of you, I found her. So thank you for breaking my heart so I could realize you never owned it in the first place.*"

I'm speechless.

His words are so confident and sweet.

Tears well in my eyes, but I wipe them away before they can fall.

"You said that before we kissed?"

"Yes, ma'am. 'Cause I knew. I was gonna give you as much time as you needed to come to terms with what was happenin' between us, but in my gut, I knew you were it for me. I know it's soon, and you might have some reservations since I just got out of a serious relationship, but lookin' back, I was checked out of it a long time ago. Findin' my way back to you has made me feel more alive than I've felt in years. So even though I didn't know when you'd be ready, I wanted to set her straight. And the sooner she realizes I'm not an option for her, the sooner she'll stay out of my life. Hell, maybe I put it out into the universe by tellin' her that."

He smirks at that last part.

My cheeks heat at his honesty, but I don't even know how to reply to something that genuine. So, I lean in and kiss him.

"I appreciate you givin' me time, but I'm ready now. At least, privately until we can go public."

"Posey, baby. I will take anythin' I can get 'cause I know it'll be worth it either way."

chapter twenty

Silas

"SO I WAS THINKIN' of goin' into town tomorrow to look for a new suit for the weddin' next weekend. Would you wanna go with me?"

Posey sits across from me, drinking her coffee and eating breakfast, before we head into work. Since it's Friday, and we don't have to be there early for yoga, I'm tempted as hell to lift her up on this table and devour her.

But after being later than usual yesterday, we can't risk being late today.

"Yeah, I was thinkin' of gettin' a new dress too. Maybe we could match." She smirks.

"Won't that make us more obvious?"

She shrugs. "Or a coincidence. We're roommates who went together. Nothin' strange about that."

I love that she's so willing to go along with keeping us a secret for now. Although she hates lying to her family, it won't be for long. I have a job interview next Tuesday, and if all goes well, I could start in the next few weeks.

"Am I allowed to wear my cowboy hat?" I waggle my brows. "Since I know it's your kryptonite."

Her eyes widen with realization. "I knew you only wore that to tease me!"

When she flicks a piece of toast at me, I bark out a laugh.

"I thought that was obvious."

"Your fan club sure enjoyed it."

"Did you see the comments on the video someone posted yesterday?"

"No, I stopped lookin' after they kept postin' sexual memes about wantin' to climb you like a tree."

I snort, smirking over the rim of my tumbler as I sip my coffee.

"Apparently someone recorded you and me interactin' and zoomed in every time we touched each other. They made an edit of us."

"Wait, really?"

"And now they're all makin' assumptions about us."

"Great..." she deadpans. "So much for being subtle. Hopefully my parents don't see it."

I'm one hundred percent prepared to quit if I need to. Of course I need this job, but it'd only be a temporary setback. After finally getting her back, I'm not letting anything or anyone get in our way.

Standing, I grab her chin and dip down until our lips meet. "It'll be okay. Stop worryin'."

"Easier said than done."

"If it helps, my mom and sisters are ecstatic to see you on Sunday. But prepare to get bombarded."

Although we're keeping our relationship a secret from her family, mine already had their suspicions so I told them with the understanding it couldn't go public.

"I'm excited to go." She smiles up at me when I move between her legs. "It'll be a nice break from my siblings sharin' humilatin' stuff about me. Now I get to hear all about you."

"Oh no...they're under strict orders not to embarrass me."

"Well, that's no fun." She pouts, yanking on my belt buckle to drag me closer. When her fingers play with my jeans zipper, I pull back.

"Uh uh...we gotta go." If I give Ian one more reason to get pissed at me, he'll rat us out before we're ready.

She gets to her feet and slides her hands underneath my shirt, taunting me with her nails dragging over my chest.

"Fine...but then I get to put this image in your head all day."

I furrow my brows and wrap a loose strand behind her ear. "What image?"

"The one of me...in the shower...with my vibrator...and lots of soap."

I growl, wrapping a hand around her neck and yanking her closer. "That's cruel."

Her flirty gaze lowers to my groin where my cock strains against my shorts.

"And now we can go!" She giggles and moves to walk past me.

Quickly grabbing her arm, I pull her back to me and crash my mouth down on hers. Swiping my tongue with hers, I deepen the kiss until she's ravaged and breathless.

"Alright, *now* we can go." I wink at how flustered she is. "I'm not the only one who gets to suffer with blue balls all day."

As promised, I found Posey in the shower with her toy after work and used it on her until she was a weeping mess. Getting her off and hearing her cry out my name were enough to make me cum all over her.

We spent the night in front of the TV with a bowl of popcorn, watching *Golden Girls*, and teasing each other as much as possible. Posey's giggle is infectious when she lets her guard down, and by the end of the evening, my stomach hurt from laughing so much.

I wake up in Posey's bed and tighten my hold on her, groaning into her neck as I arch my hips. I've always loved cuddling, so it helps that she does too.

When she feels my morning wood, she wiggles her ass against me, and slides one of my hands down between her thighs.

"Mm…" I moan, unable to resist giving her what she wants.

I suck on the soft skin below her ear and rub over her panties.

Before I can slide my fingers inside, something hits my foot at the edge of the bed.

"What was—" Leaning up, I see it. "Oh fuck. What the hell?"

As I scramble to get as far away as possible, he moves toward me.

"Stop freakin' out." Posey pulls him into her arms and nuzzles him. "It's just Teddy."

"It's a *rat*, baby. In bed with us," I say pointedly.

"At least he didn't hide for three days again. No, he didn't… he came right to his mama." She speaks in a baby voice that Teddy clearly loves, and if I didn't know any better, the bastard is gloating about it in front of me.

"Here, hold him." She pushes him into my chest.

"Oh, hell no." I jump out of bed. "I don't do rats, Posey."

"Would this be a bad time to tell you I'm gettin' another one?"

"No…no way," I argue, grabbing my sweats off the floor and aggressively putting them on.

"He needs a friend!" she whines, climbing out of bed with Teddy in her arms. "He's lonely."

"Then you be his friend. I—no…no more rats, please."

"C'mon, what's wrong with him? He's so stinkin' cute!" She squishes her face into his. "Just hold him."

"Not gonna happen." I shake my head and go out the door.

"Just one time!" She chases me down the hallway.

I can't help laughing when we're at a stalemate around the kitchen island. It's so ridiculous, but I refuse to give in.

"Marjorie released him for a reason. She wants you to be his buddy."

"Marjorie's lucky I let her stay here."

Posey scoffs. "You mean, you're lucky she lets *you* stay here."

Crossing my arms, I roll my eyes. "Let's compromise."

"Whaddya have in mind?"

"I will *pet* him while you hold him."

She playfully narrows her eyes and whispers to Teddy, presumingly to ask if he's okay with that, and then she nods. "Okay, deal. But you gotta pet him for one minute."

"Thirty seconds," I counter.

"Forty-five."

"Forty."

"Forty-two and a half."

"Fine."

She beams, then walks him over to me. "Be gentle rubbin' over his head and down his back."

I hope she realizes how strong my feelings are that I'm willing to do this to make her happy. If it were literally any other animal, it wouldn't bother me so much, but I fucking hate rats.

"Alright...start countin'."

And she does, except she counts them in Mississippi, so it takes nearly twice as long.

"There, now he thinks you're besties," she praises once I'm finally off the hook.

"How wonderful," I deadpan. "I'm gonna go boil myself in the shower now."

"*So* dramatic."

Two hours later, Posey and I are downtown shopping for wedding attire. I've also been looking at home decor and furniture ideas since I still haven't bought any, but I've not been eager about moving either.

"Any chance there's space for two in there?" Posey smirks, scanning her eyes in the dressing room. "'Cause you in this shirt with the sleeves rolled up is makin' my clit throb."

"Jesus Christ," I choke out a laugh at how unexpected her words were, but I'm not complaining.

I adore this side of Posey.

The not afraid to show affection, be clingy and needy, always wants me around side that I've never experienced before. Not even with my fiancée. It's nice to be on the same level as someone with similar love languages and not worry if you're being too much or not enough.

I tilt her chin, pressing a soft kiss to her lips. "As soon as we get home, I'll do whatever you want me to."

She grins. "Deal."

"Posey?"

A man's voice calls out her name, and she quickly pushes me back in the room, then closes the door on me.

"Hey, Colt."

Oh shit.

"Whaddya doin' here?" he asks.

"Nothin'. Well, shoppin'." She chuckles nervously. "Obviously."

Wow, she sucks at this.

"Uh…what're you doin'?" she asks.

"Findin' somethin' to wear for the weddin'. Whaddya think of this?"

I quickly change out of the shirt and back into my own so I can help her out. She's panicking for no reason.

"That looks great," Posey says. "Blue looks good on you."

"Think so?"

"Oh yeah. You should go buy it. Like right now."

I shake my head.

Opening the door, I step out with the shirt and slacks I'm going to buy and greet Colton with a nod. "Hey, man."

"Oh hey." His gaze pingpongs between Posey and me.

"She was helpin' me find somethin' to wear for the weddin' too."

"Oh, right. Cool." Colton looks at Posey, and when I follow his gaze, I stifle a laugh at how guilty she looks.

"And she's gonna help me find some things for my new place."

"You found an apartment?" he asks.

"Yeah, on Grove. It's a small one-bedroom, but it'll do for now."

"Nice. Lemme know if you need help movin'."

"Thanks, I will."

"Well…" Posey claps and speaks at hyper speed. "We should go. I need to find somethin' to wear too and whatever else he needs. Kitchen and bathroom stuff. Ya know."

"Right, okay," Colton drawls. "Have fun. See ya guys."

"Yep, bye."

As soon as he's out of view, Posey turns toward me, her eyes wide and face flushed.

"You need to relax," I tease. "He probably thinks you ate a gummy or somethin'."

She blows out a breath, slamming her head against my chest. "I told you I can't lie."

"We didn't." I pull her back, cupping her face. "We're just shoppin'."

"You know what I mean. Lyin' by omission."

"I doubt he cares that much."

After I check out, we walk to one of the boutiques so she can try on dresses and shoes. I had to glue my back to the wall to stop myself from touching her each time she showed me a new one.

"I'm thinkin' this one. Whaddya think?"

When she opens the door, my jaw falls to the floor. "You cannot wear that in public."

"You always say that."

"Yeah, but I can see your nipples. And that slit? There's no way you can wear panties underneath."

She bites her lower lip before gliding her tongue over it. "Sounds like easy access to me."

"Posey," I growl. "I'll be walkin' around all night with a hard-on."

"So?"

"So that might get awkward when I'm talkin' to your family and my whole package is tented on display."

"You can wear somethin' that'll equally turn me on and we can suffer together."

"And what might that be?"

She holds my gaze and walks toward me, then lifts a finger to my chest. "A chain hangin' from your neck with the letter P on it. I would probably lose my mind and go feral anytime I saw you wearin' it."

I'm surprised she wants me to wear one considering she's always calling me a city boy and loves cowboy hats, but fuck it. If that's what she wants, I'll make it happen.

Tipping her chin, I inch closer to her mouth. Not quite touching, but if anyone walked in here and caught us, they'd definitely know we weren't just friends.

"If that's the case, then you better be ready for me next weekend." I wink before pulling away.

We spend the rest of the day window shopping for apartment furniture and although I grab some kitchen and bathroom supplies, I don't get much more than that.

On Sunday, we went to my mom's and had brunch with my sisters, who took far too much joy embarrassing me every chance they got. Showing off old photos, telling stories from my middle and high school years, and overall, making me sound like a nerd and loser.

Posey loved all of it and joined in on teasing me. I couldn't even be mad about it because seeing her get along with my family so well was a relief. She played with my nieces and nephews and by the end of the evening were already asking when I'd bring her back.

Aundrea didn't talk or engage much, which made things awkward when I brought her to my family events. I don't even think she knew all their names.

Monday started out like the rest of the week did—with Posey and I in the shower, my new favorite morning activity of making her come, followed by my favorite evening activity of making her come. On the couch, the kitchen island, her bed, my bed, or the back of my truck.

I loved finding new ways to get her off and teaching her how to finish while I coached her.

We went to goat yoga as usual on Tuesday and Thursday, me in my cowboy hat and her in too tight spandex that had me drooling all over the mat.

The job interview was a bust, but I have another one scheduled for next week that sounds much more up my alley. A building company looking for a project manager who can start right away with great benefits, consistent hours, opportunities for promotions, and optional overtime.

Tonight's the wedding rehearsal for Landen and Ellie, which means the entire Hollis family is here along with Ellie's. They're staying at the Willow Chalet. I've helped with cleaning, getting out chairs, and setting up the past few nights, and now I'm excited to see everyone. It's been years since I've seen their cousins.

"Are you ready?" Posey asks, entering the living room and looking far too tempting.

"Goddamn, why must you torture me?"

She's in the prettiest pink dress and brown cowboy boots, hair down in long waves, and silver hoops in her ear.

Pulling her to my chest, I slant my mouth over hers. "You look breathtakin', love. Any single guys at this thing? Hope not, 'cause I might be tempted to punch 'em if I catch 'em starin' at you."

"Well...there might be." She shrugs playfully. "But they're all related to me, so you don't have anythin' to worry about."

"Good, even better." I wink before stealing another kiss.

"We should go so we aren't late."

I only tagged along because I was told to, but I mostly sat and watched the rehearsal. Warren introduced me to everyone I hadn't met yet and re-introduced me to the ones I had in previous years.

Posey and I decided to keep our distance since there'd be so many eyes on us otherwise. Plus, I wanted her to enjoy being with her family and catching up with them instead of worrying about me.

I'll steal her back tomorrow night after the reception and make her mine for good.

chapter twenty-one

ELLIE'S one of the most beautiful brides I've ever seen. Her golden blonde hair is swept up gracefully underneath a veil and her dress hugs her curves perfectly. But truthfully, it's Landen everyone was watching.

I don't think I've ever seen a man weep so much when he saw his future wife walk down the aisle. His deep love for her could be felt throughout the entire room.

Everyone was in tears when he read his vows and then even more after Ellie read hers. It's obvious how right they are for each other. She's more straightforward and driven while he's adventurous and playful. They complement each other so well in making sure they don't take life too seriously and remember to have fun too.

Halfway through the reception, I'm three champagne glasses gone. Dinner was delicious and I got to catch up with more cousins and family members. Even though Silas sat next to Warren on the other side of the table, I tried to keep my gaze off him. But it was hard since I could sense he was staring at me.

He's more obvious than I am.

But he looks so good in his black slacks and shirt with a matching black cowboy hat. It's like he's trying to get me to combust right here in front of everyone.

"Dance with me." A shiver runs down my spine when Silas's deep voice echoes in my ear.

"It's too soon," I say over my shoulder. "There's too many people still here."

"They're all *ten* sheets to the wind."

I laugh at his ten sheets joke and mocking me when I was drunk.

"No one's payin' attention, baby. C'mon…" He holds out his hand, and I reluctantly take it, glancing from side to side to see if anyone's watching. But he's right. Everyone's drinking or talking in their own circles.

A popular slow song plays and when Silas pulls me into his chest, I wrap my arms behind his neck. His palms grip above my ass, holding firm.

"In case I haven't told you eight million times tonight, you look stunnin' in this dress. I've had a hard time not starin' and imaginin' my tongue lickin' up that naughty slit on your thigh."

"Why do you think I wanted to wear it so badly?" I bite my lower lip. "I knew how much you'd wanna rip it off me."

"Posey…" he growls, pushing his hips into me so I can feel his hardened length. "You better be careful."

We've fooled around nonstop. And it's been nothing short of amazing. Each time he gives me an orgasm or I give him one is a serotonin shot directly into my brain. But I'm ready for more.

I want to feel those piercings inside me and connect with him in a way I never had before. Silas makes me feel things that are completely new. The constant rush of emotions anytime he's near. The way my heart feels like bursting when he calls me baby, love, or mama. The wild part inside me that only he's been able to activate in a way that doesn't feel wrong or foreign.

My feelings for him get stronger and stronger each day and even if we can't go public, I don't want to wait any longer to give all of myself to him.

"I read somethin' the other day that had me wantin' to try it, but I wasn't sure if you'd be on board or not."

"A…sexual thing?"

I nod, feel my cheeks heat and am almost too embarrassed to talk about it.

"I'm gonna almost always be on board for anythin' with you."

"Well…I dunno if guys actually like it or not, or if it's only good for the woman, but it's where I'd sit on your face while you eat me out. Sounds kinda dangerous, to be honest but…"

"Oh, Jesus Christ," he blurts, blowing out a breath. "Yeah, we're gonna need to leave soon. Fake a sickness, break a bone, I don't care."

I stifle a laugh, glancing down to see the tent pitched in his black slacks.

"So you like that idea, then?"

"Are you kiddin'? If I could have you sit on my face for breakfast, lunch, and dinner, I would."

"Not that I'm complainin', but I think you enjoy eatin' pussy more than most men."

At least in my experience. The guys I've dated got bored after five minutes, then would come up for air and ask, *did you cum?*

No asshole, I'm still dry.

"I enjoy it 'cause it's *your* pussy." He smirks devilishly. "Not only do you taste so fuckin' good and smell so damn sweet, but I love how you react. You practically rip out my hair and squeeze my head with your thighs. The little whimpers you make when you're so damn close but don't think you can last any longer are my favorite. Then, when you're right there and one more lick sends you over the edge, I nearly cum in my pants at how loud you moan. So yeah...I love eatin' *your* pussy."

I'm practically panting like a dog in heat by the time he finishes.

"Okay, yeah. We need to go."

"Wait, I forgot to show you somethin' earlier."

He reaches into the collar of his shirt and pulls out a silver chain with the letter P hanging from it.

My mouth pops open.

"You actually got one? Already?"

"Of course. And I got it engraved with your name on the long part of the letter."

Taking it between my fingers, I inch closer to see the tiny script letters.

"You have no idea how sexy I find this."

I'm already picturing him naked on top of me with it hanging down between us.

Yeah, we gotta leave now.

I pull him off the dance floor and grab my clutch, not bothering to say goodbye to anyone since I'll see them tomorrow at brunch. It's where the immediate family gets together hungover, eats carbs, drinks mimosas and watches the bride and groom open their gifts.

"Silas."

Warren's voice makes us both turn, probably looking guilty as hell.

"Hey, what's up?" Silas asks, casually covering his groin area with his hands.

"Aundrea's here."

"*What?*" Silas and I say in unison.

"Yeah, she's outside. We wouldn't let her in since she's not on the guest list, but she said she figured you'd be here and wanted to talk to you."

"Fuck." Silas shakes his head.

"I tried tellin' her to leave, but she said she wouldn't until she sees you. I didn't want her to cause a scene, so I told her I'd come get ya."

"Can I punch her?" I ask. "Just once?"

"No," Warren says. "Any other time or place would be fine but not here."

I roll my eyes. What a fun-sucker.

"Tell her I'll be out there in a minute."

Warren nods, glancing between us, then walks away.

"I hate her," I say matter-of-factly.

"Don't worry, baby. I'm gonna get rid of her."

"Like..." I slice my finger across my neck. "Or?"

Silas looks at me like I've lost my mind.

Maybe I have.

"What? You said *get rid of her* like some mafia cowboy, so I was just checkin'. And 'cause I was offerin' to help carry the body."

He barks out a soothing laugh. "No, I'll handle it. She can't stand rejection and that's why she's threatenin' to make a scene."

"Fine. But if you aren't back in eight minutes, I'm comin' out with my heels ready to stab a bitch."

They're five inches, so they could do some damage if I threw them hard enough.

"Okay, calm down, Ninja Warrior. Stay here."

He quickly kisses the top of my head before walking out the door.

I'm anything but calm as I sit at the table and tap my feet. Luckily, Bellamy comes over and forces me onto the dance floor, which is a nice distraction. Since she already knows about us, I tell her where he is.

"Well, she can't fight both of us. Let's go." She nods toward the exit.

"No, I'm gonna trust Silas to handle it. He knows what he's doin'."

"You're right. He's obsessed with you." She makes a disgusted face. "It's gross, really."

I playfully push her. "No, it's not!"

We continue dancing for three more songs before I spot Silas out of the corner of my eye, standing with Warren and Colton, actively trying not to stare at me. But I catch him.

"I'm gonna go," I say in her ear so she can hear me above the loud music. "Cover for me."

I'm dying to know what happened with Aundrea.

"Alright, but you owe me!"

"I will!" I give her a quick hug before grabbing my heels and clutch from the chair I set them on. Without saying a word, I glance at Silas who's already watching me.

I tilt my head toward the exit, then walk out.

We came together, but I don't need to give Warren anymore

reason to suspect us. Hell, maybe he already does, but I think he would've told Silas by now if he did.

Silas jumps in the truck less than two minutes later, hauls me out of my seat and pulls me onto his lap. Before I can even open my mouth to ask what the hell he's doing, his lips are on mine.

"I waited six hours to do that," he breathes out, kissing his way down my jaw and neck. "I want you outta this dress the minute we get home."

"I'll do you one better and take it off now."

He can tell me what happened with his ex later. Right now, all I want to focus on is him.

"Unless you want me to drive us into a tree, you need to wait."

"Fine. Then drive, cowboy." I flick his hat. "'Cause I only want you in this and that chain."

chapter twenty-two

AS MUCH AS I want to take my time with Posey, I can't stop kissing and touching her the second we get through the door.

Her legs wrap around me the moment I lift her up, then blindly walk us to her room.

"Why're your clothes still on?" she pants when I lower her to the mattress.

"Patience, love." I stand between her thighs hanging off the bed and slowly unbutton my shirt. "I need to taste every inch of you first and get you nice and ready for me."

"Oh, c'mon!" she whines, dragging her bare foot to my belt buckle. "I'm ready! I'm *so* ready."

Chuckling at her eagerness, I toss my shirt but set my hat on the bed for later. Then I kneel on the floor and spread her legs wider.

"This fuckin' slit, Posey," I growl, gliding my palm up her bare thigh. "I spent all day thinkin' about what was waitin' for me."

Pressing my lips to her skin, I pepper kisses up her leg until I reach the barrier of her thong strap. Slowly, I lift her dress and make my way to the other side, not quite touching where I know she needs, but giving equal attention with my mouth.

"Silas, I swear..." She digs her fingers in my hair, yanking.

"Where's your toy, sweetheart?"

"My vibrator?"

"Mm-hmm. I wanna play."

"Oh fuck." She gasps when I slide a finger through the fabric. "Um...it's in my nightstand along with the condoms."

I give her clit a little kiss before opening the drawer and finding her pink vibrator and a box of rubbers. "Thirty-six pack, huh?"

"They're cheaper in bulk, so sue me."

Smirking, I pull one out and bring her toy back to the bed.

"I'm gonna get you nice and ready for me. Lots of edgin', so prepare yourself."

"Silas, please...I'm dyin' here."

"I know, sweetheart." I press the button and increase the speed. "But we have all night."

Instead of removing her underwear, I press the vibrator to her clit on top but slide the fabric out of my way so my fingers can thrust inside.

Her hips arch and she rocks against my hand, climbing higher toward ecstasy. When I curl my fingers deeper, she fists the sheets and groans.

"Louder, Posey. I want the next town over to hear you come for me."

I hit the button that amps up the speed and add another finger into her pussy. She's so close, I can feel it.

"Fuck, mama. Gonna squirt for me?"

"It's so intense…"

She squeezes her eyes closed, but I can tell she's holding back.

"You gotta relax and trust me to get you there. Don't fight it."

"I'm tryin'…"

"Tell me how it feels," I demand.

The tension built up inside her usually releases when I talk her through it.

"So full and tight," she whimpers. "And like I'm gonna combust."

"Good, 'cause I need to taste your sweet cum all over my tongue."

"Yes…*please.*"

"Play with your nipples for me. Get 'em nice and hard. I can't wait to suck on 'em."

She palms her breasts and it only takes a few seconds to see the peaks of them pop up through the fabric of her dress. Knowing she wasn't wearing a bra tortured me all day.

"Doin' so good, love. Your body's ready…let go."

"Oh God…yes, it's right there."

"Look at you…so fuckin' gorgeous. Squirt all over my fingers, baby."

Thrusting harder and deeper, she unravels so flawlessly, screaming through her release and giving me exactly what I need. I toss the vibrator to the side and lift her thighs so I can lick up every drop.

Her eyes widen with heat when I flick the chain and the P charm to my back so it doesn't get in my way when I devour her. She shudders against me when I flick her sensitive button.

My face's covered by the time her breathing steadies.

"Holy shit," she murmurs. "That was so hot."

I chuckle against the inside of her thigh. "Just wait until I have you sittin' on my face next time."

My cock strains against my slacks, and I'm so desperate to get inside her, but I know her limbs need a break. Sliding my fingers into the thong straps, I slide it down her legs, then reach for her dress and add it to the pile.

She leans up on her elbows, completely bare and exposed, giving me the most delicious view I've ever had.

"You gonna stare at me or fuck me, city boy?" she sasses once I remove all my clothing.

"Better watch that smart mouth," I mock, standing next to her on the bed.

Cupping her chin, I flick her bottom lip with my thumb. "Open up."

She sticks out her tongue, ready and waiting, and I stroke myself a few times before easing into her mouth. She sucks over the piercings before taking more of me, and I hiss at how good it feels.

"Fuck, baby. That's it. Nice and slow." I fist her hair, guiding her so she doesn't take me too deep. "You listen so well when my cock's inside you."

Her gaze snaps to mine, filled with lust and obedience, eagerly sucking me between hollowed cheeks.

"Hmm...where's all that attitude now, mama?" I smirk, and she glares. "Keep goin', don't stop."

Wrapping her fingers around me, she pumps me into her mouth until my knees threaten to give out, and I pull back.

"Wait...you were so close."

Dipping down, I bring my lips to hers. "Are you ready for me, love? I need inside you."

"Yes..." She nods enthusiastically. "God, yes."

"Good...lie back in the middle of the bed."

As soon as she's in position, I grab the condom packet and rip it open with my teeth. Her sky blue eyes watch as I roll it over my hard cock.

"Are you gonna crawl to me, cowboy?" She tips her head toward the hat on the other side of the bed.

The corner of my mouth tilts up, her confidence turning me on even more.

"Yes, ma'am." I wink before placing the hat on my head. "Any other requests?"

"Fix your chain so the P hangs down."

Holding her gaze, I slowly adjust it to the way she wants, then climb on the bed and crawl over her body until I'm between her thighs.

"If the piercings are uncomfortable, tell me, okay? But it shouldn't hurt, in case you were worried."

"I wasn't, but I'll let you know."

I bring my lips to hers, teasing my tongue inside and wrapping my hand underneath to cup her ass. Once I've thoroughly devoured her mouth, I lean back and position my cock at her entrance.

"Gonna go slow, so just breathe."

She nods, widening her hips, and I push in.

When her eyes roll to the back of her head, I slide in more. "Okay?"

"Mm-hmm, don't stop," she begs. "It feels good."

When I'm fully seated inside her, I lean down and kiss her collarbone.

"You're so tight, baby. Fuck, are you okay?"

She wraps her legs around my waist and lifts her hips.

"Yes, start movin'."

Between her scratching down my back, biting my chest, and her pleading moans, I'm a goner. Every touch pierces my skin, burning me from the inside out, and when our bodies slap together in harmony, I nearly lose control. Emotions boil through me at how lucky I am to have this second chance with her and to never take it for granted again.

She's it for me.

I wanted her for years.

Years of waiting and finally getting to have her like this again feels too good to be true.

"Posey, fuck. You feel so amazin'," I groan, pushing her arms above her head before burying my face in her neck, rocking together.

I explore every inch I can touch on her body, massaging her breasts and sucking on her nipples, squeezing her sides as I thrust deeper, and rubbing her clit when her breath hitches.

When she stares up at me, she grins at the hat and chain, tells me how much it turns her on, and I swear, she'll explode any second.

But I'm not done with her yet.

"Gonna flip us. Ride me, mama."

As soon as she's on top, she rests her palms on my chest and bounces on my cock.

"Jesus Christ, you're too good at that." Digging my fingers into her hips, I lift up and meet her thrust for thrust.

She whimpers as I play with her needy clit, but when she leans back and holds onto my thighs for support, the view of her is mesmerizing. When her nails dig into my skin, I crave more of it. I want all her marks on me, claiming me as hers.

"You're so perfect, baby. Ridin' me so damn good."

"I'm almost there…" She pants out each word.

"That's it, cum on my cock. Keep goin'."

Her throat expands and she moans so beautifully through her release. Her pussy squeezes my dick, but I hold back my own climax so I can watch hers.

"Holy shit," she gasps, falling on top of me. "It's been so long since I've come durin' sex."

"That won't be a concern for you anymore." I smirk, then roll us over until I'm above her and straddling her legs. "Flip over, baby."

As soon as she does, my hand cracks over her ass, and she squeals, but I quickly rub and soothe it.

Lowering down her body, I palm her tattoo and lick over it, groaning at how sexy it is on her skin. Especially since it matches mine.

I kiss my way up and over her cheek before dipping my tongue between her crack.

"Silas, please…" she whines. "Inside me."

Leaning above her, I brush the hair off her shoulder and press my mouth to her ear. "How do you want it, love? Fast, hard, deep, slow?"

"Yes…" She nods. "All of it."

I lick my palm before sliding it between her thighs and curling two digits inside.

"So goddamn wet for me."

Positioning myself, I tower over her and slide my dick between her folds.

"Arch your back, mama. Let me in."

As soon as I slip inside her, I cover her like a blanket and drive into her. I find her mouth with mine and slide my tongue with hers, wanting that connection between us. We breathe each other in, moaning and panting, neither wanting to stop kissing the other.

It doesn't take much longer for my balls to tighten and the buildup to intensify. A shiver runs up my spine as my muscles flex and the beating of my heart pulses through my veins. The sensation hits me like a brick wall as I come fast and hard.

"Holy fuck…" I gasp at how strong the feeling hits me. "Are you okay?"

Posey doesn't move but I can hear her breathing. "I-I don't think I can move my limbs. I'm jelly. Melted butter. Paralyzed from sex."

I snort, rolling off her and cupping her face. "Are you always this dramatic?"

"Yes."

Pressing my lips to hers, I give her a quick peck before climbing out of bed to dispose of the condom. Then I bring a warm washcloth and slide it between her legs.

"Ooh, that feels good."

"Wanna take a bath?" I ask, wanting to hold her for as long as I can.

"Together?"

"Yeah, love." I kiss her forehead. "I'll get it started, then come get you."

"Sounds perfect." Her voice is muffled from her face pressing against the comforter, and I laugh at how adorably wrecked she looks.

"So…" she prompts, leaning against my chest as my hands roam over her body with bubbles all around us.

"Yes?"

"Gonna tell me what your ex wanted?"

"Ah, yes…*that*."

"She wants you back, doesn't she?"

"Yes, but I told her it wasn't gonna happen 'cause I'm beyond happy with someone else who accepts me for who I am."

"What'd she say to that?"

"She asked if it was serious and if I had feelings for her anymore. I said yes, it's serious and no, my feelings for her are gone."

"Even though you two were engaged a month ago?"

"Like I've said, I think I checked out long before that and hadn't realized how horribly she treated me or that I deserved better. I thought it was what I wanted, but after the initial heartbreak, I could see we never would've worked out long-term. She viewed me like an accessory. Someone to tag along with her as a prized possession, not a partner."

"How'd she take it?"

"Not great but it ain't my problem. She'll learn to live with it and her choices that brought us here. I told her to stop reachin' out to me and that if she comes onto the property again without permission, I'll call the sheriff and have her removed. She *really* didn't like that."

"Wow...look at you." She grins over her shoulder. "Finally grew a backbone."

"Hey, I've always had one...just didn't always use it."

She chuckles, wrapping my arms around her tighter. "Her loss is my gain. Even if you were *technically* mine first."

"Well, *technically* speakin'...we were each other's firsts. Shoulda stayed that way." I brush my fingers over her cheek. "My biggest regret is lettin' you walk away from me."

"I think it had to happen that way. We went out and experienced life, realized what we want and don't want, and now there's no lingerin' doubt we want each other."

"That's a nice way to see it."

"Now I just hope your family does too."

"Do you think Warren knows?"

"I haven't told him or Maisie, although she was on board for it, but not sure what he'll think. Though I don't think he'll be surprised either after tellin' him what happened years ago."

"If you get this job, we can tell everyone. Rip off the Band-Aid and announce it."

"Whatever you wanna do, love." I press my lips to her temple before making my way down to her ear.

"And then I get to kiss you at goat yoga in front of everyone so they know you're mine," she demands.

"Mm...I like this possessive side of you." I palm her breasts and tease the nipples. "Claim me all you want, mama. I'm yours."

chapter twenty-three

Posey

SILAS and I don't leave the bedroom for the rest of the weekend except to make coffee or food. We slept through the brunch, but I don't think anyone noticed. I'll have time to see Landen and Ellie this week since they're staying in one of the treehouses for their honeymoon.

Now that I've experienced what that man can do to my body and the many ways he can make me come, I'm addicted.

In the best way possible.

Getting out of bed Monday morning is the worst because sleeping next to a human oven has made my bed even cozier.

"I don't wanna get up," I whine, nuzzling my face against his hard chest. "Let's call in sick."

He bellows out a laugh. "Not sure that'd fly with Ian. And wouldn't look suspicious at all if we're both gone."

"We'll tell 'em you got me sick and I'm forcin' you to take care of me. Totally believable."

"The funny thing is it actually would be. You'd blame me, then make me nurse you back to health."

"Duh. And you'd love every minute of it."

He rolls me onto my back, burying his head in my neck and grinding his erection against me.

"You know I would." Pressing a gentle kiss to my jaw, he climbs over me and gets to his feet.

I stare at him, appreciating every naked inch of his body—tattoos and piercings that I want to lick and suck. Goddamn, he's too hot.

"You keep lookin' at me like that and we *will* be late."

He slides his boxer briefs on, and I pout at him obstructing my view.

"C'mon, I'll get breakfast started." He flattens his hand on my bare ass. "You get dressed."

"Oh my God," I wince at the burn. "I hate you."

"That's not what you said a few hours ago…" he taunts, walking into the hallway.

He's right. I very much enjoyed him spanking my ass.

Begrudgingly, I get ready for the day and find coffee and food waiting for me in the kitchen.

"A girl could get used to this." I beam, leaning across the counter to kiss him.

"Me too." He winks, pulling me in for another peck. "Except every time you touch me, I get hard, which is gonna make for a gruelin' day."

"You poor baby," I tease.

We manage to get out of the house and to work on time but we have to actively work on our poker faces.

"Good mornin'!" I greet Amaya when she strolls in. "You look pretty today."

I set bars of soap underneath shrink wrap so I can seal them for shipping.

"Wow, you're cheerful this morn—" Her eyes widen. "You had sex! Didn't you?"

"What? Me? No. Of course not." I laugh nervously. "No."

"Good God, Posey. You suck at lyin'."

My shoulders sag in defeat. "Shut up, okay? I don't need anyone else hearin' your loud ass."

"Tell me everythin'!" she whisper-hisses.

And because I have no self-restraint, I do.

"You're tellin' me, not only is he tatted, but he has piercings too?" She playfully fans herself. "I can't believe you even came to work."

"Me neither. I can barely walk."

"So he's big, huh?" She waggles her brows, making me blush.

"The best and biggest I've ever had," I admit shamelessly, then hold out my hands to emphasize his size.

"Damn, girl. Should've taken a sick day to ice your pussy after that."

"That's what I said!" I bark out a laugh. "Silas wouldn't let me 'cause it'd be too obvious if we were both out."

"When are y'all gonna tell your family?"

"Hopefully soon. He has a job interview this week, and if he gets it, he can put in his notice and we can finally announce it."

"How do you think they'll take it?"

"Warren, I'm not sure. Bellamy already knows. Bodie and Colton probably won't care. My parents? Also not sure. Aunt JoJo will probably offer to throw a party."

"They all seem to love Silas, so I don't see why they wouldn't support y'all. It's not like he's a criminal or has ten baby mamas." She shrugs, grabbing more supplies off the racks. "Way better than being on those damn datin' apps, let me tell ya."

"I definitely do not miss that," I agree. They've been deleted from my phone for a while now but I hope I never need them again.

"Can I be there when you tell Ian?"

"What, why?"

"'Cause he has an obvious crush on you, Posey."

"No, he doesn't!" I balk at the idea. "We've been friends for years. He's never hit on me."

"That's 'cause of your employee relations policy," she insists. "But trust me, he has heart eyes for you. We've been placin' bets when he'd finally admit it and quit."

"There's no way. I haven't noticed any signs he's into me."

"That's 'cause you're as aware as a rock when it comes to men."

"And yet, I'm the one gettin' my back cracked out of the two of us," I quip, stacking more bars of soap after they've been wrapped.

Her mouth pops open and she smacks a palm to her chest. "That was right in the jugular."

"Oh, stop actin' like you aren't hot. Maybe I should introduce you to Jackson...assumin' he's not datin' his sister by now."

"Hold up...he wants who?"

Chuckling, I tell her the whole story and how Silas insists Jackson's in love with Jamie, and then I remember I never texted her back. I'll have to get back to her later.

Amaya and I work tirelessly through lunch, wanting to get

ahead and pack more orders before we leave. By five, I'm beat and ready for a six-hour nap.

"Hey…" Silas peeks inside the room. "You ready?"

"Yep, just cleanin' up," I tell him.

"Hello, Mr. Mathiesen," Amaya says seductively.

"Uh, hi."

I snort, smacking her in the arm. "Stop flirtin'."

"Just admirin'."

"Do I even wanna know?" Silas asks, crossing his arms cautiously.

"Nope," I quickly say at the same time Amaya says, "Nine inches, huh?"

"Oh my God, Amaya! I could write you up for sexual harassment."

"Yeah, but you won't. You're too happy and high with lust."

I roll my eyes, then grab Silas's arm. "Let's get outta here before she asks you to whip it out."

"Wait, is that an option? Just for research purposes!" she calls out behind us.

"Did she—"

"Nope, ignore her."

When I glance over my shoulder, he smirks.

"Told her 'bout my cock, did ya?" he asks once we're in the truck.

"She forced it outta me."

"Mm-hmm. I bet." He puts one hand on the steering wheel, arching a brow. "What else did ya tell her?"

"Nothin'."

He shifts the gear stick and drives out of the lot. "You're an awful liar, baby."

"Why does everyone say that?"

He chuckles. "'Cause you're too honest and sweet for your own good."

Once Silas removes his clothing and we walk into the house, I immediately notice something's off.

"What is it?" he asks when I don't move.

"I dunno…" I glance around for anything out of place. "The energy is off."

"Is it Marjorie?"

"I'm not sure." I walk into the living room and notice the TV is on, but it's all static.

"Let me look. Stay here."

I wait, trying to gauge this weird feeling inside me. It's a mix of unease and weariness. Marjorie's never made me feel this way before but it's almost as if she's sending me a warning.

"There's nothin' weird or out of place in the bedrooms," Silas calls out, so I follow the sound of his voice and find him in my bathroom.

"My vanity," I point out. "Some of my creams and serums have been moved. I never leave 'em like that." They were organized before work this morning and now they're scattered over the counter.

"That's strange…" He scratches over his scruff. "Why would she do that?"

Before I can respond, a loud, muffled scream echoes from the walk-in closet.

"Teddy!" I squeal, rushing toward him, but Silas stands in front of me before I can open the door.

It whips open to a frantic Aundrea.

"What the fuck?" Silas's voice booms in a way I've never heard before.

"It's not what it looks like, I swear."

My blood boils with anger at her in my house.

"I'm callin' the sheriff," Silas says.

I rush past her and go into my closet.

"What'd you do to Teddy?" I snarl when I notice how stressed he is.

"That *thing* has a name? It tried to attack me!"

"Behind wire?" I open his cage to calm him down.

"It's possessed! He was runnin' around and his red glowy eyes kept starin' at me. As soon as he heard y'all come in, he spooked me."

"Why were you hidin' in my closet?" I demand, bringing Teddy to my chest.

Silas's on his phone, speaking to the operator and asking them to send an officer to the resort.

"Something's wrong with your house. The lights started flickerin', the TV turned on, and then the cabinets and drawers all opened and closed. Either there's a demon in here or I've officially lost it."

"Well, considerin' you broke into my house…"

"Someone will be here in ten minutes," Silas announces.

"Oh come on, please don't do this."

"I warned you, Aundrea."

"I just wanted one more chance to talk to you."

"Don't ya think he's suffered enough from your emotional abuse?" I snap. "First, he's not good enough so you try to change him, then you call off your wedding two weeks beforehand, and now, you can't stand seein' him happy with someone else. I think you're the possessed one."

She huffs, glaring. "I knew it was *you*. As soon as those videos of you two doing yoga surfaced and the comments speculated y'all were datin', I had to find out for myself."

A loud crash makes us jump.

"What the fuck was that?" she asks.

"Probably a glass. Marjorie's pissed you're here."

"W-who's Marjorie?" She spins, wrapping her arms around herself as if she's been hit with a sudden chill. "What's goin' on?"

"We're long over, Aundrea. I told you this," Silas says, neither of us openly admitting she's right.

If she finds out we're breaking the employee policy, she'll threaten to rat us out.

"But we were *engaged* to be married! Surely that means more than this bimbo you've been with for a few weeks."

"Actually—"

Silas steps closer, cutting me off. "Posey and I have history, long before you entered the picture, so before you try guilt trippin' me into givin' you another chance, you should know you were my second choice."

"You don't mean that." She sniffles, her nose turning red.

"I do," he states firmly. "Why do you think I'm not that upset you broke off our engagement? You did me a favor."

Tears well in her eyes at the words she doesn't want to hear, and I'd feel sorry for her if she hadn't just broken into my house, angered my house ghost, and scared my rat.

A knock on the door makes my heart jump. "Jesus." I hold

Teddy tighter to my chest. "I'll get it. Silas, maybe you should get some clothes on."

"Oh, shit. Right."

"Are you seriously gonna have me arrested? I just wanted to talk." I hear her pleas as I walk out of the room and answer the door.

"Hi, Sheriff Brown. C'mon in."

I lead him to my bedroom where Silas finishes putting on his shirt and Aundrea sits on the edge of my bed, looking pitiful. Perhaps she'll tell a sob story to get her out of going to jail or paying a fine, but it won't win back Silas's heart.

"What's goin' on?" the sheriff asks.

Silas and I tell him everything before giving Aundrea a chance to speak. Eventually he arrests her for aggravated burglary and when he walks her outside, we follow.

"I'm sorry, okay? I didn't expect this to hit me so hard," she admits.

Sheriff Brown puts her in the backseat of his car and then tells Silas she'll go in front of a judge to determine her bail. In the meantime, he suggested we get temporary restraining orders.

"Will do, thanks a lot."

Once we're back inside, the bad energy lifts and it feels right again.

"Well, that was weird…" I sit on the couch, holding Teddy in my lap.

"You're tellin' me." He lifts my body up and steals my spot before pushing me down on him. "Hopefully she gets some help."

"Guess we don't need to worry about your lightsaber

defendin' us, after all," I tease. "Marjorie took matters into her own hands."

He chuckles, wrapping his arms tighter. "She sure did. Who knew she was so badass?"

"She's the best."

chapter twenty-four

Silas

"IT'S yours if you want it. Think about it and let me know."

Nodding, I stand and shake Jake's hand. He's been interviewing me for the past hour, and honestly it's a great position with amazing starting pay, but I need time to decide if it's right for me.

"Will do. Thanks so much for the opportunity."

I should be thrilled for the offer, but I'm filled with dread at what it could mean if I take it. Being away from Posey after finally getting together would jeopardize everything and compromise how far we've come.

But if I don't, we risk her parents finding out and firing me anyway. And it's not like I have many options since I have no other interviews lined up and this is the best company out of all the places I sent my resume to. The alternative is searching for jobs over an hour away and commuting, but with less pay and shitty benefits.

Since I had to be here at nine in the morning, I took a half day off work, but now I need to go home and change before driving to the barn.

It's only been two days since we caught Aundrea in the house, but as expected, her father bailed her out. Then he threatened to kill me.

Safe to say, we got a temporary restraining order against him too.

And now I can't even use the job I worked at for the past two years as a reference.

If we have to keep it a secret a bit longer, then so be it, but I know she's eager to get it out there. She hates lying, especially to her parents.

"Silas," Ian says when he sees me. "Go to milkin'."

"Sure thing."

He's never been super nice to me, but ever since he caught Posey and I snuggling under the blanket the night we watched Delia, he's been extra short with me. Doesn't bother me though.

According to the farm gossip, he has a thing for her.

I'm not surprised. Posey's incredible and gorgeous, but he's had years to tell her.

Too late now, buddy.

She's mine.

I catch up with the rest of the employees' tasks, do some milking, mucking, and moving goats to different pastures to graze. It's an overall easy afternoon, but I'm eager to get home and talk with Posey.

"So I've been dyin' all day to find out how the interview went," she blurts as soon as she jumps into the truck.

I didn't want to tell her over text, so I told her we'd talk in person.

"It went really well. It's a dream offer, and I'm honestly wonderin' why they want me."

"So they hired you?"

"They said it's mine if I want it."

"Oh my God!" She bounces in her seat before reaching over to kiss me. "Babe, we gotta celebrate. As soon as we tell my family, we can go out. Dinner, drinks, dancin'?"

"Hold on, baby." I drive us toward the house, then park and sit. "I'm not gonna take it."

She unbuckles her belt and turns toward me. "Why not?"

I swallow hard, scratching over my cheek. "They'd require me to work out of state for the first year to train under another guy who's based in Louisiana."

"For a whole year?"

"Yeah, they have a hub down there. He said once that project is complete, he'd find me somethin' up here, but couldn't guarantee it."

She's quiet, fidgeting with her fingers as she processes what I said.

"You gotta take it, Silas."

"No," I say firmly.

"But you love workin' with your hands and buildin' stuff. You're good at it. And it's a great opportunity. Plus, all the benefits and—"

"I don't wanna leave you or my family. And I don't wanna move out." I finally say the words I've wanted to say for the past two weeks.

"You don't?" The corners of her mouth tip up slightly. "I thought you already found a place."

"I did, but I love being here with you, Marjorie, and even

your creepy-ass rat. I love our mornin' and bedtime routines and fallin' asleep next to you. Why would I wanna give that up? Especially after waitin' so long to be happy. You make me happy, Posey. Seein' my mom and sisters whenever I wanna make me happy. Being close to my best friend makes me happy. I'm not tradin' in that happiness for any amount of money."

She scoots over until she's able to sit in my lap, and as soon as I push the seat back, she straddles my legs.

"I don't want you to move out either."

"Good." I smile wide, brushing strands of her hair behind her ears. "I think Marjorie would riot anyway."

She laughs, wrapping her arms around my neck and leaning closer until our lips meet. "She definitely would."

I kiss her long and hard until her makeup wears off and my dick's rock solid from all her moaning and grinding on top of me.

"Why don't ya start your own company? You're experienced, smart, and have connections as well as anyone else. Plus, Warren and the family would help you."

"I don't have any collateral to get a business loan for that sorta thing. I'd need start-up money. I doubt a bank would give me one."

"Let me lend it to you. Or Warren. He has money."

I grimace. "I don't like the idea of borrowin' from people I know. What if I fail and I can't pay it back? What if somethin' goes wrong and you need it?"

"What if you succeed and everythin' goes right?" She brushes her nose against mine. "Just think about it, okay?"

"Alright, I will. But don't get your hopes up."

She scoffs. "Have you met me? We will find a way to make

this happen. Mathiesen Homes. Mathiesen Builders. Mathiesen—"

"Okay, we'll think of a name for it later. Right now, I wanna get you inside so you can sit on my face."

Her eyes light up. "Don't gotta tell me twice, city boy."

"You know I'm technically a cowboy now." I reach back for my Stetson and place it on my head. "My fans call me Cowboy Goat Yogi online."

She gags, pretending to throw up. "You're only makin' me wanna get you fired more now."

"You'd never." I give her ass a smack. "You'd miss me too much."

She rolls her eyes but doesn't deny it.

"Alright, *cowboy*. Let's go inside so I can show you exactly what a *cowgirl* can do."

Posey does exactly that. She rides my face until my tongue goes numb, her ass cheeks shine red, and her swollen clit can't take anymore. The view of her when I glance up is the sexiest thing I've ever fucking seen. Her perfect breasts bouncing and my hat on her head as she moans my name.

Once I've thoroughly devoured and made her come twice, I bend her over and slam inside her.

"Oh fuck, baby. I forgot a condom."

When I pull out, she reaches back and grabs me. "No, I want you to cum inside me."

"Posey," I growl, already on the edge and about to fall over if she's not careful with her next words.

"I'm on birth control and got tested after my last relationship."

"You're sure?" I grab my shaft and slap her pussy with it. "I got tested too before we started sleepin' together."

I didn't want to risk it since I wasn't a hundred percent sure Aundrea stayed faithful.

"Yes, I'm sure," she says confidently, wiggling her hips. "The piercings feel so good without it."

And that's all the convincing I need.

Digging my fingers into her ass, I spread her wider and slide back in.

"I'm so close…"

"Nice and loud, mama. I wanna hear you come for me."

She moves against me, slamming back with every thrust, and soon she's screaming through her release so beautifully. I love how she doesn't hold back and cries out through her orgasm until she's spent.

"Christ, love. You squeezed me so fuckin' good. I—"

Tingles shoot through my groin and up my spine as I come hard and fast, filling her so deep and full.

"Stay put," I tell her before she rolls over.

Kneeling between her legs, I lick up our joint mess, groaning at how turned on she makes me.

"Silas, I can't…it's too much," she pants.

Leaning back, I tap her shoulder and motion for her to flip. When she does, I press my finger to her mouth and she opens wide.

I wink before spitting the taste of us on her tongue. "Swallow, baby."

Once we showered together and I made dinner, we rot on the couch with our food and watch *Golden Girls*. She insists on putting Teddy in an exercise ball so he can roam around and be closer to us, but the dumbass keeps bumping into shit and getting stuck.

"That thing's gonna break and he'll get loose again," I tell her when he smacks into the coffee table leg.

"It's secure, but he's still gettin' the hang of it." She shrugs, taking a bite of her strawberry shortcake I made us for dessert. "He'll figure it out eventually."

A knock on the door startles us and we look at each other, confused who's here.

"I'll get it. Stay put," I say, setting my bowl on the coffee table.

The last person I expect to find on the other side is Ian.

"Uh hey, what's up?" I ask, not immediately offering him to come inside.

"I need to speak to Posey. Is she here?"

"Phone doesn't work?"

He glares before blinking, but I see it.

"I wanted to talk in person."

"She's in the livin' room."

When Posey sees him, her eyes widen in confusion and she quickly gets to her feet. "Ian. Hey. What's goin' on?"

"Any chance we can talk in the kitchen?"

If I step in and say no, he'll know something's up between us, so I casually sit on the couch. She glances at me, and I give her a quick nod.

"Sure."

My hands ball into fists at the fucker just showing up here uninvited. If it was a work thing, he'd call or text, or hell, wait until tomorrow. So I'm guessing it's not.

I keep the TV on mute, but I can't hear anything besides a few muffled words, nothing sticks out enough to understand what he's saying.

After a few minutes, I can't stand the tension and walk over toward the kitchen entrance, hiding behind the wall just enough so they can't see me.

"All that to say…" Ian pauses and my heart pounds in my temple. "I'm quittin'."

"Quittin', why?"

"'Cause I can't ask you out while workin' together and if I keep waitin', I might miss my chance."

"Wait…you wanna ask me out?"

Now I'm ready to punch the guy's face.

"Yeah, Posey. I have feelings for you. I have since the day we met. But I really needed this job at the time, so I pushed 'em back until…well, I guess until now. Until I couldn't do it any longer."

"Oh."

The room goes quiet.

Oh. That's it?

"I'm a little taken off guard."

"I tried to keep my distance so it wasn't obvious and things weren't weird at work between us. This job has been amazin' and I'm so grateful for it, but I finally found another one so it was no longer a barrier to datin' you."

"Wow...I—" Her feet pad around the kitchen as if she's pacing. "I dunno what to say."

You're taken, Posey. Say that!

"Would you let me take you out? Ya know, once I'm officially done here."

"No," she blurts.

That's my girl.

"No?"

"I'm so sorry, that came out harsh. I'm with someone."

"You're not single? Since when?"

Fuck no, she's not.

"No...um, it's new. But it's serious."

"How serious can it be if it's new?"

For fuck's sake, man. Read the room.

"Serious enough to know I'm in love with him." Posey's words come out at the same time Teddy's ball runs over my bare toes.

"Motherfucker!" I hiss, then clamp my mouth shut.

Posey walks over to me, eyes wide and lips pinched together.

"Whaddya doin'?" she whispers.

"Nothin'."

She crosses her arms. "Stop eavesdroppin'."

"I can't help it! He's tryin' to steal my girl," I hiss.

"No, he's—"

"Is everythin' okay?" Ian comes over because of course he fucking does.

"Yeah, fine. Teddy's ball scared me, is all. Damn rat has no sense of direction."

I laugh, hoping he'll take the bait, but when his gaze pingpongs between Posey and me, realization dawns on his face.

"I fuckin' knew it." He shakes his head, stepping back. "So much for nothin' goin' on between you two."

"Ian, I'm sorry. We couldn't tell anyone. Not until he finds a new job."

"So your father doesn't know?" he snarls.

"No, and I'd appreciate it if you didn't tell him."

"Why shouldn't I? I was willin' to quit a job I love to be with you and all along you're fuckin' him behind everyone's backs and breakin' the rules?"

This time when he raises his voice, I step toward him. "You better watch your goddamn mouth talkin' to her like that in her own house. Or any woman. But especially mine. I won't think twice about throwin' you out."

He huffs with a laugh. "You're toast, man. You'll be unemployed by tomorrow mornin'."

"Ian, get out. You're fired," Posey says, pointing toward the door. "Do not come back on my property ever again."

"You don't mean that. You need me to run that farm for you. Who else is gonna do it?"

"You're not the only person who can boss people 'round and do paperwork. I'll manage."

Obviously his job entails much more than that, but he's acting like he's irreplaceable when he's not.

"You'll regret this, Posey." He marches through the living room and then the front door slams shut.

"I'm startin' to wonder if Marjorie is attractin' weirdos to this place 'cause what the fuck was that?" I shake my head, scrubbing a hand through my hair. "Did you have any idea he liked you?"

"Only recently. Amaya said somethin' but I didn't believe her. He's never hinted he did. Ever."

Not wanting to talk about him anymore, I step closer and palm her cheeks. "Did you mean what you said in there? About being in love with me?"

"You weren't supposed to hear that," she says, pouting. "I was waitin' for you to say it first."

"Why's that?" I grin.

"'Cause I didn't wanna say it too soon and scare you after what you went through with your ex. I figured I'd wait until you were ready to hear it."

"Baby..." I lick my lips before softly brushing mine with hers. "I'm ready. I've been ready."

"So why didn't you say it first?"

"Same reason. I didn't wanna go too fast and freak you out."

"It does a little," she admits. "I've never said it to a guy before."

"Never?" I beam. "Another first you saved for me?"

She wraps her arms around my waist, tilting her head up against my chest. "Guess I did, cowboy."

"*Fuck...*" I groan. "You have no idea how hot that makes me feel."

"I bet it does." She pushes into my thickening cock and giggles.

Brushing my fingers over her face, I dip down and softly press my mouth to hers. "I'm so in love with you, mama. My feelings for you are as strong and wild as you make me feel. And for the first time in a long-ass time, I feel accepted and loved for being exactly who I am—a city boy who can't ride horses."

My heart races when she smiles wide.

"I love everythin' about you, Silas. Your heart, the way you care for me, and most importantly, how I feel when I'm with you. I wouldn't change a single thing. Even your crazed, obsessed fan groupies 'cause we agree on one thing—you are fine as hell with a cowboy hat on."

I bark out a laugh.

"Say it again," I demand.

"Which part?"

"The words you said earlier in the kitchen. I wanna hear you say 'em to me."

The corner of her eyes crinkle as a smile splits her face. "I'm in love with you. So take it. Take my love 'cause my heart is yours to keep, and I'd appreciate it if this time you didn't give it back."

"Never again, love. Not in a million years." I press my mouth to hers, sliding my tongue between her lips and inhaling her moans. "Take mine too."

When our mouths fuse together again, I lift her up and carry her toward the living room, except I trip over that godforsaken rat ball and nearly slam into the wall. Luckily, I catch myself in time before getting to the couch.

"Whew, that was close." She laughs, straddling my lap and rocking against my cock.

"What're we gonna do about him tellin' your father?" I ask, trying to distract myself so I don't explode in my pants.

"Don't worry about it. I'll talk to him tomorrow and tell him everythin'. He won't like that we lied and snuck around, but he's gonna be more upset about Ian threatenin' you."

Mr. Langston was like a dad to me growing up, especially after my own passed away, so it warms my heart to think he'll be protective of me in that way.

"You want me to go with you? I can."

"Thanks, but no. I'd like to speak to him alone first. There's somethin' I wanna talk to him about and we'll have to put out an ad to replace Ian."

"Okay, just let me know if you change your mind or when I should go over there."

"I will...but right now—" She widens her thighs and rubs faster against my erection. "You only need to worry about *one* thing."

"Mm...and what's that, my love?"

"Givin' me an orgasm."

"I think I can arrange that..." I slide my hand between our bodies, rubbing her clit over the fabric of her shorts. "You're so ready. I bet I can get you there in forty-two and a half seconds."

She grins. "Think so?"

"Yep. Start countin', love."

And before she even hits thirty-five Mississippis, she's moaning out my name.

chapter twenty-five

Posey

SILAS IS extra flirty during yoga this morning and the women are eating it up.

Even Mila can't deny it's helped more members join and the class be more fun. The goats aren't the only added bonus now.

I don't mind it because it's all in good fun. Now that people are speculating about us, we play into it more, stealing glances and not-so-subtle touches that'll have them gossiping until the next class.

It's been great for business since more people are buying goat soap from retailers in town and our website.

Landen and Ellie made an appearance at class too, which gave them time to see how we do things here. It was fun watching them try poses with goats climbing on them. We're supposed to meet up with them tonight, but it'll depend on how things go with my parents first.

"I'm gonna drive my car to my parents' house, but I'll catch up with you over lunch?" I tell Silas once we drop off the goats and return home to change. "I already told Amaya I was takin' a half day."

"Okay, baby. Text me if you need me. I love you."

"Love you too," I repeat, butterflies swarming my belly at how much those words mean to me.

Even though I've never said them to another man before, they easily slip out for him.

I gave my parents a heads up that I'd be stopping by after yoga, so when I arrive, they're both in the kitchen waiting for me.

"Mornin', sweetie," Mom greets, making pancakes at the stove. "Are you hungry?"

"Yeah, starvin' actually."

"Perfect, take a seat."

"Hey, Dad," I say, sitting across from him. He's reading a newspaper, which I find comical since everything's digital now. "Didn't know we still had those."

"Not many left."

"I could get you an iPad and you could read a handful more from all over the world."

He scoffs at the idea.

"Have you hired someone to start buildin' the new childcare center yet?"

"No, we're still gettin' bids in. Why?"

"I'd like you to hire Silas to manage the project. He has experience, knowledge, and he's dependable. He'd make sure it was done correctly over anyone else who's just in it for the money."

Which is true. Silas wouldn't let any of the contractors slide if they got lazy or did shitty work.

"Why?" Mom asks, bringing over a plate of food and maple syrup.

"Is he not workin' out at the farm?" Dad raises a brow.

"He wants to start his own home building company, but doesn't have enough assets to get a business loan. So, he could use the money he makes from this job to go toward his company."

"How much does he need?"

"I'm not sure exactly, but probably a good amount for a new work truck, professional work clothes, office supplies, new computer, maybe enough for a part-time secretary. He thinks it's too far-fetched, but I think it's possible."

"And why're you so eager to help him find another job?" Dad grabs a few pancakes before pouring the syrup on top.

Slowly, I blow out a breath. "'Cause you gotta fire him."

Dad doesn't react. "I see."

"Am I missin' somethin'?" Mom asks, taking her seat next to Dad. "Why do you wanna do that?"

"'Cause he's datin' our daughter," Dad supplies.

I'm not all that shocked he knows or at least probably assumed after catching us goofing around. Although at that time, we were only friends.

"You and Silas?" Mom's eyes light up. "Oh, sweetheart. I'm so happy for you two."

"Thanks, Mom."

Dad still doesn't look at me.

"How long has this been goin' on?" he asks.

"Shortly after he moved in," I admit, but don't go into the details of how it started. "I tried to fight it, I really did. We both did."

"Does your brother know?"

"Not that I'm aware of."

"Oh, Grady. Why're you givin' her a hard time?"

"'Cause she knew about the employee relations policy and violated it anyway."

"Oh, that silly thing?" She waves him off. "You can't help who you fall in love with."

"Lindsey, it's to avoid issues like this. He should've quit before they…things got serious."

"He's been lookin' for work, Dad. And the only company who offered him a job in the field he wants would send him to Louisiana for at least a year."

"And he didn't wanna be away from you, I assume?"

"Or his mom and sisters. Or Warren. He loves it here."

"Would you two continue livin' together?"

"Yes," I say firmly. "Marjorie likes him there, too."

"Does she?" Mom beams. "Oh, good."

"Yep, and we watch *Golden Girls* together, so she'd be sad if he left."

Dad sighs. "You realize we're talkin' about a ghost, right?"

"Her spirit," I counter.

"You know Silas has to put in a bid first, right? I can't just give him the job 'cause he's your boyfriend."

"Okay, I'm sure he knows how to do that," I say confidently.

"Grady." Mom uses her stern wifey tone on him. "Silas is family. He's been in our kids' lives since elementary school."

"What's that gotta do with anythin'?"

"If you know what's good for you and what food I put on your dinner plate at night, you'll stop being a hard-ass and be happy to see your daughter happy. Silas, too. He just went through a bad break-up."

"Not sure that's gonna help, Mom."

"Your father acts like we didn't date right after he broke up with someone." She scoffs. "We were crazy about each other within a matter of days."

"This is different," Dad argues, stuffing a forkful of food in his mouth. "She's supposed to set an example for the other employees. Now what am I supposed to do? Reward her and hire him for a different job?"

"Can't you reword the policy?" I ask softly. "Instead of no employee relations, maybe just employees who work directly together can't date. Plus, he'd technically be a contractor, not a ranch or resort employee."

"I like that idea," Mom says, sipping her coffee. "And it lets others date who work on opposite sides of the ranch and resort."

Dad grumbles as if he knows he won't win this argument.

"And maybe our other three children will find someone they're interested in on the ranch." Mom beams. "And have babies."

I snort at how eager she is for grandchildren.

"Which would be great for the childcare center," I add, trying hard not to laugh as Mom and I gang up on him.

"What does Ian think about this situation? Does he know?"

I tense, quickly shoving more food in my mouth.

"Posey?"

Swallowing hard, I wince. "Yeah, about that…"

Since I don't want any more secrets between us, I tell them everything. From when I told Ian to give Silas a hard time during his first week, to him catching Silas and I in a suggestive position, and then Ian coming clean about his feelings for me.

"He threaten y'all?"

"Yes, which is why I had to fire him."

"Never liked that kid." Dad shakes his head, frowning over the rip of his coffee mug. "Sounds like we need to find two replacements now, huh? One for Ian and one for Silas?"

I perk up. "Does that mean you'll give Silas a chance?"

He nods. "And a loan so he can start up his business right away. If he's gonna be datin' and livin' with my daughter, at least he'll be workin'."

Jumping out of my chair, I round the table and wrap my arms around him. "Thank you, Daddy. You have no idea how much this means to us. But him especially. He's not used to someone else believin' in him enough to give him a chance."

He hugs me back. "Okay, now sit so we can finish our breakfast. I wanna hear how the goat soap business is goin'."

"Sure thing, Daddy."

Once we've finished eating and talking, Dad prints out a check for a hundred thousand dollars in Silas's name. My eyes nearly fall out of my head when I see the number.

"This is a lot, Dad."

"It should get him started for whatever he needs and we'll consider the rest a sign-on bonus." He lifts his shoulders. "I'll get the paperwork started for the job. Tell him to come for supper tomorrow night so we can talk and sign the contract."

"You really are a softie underneath your hard exterior."

"Yeah, well…" He shrugs again. "I want y'all to be happy."

"Thank you. We appreciate it. And if it helps, he makes me really happy, Dad."

"Good." He kisses the top of my head. "Maybe now you can give your mother grandbabies so she stops askin' about it?"

I bark out a laugh. "Is that a condition? He has to knock me up?"

"I mean…" He grins cheekily. "You don't wanna be too old poppin' out kids, do ya? What are ya? Forty?"

"Oh my God, Dad. I'm not even thirty."

"Well, in that case…" he quips. "Whenever y'all are ready. But I'd like to walk ya down the aisle someday. Can I have that at least?"

"Yes, I sure hope so." I grin, thinking about the day Silas and I have our own wedding.

I stuff the check into an envelope before saying goodbye to my parents. It's almost noon, so I put the check in my glove compartment and drive to the barn. Amaya's been blowing up my phone. Apparently there's a ton of gossip about where Ian is.

"Fuckin' finally!" she shouts the moment she sees me. "What's goin' on?"

I grab my apron and some supplies, then start filling her in on everything with Ian and telling my parents about Silas. I don't tell her about the business idea or the check since I want him to know first.

"I told ya he had a thing for you. We all did."

"Even if I wasn't with Silas, Ian ain't my type. I think of him like a brother. Well, *did*. Now I think of him as a creepy weirdo."

"Maybe that's why his fiancée cheated on him with his stepbrother?" She snickers, and I try not to laugh, but it's impossible with her. She makes everything sound overly funny.

"It's strange 'cause he said he felt somethin' for me the first day we met but then like a year later he started datin' Sheila. But

I guess he was waitin' until he could find a different job to hit on me." I shiver at the thought of us together. "Anyway…"

"Will Silas continue doin' goat yoga with you and Mila?"

"I'm not sure," I say honestly, but it makes me sad to think he probably won't. Once he gets his company up and running, he'll be busy with his own schedule.

"Well, if he doesn't, can I vote on findin' a replacement? Preferably someone who's single, rich, and has an eight-pack?"

"I will definitely get right on that!"

"That's why I love you."

By the time my shift ends and Silas gets out of work, I'm bouncing in the passenger seat, ready to explode. I didn't have time to tell him much of anything since we were both so busy but it's better to tell him face-to-face anyway.

"Hey, beautiful." He hops in and immediately pulls me in for a kiss.

"Hello, handsome." I smirk, grabbing his hat from the backseat and placing it on his head. "There's my naughty cowboy."

"You're butterin' me up, aren't you?" He pulls back, frowning. "Your dad's pissed, ain't he?"

"He wasn't thrilled at first, but—" I pause when Silas sighs against the seat. "He came 'round."

"Really? He's not gonna rip me outta bed in the middle of the night, kick my ass, and make me goat food?"

"No…" I tilt my head, trying not to cackle. "But he did say he wants to walk me down the aisle and to give my mother grandchildren."

His brows shoot to the ceiling. "What?"

This time I can't hold it in and throw my head back, laughing at his wide eyes filled with fear.

"Okay, let me start from the top…"

He pulls out of the lot and drives us toward the cabin while I explain everything in detail that happened over breakfast. As soon as we pull into my driveway, I open the glove compartment.

"He gave me this to give to you."

As soon as he opens it and pulls out the check with his name, he stares at it wordlessly.

"Now you can start Mathiesen Homes or Mathiesen Builders. Maybe Mathiesen—"

"He just gave this to you to give to me?"

Dammit, he never lets me tell him my third idea.

"It's for you, babe. He said it's a business loan to get whatever you need and the rest is a bonus. We'll go over tomorrow night to eat and then he'll go over the contract. After that, you'll probably go over the blueprints for the childcare center and go from there. He'll pay you for the work as well. This is just to get your company off the ground so you can book other jobs too."

"I-I dunno what to say, baby." He's still staring at the check as if it'll disappear into thin air if he looks away.

"He trusts you, Silas. He knows you'll do a good job. And so do I."

When his eyes meet mine, they're glossed over, and I nearly tear up at how emotional he looks.

"No one's ever been so confident in me before. It's…" He swallows hard. "It's hard to accept. What if I fail y'all?"

Scooching closer, I pull him into my arms. "Failin' at somethin' you at least tried to make happen doesn't make you a failure. You only are if you don't try at all. You're already goin' after what so many other people wish they could do. I believe in you wholeheartedly, which means you should believe in yourself too."

He cups my face and kisses me until my lips go numb.

"I love you so much, Posey. I honestly don't know what I did to deserve a second chance, but I'm so grateful I got one."

"Love you too." I squeeze him tighter. "But now we gotta go tell my brother and the rest of my siblings the news."

chapter twenty-six

"ON THREE, READY?" I squeeze Posey's hand, waiting for her to give me the approval.

"On your count or mine?"

"Mine." Definitely not counting Mississippis while my balls are freezing.

Even though the weather's nice for mid-September, we've been jumping in and out of the cold water for the past hour.

"Okay, ready!"

I count us down, then we run and jump off the cliff. Posey screams the entire way down until we crash through the water.

Warren and I used to cliff jump into the Willow Falls River every summer growing up. It separates the ranch from the resort and has a huge waterfall up the mountain where people can jump or dive from. But once Maisie left, it took nine years for him to get back in since it's where he proposed.

As soon as we swim to shore, we run out and do it all over again.

Landen and Ellie jump in after us, then Bodie, Bellamy, and Colton go after them.

"Warren and Maisie, your turns!" Posey says.

"I don't think I can…" Maisie shakes her head. "I'm beat."

"C'mon, one more time!" Bellamy adds, then starts cheering. "Maisie! Maisie! Maisie!"

Soon, all the siblings are shouting her name.

"Oh my God, fine…" she drawls, but smirks at Warren before letting him drag her up the mountain.

After they jump, Warren pulls her against his chest and kisses her before they slam into the water.

"Fuck, that one kinda hurt," Maisie groans once they make their way back to shore with the rest of us.

Since we made plans with Landen and Ellie tonight but also needed to talk to Warren, we met at his house and ate dinner with the newlyweds. He made lasagna with cheese bread and after it settled in our stomachs, we decided to invite the rest of their siblings for a late night swim.

It was nice getting to see my best friend again because although we live on the same property, we haven't seen much of each other. He works at the stables, which is miles away from the goat farm. Even after work or on the weekends, he's usually spending time with Maisie since she only returned for good a few months ago.

The good news is Warren didn't punch me in the face once Posey told him we were dating.

The bad news is he gave me the silent treatment during dinner.

By the time we got to dessert, he got over it.

No one can stay mad while eating homemade cheesecake.

"Now that Posey and Silas are shackin' up, who's next?" Maisie teases, looking at the other three single siblings.

"Got any older single friends?" Bodie leans back on the grass, waggling his brows.

"Yes, but they don't date minors. Sorry!" Maisie grins and everyone cackles at his expense.

"Dude, I'm twenty-one!"

"Your prefrontal cortex hasn't developed."

"I can still date older women," he argues. "I can even buy alcohol."

"Wow, look at you all grown up," Posey quips.

"I am, thank you for noticin'."

Bellamy snorts. "You sleep on dinosaur sheets."

"You gave 'em to me for Christmas!" Bodie points out.

"As a joke! Just like I gave Posey goat slippers."

"Hey, those are my favorite!" Posey scowls.

"Mine too." I wink at her, still needing to find a pair of my own.

"Well, we already know Bellamy ain't ever gettin' married, and Colt..." Posey smirks at him. "He has a thing for single moms."

Everyone's gaze including mine snaps toward him because that's news to me.

"Single moms, huh?" I taunt. "Why's that?"

"Have you ever dated a MILF?" he exclaims, then sticks out his fingers to count. "They're experienced, bossy, and always have snacks in their purse. Triple-win, honestly."

Laughter ensues and it feels great to be with Posey's family and not hide our relationship. Bellamy already knew and was supportive, but Bodie and Colton didn't give me too much of a hard time. Basically said if I fucked it up, they'd kick my ass.

"I have some older friends," Ellie offers. "But you'd gotta be willin' to move to Sugarland Creek and travel with the rodeo since most of 'em are barrel racers."

"That'd be so fuckin' cool!" he exclaims. "Gonna rope me a cowgirl."

Landen snickers. "Be careful what you wish for, man. They're feisty as shit."

It's almost midnight when Posey snuggles under the blankets wearing her favorite goat-printed shorts and tank set. She clings to me, freshly showered and smelling like lavender sugar scrub. She's been catching up on goat soap orders for the upcoming holiday season for the past couple weeks and stayed late so she could have the long Thanksgiving weekend off.

After more goat yoga videos with me and her went viral, she started using them to promote Langston Soapworks and her website blew up. Even though she and Amaya post videos of their process, it was the ones of me shirtless in a cowboy hat that got the most views and orders. Eventually, they made a soap scent after me: Cowboy Goat Yogi. It's made with vanilla, leather, and sandalwood.

Instead of getting stopped at the grocery store to ask for a selfie, they ask to smell me instead.

But I don't mind. Posey loves it as long as everyone knows I'm hers.

And I have no problem reminding them of it, too.

Goat yoga is done for the season since it's late November, but they'll have to find some other tatted, muscular guy to replace me next spring since I'll be much busier, but it was fun to do with Posey while it lasted.

They already replaced mine and Ian's positions at the goat farm, so they didn't have to go long being short-staffed. Luckily, we haven't heard from him since the night he came over to confess his love for her and she fired him.

Ever since Mr. Langston gave me that loan two months ago, I've been working almost every day between managing the childcare center project and getting everything for my new business set up—including a more reliable truck for when I drive out to job sites or to meet with clients and contractors.

It's not a manual, so I let Posey use it once in a while.

I've already put in five other bids for upcoming projects throughout the state so I have consistent work for the next year. It's been a nice change of pace from working for someone else to working for myself. For the first time in my life, I'm in charge of my schedule and what jobs I do. I'm beyond grateful for her family's support and believing in me enough to give me the chance to prove I can do this.

I wouldn't be here without them.

Even my mom and sisters are passing out my business cards like candy on Halloween night. Making them proud as the youngest sibling and no longer fumbling through life feels good.

Of course the only two people who want me to fail are Aundrea and her dad. He doesn't like the competition in our small town and she's jealous I moved on without her, then got her arrested.

Her dad begged us to drop the charges, but we refused. He hired a sleazy defense lawyer, who filed a motion to reduce her aggravated burglary felony charge to a trespassing misdemeanor since she didn't steal anything or vandalize the property.

Aundrea pled no contest and started her thirty days in jail last week. The judge granted Posey and me long-term restraining orders so she can't harass us once she's out or will risk going back behind bars.

It's a relief to have all the court stuff over. I can enjoy Thanksgiving with our families and take the next five days off with Posey.

She's already getting ideas for adding onto the cabin since neither of us want to leave Marjorie, but eventually, we'll need more space. I've turned my room into an office and sleep in Posey's bed, but it'd be nice to have a larger master bedroom and use the current one as a future nursery.

"Mm, you're nice and warm. Just the way I like ya." She nuzzles her face against my bare skin, then presses a kiss above my nipple.

"Just got your comforter out of the dryer," I explain, tightly wrapping my arm around her. When she texted she was leaving work within the next ten minutes, I got it ready.

Leaning up on her elbow, she traces her finger over my chest tattoo. "I've been meanin' to ask you about this."

I rest my other arm behind my head so I can meet her gaze. "What about it?"

"Tell me the truth. Why'd you get a compass?"

Wrapping some of her fallen strands behind her ear, I grin at her question. I'm surprised it took her this long to mention it because I knew she didn't believe my explanation when she first asked about it.

"You really wanna know?"

"Yes. Tell me," she urges. "Please."

"It has an ambiguous meanin' 'cause it can be interpreted in various ways. A compass symbolizes guidance, direction, and staying on your chosen path in life. But it can also represent a love for adventure, searching for personal goals, or finding balance and stability.

"That night we argued outside of Warren's trailer and learned the truth of why neither of us talked about sleepin' together, I told you I was with someone else and couldn't kiss you. That moment changed the course of my life forever. Here I thought you regretted it, but then come to find out, you were under the assumption I had no memory of it.

"For years, I held onto that guilt of not talkin' to you about it sooner and wanted to make sure I never made that kind of mistake again. I still have the image of you embedded in my mind lookin' distraught and rejected before you walked away from me. So I got the compass as a reminder—that sometimes it's necessary to change courses when it feels right or you'll risk grieving what you missed out on by playin' it safe."

I brush my thumb slowly over her lower lip when it trembles.

"Another reason was your love for compasses and what better way to showcase an epiphany than somethin' that directly correlated to the person who helped me realize it.

"I added the roses on my bicep and shoulder 'cause of your middle name, Rose," I explain, tracing a finger where the flowers merge into a silhouette of trees that blend into the compass over my pec.

"These are 'cause of that night you were dared to kiss me. You sat across the firepit and behind you was a row of pine trees shadowed by darkness, but the moon hung between 'em and gave you the most beautiful glow."

Tears well in her eyes as she stares down at it, rubbing her finger over each tree.

"And I wanted to make sure no matter how old I got, I never forgot the view of our first kiss," I say softly, rubbing the pad of my thumb over her cheek.

"Wow...I had no idea," she whispers, choking back her emotions. "It means a lot. Even more that I never knew until after we got together."

"If I'd told you sooner, you would've called me a psycho and Warren would've sent me to the hospital with bruises and broken bones."

"Most likely." She laughs through tears. "It is unhinged behavior to do that for someone you're not even datin'."

"Trust me, I know." I shrug. "I never told my ex the truth either."

"It really is a stunnin' image." She feathers her fingers over every line. "You did a good job designin' it."

"I was thinkin' about usin' it for my company logo."

"Really?" She meets my gaze. "Did you land on a name?"

I'd gone back and forth over the past couple months on what to call the business, but nothing sounded right until I considered the path that led me here.

"Yep, which is why this was excellent timin' of you to ask."

"What is it?"

"Compass Rose Builders: Residential and Commercial Construction. Then the tagline will be: Let our compass guide your next adventure." My smile drops when she doesn't say anything. "Too corny?"

"Silas!" she shrieks. "Are you kiddin'? I fuckin' love it!"

"Yeah?" I pull her up until she's lying on top of me. "I was worried you'd be upset if I didn't use your idea."

"Well…Matheisen Hardwood Homes does have a seductive ring to it. And considerin' your online fan club, it'd totally be on brand." She giggles, rubbing her nose against mine. "But I love the backstory of Compass Rose way better. It's perfect."

"I do too." I roll us over so she's underneath me. "Do you remember what I used to call you when we were little kids?"

Her brows furrow and then her blue eyes widen. "Oh my God, wait…I do. Posey Rosey! I used to hate it!"

Burying my face in her neck, I chuckle and whisper in her ear, "Perk of being Warren's best friend was gettin' to tease you before I developed feelings."

"I secretly loved havin' your attention," she admits. "That's why I called you Stinky Silas. You'd get so mad and run after me."

Laughing, I nearly lose it because I forgot she did that. "Fuck, that's right. I'd chase you 'round the barn until I pushed you to the ground."

"And then you'd climb on me, hold my arms down, and threaten to spit on my face unless I'd admit defeat. Which was so unfair 'cause you were older and stronger than me." Realization dawns on her face, and I break out into a knowing smile. "Holy fuck. You were a spitter even back then."

"Only for you, baby," I reassure with a wink.

"You *are* a psycho!" she taunts, then tries to roll out from underneath me.

Tickling her sides, I make her laugh harder, and she kicks her legs to distract me.

"Nice try, mama." I hold her down and pin her arms above her head like I used to. "You're mine. Say it."

"No!" she says defiantly.

"Don't make me spit on you," I threaten.

She arches her hips into my already hardened cock. "And what do I get if I say it?"

"I'll still spit in your mouth, but only after you begged me for it."

Her eyes heat as if she wants to give in, but won't. "Not happenin'."

"Don't make me handcuff you to this bed."

"What? We don't have those."

"You think you're the only one with toys?" I smirk, raising a brow. "I'll cuff you to the bed rails and edge you as long as I want before lettin' you come."

"You wouldn't dare."

"Try me, sweetheart."

She sucks in her lips and pinches them closed.

"Alright...be careful what you wish for." Leaning over, I open the bottom drawer of the nightstand, then pull them out along with lube and another item. Then I go into the top drawer and grab her vibrator.

Shock spreads over her face but she remains quiet.

"Look what else I found..." I taunt, holding up a butt plug I bought for her. "Flip over, love. Unless...you're gonna say what I wanna hear?"

Without argument, she rolls onto her stomach.

"Okay, then…" I muse, knowing she wants this just as badly as I do. "Arms up."

I weave the metal through one of the rails before cuffing her wrists in place. "If they're too tight, let me know."

She rests her cheek on the pillow and nods.

"If at any point you want me to stop or you're uncomfortable, say Rose. That's your safe word. Got it?"

"Mm-hmm."

We've kept our sex life fun and interesting these past few months, but now she's trusting me to make her feel good in a way we haven't explored before. I'd be lying if I said I wasn't a bit nervous, but I'm going to take my time with her and give her exactly what she needs.

And enjoy every minute of it.

chapter twenty-seven

Posey

"SILAS, please. I can't take it anymore. Let me come."

I'm a whimpering, sobbing mess as he continues to edge me. It's been over an hour, and I'm desperate for a release.

The butt plug's securely in place with the vibrator on my clit and three fingers inside me. He curls them deep and rotates between fast and slow. And then right when the build-up intensifies, he stops.

"Say you're mine," he demands.

I refuse to give in.

My parents didn't raise a quitter, and I'm not about to start now.

"Make me," I sass back.

"Make you what?" he taunts, cracking his palm against my ass. "My baby mama?"

I'm on all fours and cuffed to the bed, so I can't look back at him, but I imagine his smug grin reflecting back at me.

"I bet you do wanna knock me up, you psycho."

He chuckles darkly, smacking my pussy with his hard cock. "Don't tempt me, love. I'll cum so deep inside you, your pills won't stand a chance."

Pretty sure it doesn't work like that, but who I am to shoot him down when him inside me is exactly what I want right now.

"Then do it. Make me cum and knock me up, city boy."

Those words must be enough to encourage him because he spreads my legs wider and positions himself at my entrance.

"Cum on my cock like a good girl, mama. Don't hold back."

He loves hearing me scream, and I love doing it for him.

Sliding in, I gasp at how full he always makes me feel. His Prince Albert piercing massages my inner walls with each thrust and when he brings the vibrator back to my clit, I nearly sob.

"Please, I'm so close...don't stop."

"Not a chance, love. I wanna feel you unravel around me."

With his free hand, he fists my hair and continues slamming into me. I don't know how he has the stamina after working all day and then cleaning all evening, but fuck—he deserves a medal.

It must be from all that yoga I made him do.

"Oh God, I'm—"

The orgasm finally takes over, floating through me like a highly anticipated sequel that's even better than I imagined. I moan and cry out between the waves of pleasure that hit me while the toy continues vibrating against me.

Every time I squeeze him, the butt plug slides in deeper. And everything together is so intense.

"Fuck, oh fuck."

Another orgasm hits me, nearly shooting me into orbit.

"Cum inside me, please...I need it," I beg.

My limbs are numb, and my body needs sleep.

"Say you're mine, baby," he growls, slamming into me harder. "I need to hear it."

"I'm yours. Of course, I am," I promise. "Always will be."

"That's my good girl." He removes the vibrator and digs his fingers into my hips. "Hang on."

I barely have time to inhale before Silas pounds into me, over and over, hitting my sweet spot until all I can see are stars in my eyes.

"You feel so good, baby. I'm gonna cum," he warns.

Warmth fills me seconds later, and I gasp in relief. Silas loves being vocal in bed, but tonight, he screams my name so loud, I'm almost certain guests in the other cabins can hear him.

"Holy shit, are you okay? Did I hurt you?"

"No…I'm great," I pant.

When Silas slides out of me, our mixed pleasure does too. Before I can ask him to uncuff me, he pushes his fingers back inside me.

"Can't let my cum escape just yet," he quips, shoving it back inside me.

"Now I'm startin' to think you really are a psycho."

"Only when it comes to you," he says playfully.

"That's not as reassurin' as you think it sounds."

"Maybe I should put the plug in your pussy instead so my cum stays in you all night. Or perhaps my tongue."

"That's how women get UTIs," I deadpan.

"Baby, play along. I'm tryin' to knock you up here." He gives my ass a little tap.

"Uncuff me, and I'll let you stick your tongue wherever you want."

"Okay, deal. Relax a little so I can take the plug out first."

As soon as he does and removes the cuffs, I groan at getting to put my arms down and roll onto my back.

"Are you sure you're alright?" He caresses my face, pressing his lips to mine for a soft kiss.

"Mm-hmm. Completely blissed out," I admit.

"I'm gonna draw us a bath. That okay?"

"Sounds perfect."

After I relieve myself, Silas leads me into the tub and presses me against his chest, gently washing over every inch of me. He softly kisses along my neck and over my shoulder, going back and forth, then sucking underneath my ear.

"Silas?"

He hums.

I smile. "I love you."

He tightens his arms around me and my head falls back on his shoulder.

"Can I tell you somethin'?" he murmurs.

"Of course."

"I know I say how much you mean to me all the time, but just in case you aren't sick of hearin' it yet, you're my whole world, baby. The love of my life. I'd be nothin' without you, and I hope I never have to experience being without you again. I wanna make you my wife someday and be your husband. Make some babies. Maybe even get a puppy. Either way, the only future I see is with you in it."

My heart swells at words every woman loves hearing. Turning my head, I capture his lips and slip my tongue between them.

"Can we get another rat instead of a dog? They're less maintenance."

His chest vibrates with laughter. "Is that all you took from that?"

Giggling, I shift my body so we're face to face and straddle his lap. I rub the P pendant on his chain between my thumb and finger, admiring how hot it looks on him.

"No, I gathered that you're a very lucky man."

"You're right about that."

"But I'm also a very lucky girl."

"Also correct."

Beaming, I wrap my arms around his neck. "And I can't wait to be your wife and have your babies someday."

After the busiest holiday season Langston Soapworks has ever had, I'm more than ready to rot on the couch for the next two weeks.

Over three thousand packages went out in the month of December, most of them with several bars of soap in their order. It was too much for the two of us, so I recruited extra help.

Amaya and I set up an assembly line with Bellamy, Mom, Aunt JoJo, and Maisie, which increased the packaging speed and number of boxes we could finish in a night.

When our videos started going viral a few months ago, we

amped up our production to be sure we had enough stock and ended up selling out of everything.

Usually I'd work in between Christmas and New Year's to get ahead for the Valentine's Day drop, but Amaya and I need a well-deserved break. Plus, I want to spend as much time with Silas and our families as possible.

"Hey, did you dump out my Frosted Sugar Cookie coffee creamer?" Silas asks, walking into the bedroom with the container in his hand.

"You know I don't touch that flavored crap."

It took him ten minutes at the grocery store to decide between that and the Peppermint Mocha flavor. Eventually, I chose for him.

"You must've used it up yesterday."

"No, it was half full." He stares at it, looking confused as hell. "I don't understand what could've happened."

"Maybe Marjorie didn't like the smell." I shrug, sinking deeper under the covers.

It's my first official day of vacation, but Silas insists on working from home for the rest of the week so he doesn't get behind. He's been filling out more bids, keeping up with the budget spreadsheets for the childcare center, and contacting the contractors to make sure they stay on schedule.

Even though he's working more hours than he did at the farm, I can tell he loves doing this a lot more. He's great with people, has an outgoing personality, and can sweet-talk anyone with his charm.

"What does that mean?" he asks. "Ghosts can smell?"

"I assume so. She once blew out one of my scented candles."

"How do you know it was her?"

"'Cause as soon as I relit the wick, it went out seconds later. I tried a third time and same thing."

"But she can't even smell my creamer. It's in the fridge."

"Maybe she doesn't like the smell of your coffee after you add in the creamer. Since you have a few cups each mornin', the smell probably lingers throughout the house."

He scrubs a hand through his hair and sighs. "This is nuts."

I shrug again. "She knows what she doesn't like."

"Yeah, well I'd like some flavored creamer in my coffee!" He huffs, throwing up his arms.

"Just put in some half-and-half and sugar like a normal person."

"Ugh, I might as well drink tar at that rate."

He walks out of the bedroom, but I can't help laughing.

Marjorie's still adjusting to all the changes we've made the past few months, but she'll get used to it.

A few hours later, I emerge from bed and go in search of my own coffee but make a fresh batch. Even though I'm not making soaps right now, I still have admin and marketing things to do, so I grab my laptop and sit on the couch with my mug.

"Hey, we got somethin' in the mail from Jamie and Jackson," Silas says when he walks inside.

I didn't even know he left.

"What is it?"

"Not sure." He slides his finger through the flap.

We haven't seen them since the weekend of our double date, but I text with Jamie periodically. Nothing more than a *hey, how are ya* and *what's new* message.

"Holy shit!" His mouth pops open and he laughs uncontrollably. "I fuckin' knew it!"

"What?"

He hands it to me with a shit-eating grin.

It's a Save the Date.

"Oh my God…" My eyes pop out of my head.

"You owe me a hundred bucks, baby!"

"They're gettin' married?" I exclaim. "Over my birthday weekend!"

"Yep, in six months. But now that I'm thinkin' about it, the bet amount should double since they're engaged already."

I'm in too much shock to even respond to him.

I have so many questions.

When? How? What did their parents say?

Who made the first move?

When did he propose?

"This is unbelievable." I stare at the words on the card, but they don't sink in. "We're being pranked."

"Nope. Believe it, mama. I was right." He fists the air and thrusts his hips.

I roll my eyes at his victory dance and flick the card on the coffee table.

"You're insufferable."

"You always say that, but I think you secretly love that about me."

I hum, ignoring him.

"Admit it."

"Never."

He stands between my thighs, caging me against the couch with his arms. "Posey."

"Fine, maybe." I lazily lift a shoulder. "Sometimes."

The corner of his lips tilt up. "How 'bout instead of the two hundred bucks you owe me, I get to give you an early Christmas present?"

"I thought we were waitin' until the twenty-third?"

Since we're going to his mom's on Christmas Eve and my parents' on Christmas Day, we wanted a night with just the two of us to exchange gifts, blast music, and eat pizza.

"I know, but I'll forfeit my winnings in exchange for one present."

"Shouldn't it be the other way 'round? You get an early one from me instead since I lost the bet?"

"Eh, who cares. Trust me, you'll want this now."

"Alright, fine. But it better be good!" I playfully threaten.

He tips my chin and crashes his mouth to mine. "It is. But I gotta pick it up from Warren's, so I'll be back in a few."

"I'll be here."

While he's gone, I finish my coffee and respond to some emails. I put up a job listing online to hopefully find another employee now that I have some downtime to go through applications. If we continue staying as busy as we have been, I could use a couple more workers.

"Babe, I'm back. Are you ready?" Silas calls out, shutting the door behind him.

"Yep."

"Close your eyes!"

"You didn't wrap it?" I ask, doing it anyway.

"You'll see why in a minute."

I lean back against the couch. "Okay, they're closed."

He walks in and sets something on the coffee table.

"Alright, love. Open up."

My gaze lands on a new and bigger rat cage with accessories and toys already inside.

"Oh my God!" I squeal, jumping to my feet. "Teddy's gonna love this!"

Movement at the bottom startles me until a gray dumbo rat crawls up one of the ladders.

"No way!" I smile at him looking at me. "I can't believe you got me a rat. He's so cute!"

He barely tolerates Teddy, so I know what a big compromise this is for him.

"Of course, baby." Pulling me into his arms, he kisses the top of my head. "I'm in love with you and want you to be happy."

My heart squeezes at how thoughtful he is and how I still can't believe he's mine.

"Even though you hate rats?" I ask, tilting my chin up on his chest.

He casually lifts a shoulder. "I figured Teddy needed a friend too."

I laugh. "He definitely does."

Opening the cage door, I offer my hand for him to smell. "What should we name him?"

"Maybe...Bear?"

"Teddy and Bear?" I giggle, reaching in and pulling him out. "I love it."

I spend the rest of the morning playing with Bear before introducing him to Teddy. Rats do best with companions since they're naturally social animals and thrive with playmates, so this was a fantastic idea.

"This cage won't fit in my walk-in closet," I tell Silas when he takes his lunch break. "But there's plenty of room in your office…"

"Not happenin'."

"Then I guess it has to stay on the coffee table," I taunt. "Or maybe I'll find a table to set it on in our room."

He sighs, his gaze shifting to Teddy and Bear climbing up and down the ladders. There's even a cute little hammock inside.

"Fine," he surrenders. "But when we add onto the cabin, they're gettin' their own room."

I smile wide. "Deal."

epilogue

Silas

"HOLY FUCK, MAMA." I whistle, scanning my eyes down Posey's body in a tight blue dress. "You're gonna bring me to my knees wearin' that."

A beautiful blush covers her cheeks. "Just where I like ya."

If only she knew what I have in store for her later.

Pulling her to my chest, I tip her chin. "I will gladly as soon as we leave the reception."

Hopefully sooner rather than later.

Although her twenty-ninth birthday is tomorrow, we're celebrating Jamie and Jackson's nuptials in Knoxville this weekend.

We've kept in touch with them much better over the past six months, getting all the details of how they confessed feelings for each other and how their parents took the news. They weren't on board at first, but they came around.

Jamie and Jackson are happy together, so that's all that matters.

"I'm wearin' five-inch heels and a corset underneath this thing, so I'm gettin' my money's worth. Which means, you're dancin' with me until my feet go numb."

"Whatever you want, love." I wink, pressing my mouth to hers.

She slides her fingers inside my collar and pulls out my chain, then plays with the P pendant. "I only want you wearin' this tonight."

Posey…" I warn. "Watch it or we're not gonna make it to the ceremony on time."

She knows what her teasing does to me, purposely getting me hard before we have to be somewhere.

"Then you better stop starin' at me like you wanna eat me." She smirks, sliding her palms down my chest and abs. "I can practically hear the dirty thoughts in your head."

I grab her wrists before she goes any lower and bring her knuckles to my lips. "Can't help it when you take my breath away."

Her blush deepens.

"Let's go, cowboy, or we'll be walkin' in after the bride." She flicks my hat, the one that drives her wild.

I smack her ass when she walks away and grab my wallet before exiting our hotel room.

Between our chaotic work and sleep schedules, we only get a few hours together in the evenings. On the weekends, we sleep in, then run errands and grocery shop.

Posey hired two more workers for Langston Soapworks, so they stay caught up on orders, and I'm planning to hire a part-time secretary this fall. That should cut some of my hours each week to spend more time together.

It's the domestic kind of life I've always dreamed of sharing with her.

And I can't wait to make it last forever.

I don't even mind the rats anymore except when I trip over their stupid exercise balls. Not a fan of holding them either, but they're growing on me.

Sadly, their lifespan expectancy isn't long, so I'm mentally preparing for the day I need to replace one without Posey knowing.

The ceremony is beautiful and wraps up within fifteen minutes. Watching them commit to each other and recite their vows makes me excited for my own wedding someday.

"Champagne?" I offer, handing Posey a glass.

"Thank you." She takes a sip, and her eyes widen. "Oh damn, this is good. Don't let me have too many of these."

Chuckling, I nod. Definitely need her to stay awake for later.

We sip on our drinks and snack on appetizers while we wait for dinner. Since we don't know most of the guests, we make light conversation with the other people at our table.

"I'm dyin' to know who made the first move," an older woman asks next to us. "And was it before she turned eighteen or—"

Oh no.

"It was recent," Posey answers. "Last year."

"How can you be so sure?"

"Well, 'cause we went on a double date with 'em last September."

The woman's eyes widen and pingpong between Posey and me. "Oh."

Yeah, that's going to give her more questions than answers.

"It was one date," I interject. "And I knew he had feelings for her even then."

"Really?" The woman's face lights up before she sips her cocktail. "How sweet."

"Sometimes you just know who your person is even when you try fightin' it." I shrug, squeezing Posey's thigh underneath the table.

Dinner music plays in the background as we eat and listen to the speeches. Their friends and family have nothing but nice things to say even if they crack a few jokes about them being step-siblings.

"Are you ready to dance, love?" I hold out my hand, waiting.

"I am." She takes it and stands, then I lead her onto the dance floor.

Between slow and fast songs, my feet ache by the time we take a break to eat some cake. When Jamie and Jackson walk through the venue, we finally give them hugs and thank them for inviting us.

"I'm so happy y'all made it!" Jamie squeezes Posey. "You two look so cute together."

"Thank you." Posey grins. "You're so stunnin' in your dress."

"Thanks, but honestly—" She leans in closer. "I cannot wait to get it off me. I can barely breathe in it."

"I'm sure Jackson won't mind helpin' with that," Posey quips.

"Not one bit," he confirms.

We chat for a few more minutes before they walk over to the next table.

Posey leans into my ear, whispering, "I think it's time for you to rip this dress off me...preferably with your teeth."

Coughing, I quickly clear my throat so I don't choke on the water I just sipped.

"Jesus." I blink at her. "I wasn't expectin' that."

She looks up at me between her dark lashes, giving me her cutest innocent face. "Take me to our room and I'll give you another surprise."

I'm the one who's supposed to be surprising her tonight.

"Okay, but me first…since it's *your* birthday and all."

Her eyes brighten and she bites her lip. "Let's go."

When we step into the elevator, I pin her against the wall and crash my mouth to hers. As I slide my palms up her sides, she gasps when I cup her breast.

"Careful, cowboy. There's cameras in here."

"Fuck," I mutter, sinking my teeth into her neck. "I'm sure it's nothin' they haven't seen before."

Although I don't like the idea of anyone but me watching her unravel.

When the elevator opens, I carry her to our room, and as soon as I get the door open, her mouth's back on mine.

The last time I had hotel sex was with her, nine years ago, and I have to say, I'm a fan. The different scenery and knowing there are rooms on either side of us make it a bit more thrilling.

I should've packed our toys, though.

"I wish they had a bigger tub here for both of us to fit." Posey sighs, resting her cheek on my chest after I've made her come three times. She's still trying to catch her breath, as am I.

We're spoiled with the one she has in her master bathroom, but once we add on, I plan to get an even bigger one.

"Do you realize this is the third weddin' we've gone to and

ended up in bed together after?" I ask, brushing my fingers softly against her face. "Goin' all the way back to Warren and Maisie's."

Our first time ever. For both of us.

"And then Landen and Ellie's," she adds.

Our first time after we reunited.

"Now, Jamie and Jackson's." I smirk, knowing what's to come this time.

"I guess we like tradition," she teases. "We can't break it now. Whose weddin' is next?"

"Well, I was thinkin'..." My heart rate kicks up as I try to find the courage to say the words I've been dying to ask for months. "Maybe we should have one of our own."

"Our own what?"

"Weddin'."

She sits up, folding her arms on my chest. "Are you serious?"

"Yes, baby." I cup her face. "I'm madly in love with you. My heart is addicted to yours. You are my home and it's my favorite place in the world to be. Marry me and let me cherish you for the rest of our lives."

Tears well in her eyes as she sucks in her lips. "You wanna marry me?"

"More than anythin', love."

A beaming smile splits her face. "Me too. I mean, yes! Yes, I'll marry you!"

Wrapping her into my arms, I kiss her until we're both breathless.

"Do you wanna see the ring?"

"You have it?"

"Of course. You think I'd come unprepared?"

She giggles and sits up when I move to grab the velvet box out of my bag.

"Here, let me do this the right way." I quickly pull on my boxer briefs, then get down on one knee.

She's half-wrapped in a sheet with her legs hanging off the bed, messy hair, and makeup smudged, looking freshly satisfied and more stunning than ever.

As I open the box and reveal the diamond, her mouth pops open, which is just the reaction I was hoping for.

"Oh my God, Silas! It's stunnin'…" She stares, eyes widening the longer she looks at it.

I take her left hand and slide it over her ring finger. "Perfect fit."

"Wow…you did so good." She holds up her hand and waves her fingers around.

"I'm not sure if you can tell, but this style is called a compass solitaire. There's four prongs placed 'round the oval diamond that represent north, south, east, and west." I point to each of them. "See?"

"Oh my gosh, you're right," she squeals. "You're unreal."

"I knew right away—that was the ring worthy of my future wife."

"I seriously love it so much." She pulls me in for a kiss. "And that it's meaningful to both of us makes it extra special."

"I agree, baby. And it's engraved, too." I carefully slide it off and flip it over so she can read it.

To our next greatest adventure.

Tears fill her eyes and spill down her cheeks. "You're the most thoughtful person I know."

Moving closer, I kneel between her thighs and cup her

cheeks. "You deserve it, my love. I wanna give you everythin' you want and need for the rest of our lives."

"You already do," she chokes out, sliding the ring back on her finger. "How long have you had this?"

"Uh…that's privileged information."

"Silas!" She playfully shoves my chest. "Tell me."

"I started lookin' around February and picked it up from the jewelers in April."

"That was two months ago! Why'd you wait?"

"'Cause Warren wouldn't give me his blessin' until I proved I was good enough to marry you."

She furrows her brows. "*What?*"

"Yep, I was tryin' to be respectful, ya know…marryin' my best friend's sister, so I asked for his blessin' and he straight up said no."

"You're jokin'."

"Nope. Ask Maisie."

"So what'd you have to do?"

I sigh, knowing I'm about to embarrass myself.

"He put together an obstacle course 'round the ranch and each time I failed to get to the end, he'd make me start over. Took me four weeks to finally complete it."

She bursts out laughing, quickly covering her mouth. "Shut up right now…"

"I swear! He said I needed to get better at horseback ridin' and wanted to be confident I'd be able to fight off any threats if someone tried to hurt you. So he made me ride to different areas, and when I'd get to 'em, Bodie and Colt would be waitin' for me."

"Oh no…"

"Yep…" I shake my head. "One tased me and the other pepper sprayed me when I wasn't lookin'."

"You've gotta be makin' this up."

"He called it *brotherly bondin'.*"

She folds her arms, looking like she's ready to murder him. "Then what happened?"

"It was pourin' rain, and I had to ride through a swampy pasture to find the next trail. But I could hardly see through the fog and accidentally led the horse down the wrong path and ended up in a muddy ditch. We were both covered and I had to ask 'em to help us out."

"Where the hell was I when this was all goin' on?"

"Workin' or with your sister and mom. That's why it took me so long to get through it 'cause I didn't want you to get suspicious."

"Did you ask my dad for his blessin' too?"

"Of course. He gave it to me right away, but it was important to me that I also got Warren's."

"You know he only did that to humiliate you?"

"Oh, I have no doubt. He took several pictures."

"I can't believe you went along with that…" She dips down and presses her lips to mine. "How'd I get so lucky?"

"I ask myself that same question every day, love."

bonus epilogue

Posey

OGLING MY HUSBAND, I admire how handsome he is in his new Stetson cowboy hat, but especially when he's driving. One hand on the steering wheel and the other squeezing my thigh.

"Why're you starin'?" he drawls without looking at me.

"'Cause you're mine and I can."

He digs his fingers deeper into my leg. "Keep givin' me those eyes and we aren't gonna make it to the hotel on time."

"Off-road backseat truck sex? Oh no, not that..." I say sarcastically.

He chuckles and brings my hand to his mouth, kissing sweetly over my knuckles while staying focused on the road.

We're headed to Sugarland Creek for my cousin Wilder's vows ceremony, but we're also utilizing the weekend as a long awaited couple's getaway.

The last time we had a vacation was when we went to Charleston for our honeymoon last summer. I wanted to see the beaches and shop. It was so charming and relaxing after a stressful year of wedding planning.

We utilized the Willow Chalet as our venue, which made things a bit easier. But since I was the first daughter to get married and Silas's the baby of his family and the last to get hitched, everyone had an opinion about everything and kept suggesting new ideas.

It was worth it, though, because at the end of the day, I married the love of my life. Warren got to be his best man and Bellamy was my maid of honor.

Letting her be in charge of my bachelorette party is how we ended up drunk off our asses in Nashville, singing bar karaoke, and riding a mechanical bull until we face-planted on the mats.

The seven of us—Mom, Aunt JoJo, Maisie, Amaya, Jamie, Bellamy, and me—had to call Warren, Dad, and Silas to come pick us up because none of us were able to drive home the next day.

But we had a blast.

Totally worth the hangover.

It's still hard to believe it's been almost two years since he proposed and that we'll be celebrating our first wedding anniversary this summer.

Time goes fast when you're living your best life with your soulmate.

After our honeymoon, we started on the cabin expansion project since the childcare center finished early and opened sooner than anticipated. Dad was so impressed with how Silas managed it and even gave him a five-figure bonus.

I was so proud of him, I gave him a little bonus of my own —a surprise clit piercing—and although we had to refrain from sex for six weeks, we found other ways to pleasure each other.

Since my cabin has plenty of land around it, we added two more bedrooms, another bathroom, and expanded the kitchen for more space.

Marjorie hated every second of it.

Silas's tools and supplies constantly went missing.

Every time he plugged in something, it'd randomly turn off in the middle of using it.

He had to plead with her to knock it off.

She finally did when he left *Golden Girls* playing on the TV for hours at a time. And then I kept her calm with a lavender and eucalyptus candle—her favorite scents.

Teddy and Bear had to stay at Uncle Warren and Aunt Maisie's for a while since the noise was too much for them. But after a few weeks, Warren got annoyed with them and threatened to feed them to his chickens if I didn't come get them.

But after nine long months, it's finally complete.

Silas worked on it in the evenings and almost every weekend since he wanted to do it himself and only contracted an electrician to make sure he didn't accidentally kill himself or burn the place down.

I did my part by picking out the furniture and decor. Most of our engagement and wedding photos cover the walls and make me smile every time I walk past them.

We moved our bedroom into the new master suite, so now there's plenty of space for the rat cage. But Silas makes me put a blanket over it when we're having sex.

I told him they can still hear us, but whatever gets him naked and inside me.

Teddy the third and Bear the second got a new sibling that we named Winnie who arrived on Valentine's Day a couple months ago.

Silas has replaced Bear once and Teddy twice after they died without telling me. He thinks I don't know, but I noticed right away and didn't have the heart to tell him.

It's either psycho behavior or extremely sweet—either way, I play along to make him happy.

It also makes it easier on me emotionally so I don't get too sad when they die only a couple years later. I got Teddy on a whim one day, so he'll always be my special first baby, but I fall in love with the new ones, too.

Teddy II didn't live long, and I think it's because he was lonely since the original Bear was in mourning after Teddy passed. So once Bear II arrived, I suggested we get a third rat so they'd have more opportunities to socialize.

And now they're all doing great.

Since we'll be gone all weekend, Amaya and her boyfriend, Jack—our new goat yoga demonstrator—are house sitting so the rats aren't left alone and Marjorie doesn't worry about us being away.

But I'm waiting for the moment Amaya texts me and finds all the cabinet doors and drawers randomly open.

But I did warn Marjorie and tell her to be nice.

The wedding is at Wilder's family property— Sugarland Creek Ranch and Equine Retreat. We used to visit there a lot as kids or they'd come up and go camping with us, but we haven't seen our cousins since our wedding. It'll be nice to catch up with everyone this weekend and actually have time to chat.

I usually hear any family gossip through my mom since her brother's wife, Dena, is her best friend and my aunt. They're always sharing each other's kids' tea, then relaying it to the rest of us.

Four months ago, Wilder and Delilah got drunkenly hitched in Vegas when they attended the National Finals Rodeo to watch Ellie compete in barrel racing.

Delilah used to date Wilder's twin brother, Waylon, years ago. But then he started seeing Delilah's little sister, Harlow, and now they're together.

It's as weird and complicated as it sounds.

But I guess everyone's happy so that's all that matters.

When Wilder and Delilah decided to stay together and not get an annulment, they planned for a summer vows ceremony for the whole family to enjoy.

But then she got knocked up with twins on their honeymoon.

So they pushed it up a couple months to April.

Funny enough, most of us met Delilah on their honeymoon since they stayed at our resort for a week.

"We're here," Silas announces, pulling into the parking lot.

There isn't enough room for everyone at the ranch, so my family booked hotel rooms in town.

"Thank God, I gotta pee!" I bounce in my seat, eagerly waiting to jump out.

"We stopped thirty minutes ago so you could use the bathroom."

I shrug. "Well, that slushie went right through me."

After I race inside and relieve myself, I meet Silas at the front desk.

The rest of my siblings are already here, so we grab our luggage and head up to our floor.

Colton's room is across from ours, Bellamy's to our right, Bodie's across from her, and then my parents are to our left.

Warren and Maisie booked a suite on another floor so they don't get bothered.

Honestly, it's smart.

Our siblings can be annoying.

"What time do we have to be there?" Silas asks.

Since the wedding rehearsal is for their immediate family only, we won't need to go until tomorrow afternoon.

"The ceremony isn't until six, but Aunt Dena said we can come at five for family photos."

They're having an intimate evening ceremony in one of their barns with tons of lanterns and fairy lights, so it'll be super romantic. Then we'll move to a big, white tent to eat dinner and dance the night away.

"Perfect, so we can actually sleep in is what I'm hearin'..." He waggles his brows.

"Sleep or *sleep*?"

"Always *sleep*."

"In that case, I need to lie down for a bit."

"Are you tired?"

"A little, yeah. But I'm a bit queasy too from that longer drive."

Willow Branch Mountain and Sugarland Creek are about two hours apart, but it's super hilly, so it always puts my stomach in knots.

"Go ahead, and I'll unpack." He kisses my forehead. "And get your dress hung up."

"Thank you. Wake me up when it's time to go to dinner."

Since my whole family is here, we made reservations to go out to a nice restaurant and I don't want to miss it.

I danced far too long, ate way too much, and didn't sleep nearly enough, but the wedding was a blast.

When I wake up Sunday morning, my head's throbbing from a lack of hydration, and I feel sick to my stomach. Silas's passed out next to me, buck-ass naked, so I crawl out of bed in search of water and maybe some crackers.

There's no water left and the bucket of ice has long melted, so I slip on my pj shorts, a tank, and sandals to go in search of something to drink and eat.

I open the door and carefully close it behind me so I don't wake Silas, but as soon as I turn into the hallway, I find Amelia sneaking out of Colton's room.

"Oh hey," I say, surprised to see her here.

She's one of Delilah's bridesmaids who lives in the ranch hand duplexes with her two kids. From what I got to know about her, she works as a receptionist at The Lodge on the retreat side.

"Hello," she says hesitantly.

"You okay?"

She's still in her bridesmaids dress with her shoes dangling from her hand and her purse over her shoulder.

"Is there any chance you could drive me back to the ranch? My friend Raven watched my kids for me last night, and I gotta get back to 'em."

"Yeah, sure. I'll grab my keys."

This time, I let the door slam behind me and shake Silas awake.

"What?" he mumbles against his pillow.

"I'll be right back. Gonna drive Amelia back to the ranch quickly."

"Mm'kay."

He probably has no idea what I said, but I kiss his cheek anyway. "Love you."

After he rolls over and gives me a sinful view, he grunts out three inaudible words that echo the same sentiment.

Grabbing my bag, I meet Amelia back in the hallway. "Okay, let's go."

"I can't believe how much I drank last night." She shakes her head as if she's disappointed with herself.

"It was a party. Everyone was drinkin'," I reassure her, driving us out of the parking lot. "Although, I only had two drinks and feel sick as shit."

"Oh really? Maybe it's somethin' you ate."

"I hope not, but I've also been queasy and nauseous, and kinda sweaty. Maybe it's the flu."

She leans away from me toward the passenger side window.

I bark out a laugh. "Sorry. It's probably not."

"If not, maybe you're pregnant."

"Wait, what?" I snap my gaze toward her.

"I had early pregnancy symptoms with my kids that sound like what you're experiencin'. Do y'all use protection?"

"No, but I'm on the pill."

She chuckles with a huff. "Yeah, I was too—both times. They're now seven and two."

"Oh shit..." My heart beats faster. "Maybe I could be."

"Might wanna stop at the store on your way back," she suggests. "Could help ease your mind on why you're feelin' this way."

"Yeah, good idea."

I try to wrap my mind around the possibility.

Silas and I have talked about starting a family, so it's not like it'll be all that surprising, but I hadn't expected to get pregnant this quickly.

"So..." I hesitate about poking into her business, but I'm nosy when it comes to my siblings. "Are you and Colt—"

"No!" she cuts me off frantically. "That was just a one-time thing."

"Does he know that?"

Colton doesn't do one-night stands.

She lifts her shoulder. "I assume so. We only just met last night and I didn't even give him my number."

"Interestin'..."

"What is?"

"Um..." I contemplate how much to share with her. "Colt doesn't really do casual hookups."

"Well, it's not like anythin' can come about it. We don't even live in the same town." She frowns. "And most guys don't wanna do the whole kids thing when it's not theirs."

I suck in my lips to stop myself from blurting out that single moms are exactly Colton's type. But she's right. Being two hours apart and living completely different lives won't make it possible for anything more.

"If you don't mind me askin', are the kids' father involved?"

"No." She swallows hard, but doesn't offer any further details, which is fine. I can tell it's not a topic she wants to discuss.

"What're your kids' names?"

"Sam and Lily."

"Those are adorable."

"Thanks." She fidgets with her fingers as I enter the long ranch driveway.

Everything is still set up from yesterday, but it looks much different in the daytime.

"I *never* go out or do this sorta thing, just in case you wondered," she blurts.

"I wasn't, but good to know."

"Colt was still passed out when I left," she admits. "We only fell asleep a few hours ago, so that's why I didn't ask him to take me home."

"What was your plan if I hadn't come out?"

"Call a ride share, though they're pretty sparse 'round here."

"Well, luckily, you found me." I grin.

She directs me where to go and once we get to the cul-de-sac, I park in front of her garage.

"Thank you a ton, Posey."

"You're very welcome."

"Good luck and congrats if you are pregnant." She smiles sincerely and a wave of jittery butterflies swarm my already queasy stomach.

I snort. "Thanks. I'll let you know through the grapevine if I am."

"I don't doubt it. No one can keep a secret here."

She grabs her things and gets out, but I wait until she's inside before pulling away.

My brain's on autopilot as I drive to a convenience store in town. After grabbing some Gatorade and protein bars, I make my way to the woman's health aisle.

Why're there so many options?

I've never taken a pregnancy test before so I don't even know what specific options I should look for.

After fifteen minutes of reading various boxes, I grab a digital test that claims to tell me six days before my missed period.

I guess we'll find out.

Considering Silas's and my history with weddings, it'd only be fitting to find out I'm pregnant after another one.

Read Posey & Silas's bonus scene on my website:

brookewritesromance.com/bonus-scenes

next in the willow branch mountain series

Take My Kiss is book #3 in the Willow Branch Mountain interconnected series featuring the middle Langston child, Colton, and his one-night stand with single mom, Amelia.

about the author

Brooke has been writing romance since 2013 under the *USA Today* Bestselling Author retired pen names: Brooke Cumberland and Kennedy Fox, and now under the Amazon top 100 Bestselling Author pen names: **Brooke Montgomery** and **Brooke Fox**. All together, she's published over 65 books.

She writes books that she loves reading about the most—cinnamon roll heroes with dirty mouths who are obsessed with their women. She enjoys writing small town romances with big families and happily ever afters!

When she's not writing, you can find her reading or listening to audiobooks. watching hockey, or cooking. Sometimes all three at once.

Learn more on her website at
www.brookewritesromance.com